AP   '09

P9-AZW-361

Benji's Sag Harbor

The Creek

The Rock   Harding Terr.

kids w/
Empty House

NINEVAH

Shore Rd.

Richards Dr.

Fist Fight!

Shootout

AZUREST

THE

HILLS

Hempstead St.

The Old House,
beware

Meredith Ave.

Walker Ave.

Harbor Ave.

Hillside Dr. W.

Found →
2 bucks here
once

Hampton St.

Lincoln St.

Lighthouse Ln.

Wildwood Dr.

to East Hampton,
the Atlantic Ocean,
Europe

WITHDRAWN

Sag Harbor

ALSO BY COLSON WHITEHEAD

The Intuitionist
John Henry Days
The Colossus of New York
Apex Hides the Hurt

Sag Harbor

A NOVEL

COLSON WHITEHEAD

DOUBLEDAY

NEW YORK LONDON TORONTO

SYDNEY AUCKLAND

Mount Laurel Library
100 Walt Whitman Avenue
Mount Laurel, NJ 08054-9539
856-234-7319
www.mtlaurel.lib.nj.us

DD
DOUBLEDAY

This book is a work of fiction. Names, characters, businesses,
organizations, places, events, and incidents either are the
product of the author's imagination or are used fictitiously.
Any resemblance to actual persons, living or dead, events, or
locales is entirely coincidental.

Copyright © 2009 by Colson Whitehead

All Rights Reserved

Published in the United States by Doubleday, an imprint of
The Doubleday Publishing Group, a division of Random
House, Inc., New York.
www.doubleday.com

Page 275 constitutes an extension of this copyright page.

DOUBLEDAY is a registered trademark and the DD colophon is
a trademark of Random House, Inc.

Endpaper map by Virginia Norey

LIBRARY OF CONGRESS CATALOGING-IN-PUBLICATION DATA
Whitehead, Colson, 1969–
Sag Harbor : a novel / Colson Whitehead. — 1st ed.
p.   cm.
1. African American teenage boys—Fiction. 2. Adolescence—
Fiction. 3. Sag Harbor (N.Y.)—Fiction. I. Title.
PS3573.H4768S35 2009
813'.54—dc22
2008013510

ISBN 978-0-385-52765-1

PRINTED IN THE UNITED STATES OF AMERICA

10 9 8 7 6 5 4 3 2 1

FIRST EDITION

For Maddie

Contents

Sag
Harbor

Notions
of
Roller-
Rink
Infinity

FIRST YOU HAD TO SETTLE THE QUESTION OF OUT.
When did you get out? Asking this was showing off, even though
anyone you could brag to had received the same gift and had come
by it the same way you did. Same sun wrapped in shiny paper, same
soft benevolent sky, same gravel road that sooner or later skinned
you. It was hard not to believe it belonged to you more than anyone
else, made for you and waiting all these years for you to come along.
Everyone felt that way. We were grateful just to be standing there in
that heat after such a long bleak year in the city. When did you get
out? was the sound of our trap biting shut; we took the bait year after year, pure pinned joy in the town of Sag Harbor.

Then there was the next out: How long are you out for?—and

the competition had begun. The magic answer was Through Labor Day or The Whole Summer. Anything less was to signal misfortune. Out for a weekend at the start of the season, to open up the house, sweep cracks, that was okay. But only coming out for a month? A week? What was wrong, were you having financial difficulties? Everyone had financial difficulties, sure, but to let it interfere with Sag, your shit was seriously amiss. Out for a week, a month, and you were allowing yourself to be cheated by life. Ask, How long are you out for? and a cloud wiped the sun. The question trailed a whiff of autumn. All answers contemplated the end, the death of summer at its very beginning. Still waiting for the bay to warm up so you could go for a swim and already picturing it frozen over. Labor Day suddenly not so far off at all.

The final out was one-half information-gathering and one-half prayer: Who else is out? The season had begun, we were proof of it, instrument of it, but things couldn't really get started until all the players took their marks, bounding down driveways, all gimme-fives. The others were necessary, and we needed word. The person standing before you in pleated salmon shorts might say, "I talked to him on Wednesday and he said they were coming out." They were always the first ones out, never missed June like their lives depended on it. (This was true.) Someone might offer, "Their lawn was cut." A cut lawn was an undeniable omen of impending habitation, today or tomorrow. "Saw a car in their driveway." Even better. There was no greater truth than a car in a driveway. A car in the driveway was an invitation to knock on the door and get down to the business of summer. Knock on that door and watch it relent under your knuckles—once you were out, the door stayed unlocked until you closed up the house.

Once we're all out, we can begin.

MY NAME IS BEN. In the summer of 1985 I was fifteen years old. My brother, Reggie, was fourteen. As for when we got out, we got out that morning, hour and a half flat, having beat the traffic. Over the course of a summer, you heard a lot of different strategies of how to beat the traffic, or at least slap it around a little. There were those who ditched the office early on Friday afternoon, casually letting their co-workers know the reason for their departure in order to enjoy a little low-pressure envy. Others headed back to the city late Sunday evening, choking every last pulse of joy from the weekend with cocoa-buttered hands. They stopped to grab a bite and watched the slow red surge outside the restaurant window while dragging clam strips through tartar sauce—soon, soon, not yet—until the coast was clear.

My father's method was easy and brutal—hit the road at five in the morning so that we were the only living souls on the Long Island Expressway, making a break for it in the haunted dark. Every so often my mother said, "There's no traffic," as if it were a miracle. Well, it wasn't really dark, June sunrises are up and at 'em, but I always remember those drives that way—memory has a palette and broad brush. Perhaps I remember it that way because my eyes were closed most of the time. The trick of those early-morning jaunts was to wake up just enough to haul a bag of clothes down to the car, nestle in, and then retreat back into sleep. Any unnecessary movement might exile you from the realm of half asleep and into the bleary half awake, so my brother and I did a zombie march slow and mute until we hit the backseat, where we turned into our separate nooks, sniffing upholstery, butt to butt, more or less looking like a Rorschach test. What do you see in this picture? Two brothers going off in different directions.

We had recently ceased to be twins. We were born ten months apart and until I went to high school we came as a matched set, more Siamese than fraternal or identical, defined by an uncanny inseparability. Joined not at the hip or spleen or nervous system but at that more important place—that spot on your self where you meet the world.

There was something in the human DNA that compelled people to say "Benji 'n' Reggie, Benji 'n' Reggie" in a singsong way, as if we were cartoon characters or mascots of some twenty-five-cent candy.

On the rare occasions we were caught alone, the first thing people asked was "Where's Benji?" or "Where's Reggie?," whereupon we delivered a thorough account of our other's whereabouts, quickly including context as if embarrassed to be caught out in the sunlight with only half a shadow: "He rode into town. He lost his CAT Diesel Power cap at the beach and went to get a new one at the five-and-ten." And the questioner nodded solemnly: Reggie's love for his CAT Diesel Power cap, fostered by '70s trucker movies, was well-known.

There was summer, and then there was the rest of the time. During the rest of the time, before we were separated, you could find us modeling gear from the Brooks Brothers Young Men's Department—smart white Oxford shirts, for example, tucked in during school hours, flapping in soft rebellion when we were home. The elementary school we went to required us to wear jackets and ties, so we did. Our wrists inevitably outran our jacket sleeves despite our mother's attempts at timely hem-jobs. The ties as a species were clip-on, but we had a few that our father tied for us at the beginning of the school year, which we then slid loose and slid tight for the next nine months, knots getting greasier and grubbier as our kiddie fingers oozed into them. We had one blue blazer and one beige corduroy jacket apiece, rotated over gray slacks and khaki pants. I was a little taller, which helped us sort out whose was whose, but not always.

What did we look like, walking down Lexington, across Sixty-second Street, side by side on our way to and from school? I remember one day in the seventh grade when an old white man stopped us on a corner and asked us if we were the sons of a diplomat. Little princes of an African country. The U.N. being half a mile away. Because—why else would black people dress like that? Looking up into his mossy teeth, I croaked a tiny "No" and tugged Reggie into the crosswalk, as my don't-talk-to-strangers/everyone-is-a-child-molester training kicked in. The TV was our babysitter, sure, so finger-wagging movies of the week were our manual on how to deal with strangers. We eagerly riffled through the literature, tsk-tsking and chuckling over tales of neglected white kids gone awry, the sad procession of zaftig and susceptible teenage hitchhikers, the pill-popping honor students turned wildcat over "the pressure to succeed." When strangers stopped us on the street asking questions, we knew what to do. Keep walking, brother. What did he look like? Senior partner in the law firm of Cracker, Cracker & Cracker. What did we look like? I don't know, but his question wasn't something we'd ever be asked in Sag Harbor. We fit in there.

Summers we branched out in our measly fashion. Freed from the dress code, what did we do? As fake twins, we couldn't shake our love of the uniform. Each day we wore the same make of shirt, but different colors, different iron-on decals. Every couple of months our mother bought us some clothes at Gimbels—security cameras capture her foraging for her cubs, murmuring "Two of these, and two of these"—and then tossed them into our cage for us to hyena-yip over who got what. Want the maroon terry-cloth shirt? Get to it first or else you'll be wearing the olive one 'til next Christmas. R2-D2 jammies for you, C-3PO for me. You had to work fast. Dibs was all.

We were a bit of a genre when you pried open a family photo album: There's Benji 'n' Reggie slouching in the beach grass, leaning on the hood of that summer's rented car, huddled on a bench outside the ice-cream parlor. One brother in a powder-blue Izod polo, the other in a crimson Izod drizzled with Rocky Road. Arms noosed around each other's necks, always wearing the same shirts but for that one crucial, differentiating detail that was everything. The same, but a little off, and it was to that crooked little corner of difference that we truly aspired.

Our expressions, picture to picture? Me: pained and dyspeptic, squinting in discomfort at the discovery of some new defect in the design of the world, the thought bubble asking, "Aren't we all just ants under the magnifying glass, really?" and "Is this the passing of our days, so much Pixy Stix dust falling in an hourglass?" The only time "early bloomer" has ever been applied to me is vis-à-vis my premature apprehension of the deep dread-of-existence thing. In all other cases, I plod and tromp along. My knuckles? Well dragged.

Say Cheese. And what's Reggie up to? Mugging, of course, cross-eyed, sneering, fingers bent into devil's horns, waving his dented beggar's cup for one extra ounce of precious attention, a rare element in our household. We knew we wanted to be separated but could only bear it in slim degrees. So when our father showed up with knockoff souvenirs from the 1976 Montreal Olympics, I snagged the javelin T-shirt, Reggie reached for the shot-put T-shirt, and we broke out of the locker-room tunnel into the arena of sunlight, summer after summer, members of the same team. It was nice to have a team, even if it was just us two.

Where is the surgeon gifted enough to undertake this risky operation, separate these hapless conjoined? Paging Doc Puberty, arms scrubbed, smocked to the hilt, smacking the nurses on the ass, and well-versed in all the latest techniques. More suction! Javelin and shot put—that's about right. Hormones sent me up and airborne, tall and skinny, a knock-kneed little reed, while Reggie, always chubby in the cheeks and arms, bulged out into something round and pinchable, soft and smooth, where I stuck out in sharp angles. We disentangled week by week, one new hair at a time. Junior high, they called it.

There were no complications on the physical separation, but what about the mental one, to sever the phantom connection whereby if Reggie stubbed his toe, I cried out in pain, and vice versa? The moment of my psychic release was occasioned by Liza Finkelstein's eighth-grade roller-disco party in the spring of '83.

IT WAS BAR MITZVAH SEASON, a good time to be alive by any measure, but particularly for die-hard finger-food aficionados like myself. As my friends underwent their time-honored initiation rituals, I experienced my own coming-of-age, culinary-wise. I had led a rather sheltered life with regards to bite-sized snacks, having only messed around with Mini Hot Dogs, La Choy Egg Rolls, and other lovelies of the Preheat To 350 school. The racy, catered pleasures of the full-tilt, bank-busting, don't-you-love-me bar mitzvah were a revelation. I remember marveling at the silver hors d'oeuvres trays as they dipped and flitted through the air like flying saucers out of a

'50s sci-fi movie, bearing alien life forms I had never reckoned, messengers of gustatory peace and goodwill. Chicken teriyaki on skewers, Swedish meatballs squatting in brown pools, all manner of dipping sauces in dark and gluey abundance—it was dizzying, and that wasn't just the thimbles of Manischewitz talking.

I was used to being the only black kid in the room—I was only there because I had met these assorted Abes and Sarahs and Dannys in a Manhattan private school, after all—but there was something instructive about being the only black kid at a bar mitzvah. Every bar or bat mitzvah should have at least one black kid with a yarmulke hovering on his Afro—it's a nice visual joke, let's just get that out of the way, but more important it trains the kid in question to determine when people in the corner of his eye are talking about him and when they are not, a useful skill in later life when sorting out bona-fide persecution from perceived persecution, the this-is-actually-happening from the mere paranoid manifestation. "Who's that?" "Whisper whisper a friend of Andy's from school." "So regal and composed—he looks like a young Sidney Poitier." "Whisper whisper or the son of an African diplomat!"

Eventually I'd have some company when the occasional R&B band showed up to drag themselves through the obligatory Motown retrospective, with the inevitable "Super Freak" thrown in . . . as Liza Finkelstein, grim and silent, squashed her place setting in her fist and cursed us all. Her parents were civil rights lawyers, not that I knew what that meant, except that it compelled Liza to blurt out "My parents were there!" on that one day a year when a teacher mentioned the March on Washington. Her parents respected all races, colors, and creeds, unless that creed was their own. According to some lefty calculus they had concluded that the traditions of their faith were bogus, and consequently Liza was going to have to wait a while before entering the world of calligraphic invitations and their little guppy RSVP envelopes.

Rebellion trickles down. Liza's "My parents were there!"s diminished in enthusiasm year by year, to be true, but I think it was bat mitzvah season, with its exuberant pageantry and lovely haul of presents, that puckered her to new pouty extremes. To be so exiled. It came to pass that one bright spring morning our hippie English teacher Mr. Johnson mentioned the March on Washington and the assembled of Homeroom 8B instinctively turned to Liza to hear her declaration for the last time. Perhaps we were feeling sentimental. We'd be in high school in a few months, split up after being together—some of us—since pre-K. This was a milestone, and we waited for Liza to give us what we needed. The moments piled up. A suspicion or fear that Liza might not provide her necessary service began to creep across the room in the same way that, gently, menthol cigarette smoke crept from under the door of the teachers' lounge. My eyes fell to her checkered New Wave knee-high socks, and I thought, Liza's not New Wave. Then she sneered a "My parents were there," rolling her eyes and kicking her feet out into the aisle between desks. Liza didn't need the whole bat mitzvah treatment. She was a teenager in that moment.

The Finkelsteins negotiated a settlement whereby the older generation would shell out for a roller-disco party of secular design and execution, and the younger generation would cut down on her use of the phrase "But all my friends" by at least 50 percent. Usually other people's parents scared me, but Mr. Finkelstein always seemed glad to have me around. Sending their daughter to a fancy private school was a betrayal of core values, paying tuition when you were supposed to support local public schools being in traitorous equivalence with eating grapes when you were supposed to boycott grapes. Those days, every nonunionized grape was a tear squeezed out of the eye of a migrant worker's child.

The fact that Mr. Finkelstein's daughter had a bona-fide black friend mitigated the situation a bit. Hey, wasn't that why they'd marched on Washington in the first place? The pictures of that day in 1963 are majestic and holy—the black-and-white mosaic of faces and stone, the force of people such that it overwhelms the pool and the monument and wipes the sneer off the face of architectural arrogance. If you were actually there, what did you think when you saw the photographs? The mass of figures was the sheer expression of human potential, making it possible to kid yourself that you could spot yourself in that sea of people—that's me in this important event, right there, as I was, before all this. It must be possible to fool yourself that you were not lost in the crowd. I had no problem with Mr. Finkelstein.

A roller-disco party was surely an artifact of the post-piñata, pre-intercourse era. Whither all the piñatas of yesterday? In a succession of finely furnished living rooms we took sticks and expressed our lust through an eager fury, assailing the poor piñatas and sending their sad paper fur flapping, their empty bulk wobbling above us, such a grubby mob we were. We needed to get inside there, split the beasts open, see their pink guts burst to loose that clumsy rain of mongrel candies that exist only inside piñatas, the dingy Zimzis, Dolos, and Shrats, sweet shreds that we scrambled after like well-dressed vultures. We wanted different candy now. For some, this period of pre-sexual limbo would be short. Not for me. Which made my inflated sense of self after that time Emily Dorfman asked me to skate with her all the more pathetic.

Emily Dorfman was the tallest person in our class, had been for a while. We called her Spider. Her arms and legs were pale scaffolding propping up her shirts and skirts, and she hadn't yet realized that growing her hair out might cover up the extra vertebrae she seemed to have in her neck—if she were an animal, she'd be nibbling those high-up leaves. While I believed she was the owner of a certain bow-legged elegance, a gangly grace, I had never thought of her as a sex object. We'd shared co-ed bathrooms as youngsters, seen each other's bald parts back in the day, and maybe that had something to do with it. No mystery.

We were on our second or third sugar rush of Liza's birthday party when Emily came over. I hadn't hit the floor that much. The skates were too tight, and I winced through wide, oafish circuits around the rink. I didn't know what size my feet were anymore. My body was having an off year basically, and I was not the kind of person to ask for the right size after I had committed, preferring to stumble around in pain for a couple of hours rather than speak up for myself. And so. I was standing with the guys over by the Aster-oids machine—all of us momentarily between quarters and specu-lating as to the training regimen of DMZ, the high scorer on the game—when Emily stepped into our circle and said, "Benji, let's go out there. I want to skate." She slapped me on the back to emphasize the casualness of her proposal.

I looked over at Andy Stern, who was my buddy. We played D&D together, went way back, to *Star Wars* marathons. I remembered he passed notes to Emily for a while in the third grade. Was this okay? Would he take revenge as Dungeon Master? Those days we expressed aggression by siccing orcs, gryphons, and homunculi on each other. Andy Stern scratched beneath his bowl haircut, eyes vacant. What was the big deal? I didn't think of Spider in that way and why would anyone think of me in that way. I said, "Okay," and we headed out.

It was all pretty innocent, just pals, as we dodged a flotilla of older kids skating together in a gossipy swarm and discovered a comfortable little slipstream on the inside of the track. Then she grabbed my hand and I almost jumped. Her hand was hot and moist. She was sweating a lot. I mention her sweatiness not to raise the specter of glandular aberration but to explain the sympathetic gushing of sweat it roused in my own hand. Guh. Our fingers slob-bered over each other. I had been dragging a little behind her on ac-count of my pained feet but I caught up and started matching her rhythm. We swooped past where our friends were hanging out but we didn't look at them. We kept them behind the aluminum rails and far from us. I did not witness any hypothetical thumbs-up Mr. Finkelstein threw my way. As my fingers slid in the grooves be-tween her knuckles, I reckoned that her spidery fingers provided more points of contact than those of our classmates. If you were go-ing to hold hands with someone, this was the hand to hold, volume-wise. My perception burrowed down into those places where our flesh rubbed together. I turned to her, she looked at me and I smiled and lifted my eyebrows, this suave tic. Then it was quickly eyes down again. Too much! I squeezed her hand twice in some kind of weird code and she squeezed back. And then my other hand occurred to me. It was empty. I wasn't pulling Reggie out of traffic or up out of bus seats so that we wouldn't miss our stop, he wasn't drifting behind me sloshing a cup of soda, he wasn't there at all. This was no threesome, I was alone with someone else. The awareness of my left hand faded and I returned to the little world of sweet contact in my right.

We were out there forever. How does one measure infinity in a roller rink? You can test the universe by asking questions—how many mirrored tiles on disco balls shooting how many pure white streaks across the walls and floors, how many ball bearings clacking into each other like agitated molecules in how many polyurethane wheels, how many inkblot colonies of bacteria blooming unchecked in the toe-ward gloom of how many rented skates. But let's say this notion of chintzy roller-rink infinity is best expressed by the number two. Two people, two hands, and two songs, in this case "Big Shot" and "Bette Davis Eyes." The lyrics of the two songs provided no commentary, honest or ironic, on the proceedings. They were merely there and always underfoot, the insistent gray muck that was pop culture. It stuck to our shoes and we tracked it through our lives. Spider and me slogged through the songs, hand in hand. Occasionally seeking each other's faces to trade brief, worried smiles.

Then "Xanadu" came on, murderer. We clomped off the track and rejoined our respective tribes, slouching male and female on opposite walls of the subterranean roller rink, never acknowledging this episode again. What made her step up? Next year we went to our separate high schools, and Emily might as well have been broken down into antimatter because we never saw each other again. Frankly, I took our moment of closeness for granted (this will be a running theme) and if I had known that that was the most girl contact I was going to have for many years, I would have taken a souvenir. Wiped her sweat off my hand with a handkerchief and cherished the hankie as an erotic aid during the long period of self-abuse that was to commence a few months later (initiated by a vision of a glistening Barbara Carrera in the minor James Bond vehicle *Never Say Never Again*, which featured many water-themed scenarios). Retrieved from its secret hiding place, the uncrumpled hankie, saturated with Emily's sweat, would have added an olfactory component to the visual artifacts I had in my mental files, mostly snippets of Cinemax movies and adolescent sex comedies of the *Makin' It–Doin' It–Losin' It* ilk, plus the odd stray tit from *National Lampoon* as I was too afraid to buy *Playboy*. The surface area of her long fingers would have left more sweat than the average eighth-grade hand. I would have huffed that hankie for all it was worth.

The night of the roller-disco party I decided I was in big-boy territory. Other kids in our class were doing more than holding hands, and the fact of other people's greater pleasure was becoming a feature of my reality. Now even I was on my way, having received what I interpreted as an omen of glorious high school–style interaction into my fetid sandbox. Freshman year was going to be great. Reggie wouldn't even be in the same building. I was relieved the day he told me that he didn't want to go to my high school. "I'm tired of being everyone's little brother," he said. (We have an older sister I haven't mentioned yet—we both bobbed in sibling wake all through elementary school.) Fair enough. I was tired of being everyone's older brother. By the summer of 1985, we were at a time when if someone asked, "Where's Reggie?," I didn't know. And it was good to say I didn't know.

MY MOTHER SAID, "We're making good time." The LIE had stopped slicing towns in half and now cut through untamed Nassau County greenery, always a good sign. Apart from the occasional lump of an office park on the side of the highway, we were in the trees. I slunk back down and tried to claw my way back into sleep. It was hard to get a nice deep sleep going when heading out there—all you could really do was splash around in shallow water—and I endured my usual messy dreams, although the reason for them requires a bit more context:

Before we started staying at the beach house, we used to stay at the Hempstead House, and behind the Hempstead House was a small white wood-frame cottage with dingy yellow trim. At night, spied through the thin wall of trees separating the properties, the light in their kitchen was the only thing alive in the dark, the constant moon of summer. The woman who lived there in the '50s, my mother reminded us from time to time, used to have a fish fry on Saturdays, selling lunches, and legend had it that DuBois came out to Sag once and ate there. I nodded in a show of pride whenever my mother told us this story even though I had no idea who DuBois was. I had learned to keep my mouth shut about things I didn't know when I sensed that I was expected to know them.

For instance: there were Famous Black People I had never heard of, but it was too late to ask who they were because I was old enough, by some secret measure, that it was a disgrace that I didn't know who they were, these people who had struggled and suffered for every last comfort I enjoyed. How ungrateful. One of my uncles would be over and mention Marcus Garvey and I'd ask, "Who's that?," as the eyes of all the adults in the room slitted for a sad round of tsk-tsking. "Who's Toussaint L'Ouverture?" I'd stupidly inquire, and my father would shoot back, "You don't know who Toussaint L'Ouverture is? What do they teach you at that fancy school I bust my ass to send you to?" Not "Iconic Figures of Black Nationalism," that's for sure.

What I did know about DuBois was that he fell into the category of Famous Black People—there was a way people said certain names so that they had an emanation or halo. The respectful way my mother pronounced *DuBois* told me that the man had uplifted the race. Years later in college I'd read his most famous essay and be blown away. And I quote: "It is a peculiar sensation, this double-consciousness, this sense of always looking at one's self through the eyes of others, of measuring one's soul by the tape of a world that looks on in amused contempt and pity. One ever feels his two-ness,— an American, a Negro; two souls, two thoughts, two unreconciled strivings; two warring ideals in one dark body, whose dogged strength alone keeps it from being torn asunder. The history of the

American Negro is the history of this strife,—this longing to attain self-conscious manhood, to merge his double self into a better and truer self." I thought to myself: The guy who wrote that was chowing fried fish behind my house!

Driving with my father, it was potholes of double consciousness the whole way. There were only two things he would listen to on the radio: Easy Listening and Afrocentric Talk Radio. When a song came on that he didn't like or stirred a feeling he didn't want to have, he switched over to the turbulent rhetoric of the call-in shows, and when some knucklehead came on advocating some idea he found too cowardly or too much of a sellout, he switched back to the music. And all these sounds seeped into my dreams. One minute we were listening to the Carpenters singing "I'm on the top of the world looking down on creation," like so:

Such a feeling's coming over me
There is wonder in most everything I see
Not a cloud in the sky
Got the sun in my eyes
And I won't be surprised if it's a dream

Everything I want the world to be
Is now coming true especially for me
And the reason is clear
It's because you are here
You're the nearest thing to heaven that I've seen

Every time Karen Carpenter moved her mouth it was like the lid of a sugar bowl tinkling open and closed to expose deep dunes of whiteness. Then the next song would send my father's fingers to the preset stations and we were knee-deep into police brutality, the crummy schools, the mechanistic cruelty of city hall. The playlist of the city in those days was headline after headline of outrage, in constant rotation were bloody images of Michael Stewart choked to death by cops, Grandma Eleanor Bumpurs shot to death by cops,

Yusef Hawkins shot to death by racist thugs. On WLIB, they played the black Top 40, and the lyrics went like this:

What I want to know is
When are we going to have our day of justice
These white people think they can kill us in our homes

Can't walk down the street
Without some cracker with a baseball bat
Trying to murder us
Murder our children, our future
When are we going to have our day?

My father announced his approval by singing along or muttering "That's just common sense," depending on the song or stump speech. Is it any wonder my dreams were troubled? Ease and disquiet weaved in and out of reception, chasing each other down, two signals too weak to be heard for more than a few moments.

My father shut off the radio once we hit the manic nowhere that was East End radio, where ads for car dealerships and ladies' night at the latest one-season wonder duked it out between last month's hits. Ads for places we never went, services we never needed rendered. At the opening of summer, the words of the local DJs and merchants were cinder blocks, rebar, I beams, and bit by bit the edifice of the summer world rose from the dirt. Avoid the fender-bender on Stephen Hands Path, red flag at Mecox Beach, no swimming. With every mention of a landmark, that place came into being after nine months of banishment by the city. The words from the radio said, Stephen Hands Path exists again, Mecox Beach exists again, pulled out of mothballs, and even the tide itself has been conjured back to the shores. For we have returned.

We ditched Route 27 and cruise control and weaved down Scuttlehole Road, zipping past the white fencing and rusting wire that held back the bulging acres at the side of the road. I smelled the sweetly muddy fumes of the potato fields and pictured the corn stalks in their long regiments. My mother said, "That sweet Long Island corn," as she always did. Reggie had been farting for the last five minutes while pretending to be asleep. My feet scrabbled under the front seat in anticipation. Almost there. We slowed by the old red barn at the turnpike and made the left. From there to our house was like falling down a chute, nothing left to do but prepare for landing.

I kept my eyes closed. A few years earlier, I would have been panting at this point, up on my knees at the window and whipping my tail at the prospect of returning to Sag Harbor. I was beyond that—anything I could have seen here was not part of summer in a true sense, just a bit of warming up. I pictured what was outside and trees and houses in gray silhouette scrolled by, the featureless, unremarkable spots I had no connection to. The gray was interrupted by places that glowed, charged in my mind by association. The charred, heaped remains of that double-wide that burned down a few seasons back—we saw the fire, rubbernecking on the way to Caldor one afternoon. The dump, expeditions to which always had me and Reggie run-walking to the Dumpsters before the over-full bags broke open. Sometimes we pushed our luck, putting off a visit to the dump during a hot spell, and writhing maggots drizzled on our sneakers.

The glowing places were previews to the main attraction, previews most definitely, because some of them had ratings. Mashashimuet Park, Rated G for General Audiences, home to the only really good playground for miles, where Reggie and I and the crew had jumped, dangled on bars, and chased one another until we were sick, vomiting Pop Rocks and cola. There was also the PG part of Mashashimuet, the scrabbly baseball field, where the boys of my sister's age group had had a few mini race wars a few years back— black city kids versus white town kids over loitering rights to dirt and burrs. Then the turn at the pond and another hundred yards to the House on Otter Pond, Rated R restricted, as it was one of my parents' haunts, where they went out to eat without us and drank and did adult stuff. And on past the graveyard, the biggest coming attraction of all, rated I for Inevitable, where custom called for you to hold your breath as you passed, no matter what age you were, lest a spirit enter your open mouth. Or so it was said.

ONE SMALL ASIDE ON MOVIE PREVIEWS, more or less germane: our local movie palace was the Olympia on 107th and Broadway, chronic matinee destination for Reggie and me, and sometimes Friday night, too, when we had no other plans, which was more frequent than we liked. Site of what little hanging out we did that year, Hangover Central, a place to recover from the weeklong bender of misfitry that was our high-school experience thus far. The Olympia had survived the bad run that was the lot of uptown theaters in the '70s, when critters of insect and rodent descent often jumped into your lap for a little popcorn and the back rows were lost in the oily fog of cheap, laced cheeba. The real grimy joints had banks of phone booths in the lobby, old-school sliding doors and everything, so you could make a deal or a plea during the slow parts, and the worst characters were always diddling the coin slots with their fingers after that crucial dime.

The Olympia had a new marquee of hot-pink neon and new seats with red upholstery, but was still beset by a few gremlins. Management couldn't get the curtains going. First came the crackling of the speakers, and then we watched as the No Smoking/No Crying Babies messages and the first half of the previews played out on the stalled, crimson curtain in front of the screen. The ruffled images continued until the audience's invective grew loud enough that the projectionist or whatever multitasking character up there in the booth hit the switch and the curtain creaked apart. Every time. A couple of years earlier and you would have been bracing yourself for the volley of bullets aimed at the white slot of the booth, no joke.

The curtains always bugged me, apart from the obvious way they bothered everyone else. The curtains were just wrong in there, considering the dingy exploitation fare we had paid to see, the slasher flicks, the low-budget pyrotechnics of time-traveling Terminators. It was a sentimental relic of the time when people came to the Olympia for the stage spectacles of a kinder, classier age, and had no place in our lives. As a former twin, I liked things separate. You are there, me over here. Be nostalgic for the old days, but do it over there on your own time. Right here is the way things are now. We're trying to watch a movie.

WE DROVE PAST the weathered and splitting shingles of the old houses on Jermain Avenue and Madison Street, and the empty porches that referred to conversations long past or yet to come, never now, then the quiet plot that was Pierson High School, where no soul was ever seen, as if to aid in the illusion that the town was switched off when we weren't around. Those of a narcissistic bent could find such proof in any old place, everything was a prop if you wanted it to be, the beaches, Main Street, the sky, all of it gathering dust and waiting for your animating grace.

We stopped, which meant that my father was waiting for an opening to cross Route 114, and then we were rolling down Hempstead, the official start of our hood. Official—the book said so. We had this book, *Guide to Sag Harbor: Landmarks, Homes & History*, which we kept handy by the couch, for visitors I suppose, except that the only people who ever visited were other summer people, so we might as well have been displaying a pamphlet called *An Illustrated Guide to Your Own Damn Hand*. The book had a nice map of the village in it, tucked in between chronicles of the whaling boom and florid salutes to the quaint architecture, and we knew where our neighborhood began because that's where the map ended. The black part of town was off in the margins.

Hempstead was where the houses started to have names, with stories and histories attached. "That's the Grables," "That's the Huntingtons," even if the Grables and Huntingtons had sold off years ago. If I didn't know the people, I populated the houses using stories I'd heard, drawing material from the inflections of the speaker and the reactions of the listeners. The patriarch or number-one son of the Franklin House, for example, was surely a skirt-chasing horndog, if my hoard of random intel was any indication. Call: "Then Bob Franklin walked in with this young little gal who looked country as hell, with that big hair like they're wearing these days and skirt up so high so everybody could get a look at her stuff." Response: Shaking of heads, sliver of a smile.

Past Yardley Florist, whose greenhouses were visible from our old tree house. Our old tree house, which consisted of two pieces of rotting plywood lying in the dirt and three nails in the dead bark of an oak tree, was actually an ex–tree house, staked out by older kids years earlier, then abandoned. Maybe it had never been more than the idea of a tree house, an afternoon's fancy. But we had come upon it one day in the woods and decided it had been a home to adventure and we would make it so again. We were always coming upon paths made by those who had come before us, retracing their discoveries and mistakes. We told each other, some more wood, some nails pilfered from a jar in somebody's basement, and we'd make it into a real hideout. We hadn't been near it in years.

Then the turn onto Richards Drive, where I clenched my eyes tighter, for extra protection from a glimpse of the Hempstead House through the trees. Soon gravel popped against the undercarriage, the car gave one last rev of exhaustion before shutting off, and we had arrived. The bay could wait, the house could wait—they never changed so there was no need to appraise them, coo over them, honor them in any way—and me and my brother beat it to our bedroom for some proper sleep. Since my sister went off to college, Reggie and I had separate bedrooms after sharing a room our whole lives, either stacked on top of each other in bunk beds or head-to-head in a twin-bed L along the walls. Having our own space was wonderful. But out in Sag, we were back to sharing a room and we despised being so reduced in circumstance. The indignity of it all. There was an invisible fur covering everything, a musty coat, and it would linger for a couple of days until the house aired out.

It was six-thirty in the morning. That was that. We were out for the summer.

ONCE THE SEASON WAS IN FULL SWING, you came across one of the tribe and they asked, Do you know who else is out? The tantalizing inflection meant that they'd run into someone who hadn't been seen in a long time, some unlikely soul who'd gone missing in the big wild world. Bobby Hemphill, they said, Tammy Broderick, they said, and all the ancient stories and escapades bubbled up, nods and winks all around before you got to the business of trading rumors, the undermining of cover stories. Heard he got his pilot's license, he told me he went back to dental school. Rehab. She followed the trail of hang ups and odd receipts to her husband's mistress, dumped him, and decided to start coming out again. What were they up to? "A little this, a little that, you know, making some moves." That golden oldie: "Getting some stuff off the ground." Vague as hell, but persuasive if the speaker quickly changed the subject with a "How's your mom and pops?" They were back out to see if it had changed, if it was still the same, to recoup, recover, catch a breath. It was the bed you knew the best and all that entailed. We tried not to smirk at their predicaments, smirk at home maybe but not out there in public. It's such a nice day and we were raised better than that. By that strict generation.

There was something so sad about Those Who Didn't Come Out Anymore. Sometimes we knew why they didn't come out anymore, sometimes we didn't. Slander by their name if we suspected they thought themselves better than us. Good old Bobby, Good old Tammy. We called them by the old nicknames after all this time because it kept them in our clutches no matter how they struggled. They were branded by their pasts as much as we were. It was a close community and we all had dossiers on one another.

When I woke up, I heard my mother working the phone, trying to find out who was out, if the people who said they were coming out were indeed out, or if they had yet to arrive. No one was answering. Traffic or catastrophe, who knew. Reggie was already out of bed. In the kitchen, my father was bent over the grill scraping off last year's residue, strumming his harp with a pinkly foaming scouring pad. The pink reminded me of something and I went to check it out.

The doors to the storage space beneath the deck were secured by a cheap bolt from the Hardware Store in Town, as it was always referred to. No one ever tried to break in. I waded into the slatted light, swatting spiderwebs and half-digested creatures from my hair. I stepped over a spaghetti plate of hose and our three prizefighter rakes, one full smile between them, and approached the blue slopes of Mount Fuji. I pulled the tarp from the bike, spilling the dirty lakes that had accumulated over the winter. Reggie's bike lay a few feet away, wheels poking out from under plastic. It had fallen over at some point while we were away.

I tugged the red Fuji outside. The bike had been too small for me for a long time but now looked hopelessly lame. The grip tape on the handlebars, once a brilliant red, had faded to an inexcusably girlie pink. I'd raised the bike seat the last few summers, thin rusty scars marking the bar like the growth rings in a tree. When I raised the seat up this year, it'd be a clown bike. It needed air, and oil, and when I lifted it, it felt as light as a ball of aluminum foil.

"Reggie!" I yelled. He didn't answer. "Reggie!"

I found him up on the deck, hunched over the side of a chaise. At his feet, on some newspaper, I recognized an ancient bottle of ammonia from under the kitchen sink. It was older than I was. Reggie dipped a toothbrush into the bottle and then slowly rubbed it against the foxing of one of his new sneakers—puffy white Filas, B-boy specials he'd started wearing the week before. They weren't his usual style of footwear, a little further out into the Street than we ever ventured. He appraised the sneaker, rubbed the toothbrush against some tiny scuff, returned to the ammonia, and repeated the process. It was the most gentle I had ever seen him.

"What are you doing?"

"What's it look like? Cleaning my kicks."

Such an alien thought, keeping your sneakers clean. I'd switched over to black Chuck Taylors that spring, a gesture toward punk by my sights (no one cared), and the days had not been kind to them.

The black canvas had sickened to uneven gray, and the toe bumpers a jaundiced yellow. But the true shame was the shoelaces, which were too long to begin with, and which I ineptly tied in addition, and had over the months dragged across whole marathons of Manhattan pavement. Perhaps you have seen documentary footage of a dry lake bed in the Kalahari, where it rains once a year for one precious hour. The lake bed transforms into an all-star tribute to the dynamism of creation. Dried-out seeds explode into flowering vegetation in an instant, nearsighted pollywogs and gangs of winged bugs suddenly hatch out of microscopic eggs, and all the parched animals who have been dying for a drink scurry out on their skinny legs to fill their humps and canteens. A whole, ragged world erupting from that one thunderclap. Now imagine the germy legions and bacterial hordes slumbering in the sidewalks of New York, waiting for a little moisture. On rainy days, the shoelaces were their floppy refuge, soaking up these misbegotten life-forms and granting them salvation. They were a holy land.

I heard about his sneakers before I saw them. Reggie was an easy sleeper who occasionally talked in his sleep, and I was an apprentice insomniac and eager audience for his nocturnal soliloquies. I usually tried to engage his gibberish and get a conversation going but it never worked. His mouth was awake but his ears slumbered. The week before we went out to Sag, we were watching TV in the living room when Reggie fell asleep and began to mumble. I waited for an opening. Maybe this time I would unlock the secrets of his unconscious mind, and use what I learned against him later.

"My new Filas . . . the brambles."

"Tell me about the brambles," I said patiently.

Reggie turned into the cushions. He said, "My new Filas . . . are . . ." And that was it.

I saw now that the missing word was *white*. His new Filas, following his ministrations, were a sheer gleaming white. He had his hand deep in one sneaker and held it up to the sky, scrutinizing it, tilting slowly to and fro, as if it were a piece of cloud that had broken off and conked him on the head. "The brambles" I interpreted as the unjust world, the vast array of malevolent forces out to blemish or mar his blessed kicks. I'd talk in my sleep, too, if I had such heavy thoughts roiling in my brain. (Maybe I did talk in my sleep but there was no one to hear me.) I wanted to know the origin of Reggie's behavior. Why Filas? Who told him about using ammonia? I said, "Let's go riding around."

"I gotta wait for them to dry."

Half an hour later, I was waiting in the driveway. Three months, I thought. In idle moments, I retreated into that early-summer dream of reinvention, when you set your eyes on September and that refurbished self you were going to tool around in, honking the horn so people would take notice, driving slowly around all the right hot spots: Look at me. I had a Plan coming together, and three months to implement it. Surely I was not alone in my delusion, although that wouldn't have occurred to me then. All over the world the teenage millions searched for routes out of their dank, personal labyrinths. Signing up for that perfect extracurricular, rehearsing fake smiles before toothpaste-flecked mirrors, rummaging through their personalities to come up with laid-back greetings and clever put-downs to be saved for that special occasion. Lying sprawled on their beds, ankles crossed, while they overanalyzed the lyric sheets of the band that currently owned their soul, until the words became a philosophy. Running up to bordering cliques and hurriedly exclaiming, "I want to defect!" All of them stooped and hungry, lurching after that shadowy creature, the New Me. An elusive beast, but like I said, I had three months to get my shit together.

"Come on!" I yelled.

My little bike. I leaned it away from me so I could get a good look. Flat tires, rusted joints, peeling paint, out of scale. Only a buffoon would climb on such a thing, but I'd been marked as such for a while now—some grave mistakes the first week of freshman year, and I'd derailed all my junior-high schemes of social improvement. I was one of those dullards who thought that "Just be yourself" was the wisdom of the ages, the most calming piece of advice I had ever heard, and acted accordingly. It enabled these words, for example, to escape my mouth: "I can't wait for Master of Horror George A. Romero to make another film. *Fangoria* magazine—still the best horror and sci-fi magazine around if you ask me—says he has trouble raising funding, but I think Hollywood is just scared of what he has to say." And also: "It seems like we—all of us—made a mistake by switching over to Advanced D&D. The Basic game was . . . purer, you know?" Statements (of simple truth!) that had been harmless weeks ago were now symptoms of disease. And possibly catching. I was just being myself, and I was just being avoided. For whole, contaminated semesters now.

Reggie didn't talk about his first year of high school. But he didn't look happy, and if I was faring poorly, logic said he had to be doing worse. I had always been the capable one, if you can imagine.

"Where's your bike?" I asked, when he finally showed up.

"Nah, I'm going to walk."

This was a breach of protocol. Riding around meant riding.

"You can ride if you want," Reggie said. "I'm going to walk." He looked down at his sneakers with great meaning.

It was the last time we'd start the summer that way. It was how we always did it, that first day—get out the bikes and take the measure of things. Tour the developments to see who else was around, recruit, then hit town, the five-and-ten, the Ideal, get a slice at Conca Doro. This was our system, skidding down the streets like some fraternal tumbleweed gusted about. Technically, we were hitting the reset button on our twinhood, but it didn't seem like that much of a cheat. Maybe it didn't matter what went on during the rest of the year. Sag Harbor was outside the rules.

"I'm not going to wait for you," I said. But I didn't leave him. I wobbled in foolish loops around him, out in front then doubling back. My long legs zagged goofily about. Each time I turned, the flat tires made long farting noises as the rubber collapsed into the asphalt. Reggie kept a solid pace as we headed up Walker Avenue. There were three housing developments in our summer world— Azurest, where we stayed, Sag Harbor Hills, and Ninevah. But Ninevah was a bit of a hike, and only Bobby lived there, and we'd trained him over the years to come to us, so it was off our itinerary. Azurest, check out the Hills, then town.

I didn't see a lot of parked cars. The summer people were trickling in. This was when there were still plenty of unimproved lots and people hadn't started building the really big places. The majority of the houses were two- or three-bedroom jobs built in the '6os. Snubbed-nosed, single-story ranch houses with cement patios and screened-in porches sat next to pastel-colored split-levels with oil-stained carports and unruly hydrangeas for that extra dab of color. Occasionally you came across a harsh-angled beach house, sheathed in rain-streaked gray pine and introduced by dark gravel that leaked out into the street after every big storm. No matter the size or make of the house, the early arrivals were tormented by the same questions. Did the roof keep through the winter, did the pipes hold, did a townie or local bad kid break in and steal the television, or was it just the raccoons and squirrels who had given the place the once-over? Is it still here or did I just dream it?

We passed the house that we always called "haunted," and for the first time we skipped our ritual, in which one of us dared the other to knock on the door, we argued about it for a few minutes, and then somebody threw a pebble at one of the windows as we ran away screaming. It was a tiny box of a house, shrinking every year into further dilapidation as more roof shingles flew away and the paint scabbed off. A motorboat on its hitch was barely visible for the weeds and bushes, beached there in cracked fiberglass after the Great Flood, and an old barbecue grill lay on its side, half in the woods, legs poking up, like a potbellied animal that had crawled there to die. Like we said, haunted.

There were a bunch of these ramshackle abodes scattered throughout the developments. The hedges grew out into—let's face it—a nappy riot, grasses filled the tire ruts of the driveways, and the front yard became a minefield of old phone books, the swollen pages of info straining against their plastic sheaths. The houses of Those Who Didn't Come Out Anymore. Who knew the stories behind them. Ask my mother about this or that house and she'd say, "They Don't

Come Out Anymore," in such a way that you saw the weeds grow-ing up around her words. There were obvious reasons—economic reversal, no longer living in the Northeast—but my thoughts always tended to the melancholic. Like, the red house on Milton was one generation's gift to the next, but the kids and grandkids neglected it, didn't appreciate the treasure they possessed, and left it to rot. Or, the people who lived on Cuffee Drive hadn't come out in decades, but if they sold the property, what did they have? It was the most impor-tant thing they had in their lives and they held out hope that one summer they would return. Maybe the missing neighbors absorbed all our bad luck so that we could have it easy.

Over the years I discovered that there was a variety of haunted. There were houses that were immaculately maintained, but where you never saw any people. The gutters sparkled in the sunlight, the hedges were grazed into clean, perfect geometry, the curtains in the windows just so. The lawn mowers appeared the first day of spring, shredding up and down the rows twice a week, and the sprinklers maintained sure, sibilant order, calibrated to wet one molecule's dis-tance from the property line and no farther. But you never saw a hu-man presence. No lights, no cars, no life-affirming barbecue smoke rising from the deck in the backyard. The houses waited all summer for their owners to appear, and then one day the lawn guy made his last visit and that was that. Well, taking into account people's sched-ules, it was possible that you might miss seeing your neighbor, never pass them on the street. You could coexist in this Sag Harbor galaxy in perfectly alienated orbits, always zipping into each other's blind spots, or hidden on the dark side of the moon. Of course that could happen to people who lived on the same street. Sometimes it hap-pened to people who lived in the same house.

Someone was writing the maintenance checks, doling out cash to LILCO and the water company, but somewhere they got stalled out. There was a malfunction. I couldn't wrap my head around it. That kind of house was different from the ones that were kept up all sum-mer but were only inhabited one weekend a year, usually Labor Day. The one-weekenders were a familiar group, not known for their planning skills. And for completion's sake, we should also respect that renaissance house, haunted for long years but rediscovered by a new generation out to reclaim some shred of childhood joy, or by new arrivals who finally owned their little piece of the Sag Harbor mystique after so long. They fixed the roof, redid the patio, finally put in a decent water heater that didn't go into a coma after one shower. Performed an exorcism. Kudos.

WE ROUNDED THE BEND on Walker. Marcus was first up in our circuit. The Collins House was a lime-green split-level where we were never allowed upstairs. Marcus's bedroom was on the first floor, next to the rec room, and there we had often loitered around the old Trinitron, but going upstairs was off-limits to kids. Periodically, his mother shouted down directives we couldn't decipher, and Marcus would curse, stomp upstairs, and disappear for a while. When that happened we knew we were getting kicked out into the street. We were already standing when Marcus eventually reappeared, tossing excuses, and we beat it out the sticky screen door to the next afternoon oasis.

The telephone book was still waiting on Marcus's front step, and this year's Oldsmobile, the next in a proud line of Collins Oldsmobiles, was not to be seen. "Let's take the shortcut," Reggie said. Walker was the last street in Azurest before Sag Harbor Hills, so it was convenient for taking a shortcut to the other side.

We loved shortcuts. For a long time, it was hard to top the thrill of slipping into a slim corridor into the woods, undetectable except for the small mound of kicked-up soil by the side of the road. Sometimes a shortcut was half woods and half a sprint through someone's property, but the best ones cut through two unimproved properties, one in Azurest, the other in the Hills. Even though you were only making your way across two quarter-acre lots, it was like hacking through primeval forests, the gigantic fronds of an alien planet. The only people who had preceded us were fellow explorers. Each time the branches shivered closed behind us, we exited our juvenile existences and joined the fraternity of the brave. I never discovered any shortcuts on my own. I only found out about them when the rest of the gang initiated me. Didn't have the eye, apparently.

The real woods outside of the developments were the true frontier, enigmatic and intimidating. Behind the gas station, or leading out from the paths behind the park, we tramped farther and farther from the roads we knew, each fork thoroughly debated—left is madness, right is the buried treasure, the gold doubloons to be divvied up according to age and status. We stumbled across shotgun shells, remains of fires, crushed beer cans, fresh tracks gouged by motorbikes—dangerous characters were up to inscrutable things between towns. Who had left these things, who was lurking in the shadows? "The KKK" was the usual answer, the reliable if unlikely boogeyman, tossed out there to amp up the feeling of danger. Statistically speaking, there may have been some members of the KKK in the near vicinity—it was the Hamptons, a "resort community" after all, and even the worst America has to offer occasionally need to unwind, catch some rays—but it was unlikely that they were patrolling on horseback, in full getup, complete cracker regalia, behind the dirt trails of Mashashimuet Park. Nonetheless, everybody immediately traded versions of how they were going to outrun the KKK—"I'd be out in front of you dummies with a quickness," "Knock your ass down to buy me some time"—while I kept silent, thinking of how I was going to save Reggie. Grandiose scenes of self-sacrifice came easily to me, wherein I distracted the Hooded Menace long enough to allow him to escape. He was my little brother.

When we got to the shortcut in question, there was nothing to say beyond Reggie's verdict: "That's messed up." We were used to emerging from the woods to see a car in the driveway of a shortcut house and having to hightail it back. We were not accustomed to the woods disappearing. The old oaks and chestnut trees and low-lying sticker bushes had been uprooted and cleared. In their stead, moist orange dirt was heaped in piles, and the freshly laid cement foundation gaped at us. It was messed up, some newcomers taking over land we had claimed. It wasn't hard to picture the future. First this lot, then the rest. One by one, the new Sag Harbor would replace the haunted houses in all their forms.

"I hate that," I said.

"That's messed up," Reggie repeated.

We took the long way around. Not a lot of people in the Hills, either. Clive's house looked dead. The brown kente-cloth drapes behind the sliding glass doors to his living room were tight. Usually, they were open from May to September, inviting us in. The grass had been cut, though, so this was a promising sign. Maybe next weekend.

"I think we're the only ones here," I said. Private schools were done for the year, but not public schools yet, and I didn't know about the Catholic schools. Maybe it was just us.

"Ma-a-nn," Reggie said.

Then we heard a far-off call. We listened and nodded to each other. One two three. Pause. One two. Pause. It was the metallic squeal of a basketball on asphalt, the teenage Morse code of indolent boys that said: I AM OVER HERE. We followed the trail.

We saw NP bouncing about in his familiar rhythm. To observe NP was to witness a haphazard choreography of joints and limbs. His invisible puppeteer had shaky hands, making it seem that NP was always on the verge of busting out into some freaky dance move. Looking back, his condition was probably caused by him trying to keep his freaky dance moves in check, whatever convulsive thing he'd taken notes on at a party the week before and had just finished practicing in his room. That I wouldn't have heard of the dance was a given—the Phillie Bugaloo, the Reverse Cabbage Patch. Hanging out with NP was to start catching up on nine months of black slang and other sundry soulful artifacts I'd missed out on in my "predominately white" private school. Most of the year it was like I'd been blindfolded and thrown down a well, frankly.

Not that I didn't learn anything in school, culture-wise. The hallways between classes were tutelage into the wide range of diversions our country's white youth had come up with to occupy themselves. When I had free time in between engineering my next humiliation, I was introduced to the hacky sack, which was a sort of miniature leather beanbag that compelled white kids to juggle with their feet. It was a wholesome communal activity, I saw, as they lobbed the object among one another, cheering themselves on, and it appeared to foster teamwork and goodwill among its adherents. Bravo! There was also a kind of magical rod called a lacrosse stick. It directed the more outgoing and athletic specimens of my school to stalk the carpeted floors and obsessively wring their hands around it, as if to call forth popularity or a higher degree of social acceptance by diligent application of friction. You heard them muttering "hut hut hut" in masturbatory fervor as they approached. Good stuff, in an anthropological sense. But these things were not the Technotronic Bunny Hop, or the Go-Go Bump-Stomp, the assorted field exercises of black boot camp. And as with DuBois, I knew I couldn't ask what these things were. I had to observe and gather information.

Switch off this, switch on that. We hung out with each other every day, all day, all summer, and then didn't see each other for nine months.

"Benji 'n' Reggie, Benji 'n' Reggie."

We exchanged friendly outs ("This morning," "Us, too") and told him we'd be out for the summer. There was also the language of prison in there, in how long are you out for. Time on the East End was furlough, a day pass, a brief visit with the old faces and names before the inevitable moment when you were locked up again. That hard time that defined the majority of our days. You did something wrong, why else would such a thing like the city happen to you. For a couple of weeks each year us habitual offenders got together and got up to no good before the handcuffs pinched our wrists again. Earlier, I described Sag as a kind of trap, but the place also attracted the language of freedom. I don't know which is worse, the trap or the prison. Either way, you're stuck.

We called him NP, for Nigger Please, because no matter what came out of his mouth, that was usually the most appropriate response. He was our best liar, a raconteur of baroque teenage shenanigans. Everything in his field of vision reminded him of some escapade he needed to share, or directed him to some escapade about to begin, as soon as all the witnesses departed. He was dependable for nonsense like, "Yo, last night, after you left, I went back to that party and got with that Queens girl. She told me she was raised strict, but I was all up in those titties! She paid me fifty dollars!"

Nigger, please.

"Yo, yo, listen: I was walking by the Miller House and I went to take a look at their Rolls and get this, I was like, they left the keys in the ignition. You know I took that shit for a spin, I was like Thurston Howell the Third up in that bitch! With Gilligan!"

Nigger, please.

Shortened to NP because the adults gave us trouble when they heard us using the word *nigger*. For understandable reasons. Like most authority figures, they had a hypocritical streak, as they used the word all the time, in its familiar comrade sense, but also to distinguish themselves from those of our race who possessed a certain temperament and circumstance. The kind of person that made the announcer on the evening news say, "We have an artist's rendering of the suspect," quickening your heart. There were no street niggers in Sag Harbor. No, no, no.

But we all had cousins who . . . you know.

We thought we were being smart with his nickname until one day we were over at NP's house and his mom started getting on his case for some chore or other that he had neglected. He began some elaborate explanation—meteorites had squashed his bike and he couldn't make it home—when she lost her patience and cut him off with a sudden, shrill, "Nigger, please!" Mrs. Nichols's hand shot to her mouth, but it was too late. His nickname had approval at the highest levels. For all we knew, she'd coined it in the first place. One can only imagine watching the boy grow up in your house and knowing you were partially responsible.

Like us, like all of us, present or as yet unaccounted for, NP had come out here every summer of his life, and even before he was born, as his mother had waded into the bay to cool her pregnant belly. We had beaten each other up, stolen each other's toys, fallen asleep in the backseats of station wagons together as we caravanned back from double features at the Bridgehampton Drive-In, the stars scrolling beyond the back window. We were copying our parents, who went back just as far, beating each other up thirty years ago under the same sky. Eating each other's barbecue, chasing each other down the hacked-out footpaths to the beach before there were roads, beach houses, a community at all.

"Hey Benji, watch it!" NP cried out. "You're messing up my kicks!"

I had been circling around him and Reggie, and my front wheel had squeezed out a pebble and sent it flying. The pebble collided with NP's sneaker, which I now noticed was the Fila model that Reggie was wearing. And just as white.

I didn't see any mark. NP pulled a white handkerchief from his pocket, licked it, and rubbed it against his sneaker.

"Sorry about that," I said.

"These are my Filas."

"There is one thing, though." I cleared my throat. "I'm not going by Benji anymore. I'm going by Ben."

"What?" NP looked at Reggie for confirmation. I hadn't broken the news to Reggie yet. He tilted his head.

"I want to go by Ben," I said. "You know, have people call me Ben instead of Benji."

Harkening back to the aforementioned Plan: No more of this Benji shit. It was a little kid's name, and I was not a little kid anymore. Ben, Ben. Case in point: stuck there next to my brother in that "Benji 'n' Reggie" construction—it was demeaning. Benji was the name of a handholder, not a fingerfucker or avid squeezer of breasts, or whatever tyro sexual-type act I would engage in once I found a willing subject. One step at a time, and a step away from Benji was a good one.

"Okay Benji, whatever, homie." NP yawned.

Reggie shook his head. "Let's go to town."

The three of us started back down the street. I was pretty excited to get out of the developments and grab a slice. To see if everything was where it was supposed to be. But when we should have been turning right, NP steered left, and Reggie followed.

"Where are you guys going?" I asked.

"We should take the beach," NP said. "It's faster."

"I can't take my bike on the sand."

A moment passed where we all looked at the Li'l Red Fuji. And its pretty pink handlebars. It should be noted that they were not a pristine pink, but one much-grubbed by years of sweat and assorted boyhood antics. Nonetheless.

"I told you," Reggie said.

"It's a shortcut," NP said. He dribbled his basketball for a second, then tucked it under his arm. "We'll meet you there. I ain't getting my bike out," he said. "The tires are flat. Mess up the rims."

I looked to Reggie for backup. He was looking down at his sneakers.

"Where are you going to be?" I exhaled loudly. Town wasn't that big, but still.

"Conca D'Oro, whatever," NP said. "You'll find us."

They disappeared down the path to the beach, that narrow aperture into water and sunlight. There was that one variation of out, Who else is out?, which was the most important out of all. Everything depended on it. Who else is out? We asked each other. We needed to know, Is it just you and me or is there another to save us from each other?

The
Heyday
of
Dag

THERE WERE SOME WHITE PEOPLE COMING UP THE beach so we got out the binoculars. White people owned the waterfront behind town, but the beach was ours, and any infiltration had to be checked out. The front wall of our living room was glass, giving us superior angles of surveillance, and my father kept binoculars handy for this very purpose. He owned two pairs, one for here and one for the city, where we faced West End Avenue and teeming beehives of naked potential. At any given moment, a nice percentage of apartments had their blinds up, their curtains spread, and you never knew what drama might emerge if you were on the lookout. Best to keep the binoculars close.

"That's trespassing," NP said.

Bobby raised the binoculars. "It looks like two fags holding hands," he said.

It was the heyday of fag. Get a bunch of teenage virgins and future premature ejaculators together, and you were going to hear *fag* a lot. Get a bunch of kids together who felt punked out in various ways, and the collective mind sought ways to punk out others. A touch of homophobia was also good for hiding any nascent predilections and/or yearnings lurking about. Binoculars: a device that facilitates looking down on people.

"They better not try to come up here," NP said. "I'll bust their ass."

"Shit, you'd be like, 'Come up here, sailor, I just dropped the soap.' "

"Dag."

It was also the heyday of dag. Dag was bitter acknowledgment of the brutish machinery of the world. It was a glimpse into the cruel void, as evidenced by the fact that it was often followed by "That was cold." In the heyday of dag, we accepted our duty to call attention to such moments, taking turns at this minor masochism. It passed the time.

I took the binoculars from Bobby. The intruders were actually a middle-aged man and woman, soft and shuffling. They clutched their shoes and dug their toes into the damp sand. Every few steps, one of them pointed at some feature of the landscape—the lighthouse squatting on its nest of rocks, the green Mohawk of seaweed on a black stone, the pale carcass of an overturned horseshoe crab— as their companion gaped in wonder. The gender confusion—apart from some wishful thing on NP's part, as he was always trying to start some shit—came from their shapeless clothes, the way they disappeared into the T-shirt–khaki shorts combo that was the official uniform of tourists the world over.

"We should go down there and tell them to get off our beach," Bobby said. He lived in Ninevah, down the way, hence his interest in keeping the sands undefiled by outsiders, but everybody in the developments, whether they lived on the beach or not, felt that selfish tug of ownership when they saw strangers—i.e., white people—on our little stretch. Most of the strollers came from the Public Beach, visiting friends for the afternoon and then letting their curiosity draw them toward Azurest. We made noises of outrage, but never did anything. There was an older lady or two of the first generation who were known to fly across the sand and admonish strangers that dogs weren't allowed on the beach, if the people in question happened to be chaperoning some yapping enthusiast off-leash, but mostly we grumbled to remind ourselves we had rights to assert, and that was enough.

Already the couple was turning back. Visitors never made it that far up the beach in those days. Watching them slow down, stop for a conference, and then turn back made you an audience to a familiar pantomime. Something was off. Everyone was brown. The ladies plopped on striped beach chairs and towels, the kids stirring sand with plastic shovels and chipped clamshells. They were every shade in the dessert menu of words beloved by romance novelists to describe African American skin, chocolate and caramel, butterscotch and mocha. Black eyes glared down from the beach houses, the lookouts on the decks of our armada. Yes, something is off, let's head back.

They rarely made it past the Rock. The Rock was a few houses down from ours and a powerful psychological meridian. Kids told each other, "I'll race you to the Rock," because it was an impossible, panting distance. Parents warned, "Don't go past the Rock," to keep their offspring in view as they gossiped and sipped Fresca. Parents let their attention lapse, argued, flirted, dozed—as long as the kids didn't stray past the Rock, nothing would happen to them. Perhaps this has happened to you, on beaches: you start drifting off while lying on a beach blanket, close your eyes and shut down your ears only to find yourself revisiting some personal torment still powerful enough after all these years to suck you into its undertow. Don't know what I'm talking about? Never mind. Take my word, friend, the Rock was an anchor to keep you from drifting too far.

It was our almanac, registering all things tidal, every off-season cataclysm. In the autumn and winter, nor'easters came to play in Sag

Harbor Bay, big dumb children that never cleaned up after themselves. The great storms mucked up sand in impressive tonnage, shoving the tide line snug up to the beach grass one year, almost no place to walk, then clawing it back the next year so that low tide became a strictly ankle affair, wearying you to get halfway wet. Wade, wade, wade. You never knew how much beach you were going to see at the start of the summer, what kind of state the Rock was going to be in that year. This season, the Rock was high and proud, next season it had been brought down low, up to its neck in sand. But it was always a real trooper, bird-shitted and buried or no. After eons of being kicked around by glaciers, and then deposited on some random strip of beach, it must be hard to faze you.

The Rock, the Creek, the Point: the increments of our existence. Earth, solar system, galaxy. The shallow waves of the Creek put an end to the line of beach houses, and on the opposite bank the wetland outskirts of East Hampton whispered in their eternal huddle. Watching over a scrabble of inhospitable beach, the wetlands curved up to Barcelona Neck, aka the Point, and beyond that maps failed. Even the animals changed, so extreme the border between Sag Harbor and East Hampton. Crescent rinds of dried-out sand sharks littered the shore and this new breed of horseflies, the juvenile delinquents of their set, taunted and nipped the whole way to the Point, trying to suck the moisture on your legs. The Horsefly Shuffle was the one dance I could do, no hassle: bat at thighs and calves, skitter a few feet in a serpentine style, repeat. Also: shout "Dag!" whenever a horsefly raised a welt. Who knew what kind of fauna lurked around the bend of Barcelona Neck? Pterodactyls wearing ascots and sipping gin and tonics, trust-fund duck-billed platypuses complaining about "the help." It was all hoity-toity over there.

When we were small, we were impatient for the day when we'd be able to undertake an expedition out to the Point. Sandwiches in baggies, orange soda, baleful glances backward after the soothing sight of our homes. By 1985, we knew it wasn't worth it, and had decided the same was true of the entire beach. This grousing about beach rights and intruders was beside the point because we never hung out down there anymore. The beach was for little kids and old people. We preferred the ocean, on the other side of the island. Especially now that we had access to a car. The ocean, in fact, was our destination that afternoon, once the guys finally showed up.

So forget the beach and the rest of it, the quality of the sunrises and sunsets . . . although it must be said that those two things were top-notch. Waking up early in that house was science-fiction stuff. The sky over the wetlands was a fine, simmering blue, slowly boiling up morning. Before you lay the dead, misty surface of the bay, an imperturbable line of dark gray, a slab of ancient stone come out from under the earth. A reversal there: the sky was liquid, the water a solid screen. There were fewer boats then to zit the surface of the bay. No one to be seen at that hour, emboldening that cherished dread of early risers, that you were the only being alive and awake in the world. Occasionally some drowsily dipping seagull shot into the water after low-tide crab, seized its quarry in its beak, and swooped back up to the sky, dropping the bits of shell after it nuzzled out the meat so that the dead pieces briefly rippled the water before all was silent again. A mute, primordial theater.

Sunsets unfolded above the big houses in North Haven. The sunset made it appear that the sun and the sky were not separate things but different states of the same magnificent substance—as if the sky were a weakened diluted form of the sun, the blue and the white merely drained-away elements of the swirling red-and-orange disk sitting on the horizon. I'll wager on this: the sunsets closed the deal for that first generation, the ones who came here originally, my grandparents and their crew. After walking down through the woods off Hempstead Street, the meek trails that would one day be roads, it must have been wondrous to emerge on that unspoiled beach and see that sunset. No houses, no footprints even, just beach grass whispering to itself. Saying—what? You'd have to spend some time to learn its language. That first generation asked, Can we make it work? Will they allow us to have this? It doesn't matter what the world says, they answered each other. This place is ours. Over the years I have learned that the sunrises and sunsets of that beach are rare and astonishing but I did not know this then. Sunset meant that the damned gnats were coming out, that was it.

NP SAID, "Benji, can I get a Coke?" His head was in the refrigerator.

Cokes were no problem. My parents kept a healthy store of mixers and such. With their friends coming up from the beach for drinks, and now me and Reggie's gang spending so much time hanging out on our couch all day, they had adjusted their mixers supply. Food was something else, however, with Reggie and me on rations.

That summer we switched from a Kid with the Pool–based hanging out economy to a Kid with the Empty House–based hanging out economy. Before his family moved to California and he stopped coming out, Kevin had been our Kid with the Pool, and the fact that we never saw his mother made it a prelude to the days of Empty Houses. I think I saw her once, when I was little. I think. We knew someone was in there—the afternoon soaps blared kissing music or about-to-kiss music through the windows and once in a while a hand clawed back the curtains overlooking the pool area. Safe to say we were unsupervised. As we horsed around in the pool, we pretended that we lived in a world without parents, but actually it didn't take that much pretending.

We'd been moving toward Empty House status for a while. For years, we'd skulked in basement rec rooms, on screened porches, played tag on cracked patios. We heard footsteps above, inside, over there, but never saw who they belonged to. In every house there were secret rooms with locked doors and if you asked who was in there watching TV, the kid always said, "My grandma," in the same dead tone. The moms ran through their summer itinerary, off to the beach with a folding chair under one arm and an overflowing wicker bag in the other, off to "a luncheon," a cocktail party in the Hills, or an art opening in the backyard of someone who had a cousin with a bunch of friends who were said to be talented and known in Harlem galleries. The dads were in the city, making money, making something happen, reappearing on the Friday evening 7:25 train in East Hampton, staggering off the club car with big smiles: Showtime.

That summer we just made it official. Reggie and I were the Kids with the Empty House, and the gang changed their schedules and routes accordingly. Our parents only came out on weekends, which meant that now me and Reggie had the place to ourselves most of the week. Our sister, Elena, used to be the one in charge, bossing us around with such relish that history's great lesson, "Power corrupts," played out in intimate scale in our living room. How we cringed as she kept us in line with her powerful club, "I'll tell Daddy on you." But she was gone now. Once you were old enough to go to college, you stopped coming out to Sag. It was kids' stuff, it was too bourgie, the city summoned, etc. Graduate from high school, and you graduated from Sag as well. Until you were called back.

"You're men now," my father told me when I asked who was going to look after us. "You can take care of yourselves." Men? A compliment and a curse: no more excuses, no one to blame. At first I thought he was joking. But there we were—me and Reggie alone during the week, and my parents only coming out on weekends. If then.

Now that we had a free house, what did we do with it? Sit around and talk shit. That day it was me, NP, and Bobby. Reggie was working at Burger King. The smell of Reggie's grease-infused clothes crept from our bedroom, from the corner where he tossed his work duds, making us hungry whenever a breeze swept through.

"You want sprinkles with that Coke?" Bobby asked. NP had a job at Jonni Waffle, the new ice-cream joint in town, and when we went to visit him for freebies we taunted him over the stupid shit he had to say all day. Whip on top, waffle cone, slob your knob? NP had also been ribbing Bobby about his "Scarsdale mansion" lately, causing Bobby to push back a little.

"Shut up, you pleather Members Only–wearin' motherfucker," NP said. Which might appear to be a non sequitur, as Bobby was wearing a T-shirt and shorts, but there was history there, context. It was a reference to some intel from Clive, who had informed us that he'd run into Bobby during the school year, and described how Bobby was wearing a Windbreaker that looked suspiciously like a knockoff Members Only jacket. No small misdemeanor, that, and Clive's alpha-dog status only magnified the dis.

The trend that summer, insult-wise, was toward grammatical acrobatics, the unlikely collage. One smashed a colorful and evocative noun or proper noun into a pejorative, gluing them together with an -in' verb. I'm not sure of the syntactical parentage of the -in' verbs, so I'll just call them the -in' verbs. Verbal noun, gerundlike creature, cog in the adjectival machine, who knew—as was the case with some of the people in my living room, there was a little uncertainty in the bloodlines. "Lookin' " was a common -in' verb. Like so:

MODIFIER 'IN VERB OBJECT

ANGELA DAVIS   MOTHER FUCKER
GORBACHEV   LOOKIN'—BITCH
GEORGE JEFFERSON   NIGGER

"Wearin' " made the rounds as well:

MESSED-UP GARANIMAL-ASS   MOTHER FUCKER
99 CENT —WEARIN'—BITCH
GOLD CHAIN
FAKE ADIDAS   NIGGER

You could also preface things with a throat-clearing "You fuckin'," as in "You fuckin' Cha-Ka from *Land of the Lost*–lookin' motherfucker," directed at Bobby, for example, who had light brown skin, light brown hair, and indeed shared these characteristics with the hominid sidekick on the Saturday morning adventure show *Land of the Lost*. "You fuckin' " acted as a rhetorical pause, allowing the speaker a few extra seconds to pluck some splendid modifier out of the invective ether, and giving the listener a chance to gird himself for the top-notch put-down/splendid imagery to follow.

True masters of the style sometimes attached the nonsensical "with your monkey ass" as a kicker, to convey sincerity and depth of feeling. Hence, "You fuckin' Kunta Kinte–lookin' motherfucker . . . with your monkey ass." You may have noticed that the -in' verbs were generally visual. The heart of the critique concerned what you were putting out into the world, the vibes you gave off. Which is what made them so devastating when executed well—this ordnance detonated in that area between you and the mirror, between you and what you thought everyone else was seeing.

There was a loud squeaking noise. "Hear that?" I asked. It was Marcus on that messed-up bike of his, you heard him changing gears two miles away.

We all sighed with relief. Marcus was a key player in that he reassured us that there was someone more unfortunate than ourselves. He possessed three primary mutant powers; we had all seen them in action: 1. He was able to attract to his person all the free-floating derision in the vicinity through a strange magnetism. 2. He bent light waves, rendering the rest of us invisible to bullies. When Marcus was present, the big kids were incapable of seeing us, picking on him exclusively, delivering noogies, knuckle punches, and Indian rope burns to his waiting flesh. Indian rope burns always put an end to the torture, because everybody got distracted while bonding over their smidgen of Indian blood, one-eighth, one-sixteenth Seminole whatever, and that was that. 3. Superior olfactory capability. We heard his bike from two miles away; he smelled barbecue from twice that distance, attaining such mastery that he could ascertain, with the faintest nostril quivering, if the stuff on the grill had just been thrown on or was about to come off, and acted accordingly. Like a knife and fork, he appeared around dinnertime. I think there was a summer or two when he ate over every night, guzzling Hi-C and waving a plastic-coated paper plate around for seconds, more, more. Not until later did I wonder why there was no dinner at his house, why no one missed him at twilight. Call him a mooch to hurt his feelings, and he'd just smile, wipe his mouth with his wrist, and snatch the last piece of chicken, probably a wing, damn him. He was always hungry, like we all were, but at least he had the good sense to eat.

Marcus pried open the glass doors. They were sticky. Decades of sand filled their tracks. "What's up?" He had his beach towel around his neck, and he wore dark-green-and-gray plaid shorts, and a T-shirt that read BOY'S HARBOR JULY 4 FIREWORKS 1983. He extended his hand to Bobby and I witnessed a blur of choreography.

Yes, the new handshakes were out, shaming me with their permutations and slippery routines. Slam, grip, flutter, snap. Or was it slam, flutter, grip, snap? I was all thumbs when it came to shakes. Devised in the underground soul laboratories of Harlem, pounded out in the blacker-than-thou sweatshops of the South Bronx, the new handshakes always had me faltering in embarrassment. Like this? No, you didn't stick the landing: the judges give it 4.6. (The judge from Hollis, Queens, was a notorious dick, undermining everyone from the other boroughs.) No one ever commented on my fumbles, though, and I was grateful. I had all summer to get it right, unless someone went back to the city and returned with some new variation that spread like a virus, and which my strong dork constitution produced countless antibodies against.

NP slapped Marcus's hand. "Hey, Act—" NP began, before cutting himself off. He was about to use last year's nickname.

We used to call Marcus "Arthur Ashe." Two summers ago, Marcus had suffered a dry patch—actually multiple dry patches, on his elbows, knees, in the webbing between his fingers and toes. "Why'd his mother let him out the house like that," we'd all wonder, but never say aloud, because talking about someone's mother was, well, talking about someone's mother. Talking about someone's mother was talking about your own mother: it opened a door.

Obviously the nickname affected him deeply. Perhaps the sight of a tennis racket mortifying him, all those long months of the school year, or a chance encounter with someone dressed in crisp white clothing curdling his mood. All I know is that the next summer Marcus returned so profoundly moisturized that there was nary a flake of ash to be seen on his skin. In fact his skin was so lubed up that he glistened mightily whenever the sun hit his flesh, and even when it didn't. He had become, sadly, a living Jheri Curl.

"Hey, Activator!" NP called out one afternoon, while making little spritzing motions about his head, and Arthur Ashe was now Activator until Labor Day.

It was the last week of June, still early in the season, so there was no telling what kind of handle Marcus would get this year. Whatever nickname he got, it was likely to be of the kinder variety—he had grown four inches over the year and started lifting weights, or tied-together phone books, some kind of heavy object. Maybe he'd cast his disappointments in lead. No one had put him to the test yet, but powwows over the matter, even our diluted one-eighth or one-sixteenth powwows, decided that he could kick all our asses, and we had it coming.

I did a head count: four of us, Randy and Clive on their way. There were five seats in Randy's car.

"They're not here yet?"

Bobby sucked his teeth. "Waiting on them all day."

"It's going to be dark by the time they get here."

"It's going to be six of us?" I asked. I was trying to get the fight started over who was coming in the car. Let everybody get their arguments for inclusion going beforehand, and see where I stood.

"Shit, I know I'm going, I had to ride my bike last time," Marcus said.

"I know I'm going—he's my cousin," NP countered.

I decided to make some lunch, to fortify myself for the battle to come. Reggie and me didn't agree on much when it came to food, but we were both partial to Campbell's Homestyle Chicken Soup with Egg Noodles. It was the Cadillac of canned soup, the noodles firm yet pliant on the tongue, the ratio of celery and carrots consistent and reliable. The tiny amber globules of fat shimmered on the surface in an enticing display, to delight the eye. There was one can left; I'd traded it with Reggie that morning for a bag of Lay's Potato Chips and two ice-cream sandwiches. Every couple of days, Reggie and I walked over to Frederico's and stocked up on food. Our family had a credit account there.

Everybody had their brands, black kids, white kids. Sperry, Girbaud, and Benetton, Lee jeans and Le Tigre polos, according to the plumage theory of social commerce. If the correct things belonged to you, perhaps you might belong. I was more survival-oriented. The brands I worshipped lived in the soup aisle, in the freezer section behind glass. I'm talking frozen food here. Swanson, of course, was the standard, the elegant marriage of form and function. The four food groups (meat, veg, starch, apple cobbler) lay pristine in their separate foil compartments, which were in fact, presto, a serving dish. Meal and plate in one slim rectangle—this was American ingenuity at its best and most sustaining. Fried Chicken, Turkey, Salisbury Steak, that was three days of the week right there.

All hail Stouffer's! Pure royalty, their bright-orange packaging a beacon in refrigerator sections across the NY metro area. French Bread Pizzas—so continental! Turkey Tetrazzini, Chicken Pot Pie, Beef Pot Pie. Friday, Saturday, Sunday. Stouffer's employed the best minds the prepackaged food industry had to offer, no doubt luring geniuses from rival firms with groovy perks and extensive benefit packages, ultimately producing that sublime Boil-in-Bag technology, up there with penicillin and the microchip in the pantheon of twentieth-century scientific achievement. I will admit to an unwholesome fascination with Boil-in-Bag technology. Chicken à la King, Swedish Meatballs, Beef Stroganoff with Parsley Noodles—'twas satisfaction itself that oozed out of the plastic bags and murked our waiting bowls.

There were, as well, renegades to whom we had given our hearts, like Howard Johnson's Tendersweet Fried Clams, 95 percent batter plus a special ingredient that made you forget that they were 95 percent batter the next time you reached for them in the supermarket.

And the rare and valued Weight Watchers Chicken Cutlet & Veg-
etable Medley, tough to find on account of some complex distribution quirk beyond my ken, and entering our menu rotation by
accident; my mother had bought a box for herself one time, and in
a famished episode I had devoured it and become addicted. I felt
ridiculous buying a Weight Watchers meal, the sight of the pink box
sliding across the scanner rousing my sundry manhood issues, the
gentle ping of the bar-code reader becoming in my mind a gigantic
church bell ding-donging my worthlessness throughout Food Emporium and beyond, to the entire zip code, but there was no denying
the tantalizing breading on the cutlet, featuring a blend of spices so
well-calibrated for delight that it was hard to accept that it had been
squirted on by machine, for surely this was human tenderness and
love of craft before you, and the orange butter sauce, yes, the orange
butter sauce, more of a chutney really, covering the veg medley. Believe this one truth in my story if nothing else.

Finally, soup. Broth of life. We were Campbell's men, had been
for years, and nothing took the edge off like the talent in their bou-
tique Chunky line. We adopted the advertising slogan of Chunky's
Soup as our rallying cry and motto—it was indeed the Soup That
Eats Like A Meal. Or we forced ourselves to believe this over time by
necessity. Like I said, I was survival-oriented.

Mondays we usually ate leftover barbecue from the weekend, but
our parents had told us on Friday that they weren't coming out after
all, so our stash took a big hit, plus the last time we went to Frederico's, the manager told us that we'd maxed out our credit, those
boxes of Yodels pushing us over the edge a couple of days ago, and
our mother was going to have to give them a call to discuss it. Which
I didn't know if she had. After the can of Homestyle Chicken Soup
with Egg Noodles, there was one can of Hormel Chili with Beans left
for Reggie—I couldn't abide the stuff—and the legendary icicled
box of Macaroni & Beef with Tomatoes. If Stouffer's was royalty, this
guy was the inbred dolt everyone feared ascending the throne. Reggie and I sometimes spooked each other with tales of its wretched-
ness. It was hard times when you opened the freezer door to discover

that you were sentenced to Macaroni & Beef with Tomatoes. Purchased by accident a few years prior (in a hurry we had mistaken it for Lasagna with Meat Sauce), the sight of that accursed package, nestled in there with its frosted cohort of aluminum foil–covered enigmas, was an indictment of our character: if that was your only choice, you deserved to eat it. We prayed against that day.

I gobbled my soup as we watched TV. *Raiders of the Lost Ark* was winding down on Showtime, one of our favorite parts, The Burning of the Nazis by Heaven. If we had a VCR, we'd be playing the sequence frame by frame, so as not to miss a second of the elaborate special effects, which had merited a cover story in *Fangoria* magazine, although I now knew better than to admit to this knowledge.

"God's gonna melt that Nazi," Marcus said.

"You better melt that Nazi-ass motherfucker, God!" NP said. Then we heard Randy honking and we were outside in five seconds flat. Firemen had nothing on us when it was time to roll, the emergency we waited for.

RANDY DROVE A MOSS-GREEN TOYOTA hatchback that he claimed to have bought for a hundred bucks. Its fenders were dented and dimpled, rust mottled the frame in leprous clumps, and the inside smelled like hippie anarchists on the lam had made it their commune. But who was I to cast aspersions? Randy had a license, he had a car, and our world had changed.

Clive was in the passenger seat, radio and cooler at his feet. "What's up, what's up, what's up?"

"You guys ready to go?" Randy asked, a bit exasperated, as if it were him who had been left waiting.

"Maybe we should do a head count," I said. Again: there were six of us, and five seats. Needless to say, this was a no-lap situation.

"Your car only fits five, cuz," NP said.

"We can't all fit," I said.

"I got left behind last time," Marcus said.

We scanned one another's faces for weakness. "I'm skinny," I added. "I have skinny legs." There was no denying the twiglike nature of my legs.

"Right," Randy said, "Benji has skinny legs. Look at those Christmas hams you got there, Marcus—you take up two seats as it is." The fix was in. He pretended to consider the options. "Maybe you could rock shotgun, but Clive has shotgun."

"I have shotgun," Clive said.

"And it wouldn't be fair to take that away from him," Randy mused. "And Bobby, he got left last time."

"I was left last time!" Marcus said. He gripped his beach towel around his shoulders like a yoke.

"That was two times ago," Randy improvised, "on Thursday. On Friday we went to Bridgehampton and there was no room for Bobby, so he had to stay behind. That means you got left two times ago." Randy looked at Bobby, and Bobby made a show of feeling wounded by this fictional abandonment. "Plus, you got your bike. You can ride your bike and meet us there."

"My bike is busted," Bobby said.

"I don't even have a goddamned bike," NP said.

"If you start pedaling now," Clive said, "you might beat us there." We all knew this was ridiculous.

"Yeah, you better start pedaling now, nigger!" NP said.

Marcus shook his head, reconciling himself to this brutal calculus. "Dag, y'all." He got on his bike. "Can you at least take my towel?" he asked.

Randy looked at him skeptically. "Is it . . . dry?" he said, wrinkling his nose.

We were on the road a few minutes later, Randy ahem-aheming about gas money before we even got out of Azurest. I didn't approve of how Randy handled being the Kid with the Car, how swiftly he had been corrupted. The day before the summer started, he was a nobody. Now he was a sneering despot, honking his sick little horn. He rewarded brownnosing with a "I'll give you shotgun for a week," punished with a "Just forgot to pick you up" for whatever critical mission was going on that day, the movies, Karts-a-Go-Go, the ocean.

Even if there had been only five of us, he might have left Marcus behind. The backseat of his Toyota possessed this extradimensional quality where it fit max two or max three people depending on Randy's whim. Reggie and I kept our sliding doors open, no attitude.

Aiding Randy's schemes was the fact that there were no girls around to distract us. Our troupe, at first glance, defied birth statistics. My sister's age group, four years older, was balanced between boys and girls. There were twenty or so kids in my sister's group, and over the summers they all dated one another, nursed crushes across years, traded first loves and first kisses and assorted first fondlings between them. One summer Elena dated Bill, two summers later she was driving around in Nat's convertible, and so on. Reggie and me benefited from this situation. The big kids had to be nice to us, lest word of their bullying misdeeds get back to our sister and ruin long- or short-term plans. The older boys ferried us in their backseats to the ocean, to the movies, they bought us comics at the Ideal in town, forked over the cash for ice cream at the Tuck Shop. Not bad at all.

Then Elena's group turned eighteen, grabbed their diplomas, and stalked off into the big wide world, ceding control of the developments to our gang. We were a different breed. Whether it was martinis or cigarettes or the deleterious effects of ambient Nixonian radiation, '68 to '72 turned out to be a hard time for X chromosomes. The girls were scarce. Look at us in the car there. Boy's town.

Blame for Randy's sudden appearance in our group should fall on his parents' lovemaking schedule. He was an in-betweener, living like a weed in the cracks between the micro-demographic groups of the developments. Too old to hang out with us, really, and too young to be fully accepted by my sister's group, he had wafted in a social netherworld for years. Frankly, before he started putt-putting around town in his Toyota, I had little idea who he was, never saw him except at the annual Labor Day party. Randy had just finished his freshman year in college, but against usual custom, he still came out to Sag. No Great Exodus for him—why leave when the pond was so small, and you were so big? He relished his new status. He had a car, he was old enough to buy us beer, and for this we accepted him into our tribe. It has been observed by wiser men than me that kids who hang out with kids who are too young for them often make themselves useful in the transportation and beer-buying sectors. We overlooked his shortcomings.

The No-Girls thing was true in essence, although there were a few exceptions. Let us open the case files. Marnie was two years older than me, but had never been part of our group, even when we were very young and the boy-girl divide a nonissue. The girls of Elena's group kept her as a sort of mascot, ditching her only when it was rec-room slow-jam time or walk-down-the-beach-at-night time, and once they left Sag Harbor, she started spending her summers in the city as well, in premature exit. And then there was Francesca, whom we had barely seen for years. She was a bit of a debutante, popping out of her mother's womb with elbow-length white gloves, so it was said, and come junior high she spent all her time on the ocean side with her finishing-school friends. Occasionally we'd see her being dropped off in a white Porsche or similar chariot, and she'd delicately wave in our direction and run inside her house as if we were swarming paparazzi. So in truth, there were girls our age—they just didn't want to hang out with us, and frankly who could blame them. This was to change in a few weeks, but we didn't know that yet.

"Look at that goofy motherfucker up there!"

We passed Marcus on the turn to Sagg Road, which was a dead shot through the South Fork to the Atlantic. Marcus'd made good time. For his efforts we heckled him. Fists and catcalls out the windows.

"Better change that gear!"

"My grandma goes faster than that in her wheelchair, sucker!"

Check out Marcus huffing away. What had formerly been the embodiment of cool—ten, count 'em, ten speeds!—was now the ultimate signifier of lameness. That summer you walked like a man, a summering desperado, or drove, behind the wheel or shotgun. Marcus was making good time, but let's face it, he was on a bike.

"Leave him alone," Clive said. And we did. Except for some obscene gestures through the tiny Toyota's back window as we pulled ahead.

The houses thinned out, dangling in mystery at the end of snaking driveways, and we entered the no-man's-land in the middle of the island. Outside our black enclave and lighting out for the white side of the island. It was only a few miles to the ocean, but our sense of scale was off from spending so many summers in our safe little circuits. We had formed scouting parties to explore the dirt trails behind Mashashimuet Park, striking out toward Bridgehampton, and made occasional forays up 114 to the twisty, forsaken bends of Swamp Road, in a tentative East Hamptonly salvo, but generally we confined our shenanigans to the developments, to obsessive loops up and down Main Street in town. The coming of the cars changed all that.

My mother used to say that the white people went to the ocean beaches in the morning and the black people in the afternoon. I don't know how much of that was flat-out segregation or a matter of temperament—white people getting a jump on the day to do white-people things, and black people, well, getting there when they get there. Certainly that first generation claimed and settled on Sag Harbor Bay because the south side was off-limits—the white people owned the coastline, South Hampton, Bridgehampton, East Hampton. And the Jersey shore, and every other sandy stretch of vista-full property in the tristate area, the natural places of escape from city life. No Negroes, please. That first generation came from Harlem, Brownstone Brooklyn, inland Jersey islands of the black community. They were doctors, lawyers, city workers, teachers by the dozen. Undertakers. Respectable professions of need, after Jim Crow's logic: white doctors won't lay a hand on us, we have to heal ourselves; white people won't deliver us to God, we must save ourselves; white people won't throw dirt in our graves, we must bury ourselves. Fill a need well, and you prospered. Prosper and you took what was yours. Once The War was over (there was only one War when the old heads took us to school), finished, and the new American future beckoned—with bony skeletal fingers, but beckoning nonetheless, don't quibble—and why shouldn't they answer? They had fought to make a good life for themselves, vanquished the primitives and barbarians out to kill them, keep them out, string them up, and they wanted all the spoils of their struggle. A place to go in the summer with their families. To make something new.

If only they could see us now. O Pioneers!

Through the rusted hole in the backseat floor, I watched the asphalt blur. Randy warned us constantly to be careful around the snowflaked edges of the hole, so as not to make it worse. Every big bump in the road, bits of it fell away into the void. I nudged the rusted edge with my foot and saw it disintegrate and fly away. Up front, Randy started in with a story of last night's shift at the Long Wharf, the restaurant on the town pier. His work stories invariably revolved around tips, elaborate up-and-down melodramas full of defeats and sudden, triumphant reversals. "At first we thought it was going to be a slow night . . ." I remembered to ask NP about his job at Jonni Waffle.

"I like working there. The manager is cool," NP said. "And sometimes they let you bring a pint home."

"Can you get me an application?" I asked. I'd put it off, but I needed a job. I was out of money, we needed TV dinners for the next few days, and as it stood now Reggie was going to have to pay for them out of his Burger King paycheck. My mother would reimburse him when they came out, but I didn't relish having to beg soup money from him. So: fill out an application for Jonni Waffle and take it from there.

We rumbled across the wooden bridge over the railroad track, and traversed 27 after not too long a wait. Before July Fourth weekend, crossing Route 27 was a minor hassle. But after the Fourth, the crypts up-island disgorged their Hamptonite Undead in earnest, and you never knew how long you'd spend stranded, waiting for the caravan to thin. (Helpful Hint #236 for the Hamptonite Undead: sunscreen slows down the rate of decomposition by solar rays when you are riding around with the top down.) Then we were in Sagaponack, popping into the roadside deli for supplies, and a few minutes later we pulled up at Left Left, the beach down from the town beach. No permit needed, no lifeguards. And this year, no parents.

WE TRUDGED IN FORMATION UP THE DUNE, beach grass lashing our calves, entering that strange zone of black sand at the head of the beach. The black sand was twice as hot as the rest of the sand on the beach, inspiring cartoony cries of "Ow, ow, ow!" in former times, and a stoic teeth-gritting today. There weren't many people. We had our pick of spots.

"Let's go over there," Randy said.

"Over here," Clive countered, and we followed him to a spot above the tide line, demarcated by a garland of dried seaweed. Clive had always been the leader of our group. He was just cool, no joke. I pitied Marcus for his victimhood; I pitied Clive because he had to hang out with us. He was that rare thing among us: halfway normal, socialized and capable and charismatic. Like—he did sports. Basketball and track, captain of one of the teams at his school, I can't remember which, he was good at both of them. Sometimes he tried to get a basketball game together, two-on-two, but after a while we just started playing three against him, and he still won, leaving us a sorry sight at the side of the court, bent over and dizzy, palms on our knees and reaching for imaginary asthma inhalers. Imaginary asthma inhalers created a placebo effect, which was better than nothing.

Before Reggie and I had an Empty House, and thus the meeting place/departure point for expeditions, the one sure way not to be excluded from that day's adventures was to be the first one over at Clive's crib, where all the major decisions went down. Crack of dawn was a bit excessive, but the thinking went that you couldn't be ditched if you stuck close to Clive. Tall and muscular, he had the physical might to beat us up, but he broke up fights between us instead, separating combatants while dodging their whirling fists, and no one complained. A reluctant Solomon with a soul patch, he ended disputes over the important issues of the day, such as who called shotgun first, who had next on the diving board, who was up on Punch-Out, the video game in the lobby of the East Hampton movie theater that we worshipped like a pagan totem while the white people stared. He knew how to talk to girls, had girlfriends, plural. Good-looking girlfriends, too, from all accounts, with all their teeth and everything. Last summer he'd even dated an older woman—in her twenties! Who lived in Springs! Who had a kid! He had his problems like the rest of us but he hadn't let them deform his character yet. Not back then.

We picked our spots around camp, laying our towels down, weighing down their edges with sneakers and sodas to keep them from flipping up. And it happened, like that, after an increment of time so tiny that neutrons and protons were the only witnesses: we got sanded. In the towels, scalps, clumping on sweat along our limbs. It had begun, the gritification of the day. Some windy afternoons, the wind agitated the sand into a needling layer two inches thick. It hovered above the beach, the atmosphere of a different planet, saying, You should not be here. But what was another warning among so many?

We were the only black people on the beach. My sister's group was grown up, dispersed, and most of the moms from our neighborhood frequented the town beach, which had a lifeguard. "Stay within the markers!" There was a nice bit of suspense when you rounded the bend to the town beach and saw the flag—red, yellow, or white—signaling how rough the surf was that day. On red-flag days you heard the thunderous hammer of the waves before you got over the dune and saw the mist of smashed-down water floating above the battered shore. On calmer days the most important sound was the lifeguard blowing his "Shark Attack!" whistle. Everybody wanted their *Jaws* moment. Seeing the fin of the "must have been a Great White" gliding in the waves was cool, and bonus points if you were in the water when the whistle blew and you had to paddle to the shore for dear life.

One important fact: the town beach did not allow radio playing.

Pure fascism. As soon as he was settled, NP cranked up the volume on Clive's radio, a yellow waterproof Sony. It was a mix tape he'd recorded off the radio, KISS FM, lighthouse to the lost. On clear days the signal came through all the way to Sag, and we crowded around the radio like people in the olden days. You say Martians have touched down in Grover's Mill, New Jersey? Or are these far-off sounds an invasion of metropolitan funk, a different kind of alien altogether?

The songs started ten seconds in, the time it took NP to run across his bedroom, dodging mounds of dirty clothes and comic books, and press Record. The songs ended with the DJ's truncated explications: "Alright, that was the boombastic—" "That's for all you in the Queensbridge Houses, Boogie Down Bronx—"

"Doug E. Fresh stole my cousin's rhymes," NP said, apropos of nothing.

"I thought you said Doug E. Fresh was your cousin," I said. NP was a notorious "that's my cousin"-er. I certainly didn't remember him claiming Randy in his kinship group before Randy got wheels.

"What are you, high? Think I don't know who my own cousin is? No, he bit them, check it out, I was at this house party . . ." and he trailed off on one of his chronicles. I looked up at the sky and his words were sucked away by the wind. A small plane chuggered parallel to the shoreline, a banner slithering behind it: VISIT BUZZ CHEW.

I walked up to where the beach crumbled away into the ocean. Left Left faced the Atlantic, not that meager, lapping bay crap. Not big enough to surf in except in front of an advancing hurricane— you had to go up to Montauk for that, and none of us was so inclined. There were no houses beyond the waves, no slim spits of land, as on our turf. Just invisible continents. It was the Edge of Things, and the Edge liked to grab at you, pull you in. I wasn't even toe-deep in the water when I heard my mother's warning in my ears, "Watch out for the undertow!," which wasn't a bad philosophy, really, applicable to most situations in a metaphorical sense, but I hated being so conditioned. I never went past where I could feel the bottom beneath my feet, so riptides and undertow weren't much of a concern. But you could feel it, even in the shallows—the ravenous pull when the ocean sucked back into itself to gather for the next wave, the next volley in its siege against land and landlubbers—i.e., you. The ocean was kidnapping arms and a muffled voice that said, You ain't much at all, are you? Nope, not much at all. Sand beneath my feet, that was my rule.

"Aren't you hot in that shirt, man?" Clive asked when I sat back down.

"No. Why?"

"Black absorbs light," he said. "So it heats up—that's why on a hot day you're more comfortable wearing light clothes."

I didn't know that, but as I looked around, I didn't notice anyone wearing black. Maybe there was something to it.

"Hey! Hey! Yo!"

Marcus hot-footed it over the black sand. He'd made good time, but then he was putting in a lot of biking time to and from work. Marcus had only been out for a week and he was already on his second job. Every summer he went through a dozen, easy. He got his foot in the door no problem, spinning his dismissal from his last job to his new bosses the same way he spun them to us. "The day manager was out to get me," he'd tell us, or, "I had a personality conflict with the cook." "The owner was all coked-out," he explained, pointing toward the realities of the mid-'80s resort-town restaurant business. Most of those people were coked-out, basic fact. If we knew that he got the ax for stealing booze—not a bottle or two but a whole crate—he trumped us with, "They were some straight-up racists." Which always worked. In any sphere. Who among us could refute such a judgment? It was like saying "It's hot" during a heat wave. No dispute.

"Where's my towel?" Marcus asked.

We shaded our eyes with our hands and squinted up at him.

Randy said, "You said, can you bring it in the car, not can you lug it down the beach for me." He gave Marcus the keys and Marcus returned to the dune.

"Dag," Bobby said.

"That was cold," Clive said.

Randy yawned and stretched. He turned over on his back, exposing his great mammaries. They bobbed on his stomach. "Ain't nothing but a thang," he said.

"Why don't you put your shirt back on, Randy," NP said. "You're going to scare the white people."

"Yeah, Randy, shit," I said.

"Sh-ee-it," Randy said, slapping his chest vigorously. He was in a good mood, or else he would have thrown out "You want to walk home?," his now-standard, signifying-ending response.

"Shit, I'll show them something to be scared of," Bobby said.

"What are you going to show them, you fuckin' albino-lookin' bitch?" NP said.

Everybody cracked up except for Bobby, who growled, "Shut the fuck up," and turned over to even up his tan. He was a fierce and aggressive tanner in the early part of the summer, to giddyap his skin to a level-playing-field brown. By late July, albino wouldn't apply as an insult, except in a retro kind of way when you couldn't think of anything else. It was always nice to have a spare.

These were the early stages of Bobby's transformation into that weird creature, the prep-schooled militant. We were made to think of ourselves as odd birds, right? According to the world, we were the definition of paradox: black boys with beach houses. A paradox to the outside, but it never occurred to us that there was anything strange about it. It was simply who we were. What kind of bourgie sell-out Negroes were we, with BMWs in the driveway (Black Man's Wagon, in case you didn't know) and private schools to teach us how to use a knife and fork, sort *that* from *dat*? What about keeping it real? What about the news, statistics, the great narrative of black pathology? Just check out the newspapers, preferably in a movie-style montage sequence, the alarming headlines dropping in-frame with a thud, one after the other: CRISIS IN THE INNER CITY!, WHITHER ALL THE BABY DADDIES, THE TRUTH ABOUT THE WELFARE STATE: THEY JUST DON'T WANT TO WORK, NOT LIKE IN THE GOOD OLD DAYS. Hey, let's stop pussyfooting around and bring back slavery already, just look at these dishpan hands.

Black boys with beach houses. It could mess with your head sometimes, if you were the susceptible sort. And if it messed with your head, got under your brown skin, there were some typical and well-known remedies. You could embrace the beach part—revel in the luxury, the perception of status, wallow without care in what it meant to be born in America with money, or the appearance of money, as the case may be. No apologies. You could embrace the black part—take some idea you had about what real blackness was, and make theater of it, your 24-7 one-man show. Folks of this type could pick Bootstrapping Striver or Proud Pillar, but the most popular brands were Militant or Street, Militant being the opposite of bourgie capitulation to The Man, and Street being the antidote to Upper Middle Class emasculation. Street, ghetto. Act hard, act out, act in a way that would come to be called gangsterish, pulling petty crimes, a soft kind of tough, knowing there was someone to post bail if one of your grubby schemes fell apart.

Or you could embrace the contradiction, say, what you call paradox, I call *myself*. In theory. Those inclined to this remedy didn't have many obvious models.

In Bobby's case, his birthright, if we can call it that, made him a premature nationalist. The customary schedule for good middle-class boys and girls called for them to get Militant and fashionably Afrocentric the first semester of freshman year in college. Underlining key passages in *The Autobiography of Malcolm X* and that passed-around paperback of *Black Skin, White Masks*. Organize a march or two to protest the lack of tenure for that controversial professor in the Department of Black Studies. Organize a march or two to protest the lack of a Department of Black Studies. It passed the time until business school. Bobby got an early start on all that, returning to Sag from his sophomore year of high school with a new, clipped pronunciation of the word *whitey*, and a fondness for using the phrases "white-identified" and "false consciousness" while watching *The Cosby Show*. It caused problems as he fretted over his zip code ("Scarsdale ain't nothing but a high-class shantytown. It's a gilded lean-to") and how changing his name might affect his Ivy

League prospects ("Your transcript says Bobby Grant, but you said your name was Sadat X").

We used to make fun of him for being so light-skinned, and this probably contributed to some of his overcompensating. The joke was that if the KKK came pounding on Bobby's door and demanded, "Where the black people at?" (it's well known, the fondness of the KKK for ending sentences with a preposition), he'd say, "They went thataway!" with a minstrel eye-roll and vaudeville arm flourish. He rebelled against his genes, the Caucasian DNA in his veins square-dancing in there with strong African DNA. It's a tough battle, defending one flank against nature while nurture snuck in from the east with whole battalions. He directed most of his hostile talk at his mother, who worked on Wall Street. "My mom wouldn't give me twenty dollars for the weekend. She's sucking the white man's dick all day, Morgan Stanley cracker, and can't give me twenty dollars!" In two weeks, his parents were going to give him a used Saab for his birthday, generosity that created a whole new genre of bitterness. "My mother's so busy trying to get a pat on the head from Massa that she can't give me gas money. Telling me I should get a job— doing what, sucking the white man's dick?" His mother bore the brunt of his misguided rage, even though his father worked at Goldman Sachs, so it's not like he was dashiki-clad and running a community center somewhere. Get a bunch of teenage virgins together, and you're bound to rub up against some mother issues. Let he who is without sin cast the first stone, cast the first plucked-out orb of Oedipal horror.

"Well," NP said, "I think it's time for this Negro to get himself down the beach and see if he can check out some titties."

"There's nothing down there, man," I said. It was an old game, and rigged. Every summer we hiked off in search of that cloud-cloaked Shangri-la, the nude beach. Legends had circulated for years, in hushed tones delivered to wide eyes. Our mothers occasionally sniffed about "those French people lying around with their tops off," and older kids wowed us with tales of long-limbed honeys sun-bathing in little packs. If at long last you discovered their nesting grounds, there was one last hurdle. They might be lying on their stomachs. Tough luck that. But maybe they were on their backs, and if the stars aligned you saw them turn over—in unison, glorious unison—to expose their gifts to the world. They were ambassadors of the international jet set, the kind of lovelies populating James Bond movies and Duran Duran videos. I heard "Watch out for the undertow!" when I looked at the water, and a voice cooing "Oh, James!" when I looked down the beach, in a kind of Madonna/Whore whiplash.

For years we told our moms that we were "going for a walk," while visions of empty bottles of Bain de Soleil and supermassive fried-egg areolas danced in our heads. We walked and we walked and we never saw anything, returning, forever returning, with slumped shoulders and a faintly mumbled "Next time." Some of us still held out hope. I knew better, my learned helplessness enjoying a banner year.

"I'm down," Bobby said. He stood, holding up his arm and inspecting his skin for the slightest change in shade. He seemed pleased.

"That's what I'm talking about," NP said, thrusting out his hand so that his jive-ass flutter smashed into Bobby's more aggressive pump-'n'-dump, the two quite different shake styles misfiring before finding common ground in the two-finger snap. As if their historic hand summit had come off magnificently, NP yelped, "Alright!" and turned to admonish us. "You'll see what happens when we get back and tell you about the monstrous, most bodacious ta-tas you missed. You'll be like, 'Damn I shoulda gone!' "

That left me and Randy and Clive and Marcus. I think I dozed off for a while. I did not dream. I woke up, disoriented, to the sound of an alien spaceship landing. Afrika Bambaataa and Soulsonic Force's "Planet Rock" clanged out of Clive's radio.

"That's a classic joint right there," Marcus said.

"I haven't heard this in a while," Randy said. "We used to open up parties at my fraternity house with this." Clive and I smirked at each other. Randy's constant references to his frat amused us, frankly. The way he talked about it, it sounded like nonstop back rubs and "hey, let's wrestle"–type horsing around. But he had a car.

" 'C'mon ladeezz!' " Marcus sang, his bobbing head loose on his neck.

"You know they bit that off Kraftwerk," I said.

"Bit what off who?" Marcus asked.

"That part right there." I hummed along. "Kraftwerk is this German band that pretended to be robots. They have this song, 'Trans-Europe Express,' that has that 'Da Dah Da' part."

"Afrika Bambaataa didn't steal anything. This is their song."

"I'm serious, it's true," I said.

"This song came out first."

Afrika Bambaataa and Soulsonic Force said, "Keep tickin' and tockin', work it all around the clock."

"No," I said, " 'Trans-Europe Express' came out in the late '70s, I'm tellin' you. Elena had the eight-track." Reggie and I inherited her old stereo when she went all high-tech and futuristic with cassettes, which was great, except that somehow we only ended up with two eight-track tapes: *Trans-Europe Express* by Kraftwerk, and *The Best of the Commodores*. It was a grueling couple of months, listening to those two albums over and over—so I knew I was right.

I didn't understand back then why Marcus was hassling me, but I get it now. A couple of years later, if someone said "I stole that off an old Lou Donaldson record," and the sample kicked it, you got respect for your expertise and keen ear. Funk, free jazz, disco, cartoons, German synthesizer music—it didn't matter where it came from, the art was in converting it to new use. Manipulating what you had at your disposal for your own purposes, jerry-rigging your new creation. But before sampling became an art form with a philosophy, biting off somebody was a major crime, thuggery on an atrocious scale. Your style, your vibe, was all you had. It was toiled on, worried over, your latest tweak presented to the world each day for approval. Pull your pockets out so that they hung out of your pants in a classic broke-ass pose, and you still had your style. If someone was stealing your style, they were stealing your soul.

But I didn't say this to Marcus. I didn't know it myself. I just knew that it was okay to like both Afrika Bambaataa and Kraftwerk, and I liked what Afrika did with Kraftwerk. Across the ocean right there, the Germans banged out tunes on state-of-the-art synthesizers. Soulsonic Force, they had the reverb up so high it sounded like they were playing that "Trans-Europe Express" melody on some floor-model Casio job from Radio Shack, the dying C batteries croaking out through broken speakers. I pictured the beat box covered in electrical tape, only working if you kept it propped at a forty-five-degree angle due to a loose wire inside, envisioned them recording the song in a janitor's closet deep in the bowels of some uptown high-rise. They dismantled this piece of white culture and produced this freakish and sustaining thing, reconfiguring the chilly original into a communal artifact. They yelled, "Everybody say, 'Rock it, don't stop it,' " and the crowd yelled back "Rock it, don't stop it" in dutiful assent. How could they not? Probably it was up on Planet Rock where I wanted to be half the time, where they transported all us unlikely chosen, *Close Encounters*–style. There were other places besides this, the song said. I wasn't trying to rag on Afrika, but salute his oddball achievement. His paradox.

Marcus wasn't having it. Because I didn't say it.

"You're lucky the Zulu Nation ain't around," he said. "They'd scalp your shit, bury you up to your neck in the sand, and let the tide roll in. They ain't playing, son."

I looked at him blankly.

He shook his head. "I was at this party one time and this sucker from Bed-Stuy was all, 'Fuck Manhattan, Bed-Stuy blahzey-blah, Bed-Stuy blahzey-blah' and these dudes from the Zulu Nation came up and wailed on him. My boy was like blubbering with blood and saliva and shit running down his face. You better watch what you say."

"I was just trying to share some information."

"Yeah, right, I forgot you like that white music, you fuckin' Siouxsie and the Banshees–listenin' motherfucker." He scratched his chest and thought for a moment. "With your monkey ass."

Let the record show that my black T-shirt was in fact a Bauhaus T-shirt, purchased the previous fall down in the Village on the very first of my weekly trips to scavenge for new albums, generally vinyl dispatches from the world of the pale and winnowed, but it was true that I had worn my Siouxsie and the Banshees T-shirt the week before. I didn't buy rap—I heard it all the time, Reggie and Elena had all the good stuff, so there was no reason to spend my allowance on it. Rap was a natural resource, might as well pay for sunlight or the very breeze or an early-morning car alarm going off. No, I spent my money on music for moping. Perfect for drifting off on the divan with a damp towel on your forehead, a minor-chord soundtrack as you moaned into reflecting pools about your elaborate miserableness. The singers were faint, androgynous ghosts, dragging their too-heavy chains across the plains of misery, the gloomy moors of discontent, in search of relief. Let's just put it out there: I liked the Smiths.

"I don't know what you're talking about, Marcus," Clive said. "I put on that Tears for Fears song last night and you were all, 'That's the shit.' "

Marcus winced. "I like that video, man. It's a good video."

With that, the argument ended, the latest meaningless border skirmish in the long war over what white culture was acceptable and what was not. We redrew the maps feverishly, throwing out our agreements and concessions. This week surf wear was in, and we claimed Ocean Pacific T-shirts and Maui shorts as our own. Next year, Lacoste was out in enemy territory again, reclaimed by the diligent forces of segregation. There was one rule, though: Clive trumped everything. If Clive gave his blessing, it was okay, whether it was Donny and Marie or Twisted Sister. Golf, whatever. But for the rest of us, the rules changed daily. It kept you on your toes.

AFTER A TIME, we stood one by one, and looked at the waves and one another and nodded: time to go in. The sun was a sick death ray cutting through the cloudless sky—ever since Clive told me about the heat-gathering qualities of black T-shirts, an oven of 50-50 cotton-poly had broiled my flesh. I was pretty suggestible. Clive and Marcus shouted war cries and dove into the water. I ran down to the surf once, ran back, ran down again, ran back (I had a system), then burst into a full-speed wade, grimacing at each frigid centimeter's advance up my belly, holding my arms above the water as if battling quicksand. Randy dipped in a toe and padded back to his blanket.

No, I cannot swim in the conventional sense. To this day. Over the years I have learned how to generate forward movement in a liquid medium through a combination of herky-jerky flip-flapping arm-and-leg movements, but nothing that approaches the standard definition of a stroke. I can float on my back—that counts for something, right? In the doomed-ocean-liner movie that runs in my head, more frequently than I like, I float on my back to the eventual safety of the rescue boat or deserted island. Splish-splashing around with a healthy stroke, hell, that's calling attention to yourself, alerting sharks, who are attracted to movements that resemble those of an "animal in distress," according to what I read in my shark books in elementary school. Might as well be a traveling chum salesman. Best to float and pretend to be dead, or so my thinking went back then—and in calm water I found nothing more peaceful than doing that very thing. Letting my body go, as if I didn't have a body at all and there was no barrier between me and the sea, while waiting for one of my friends to flip me over or pull me under, because that's what friends do, but if I could get a few minutes alone out of the world I was happy.

I wasn't doing any of that freewheeling floating in the ocean. I needed to know where the bottom was. Anytime I strayed into a drop-off, where I knew there had to be a bottom and yet suddenly there wasn't, I panicked. Especially at Left Left, where there was no lifeguard. Clive and Marcus swam out and I stayed behind, up to my waist, turning around every minute to check out the next wave sneaking up on me.

I lumbered down the shore a ways so I could take a whiz without the sudden warm patch wafting over to my friends, jellyfish-like.

From down on the beach, you could only see the tops of the Saga-ponack houses, but from the water you got a better view. Our houses on Sag Harbor Bay were bunched up all over one another, and it created a close-knit beach culture. Here the houses were moored behind the dunes like battleships. These were no quarter-acre lots like the ones around our way, who knew what was between these houses, Olympic pools and tennis courts. Croquet arenas where the players swatted human skulls across the grass. Behind the big windows, eyes considered and surveyed all, the gigantic tidal events as well as the minor human ones, the ones wearing bathing suits and sunblock. Behind the windows someone said, There were some black people coming up the beach so we got out our binoculars.

From the water, I saw the long arms of the beach, east and west. I saw Bobby and NP coming back, but no one else out strolling. On the bay, there was always somebody. Some galoot or other. The middle-aged ladies camped out in front of someone's house each afternoon, usually ours, as folks from Azurest and the Hills and Ninevah promenaded by, making the rounds, leaving footprints that were physical traces to a dozen conversations. Trading information—who's up, who's down—while the tiny waves nibbled at the shore. That was the social scene. They came up the steps to our house to fix themselves drinks, to use the bathroom, whether our parents were out or not. We sat up straight, stopped cursing, got into raised-right mode. They made gin and tonics and screwdrivers, moved TV dinners aside to get at the ice-cube trays, and asked when our parents were coming out.

I believed my parents when they said they were coming out, odds be damned. Retrieving the soup cans from the sink, rubbing the dried brown stains off the stove top. Even if in the end they didn't show, the threat kept the house from falling completely into utter teenage entropy. When they called to say they weren't coming, it was always a few minutes after we finished cleaning, as if they had us under surveillance. It kept us in line, the necessary illusion that they returned every Friday. Who knew how Reggie and I would have lived if we truly lived in a world without parents. When we told their friends that they weren't coming out, we got smirks and shakes of the head before they retreated down to the beach to continue their circuit, ice clacking in their plastic Solo cups.

A wave knocked me down and sent me cartwheeling in swirling sand. I walked out farther to be safe. I thought, If they're going to keep skipping weekends, I was going to have to adapt. We needed TV dinners to survive. If the job at Jonni Waffle didn't come through, there was a dishwashing job at the Sandbar that Marcus told me about. I looked up and saw that Bobby and NP were back. Randy was up on his feet. NP said something outrageous—his arms spun in deep anecdote theatrics—and then I saw something strange. The three of them were laughing, and then NP extended his hand and Randy put his hand out, and the hands grew closer, almost in slow-mo, and then I could see it, even from that distance, as if I had binoculars, the most botched handshake of the day. NP approached serpentine, attempting to replicate the pump-'n'-dump that Bobby had used on him, adding a wiggle closer, but Randy was expecting something else entirely, going with a fingertip pull, double squeeze, before winding up with a shoulder-to-shoulder manly half-hug. They recovered and NP continued his story, Bobby nodding in enthusiasm.

It was unmistakable. Everybody was faking it.

A big wave lifted me off my feet and when it rolled past, I sought the bottom, but it wasn't there. My toes poked around, but I couldn't feel anything. I had been pulled out, and my dog-paddler's mind tripped into full fear mode, my fight-or-flight imperative kicking in with a fury. (Thank you, reptilian brainstem.) I understood instantly that the water wasn't merely an inch over my head, but fathoms. I was in the undertow, en route to Europe, there were sharks, and no shark whistle to signal that I was in danger. My hands reached out. I tried to make the water into a rope—from the outside I'm sure it looked as if I was pulling myself toward shore, hand over hand. But I made no progress. My chest tightened and my feet scrabbled vainly for the bottom again and my chest tightened even more. Clive said, "I'm going in." He was right next to me.

"Hey! I need—can you give me a hand?" I asked.

He looked confused, then stuck out his hand and towed me in half a foot.

I felt the sand beneath my feet, or tippy-toes specifically. I had water up to my neck and I was loving it. I started to explain the situation but Clive cut me off. "Hey, no problem," he said. "They're back," he said, pointing. I saw that Marcus was already out of the water and heading toward the others.

NP debriefed us when we joined them. "There was no one out there but this old white man out walking one of those horse-lookin' dogs," he said. "Dog came up to his chest, lookin' like it wanted to eat him, if you ask me. So this guy sees us walking up to him and he starts frowning like we were trying to move in next door to his house."

"Looked like a prune," Bobby said.

"Prune-ass bitch. We kept going, but we didn't see one naked lady. They must be farther down the beach, I don't know where they're hanging out. But you know we're not going to walk all the way to Montauk."

"So we turn around."

"Bobby's like, 'I'm tired,' and we start heading back and who do we see again but that old white man and his big dog. And he's eyeballing us again. Just flat-out staring. So I'm like, he wants to look at something, he can look at this, and I pulled my shorts down and mooned his funky ass. I was like, 'Kiss my black ass,' " he said, making a robotic self-spanking motion. " 'Kiss it!' "

We busted out laughing. Lying motherfucker.

"He looked like he was going to have a heart attack right there. And you know that dog would have ate him, too. Be all," NP put forth his best shaggy-dog voice, " 'I'm sorry you're dead, master, but a nigger's gotta eat.' "

Randy shook sand out of his T-shirt. "I'm ready to head back," he announced. He was the driver. That was that. We packed up our stuff.

We walked up the dune in single file, end-of-the-afternoon

weary, casting our familiar silhouettes. Five o'clock June light, wrung out by the sun, sanded and damp—this day was one in a long series. We had been doing this for years, making adjustments at the beginning of the summer, fine-tuning, to get used to each other again after nine months stuck in our different corners of the city. Figuring out the next version of each other. Somebody was coming with the stuff from their neighborhood, the other guy was bringing the stuff from his neighborhood, and they collided. By the end of the summer we were all on the same page. I was already saying *def* and *fresh* at quadruple my off-season rate.

We didn't change all that much year to year, we just became more of ourselves. Where were we the next summer? A few inches closer to it. Bobby returned with a more refined version of his misguided Black Panther–ness, as interpreted by a privileged Westchester kid who hadn't read that much. NP reappeared with a more durable clown persona, getting the gestures and punch lines down, understanding the pauses and various cues that trained your friends and family into being your audience. Everybody on their own trajectory, although we sometimes intersected. And me? Keeping my eyes open, gathering data, more and more facts, because if I had enough information I might know how to be. Listening and watching, taking notes for something that might one day be a diagram for an invention, a working self with moving parts.

Until then fumbling, trying to get a sure grip. Hoping no one noticed.

"Get all the sand off your feet before you get in," Randy ordered. "I don't want you messing up my car. You know you're some sand-gettin'-in motherfuckers."

We rolled our eyes and clubbed our feet with our towels. We slammed the doors shut. I looked out the back window to watch Marcus disappear around the bend. We became more of ourselves, but what did that mean in Marcus's case? He had a long ride ahead.

Ten minutes later we were still sitting there. The car wouldn't start. There was a pay phone over at the town beach, which we could use to call a tow truck, but not at Left Left. We went to Left Left to be left to ourselves.

Randy tried the engine one more time. Nothing happened. I pictured rust sprinkling down into a pile underneath the motor each time he turned the key.

We sat for a minute.

"Dag."

If I
Could
Pay You
Less,
I Would

IT WILL HIT ME WHEN I LEAST EXPECT IT, CARRIED on the gusts of a restaurant's ventilation system or smothering me at the threshold of a friend's apartment as I'm greeted and told of the goings-on in the kitchenette—the tale of the handed-down recipe relayed over the telephone by an aged relative, the botched first batches. It is the smell of dessert, the smell of chocolate and sustenance shared, the aroma of waiting treasures, anticipation itself. The smell of normalcy. It is dessert, and the sugar-delivery system in all its guises—cookies, pies, cakes, the elaborate confections that are tribute to the creativity of the human mind. It reminds me of ice cream. It makes me gag. It makes me want to puke. After all this time.

That summer was my first tour of duty at Jonni Waffle and the beginning of my exile from the world of decent people. Not that I knew the ultimate ramifications of taking a job there, I just knew I had to make some money. A comedian once said that minimum wage is your boss's way of telling you, If I could pay you less, I would. Certainly, when I first started working there, Martine, the owner of Jonni Waffle, paid me the lowest amount allowed by law. In other words, and I feel I should stress this point, *it would have been illegal for him to pay me less.* If you lasted, every four weeks he doled out five- or ten-cent raises. How much you got was determined not by competence but by charisma, how much he valued your company. You can guess which schedule I was on.

The nickels added up, but it cannot be said that cash was our true compensation, especially if one considers with a cold and sober eye the hazards of the job. No, our actual reward came in the form of a much more ephemeral tender: we ate ice cream. As much as we wanted. Every shift. Whatever we could cram down our gullets. Chocolate ice cream for breakfast and lunch if I had a day shift, chocolate ice cream for lunch and dinner if I had a night shift. Whatever flavor we desired, washed down with as much soda as we could stand. The soda machine was stingy with the carbonation, making everything into a kind of syrup, but this was only appropriate, in keeping with the consistency of everything else we sold. We were apprentices of ooze, specializing in things that melted out of a solid state into a sticky liquid or otherwise flowed slowly, like the soft ice cream we lever-dispensed from a humming metal box, and the chocolate fudge and strawberry sauce we ladled on with gusto. There was all this candy stacked up in the back of the store—Heath bars, Reese's Pieces, Gummi Bear knockoffs that perspired rainbows on hot afternoons—that we jabbed into the ice cream as toppings. This was fair game as well. If we sold it at Jonni Waffle, you could eat it. In theory, if you had a fetish for wafer cones, this was your chance at wafer-cone-eating nirvana, and you were free to chomp your way through whole boxes, stack after stack, when the compulsion seized.

But wafer cones are not central to this chronicle. It was all about the waffle in there, the new-fangled Belgian waffle cone. There was no escaping it. The dust of the waffle mixture swirled in the air like asbestos in the guts of a condemned factory, roosted in the soft warrens of the lungs, clung to hair like sweet dandruff, commingled with sweat and congealed into salty concoctions unreckoned by the makers of the secret recipe. When you worked the waffle grills, the steam of the cooking cones became a localized atmosphere, the tar-pit exhalations of an ancient, stunted planet. You learned not to pick at the soft stuff if you noticed it on your arm—sometimes it was a drop of batter, sure, but sometimes what appeared to be batter was actually your melted skin, accidentally burned while trying to maintain the crazy hustle of the irons, and what you were actually peeling off was a bit of yourself.

ONE AFTERNOON, not long after I joined the Jonni Waffle family, I was practically cocooned in the stuff. The electricity in the house was out, so we didn't have any hot water, which meant I hadn't taken a shower and my every pore was still plugged up and battered down from the previous night's shift. I'd forgotten to wash my spare Jonni Waffle shirt (Martine, with some ceremony, presented you with two Jonni Waffle T-shirts on the day of your first shift) so I had to wear it even though it was soiled, covered with batter and befudged from a sundae mishap. I dabbed at Peanut Butter Chunk stains with a wet sock and crossed my fingers that by the time I got to work they'd dry into invisibility. It was going to be a smelly couple of hours. I prayed that my waffle musk would be camouflaged by the greater, wafflized environment of the store.

Reggie came in and told me about the electricity that morning. It was my turn in our parents' bed—we switched off sleeping in our parents' room when they were in the city. As soon as they pulled out of the driveway, whoever's turn it was blurted out, "I got their bed," to lay claim, to head off any argument over who had dibs.

Which was ridiculous. Dibs was dibs, we didn't have to call it. Ever since we were born, we'd lived according to the rough frontier justice of even Stephen, and even Stephen had a perfect memory. Whose turn was it to drag the garbage bags out to the curb, whose turn to decide what channel to watch, whose turn to pick the first piece of chicken—that freshly carved chunk of breast posing on top of the serving platter with a crisp piece of skin coyly slipping off it, obviously the best piece of all, the meal-maker. It was all recorded in even Stephen's immortal ledger, and we obeyed. As former twins, Reggie and I were driven by the fear of being shortchanged, that the other might get a bigger portion of the available resources in our household, whether they be emotional, material, or entirely imagined. Your brother, your de facto opponent in a hundred battles a day, big and small, must not receive more than his share because that meant that you were receiving less than your share. We were terrified of proof of what we understood to be true.

Occasionally the system broke down. The day before the electricity went out, in fact, we had just such a situation. A cornerstone of jurisprudence in our two-man country maintained that you were not liable for your brother's responsibilities, hence the constant declarations of "That's not mine, that's Reggie's" with regard to property placed where it shouldn't, and "It's Benji's turn" with respect to some duty or chore. Blame and responsibility were synonyms in our dictionary, and we disavowed all association until there was no avoiding it.

One law that came into play quite frequently, given our love of prepared meals, was Thou Shalt Not Clean Thy Brother's Soup Pot. There was one go-to pot that was ideal for warming a sixteen-ounce can of soup to eating temperature, celebrated for its heat-conducting properties and an elegant surface-area-to-height ratio that enabled it to heat up fast without boiling over if we suffered a spell of teenage distraction and forgot about it. According to our highly ritualized pot etiquette, if you used it last, you had to clean it if the other person needed it for their soup—instantly stop whatever you were doing, bust out the sponge, and rub away the residue of Chunky Beef Stew.

What happened in the episode in question was that my mother had made tacos for us the night before she and my father went back to the city. Distracted, she hadn't washed the pot out, and it sat on the far burner of the stove for days. It was during a heat wave, and we didn't have air-conditioning. Making the place even hotter was the fact that the windows were closed. My father had been yelling at my mother with such volume and ferocity the night before they left that I had been seized by a deep humiliated feeling, which usually paralyzed me but on this occasion sent me scurrying around the living room closing all the windows. The houses on the beach were quite close together, you see, compared to the interior streets of the developments, to maximize the use of the lot. In the city, when my father raised his voice, it was more or less swallowed up by the ambient noise of the city and absorbed by the walls of our prewar building, which were the product of the construction ideas of a better era and meant to take a licking.

The sound of my father's voice still escaped through the screen door, but by shutting the windows I thought I might cut off the most direct routes to our neighbors' ears. I imagined the progress of the sound waves through the air, as depicted in my *Introduction to Physics* textbook: the yelling bouncing off the closed windows and remaining trapped inside the house, ricocheting around us off the refrigerator and the media stand and the framed watercolor of the Long Wharf, which was the only thing hanging on our walls, and then some of the yelling sieving through the screen doors and flying out over the deck before being lost and diminished in the immense void of the bay, where there was no one to overhear. My parents ignored me on my window-closing mission or did not see me. They didn't mention it.

The thing was, now that Reggie and I were out working, the glass doors of the living room were shut more often than usual, and during the heat wave the house really became an oven, what with the windows closed, too. I had neglected to open them again after my parents' departure. In the taco pan, a wide and beloved skillet of varied purpose, nature took its course.

"What's that smell?" Reggie said when he got back from work. I had smelled something, too, but wasn't bothered enough to investigate. Reggie and I sniffed near the likely sources. The trash can, which we emptied only when overflowing. According to the even-Stephen system, and its preference for last-minute choring, there was no reason to take out the trash if it was possible to close the lid of the trash can or if it tilted open, propped up by garbage, at an angle of less than forty-five degrees. But the trash can didn't stink too much. We moved the dishes out of the sink. In our logic, we didn't clear the sink unless all sink-related tasks had become impossible by the jutting, ziggurat mess, and consequently food sometimes loitered under the plates and bowls and moldered. But the clumps of browning food didn't stink that much. The smell came from the stove.

"What's in there?" I asked Reggie, referring to the pot.

"It's not mine," he said, testifying under oath.

"It's not mine," I said, with equal gravity, and now that we had pleaded not guilty to whatever charge was about to be read, I lifted the lid off the pot.

The stench burst forth. The pale boil of maggots writhed, bumped, and grinded in the decomposing ground beef and orange lumps of solidified fat. They slithered, slightly tinted pink by the Taco Mix Flavor Packet.

"Gahh," I yelled.

"Arrggh," Reggie screamed.

We were brothers.

I slapped the lid back on the pot and we conferred. I pressed down on the lid as if leaning against the rattling Gates of Hell. The problem was that this situation lacked precedent. The pot was outside the reach of the law, over the state line. Who had jurisdiction? It was my mother's pot. Eventually it would be cleaned on an eve-of-parents'-return cleanup, and whoever was on kitchen duty that day would have to scrub it out. It was Reggie's turn coming up, in fact. But that was in the future—our parents wouldn't return for days. Did Reggie's impending responsibility apply retroactively? No, he argued, just as I argued the reverse—and had the roles been switched, we would have argued the opposite just as learnedly and emphatically. The pot, in the eyes of the law, did not exist as such. It wasn't my pot, or Reggie's pot—it was society's pot.

The smell, however, was no hypothetical. I made a suggestion. I'd get rid of the maggots, but Reggie would scrub it clean. Motion passed. Afterward, I opened the windows. We didn't yell at each other that much anymore, those days.

Episodes such as these, when even Stephen was put to the test, made us run to the safety of our parents' queen-sized. When you got the big bed, you had it until our parents returned, which meant that when they skipped the weekend, you had it for like eleven days straight. Bonus.

Reggie stuck his head in the door. "There's a blackout," he said. I got up to check it out. The power went out a lot. Any big storm knocked down a power line or two somewhere across the Long Island grid. Sometimes it was our neck of the woods, sometimes it wasn't. The power went out for a couple of hours, or, in the case of hurricanes, days. Our stove was electric, and we needed electricity for the hot-water heater, but the power usually returned quickly so blackouts were rarely more than a minor nuisance. You broke out the candles, cursed yourself for not buying more batteries after the last blackout even though it had occurred to you plenty of times, and went to bed. By the time you got up in the morning the lights were back on. Usually.

It was beautiful and blue outside. But nothing turned on as I toured the house, flipping, switching, opening the refrigerator. I slipped out the side door to see if I could hear Chuck Woolery's voice booming from Mrs. Johnson's TV—she was a big *Love Connection* fan and from all evidence had discovered a twenty-four-hour *Love Connection* channel—and saw the ticket noosed on the doorknob. LILCO had cut off the juice for nonpayment. There was no blackout. It was just us.

"Dag," Reggie said.

"That's cold, right?" I said.

Reggie went to catch the bus to his job at Burger King and I called our mother at work. "Any message?" her secretary asked. I told her no. Telling my mother's secretary that the juice was shut off, that was impossible. I was wired not to let other people know our business. What happened in the house stayed in the house, caroming off the walls and furniture and us, until it was absorbed or forgotten. When my mother called back, she seemed unconcerned. "That's just a payment mix-up," she said. "I'll take care of it." She told us they'd be out on Friday. She'd see us then.

AT A QUARTER TO FOUR, I headed off to work. I sniffed my shirt again: funky. Martine was going to be there to oversee the weekend delivery, and NP was on duty, so I was going to get ribbed over the Head-Patting Incident. Plus, on Thursdays people got an early start on the weekend, dribbling in with their crumpled bills and thirsty stares. It was going to be a tough shift.

The wind had picked up. Maybe it was going to rain, but not anytime soon. I could take the beach shortcut. Taking the beach meant you skipped a bunch of streets, Terry Drive and the rest, emerging on Bay Street with a nice head start. Terry Drive was named after Maude Terry, the spiritual architect of the developments, and, if one followed the long stream of cause and effect, the series of consequences rippling across the generations, responsible for every second of my Sag Harbor life. On old Maude Terry's shoulders lay the blame for all of it.

She was part of a group from Brooklyn and Queens who started coming out in the '30s and '40s, staying in the Eastville section, near the Hempstead House. Eastville was where the black and Indian workers settled during Sag Harbor's whaling boom, working the ships. One day our Maude, after walking through the dirt paths summer after summer to what would become Azurest Beach, decided to investigate who actually owned those woods. Which meant that she had already conceived of some idea of the developments, right? Why investigate unless you had a plan. What incident put the idea in her head, what kind of day or evening did she have to make her hope and scheme, think up such a thing? That was one story not handed down.

The twenty acres belonged to a man named Mr. Gale, who'd been trying to unload them for some time. No one wanted the parcel. It wasn't on the Atlantic, like the prime acreage of Bridgehampton, South Hampton, etc. Terry hatched a plan where she'd sell the lots for him—to her friends, to her friends' friends, and so on, the middle-class black folk of their acquaintance—$750 for an inside lot, $1,000 for a beachfront lot. The word went out. One by one the houses went up.

Cut to forty years later, to me, more specifically, as I made my way to work and confronted one small hitch. Taking the beach shortcut meant running a gauntlet of forced social interaction. That afternoon, I saw as I walked along the side of the house down to the bulkhead, I caught a break. There was only one of my mom's friends on the beach in front of our house. It was Mrs. Collins, Marcus's mother, a copy of *People* magazine in her lap. Her hand dangled over the side of her beach chair, falling on the rim of her glass of white wine. Sand clumped to the condensation on the glass like rust. There were three empty beach chairs. I saw bathing caps in the water. Good timing.

"How are you today, Mrs. Collins?"

She looked at me over the rim of her sunglasses. "Fine, fine," she said. She inspected my dirty shirt. "You headed off to that Jonni Waffle?"

"Yes."

"You going to bring back a little of that Rocky Road?" she asked, as she did every time she caught me on my way to work. I was such a square that I always took her literally, and my mind reeled into desperate scenarios where I was forced to smuggle out a pint under and between laser beams, past infrared sensors. Martine allowed us one take-home pint a week "for our families," and the mothers of Jonni Waffle employees gleefully spread the word, lording over their access to Candy Apple Praline and Vanilla Nut Swirl. Mrs. Collins and I were not related. If I brought a pint home for a family friend, was I breaking Martine's trust? Did I care about Martine's trust after the Incident? Contributing to my neurotic back and forth was that we didn't carry Rocky Road, that flavor being too pedestrian for the full-tilt exotic cavalcade that was Jonni Waffle. Not only was she asking me to steal; she was asking me to steal something that didn't even exist. A thought problem: the Moron's Dilemma.

To repeat: "You going to bring back a little of that Rocky Road?"

I nodded.

"When are your parents coming out?"

"Tomorrow," I said.

She smiled. It was a merry joke, when our parents were coming out. "Alright then," she said.

I went on my way. Most of the houses on the beach back then were modest bungalows, fronted by decks that stabbed out toward the bay or by sloping grass lawns that slunk down to the bulkhead. The exception was the Martins', which squatted over three lots and was a real Hamptons-style modern beach house, one you might see in a magazine when they ran out of white Hamptons houses to feature. Which was never. It was the biggest house in Azurest at that time, a refugee from the other side of the island, its great windows pretending to overlook some tonier stretch of beach. Mr. Martin owned a few R&B stations in the Northeast and was pretty loaded. There were always pickup trucks parked outside belonging to the gardeners, the pool guys, the dudes performing who knew what upgrades and installations inside. I'd never been inside—everyone's parents went to the parties, but kids weren't allowed.

Everyone still talked about Mr. Martin's fiftieth birthday party, when he hired Gladys Knight and a Pip to perform. They could only afford one Pip after all the food and liquor. It was a new breed of bash. Bobby's grandfather, who was part of the first generation, used to tell us how when the houses first started going up, on the dirt roads before the developments got paved, everyone was welcome when you threw a party. Maybe you didn't know each other personally, but you all had the same story, right, when it came down to it: after a long journey you had found safety on this shore. Survivors and neighbors. Weekdays were quiet, run by the wives, who took care of the kids, hit the beach, and tended to the developments with matriarchal care. The men came out on Friday, and the socializing began. If you saw the lights or heard the music, according to Bobby's grandfather, you walked on up and pushed in the screen door, whether you knew the person or not. And once you walked in, you were blood brothers.

That sounded crazy, frankly. The custom of a better time. Half the fun of having a party, it seemed—and I speak as someone who was not invited to parties, and thus had an outsider's perspective— was in excluding people, especially your neighbors, who would be forced to listen to the music and laughter, closing their windows to keep noise out as some closed windows to keep noise in.

The houses ended at Azurest Beach proper, where you set up your blankets and gear if you weren't hanging out in front of the house of someone who lived on the beach. It was where Reggie and I and Marcus and Bobby had spent most of our sunny afternoons as children, doing the standard kid-on-a-beach stuff, making things out of sand, throwing dead crabs at one another. Our replacements were there, reenacting our botched creations, our futile pastimes. And one day they'd be passing their own replacements as they tromped off to work in town. I didn't recognize any of their mothers, but waved anyway, and they waved back. We were neighbors.

I jumped over the tiny trickle we had always referred to as the Minnow, but what anyone with any sense called the Drain Pipe, which was less romantic but more honest. It was where the street runoff trickled into the sea. Tiny silver minnows hung out there, which we used to use for bait. We dragged an old bedspread up toward the ridged pipe, scooping up dozens of fish into our dingy net. When we hoisted the cloth between us, straining against the weight of the water as it drained out, the minnows hopped and flopped on the dirty threads. We drove our hooks through them, twisting their slender bodies on the metal as their guts and eyes popped out. We dropped our lines off the Long Wharf or dry-cast off

Azurest, hoping for a nibble from the porgies and baby snappers. We hadn't fished in years.

The Minnow meant that I'd reached the Public Beach, another neglected haunt, although this was to change next year when we started getting high in the parking lot, in Bobby's car. The Public Beach—which was open to all of Sag Harbor, i.e., the white people—was now key in that it provided the second half of the shortcut to town, to work. The commute to Jonni Waffle, indeed everything Jonni Waffle–related, occupied such prime real estate in my brain that I had even stopped having swimming-lesson flash-backs when I got to the Public Beach. Quite a feat, given the tor-menting echoes of my failure and their reverberations through the years. The ghostly phrases—"Blow out your nose!," "Now float!," "Let go of my arm, goddamnit!"—were just a whisper, barely audi-ble over the tide. Swimming Instructor, Prison Camp Guard. It was my first lesson in true uselessness. Guppy, Snapper, Shark—I can't remember the specific benchmarks because I never reached them. I was left back three years in a row, the tallest Guppy on the beach, looming over the little kids like a gawky monument to ineptitude, whereupon my mother washed her hands of me. A Sag Harbor Baby was someone who had been coming out here since birth, like my mother, like Reggie and me, like those kids I had just passed on Azurest Beach. A Sag Harbor Baby who couldn't swim was a shame on the whole community, a deficiency in that area being a widely recognized predictor of later deviancy. Red Tompkins, for example, was a notorious nonswimmer, and we all know how he ended up de-spite all the advantages. Glug glug.

I walked through the parking lot and up the road, splitting off to hit the last leg of the shortcut, a shunt of woods that let out on Bay Street. There's a house there nowadays, so you have to take the long way around. I've retraced my old routes to make sure what I know is plausible in the retelling, and to give a sporting chance to the For-gotten and the Repressed, those two overlooked cousins of ours there in the corner avoiding eye contact. (Chime in whenever, guys.) The house is cool, stark-angled, a gray gargoyle of hip, and I like it even though it doesn't fit in with the rest of the houses on Bay Street, the Dutch colonials with long capacious porches, the Gothic revival abodes, inevitably festooned with red-white-and-blue bunting come July Fourth. The last time I visited, the new house had a plastic playground set in the yard, which seemed odd, because the public beach's playground was so close. But then kids don't play out there like we used to.

The shortcut slingshotted us into White Sag Harbor and had the bonus of zipping us past the house on the corner of Bay and Hempstead, where a pack of dogs, pampered Labs and well-brushed spaniels, always burst out from under the porch to taunt and snarl at the passersby. It also took us past the shabby green house where the pickup truck with the Confederate-flag bumper sticker parked, forcing us to say "Fuckin' rednecks" whenever we passed it. Over the years, the "Fuckin' rednecks" tally really piled up. We were sick of saying it and sick of seeing the truck every summer.

Round the bend, past High Street, and I was practically in town. I passed the Cormaria Retreat House, known in our neck as the Nunnery. Per custom, I paused for a minute to picture what went on at the end of the driveway, generally intimations of lesbian love. Informed by late-night cable flicks, my imagery that summer featured wispy young women who cavorted in nighties, holding candlesticks in the moonlight and giggling as they chased each other across the grounds. The scenes generally ended up with a lot of petting, with roommates saying, "You be the boy and I'll be the girl and we'll practice kissing open-mouthed."

I reached the sleepy marina, home port in those days for small motorboats, secondhand Chris-Crafts, fishermen's specials with Budweiser in the cooler, and the odd swanlike sailboat, resting in our humble cove between excursions. Occasionally someone's sleek cigarette boat, straight out of *Miami Vice*. The bigger boats were rare, but it was already starting, the migration of the boors, as the marinas of the Hamptons filled up berth by berth and the rich people on the other side of the island discovered Sag Harbor as a place to moor their extravagantly gaudy yachts.

It had been a long time since Sag Harbor got its start as a shipping port, first as a conduit for goods from the Atlantic and Long Island to Connecticut—lumber, food—then hitting its stride during the whaling boom. Hard to imagine the ships that used to drop anchor there. The town is mentioned in *Moby-Dick*—it's a Sag Harbor ship that takes Queequeg from his South Sea home to America. Perhaps you've heard how that turned out for him. Even his no-doubt Shark-level swimming skills couldn't save him from his fate. I'll point out that Queequeg had a bit of double consciousness about him, to embroider a theme: "And thus an old idolator at heart, he yet lived among these Christians, wore their clothes, and tried to talk their gibberish. Hence the queer ways about him, though now some time from home."

It must have been quite a sight, sleepy Bay Street swarming with the antic commerce of the whale trade—cockeyed captains harrumphing down the gangplanks of assorted schooners and great ships, salty dogs of all shape and temperament and color dragging harpoons, humming the latest sea shanty, and generally roiling about where what is now orderly sidewalk, tamed grass. As I begin to describe the kind of work I used to do in Sag Harbor, the scooper's trade, I try to picture what things were like one-hundred-fifty years earlier, and of course it's dim. All I can muster, truly, is an image of the black sailors trudging home at the end of the day to Eastville, the direction I had just come from. I tipped my hat to ghosts as we passed each other.

At the stoplight, Bay Street ended and I had a choice. Turn left, toward the Corner Bar, or turn right, onto the Long Wharf. I turned right. The wharf has more than enough to keep us occupied, especially on warm summer days like the one in question. I was on my way to work, and it was the Long Wharf that Jonni Waffle called home.

The Long Wharf was the main drag during the whaling days.

Now it served a different trade—tourism and leisure, although given national statistics on obesity, blubber still had its niche. Bayside, the discotheque anchoring the wharf, was a new Hamptons beachhead for partying New Yorkers. Their concerts featured big pop names and the regular club nights generated crowds and traffic of a kind the town had never seen before. There was no going back. Adjacent to Bayside was the Long Wharf Promenade, a warren of well-hexed seasonal shops that never lasted long. Antiques stores collecting sixty years of lapses in taste vis-à-vis summer-home decoration. Bright and shiny preppie clothing stores selling weird things like pre-tied sweaters—sweaters that could not be worn in the conventional fashion as they were in fact fat cotton necklaces, meant to rest on the shoulders in immaculate WASP style. A comic-book store came and went, and a video store. The manager of a cigar shop incorrectly calculated the rate of Hamptonization—the body of scientific lore on this subject was still small—and his establishment quickly disappeared. The only survivor, and it is there to this day, was Jonni Waffle.

The Long Wharf Restaurant rounded things out, providing overpriced American fare in exchange for the view. Any spot on the wharf specialized in the picturesque and dared you to dislike it. A lithe bridge arced over to North Haven, and a replica of a windmill, festooned with a historic plaque or two, provided a handy Polaroid spot. Shelter Island brooded across the water, dumb and stoic. The restaurant overlooked the marina, and this was before big yachts took over the east side of the wharf, so there were still plenty of spots for fishermen to drop red-and-white bobbers over the side, their catch flailing in the buckets at their feet. The tiny fish you got off the wharf—snappers, porgies—was a parody of the old trade, but tasty when fried in a skillet.

The wharf was twice as long during its heyday. I don't know what happened. Maybe it burned up. Dip into a local history (of anywhere, really) and you'll constantly read about things being "destroyed by fire." In 17-whatever, Main Street burned down, "destroyed by fire." In 18-something, Bay Street was incinerated, "destroyed by fire." And then they rebuilt in the new style. By 1985, there was a different kind of fire sweeping through Sag Harbor rebuilding the place. A local character used to produce bumper stickers that said I HAD A WHALE OF A GOOD TIME IN SAG HARBOR, as a winking whale waved its tail. I hadn't seen one in a long time. I think there was a direct correlation between the disappearing bumper stickers and the emergence of Hamptonsy establishments. That each time a car with a I HAD A WHALE OF A GOOD TIME IN SAG HARBOR sticker on its fender went off to the wrecking yard—a dark-blue Chevy with a vinyl top, a brown Ford station wagon with faux-walnut paneling—a nouvelle cuisine restaurant popped up, a day spa opened its doors, a jet-set pet store marked up prices on their handmade chew toys. That for every disappearing winking whale, a Jonni Waffle took its place.

BRISTOL'S ICE CREAM had their truck parked outside Jonni Waffle. Martine shifted the cans on the dolly to double-check them against his list of what had been pillaged in the preceding seven days. White mist boiled off the cans, disappearing in the afternoon heat. "Hello Benji," Martine said, barely looking up.

I no longer winced when he called me Benji. My great plans at the beginning of the summer of going by Ben had been disappointed, so I had given up on friends and family making the switch, concentrating instead on the understanding strangers of my future acquaintance, my hypothetical and impending easygoing chums. NP had fixed me in Benji-dom before I even got in the door. He'd brought me an application, which I filled out on the spot and gave back to him. Martine called me in the next day. "So you're Benji," he said, right off the bat, and I knew I wasn't going to get out from under my name. Seeing that I was another one of black Sag Harbor's mysterious middle-class boys, Martine gave me a few spots in the rotation. My first job.

I followed the delivery guy inside. The front of the shop, the customer side, wasn't that large, which made it all the more terrifying when you looked up from the vats during the evening rush to see such a ferocious throng. So much menace per square inch. When you walked in, the vats were right in front, and a gentle current of lust drew the customers forward to the glass, where they marveled at the frosty bounty before them. Before I went to work there, my idea of an exotic flavor was Mint Chocolate Chip, the Baskin-Robbins version of pushing the envelope. The labels on the vat windows inside Jonni Waffle destroyed my provincial notions. What the hell was a praline, and what would possess someone to insert it into a creature called Cran-Mocha? These were nefarious doings. But then, the secondary gimmick of the place, after the waffle cone, was infinite recombination. One scoop of this with another scoop of something else, and then cap that off with a topping. When all else failed, stick in some marshmallow.

Again, I knew about sprinkles, but that was as far as things went for me, toppings-wise. Jonni Waffle had a vast Toppings Bar, featuring all kinds of wondrous things laid out in a gaudy pageant of gluttony American-style, freedom served as-you-like-it. A Plexiglas barrier protected the bar from the customers, I swear it was bulletproof and riot-tested. Is the toppings bar ready for its close-up? Let us cue the orchestra as we pan lovingly, lingeringly, over the delights in the tiny containers. Fragments of candy bars, chopped up Heath and Mounds, splinters of Snickers, Gummi Bears that we shoved headfirst into vanilla bluffs, M&M's and Reese's Pieces, containers of raspberries and blueberries that wore haloes of circling fruit flies. Chocolate chips, jimmies, shavings of coconut. We jabbed these items into the scoops, extra points if you heard a crack as the cone buckled under the strain, we dolloped on hot fudge and butterscotch on command with a fetishist's care. During slow stretches, the managers directed us to clean up the bar, and we scraped a sponge between the containers and swept the grisly dregs into our palms. The very residue of desire. At the end of the night the floor was tackier than the aisles of a porn theater, and our sneakers made creaky-sticky noises as we walked.

Next to the vats was the huge freezer where Martine stored the unopened containers. The waffle apparatus was by the window. Squeeze past that and you were behind the counter, where, on that afternoon, Nick leaned against the Soft Serv machine. "What's up, Benji?" The toothpick bobbed on his lip.

I saw he had a new gold chain. His old one said NICK in two-inch letters, and was studded with tiny white rhinestones. His new chain said BIG NICK in two-inch letters, and was studded with tiny white rhinestones that glittered more exuberantly than those of its predecessor, the ersatz diamond industry having made admirable strides in the last few months. "Nice," I said.

"Got my man in Queens Plaza to do it," he said, peering down at his love. Nick was out full time now so he made a point of going back to the city a lot. He'd been a summer kid, one of our gang through many adventures, but something had happened between his parents—we never asked about family processes, only accepted the results when informed—and now he and his mom were living out in Sag Harbor Hills full time. *Shudder*. He went to Pierson High School, was technically a townie by definitions that he himself would have upheld, and was embarrassed by this. When his schoolmates entered the store, he went all casual, downplaying the connection, muttering "What can I get you?" with true summer-job contempt. "This whole Sag thing is just temporary," he frequently told us, to reassure himself.

My father would've kicked me out of the house if I walked in with a gold chain around my neck. Not that it ever would've occurred to me to get a gold chain. "Who does he think he is?" I can hear my father say. "Where does he think he comes from, the Street?" The Street in my father's mind was a vast, abstract plane of black pathology. He'd grown up poor, fighting his way home every day off Lenox Avenue, and any hint that he hadn't escaped, that all his suffering had been for naught, kindled his temper and his deep fear that aspiration was an illusion and the Street a labyrinth without exit, a mess of connecting alleys and avenues always leading back into itself. So no gold chains, no.

The stereotype stuff was hard, no joke, no matter where you

came from. Look, we had all kinds in Azurest. We had die-hard bourgies, we had first-generation college strivers, fake WASPs, the odd mellowing Militant, but no matter where you fell on the spectrum of righteousness, down with the cause or up with The Man, there were certain things you did not do. Too many people watching.

You didn't, for example, walk down Main Street with a watermelon under your arm. Even if you had a pretty good reason. Like, you were going to a potluck and each person had to bring an item and your item just happened to be a watermelon, luck of the draw, and you wrote this on a sign so everyone would understand the context, and as you walked down Main Street you held the sign in one hand and the explained watermelon in the other, all casual, perhaps nodding between the watermelon and the sign for extra emphasis if you made eye contact. This would not happen. We were on display. You'd add cover purchases, as if you were buying hemorrhoid cream or something, throw some apples into the basket, a carton of milk, butter, some fucking saltines, and all smiles at the register.

For argument's sake, let's say there was a brand of character who was able to say, Forget that, I'm going to walk up and down Main Street with a watermelon under each arm! And one between my legs! Big grin on my face! Peak o' rush hour! Such rebellion was inherently self-conscious, overly determined. It doth protest too much, described an inner conflict as big as that of the watermelon-avoiders. We were all of us stuck whether we wanted to admit it or not. We were people, not performance artists, all appearances to the contrary.

But Nick! Nick embraced early '80s fashion of young black boys with verve and unashamed gusto. He loved two-tone jeans, gray in the front, black in the back, months out of fashion but authentic city artifacts in Sag. The fat laces on his Adidas were puffy and magnificent, and if he wasn't wearing his Jonni Waffle shirt with the sleeves rolled up juvenile delinquent–style, he wore a Knicks jersey that showed off his muscles. Said muscles which had been produced by lugging his radio around.

His radio was the most ridiculous thing, the biggest radio any of us had ever seen or ever would see. For the most part, the consumer-electronics industry focused its innovation toward miniaturization, the lighter Walkman, the more compact stereo. They reserved their passion for the gigantic for their televisions—except in the case of Nick's radio. In this one area, did they spare themselves their love for the discreet, the handsomely detailed diminutive. His radio was a yard wide, half as much tall, a gleaming silver slab of stereophonic dynamism. It didn't do much. Played the terrible East End radio stations. Played cassettes. Made a dub at the touch of a button. For all I know it was mostly air inside, save for the bushel of double-D batteries it took to power the thing, and which Nick spent most of his wages on. That, and the gold. Its only true talent was in the realm of volume, of producing the sound promised by its formidable frame. Nick never turned the dial past 7, after an incident he refused to describe. The two speakers were like big black eyes glaring out from the face of defiance itself. The radio said, I am, and what of it?

When we walked down the street with it—I could barely carry the thing, I'll admit—white people stared and elbowed each other in the gut and made little jokes to each other, which we could not hear because the radio was so perversely loud. Our parents shook their heads when they saw it, and said, "So, that's some radio Nick has," when they saw his mother. We all worshipped it, and Nick was one of Martine's favorites so the radio had its own perch by the window.

"I'M BEAT," Nick said.

"You're telling me," I said. We'd both been on last night's shift. Wednesdays were the slowest days—it wasn't the rush that killed you, but the boredom. Boredom made you eat. Some more ice cream, another milk shake. Then when we had to mop, swab the decks out front, we could barely prod the bucket across the floor.

Martine held the freezer open for the delivery guy, directing the Oreo to the top for easy access. We went through Oreo pretty quickly and Martine had a keen sense of his customers' habits, the ebb and flow of their cravings. He was a new kind of entrepreneur in our sleepy hamlet, indeed the East End in general. A harbinger.

For years we'd hit the Tuck Shop for all our ice-cream needs. It was just around the corner next to the bank, and home to the town's video games. We spent a lot of time there, buying sodas, candy, and the occasional cone from Gabe, the owner and sole employee of the joint. We slapped our quarters down for next-up on Asteroids, Robotron, Galaga, Berzerk, the whole beeping-and-blipping rogues' gallery, establishing dibs by laying our coins next to the brown wounds in the plastic where the big kids had set down their cigarettes.

Gabe was a strange guy, an aging beatnik shipwrecked in Sag Harbor after what must have been a long unlikely story. Had he won the Tuck Shop in a weeklong poker marathon, or had it been left to him by an estranged uncle who wanted to make a man out of him? We saw him every day and didn't know anything about him. Tall and gaunt, his long dark hair rubber-banded into a ponytail, he wore a gray tweed jacket even on the hottest days and liked to pace out in front of the store smoking Pall Malls. He'd look out toward the water, smoothing out his Vandyke in thought, leaving us alone inside, trusting that the black boys wouldn't steal anything. And we didn't, though we obsessed over the fact that he left us alone. "That's a crazy white man right there."

We'd graduated to different diversions and more pressing business and didn't loiter at the Tuck Shop anymore. The rest of the town, too—how could the humble Tuck Shop, with its paltry sugar and wafer cones, compete with the waffle, which was the future itself? Get outta here with that horse-and-buggy shit. Nope, Martine had the gimmick that got the people in the door and kept them coming back. The Sag Harbor Jonni Waffle was his third shop—he had two others up-island somewhere, successful enough for him to expand. It wasn't much of a gamble.

Martine was a stocky Dominican dude with pale eyes and stiff, short-cropped orange hair. He'd come to America as a teenager and described himself as "a real immigrant success story," having worked his way up from bag boy at a grocery store in Queens to manager, to owner of that store and others. Recently he'd sold his empire and moved to Long Island, where he got into the ice-cream trade. I can see Martine sitting in the lounger of his new living-room set, plotting what to do with his grocery-store profits, flipping through a fat binder of franchise brochures. He comes to the Jonni Waffle pamphlet—"True Belgian Flavor!"—and the pictures and text address something deep in his nomad soul. "This is a nation of immigrants," he'd say in wonder, when he came in on Monday and surveyed the damage of the weekend rushes. Which didn't make much sense—was he saying that our customers were literally immigrants, or was he addressing a larger notion of universal dispossession briefly remedied by ice cream? "Immigrants!"

"Some of us came on slave ships," NP would say.

"Always so negative!" Martine responded. NP was on the ten-cent-raise track. So you know.

Martine had plenty of philosophical nuggets he'd scoop out and share from time to time, mostly related to the intersection of certain theories he had about human behavior and ice-cream-store management. "No one wants to look at fruit flies," he'd murmur to the Toppings Bar, while shooing away the tiny swarm hovering over the raspberries, the tenor of his voice making it clear he wasn't really referring to fruit flies but something else. Some elusive profundity. "Heavy cone, light of heart" was another favorite, expressing his joy at the sight of a customer's arm dipping under the weight of a triple-scooped extravaganza. "People come here for a crunchy flight of fancy" was an end-of-shift declaration of satisfaction at his life's course.

Obviously, he was black.

"Don't pull that shit on me," NP told Nick, the architect of this provocation. "He has blue eyes and blond hair."

"I'd say they were hazel, shit, your sister Mary has those hazel eyes," Nick countered, anticipating this attack. "And his hair is that red you see on those Caribbean niggers sometimes, and that's where he's from, Dominica."

NP shook his head.

"What about Little John?" I said. Little John was Bobby's cousin. He had straight dirty-blond hair, gray eyes, and an indisputably

Caucasian cast to his features, profile-on-a-coin Caucasian cast. But he was Bobby's cousin, and he acted black enough . . . frankly we never really talked about it. In fact, maybe we made an extra effort not to talk about it.

"Exactly!" Nick said.

"But that's Little John," NP said dismissively.

"Martine keeps his hair short because it's kinky as hell," Nick said. "You know that."

"He's not no black Dominican."

"They got Dominicans walking round blacker than all of us."

"But if you called them black they'd punch you in your face."

"That's true," Nick had to concede.

NP looked at me. "What do you think, Benji?"

"I don't know." I shrugged. "You never know."

It was Nick versus NP in this quarrel, which went on for weeks, with each side coming back with their new evidence to bolster their cases.

"Why do you think he hired so many of us?" Nick demanded one evening when the last of the rush trickled out. "You know these white people out here don't want to have black people behind the counter."

"Because he pays minimum wage?"

One shift, Nick had been on edge. Messing up more than usual. Giving the incorrect change, confusing Chocolate Banana with Chocolate Banana Hazelnut, peeling mealy waffles off the grill— rookie stuff like that. Martine was in the store that day, in the back making a lot of calls. I noticed that Nick kept eyeballing him. When Martine said good-bye and walked out of the store, Nick summoned us excitedly to the window.

"You see! You see!" Nick said.

"What?"

"Martine walking to his car."

"What about it?"

"You can't tell me that's not a black walk!"

"I don't see it."

"His arms! His hips!"

A couple of days after that, Smokey Robinson came over Nick's radio and Martine started in on a lumbering shuffle while talking to a distributor on the phone. He was a bit stiff, but well within the range of Middle-Aged Black Man Getting His Groove On. Nick elbowed me in the stomach and I heard a crack—in surprise, I'd fractured the Two Scoops Raspberry Swirl in a Waffle Cone that I'd been packing. Nick tipped his head toward Martine and glared. You see? You see?

See indeed. We'd strayed into deep eye-of-the-beholder terrain. And you know we weren't going to ask. If he wasn't, he'd fire us for thinking that he was, and if he was, he'd fire us for it not being obvious. The question would have remained academic if not for the Head-Patting Incident, which raised the stakes. Drawing me in, actually, even though I'd tried to stay on the sidelines.

THE DAY OUR ELECTRICITY WENT OUT, NP sauntered in late, wearing a fresh Jonni Waffle shirt his mother had washed for him. His mother was no weekend parent. She was a teacher by profession, and dashed out to Sag, packed for the summer, as soon as the final school bell of the year started ringing. He said hi to Nick, slapped my hand, and then looked at my hair and, with a glance at Martine, said, "You sure you want to leave it all exposed like that? You want a hat?"

I said, "Shut up, bitch." I'd been experimenting with "bitch," trying it out every couple of days. Going well so far, from the response.

Nick flicked NP's arm with his finger. "Why you got to instigate something all the time?" he asked.

NP headed straight for the soda machine and shouted out, "Martine, you get enough Pistachio this time?" winking at us over his fake diligence.

The Head-Patting Incident had occurred the week before, after a post-lunch rush. It was a hot day, steaming, riling the natives. The waffle-cone supply was low when the rush hit, and of everybody on shift, I was known as a clutch waffle-roller, knocking them out at an enviable rate when the pressure was on, not that such a skill was worthy of envy, but you get the point, I got the job done without sacrificing quality and with few rejects. The rush ended on a brutal note when a family of six, mom and dad and their nattering brood in every species of khaki shorts—Sansabelt, pleated, hip-hugging elastic—decided it would be neat if they all had banana splits. Which were our absolute bane because everyone thought the banana split was very exotic and so they eyeballed every step of the construction process and traded notes afterward, with one of the group inevitably complaining when their split had a smidgen less fudge than their companions'.

Eventually, the family beat it out the door. The guys behind the counter, and me in my waffle perch, began to relax. Martine emerged from the back and, observing my accomplishment, the stack of cones, said, "Great job, Benji, those are some real cones you got there," and he patted me on the head. Two bounces.

I stiffened. I think I heard NP's jaw drop. Martine was out the door with his briefcase.

"What the," I said.

NP came around the counter. "Yo, Martine just patted you on the head like you were a pickaninny."

"I'm not his—" I started.

"White man patted me on the head like a pickaninny, I'd kick his ass, shit."

"Martine is black," Nick said. "He was just saying, 'Good job, brotherman.'"

"That's some racist shit right there," NP said. "Pat a black man on the head."

There has been far too little research done in the area of what drives white people to touch black hair. What are the origins of the strange compulsion that forces them to reach out to smooth, squeeze, pet, pat, bounce their fingers in the soft, resilient exuberance of an Afro, a natural, a just-doin'-its-own-thing jumble of black hair? It's only hair—but try telling that to that specimen eyeing a seductive bonbon of black locks, as the sweat beads on their forehead and they tremble with the intensity of restraint, their fingers locked in a fist in their pocket: I cannot touch it, but I must. A black-hair fondler has a few favorite questions that they like to ask when they fondle. "How do you comb it?" "How do you make it do that?" "How do you wash it?" With a pick; just does it; shampoo. Jerkoff.

A good starting point for such a study might be a metropolitan preschool, where the races are *forced to mix with each other*. Let the camera roll. The hours of footage, capturing the white school-teacher's pats of her charges' nappy heads—good-morning hello, after-recess howdy, end-of-day farewell—will be a fruitful avenue of research. It's an ancient curiosity, no doubt, one that finds its first full expression during slavery. The contact of the two races on a daily basis, on New World soil, as they breathe its strange air. Picture the slaveholder as he surveys his property, both animate and inanimate, walking between the rows of the slave shacks, the field niggers standing at attention. He passes a young boy with bright eyes, round cheeks . . . and an irresistible 'Fro, untamed, almost flirtatious. Is it . . . can it be . . . winking at him? He will pet his property and pet is the correct verb, for these are animals before him.

I had punched a white classmate or two or three, some boys and a girl, in the stomach or the eye, during my early elementary-school years for inappropriate 'Fro-touching. "I just wanted to see what it felt like." I punched them according to my father's lessons. In each case, the principal called our house that evening, my mother answered, my father listened to one side of the conversation, came to a boil, asked for the phone, and then schooled Mr. Aletta in the finer points of black history, patiently, inexorably. That was a long time ago.

NP started a campaign. In slow moments he'd whisper, "It's like lamb's wool," with a tone of wonder in his voice.

When I returned from my ten-minute break, he'd squeak excitedly, "I love its kinky texture."

And also, "It springs back so fast."

And merely "Nappy!" if he was feeling pithy.

Nick said, "He's black, I'm telling you," and that's how things went for a time. What had been Martine's intent? Caught between NP's indictment that I'd been punked, and Nick's vision of racial solidarity. I was in the middle, bending as usual in the direction of whatever breeze was blowing through me that day. The day our electricity went out, I inclined toward NP and his vision of eternal, unending race warfare.

What are you going to do about it? What are you ever going to do about anything?

MARTINE DIDN'T STAY LONG after the delivery guys left, driving off to "check out the other stores," leaving us in the care of Bert, our noble skipper. Bert made a good show of being upright when Martine was about, but once the boss left he spent half the shift in the bathroom, shivering in hangover. I didn't know much about hangovers at that point, so in the years since my Jonni Waffle time, Bert has stayed with me as Patient Zero of Morning-After Incapacitation. It was always nice when Bert came up on manager rotation. He made the tough shifts easier, too preoccupied with his nausea and that night's plans for him to get in a fever over refilling the carob chips or too-generous scoops.

The final member of the Thursday night shift joined us in the form of one of the Cousins, Meg, and I was immediately reminded of my shirt. Why did I have to stink today? "I thought Marsha was on today," I said, then realized that it might appear as if I were overly familiar with her schedule. Which was true.

"We switched," Meg explained. Marsha had a date with one of the boys, one of the Teds and Derricks and Sammys who populated the Cousins' lull-period conversation and hovered outside near closing time. The Cousins were fun. Marsha, a plump little thing with dyed red hair, lived up-island in Center Moriches, and Meg had come down from her home in Rhode Island somewhere to spend the summer with her kinfolk. Meg pushed my buttons, mostly due to her New Wave haircut, which sliced across her face in a nice, hard angle.

It was a couple of weeks before I noticed, as she bent over one day, that she cut it that way to cover her lazy eye. That I knew her secret made it even more exciting when her breast grazed my elbow, or my elbow grazed her breast, depending on your perspective, although I have my perspective and I'm sticking to it.

My elbow smooshed her breast at least once per shift. It was a tight fit, there in the vats. We reached past each other, leaning in, accumulating our little shavings from nearby or adjacent flavors, sometimes competing for the same flavor, trading scoops one after the other. Breathing each other's cooled breath. So there was plausible deniability vis-à-vis the tit collisions, between gravity working on her body, and my long, skinny arms. But the thing is, it never happened with Marsha or Arianna, the other girl I worked with sometimes. And it happened every shift, which was outside probability. I always murmured a quick "Sorry, sorry," and Meg said, "No problem," and we continued on our cones or sundaes.

One scoop dread, one scoop excitement—such was my portion when I worked with Meg. As a shift progressed without a tit collision, I'd think, the spell is broken, and then a few minutes later— smoosh, that soft inevitability. Sorry, sorry. All these years later, I can only come to the conclusion that she was steering her breasts into my elbow the whole time, as a joke or a thrill, I don't know, other people's kicks are as mysterious as my own. (Holding hands in the roller disco, a tit collision in the ice-cream vats—an arc seems to be shaping up here, or, given that there are only two points, a straight line of ascent, Team Man-Child coming from behind in the second half.) When I think about it, the memory calls up this odd mix of sensations—the heat of her breast and the cold gusts of the freezer, the latter overpowering the former so that desire was cooled off and extinguished the moment it came into being. Sounds about right.

The Cousins had a car, and a network of party tipsters, and were generally having a much better summer than I was. Meg invited me—or us, really, me and NP and Nick, so I can't say it was a personal invite—to join them at one of the parties they heard about every weekend, at some arcane West Hampton address or sinister-sounding

East Hampton beach I'd never heard of, Plow-Buddy Bluffs, Sugar-Bang Drift. I wanted to go, but didn't want to go alone, and NP and Nick weren't interested in the Cousins' lifestyle. Of Marsha, they opined that she "need to shave her arms" and "got some booty," and regarding Meg they offered that she was "too skinny," had a "flat ass," but was "okay in the face." Imagine if they knew about the lazy eye! They weren't interested, but there was something else there, too, a fear of going off-map, of traveling to a part of the East End that we didn't know. Where we didn't know where the exits were in case something racial went down, that small radius of light created by a beach-party bonfire magnifying the deep mysteries that lay beyond it, that greater darkness. Fuckin' rednecks.

Four to six was dead. Everyone at the beach or washing sand off their feet, tugging down the edge of a swimsuit to inspect tan progress. Nick was making batter in the back, and NP and Meg and I took turns with the few late-afternoon stragglers. I hadn't eaten all day, so I made lunch—a chocolate milk shake, heavy on the syrup. There was a hot-dog machine on-site, where the franks spun eternally like grisly grim planets, and occasionally I'd make a wretched feast of one, and every so often I'd grab a slice of pizza from Conca D'Oro or a burger from the Corner Bar, but most of the time I ate ice cream. Chocolate in a plastic cup with rainbow sprinkles, chocolate milk shakes, chocolate ice-cream sodas, chocolate twist dispensed by a lever into wavy, brown, short-lived peaks. I mean, it was free, and all you can eat, without limit, and it was nice to live like a glutton for a change, unchecked and unreserved. It was new for me. I was nauseous at the end of each day but that seemed a small price, and by the next shift I magically forgot how sick I'd been and started all over again.

"Your shirt smells kinda funky, Benji," NP said.

"Yeah, I forgot to wash it." I sneaked a peek at Meg. She was frowning at her fingernails, oblivious.

"Smells like . . . smells like . . ." As NP reached for the appropriate analogy, Bert staggered out front and put Nick on waffle duty.

"Dag," Nick said.

"Better to get it now, than when all those people out there staring at you," I said.

"Smells like the Funk of Forty Thousand Years," NP said, finally.

I have not described the making of the waffle cones, I know. I've been putting it off. There was a bit of theater involved. "Look at what he's doing, Mommy!" You sat on a special perch in the front of the store for all to ogle as you ladled batter onto the four waffle grills, which were mounted together on a wheel. Spin the wheel, remove the cone, roll it up in the mold, spray on the nonstick cooking spray, add more batter, spin the wheel, and on to the next. "I want one, Mommy!" Sound easy? Go fuck yourself. Move too fast and the cones peeled off limp and useless, move too slow and they turned out as brittle as ashes and disintegrated at a glance. We wore thick gloves but often burned our forearms on the grills, hence the beat-up tube of vitamin-E ointment to prevent scarring, never far from reach. When the batter overflowed, squeezed out when the grill top came down, we scraped off the stalactites of batter with a paint scraper. Is a paint scraper a standard food-preparation utensil? You had become a living advertisement for the waffle cone, a cog in a Belgian dessert combine. "Smells so good!" The hungry ones watched your every move, a grubby mob eager for this spectacle.

The human epidermis is a wondrous thing. When you pulled waffle duty, a Plexiglas barrier separated you from the hordes, and this was no small boon, especially during the weekend rushes. By the end of the night, the accumulated swabbed-on oils from untold foreheads and forearms and hands covered the glass so thoroughly that our oppressors were lost in the fog of their own plenitude. "If I cannot see their faces, I will not have the nightmares," I whispered to myself, as steam puffed out from the sizzling grills: Windex by the crate, you can imagine.

A tall man in a Hawaiian shirt came in, his face so red and peeling that he must have had sunburns on his sunburns. It was beginning, Thursday night in all its humanity. At the start of the shift, we played You're Up, trading off customers until the numbers made it impossible.

"All yours, Benji," Meg said, looking up from that week's *Dan's Papers*. She was deep in the club pages, reconnoitering the weekend.

"Why am I up? You just got here."

"I'm taking my break," she said.

"Huh?"

"I'm taking my break at the start of the shift," Meg said. "What? There's no law against it."

I looked at the customer and knew he was one of those Rum Raisin Imbeciles. Of course over time you got to know what people were going to order as soon as they walked in the door—the inner was written on the outer. Rum Raisin Imbeciles looked like they were wilting. They had a distinctive sag to their postures, their faces slack and loose, as if their day-to-day had drained away something essential. One bite of Rum Raisin, though, and they instantly perked up, standing up straight, eyes a-sparkle. It was weird.

He took a number even though he was the only customer in the store. I waited for him to speak. Rum Raisin Imbeciles always made a show of considering other flavors—cooing "Oh, that looks good" and "I've been meaning to try that"—before settling on their favorite, the polyester of ice cream. Innovative in its time, perhaps, Rum Raisin was loud plaid shorts next to a fresh can of Double Mocha Bombasta.

"Rum Raisin, please."

"In a waffle cone?" I asked in a pleasant chirp. Martine wanted us to push the waffle. At the peak of a rush, our collective *In a waffle cone?*'s trilled throughout the store like beautiful chimes.

"I've been meaning to try one of those . . ."

I exhaled with impatience. I knew where this was going.

"A sugar cone is fine."

I started scooping. One nice thing about Rum Raisin, it was soft. Especially after it had been in the vats for a while. A new container fresh out of the freezer was a horror. All you could scrape out were these tiny ribbons that made it look like you were peeling a carrot while parents lifted their whelps up to the vats so they could see us working away, the kids' noses dragging greasy smears across the glass. The shavings added up over time, but with those beady little eyes hawking you it was a real hassle.

I rang him up and he left the store, newly energized and licking thoughtfully. My shake had melted so I poured it out and made a chocolate ice-cream float, easy on the seltzer. Time disappeared into the service-industry void. You looked at the clock and saw twenty minutes had passed. What happened? I saw NP mashing some Oreo into a pint cup. He noticed me and said, "My mom wants some for this weekend."

"Didn't you get a pint yesterday?" Which was true. Mrs. Collins's Rocky Road requests weighing on my mind, I took note of my friends' pint-making habits in hopes of figuring a way out of my problem.

"Dag, Benji. What are you, the Jonni Waffle police?"

I had a thing about stealing. I discovered this in fifth grade, the first time my white classmates started their daily swiping runs through the candy racks of the Gristedes next to school. Andy palmed a roll of Mint Certs and winked. I stood behind him with a grape Fruit Roll-Up I intended to pay for, according to social norms. He whispered, "Take something, man," but before I could even think about it, I heard Sidney Poitier's voice in my head and in that crisp, familiar, so-dignified tone, he declared, "They think we steal, and because they think we steal, we must not steal."

Andy paid for his sour pickle, the ill-gotten Certs secure in his coat pocket. I paid for my Fruit Roll-Up, half intoxicated with a new self-righteousness. The next couple of years, I shook my head in disapproval when one of my friends stole something. I spent my allowance on Starbursts and Jolly Ranchers, legit all the way.

Stealing, Sidney Poitier said, was for the white kids. Let them pull their petty crimes if they wanted—we were made of better material. There was no real harm in it, ripping off a candy bar or box of cough drops here and there unless, and everyone agreed on this point, you were one of the miserable, anonymous Klepto Kids, those unfortunate souls who channeled their home-turf dysfunction into schooltime acting out, rummaging through people's coats during recess, shaking down unsecured lockers at key moments of opportunity. (Bettina, Bettina.) It was easy to picture the forbidden troves underneath the Klepto Kid beds, twenty floors above Park Avenue—the shiny mound of Timex watches, Fiorucci sunglasses, electronic calculators, and bracelets engraved with the names of happier children.

So it went until high school, when the rules changed, as usual. Now the good boys of my Sag Harbor crew pulled the occasional crime—smuggling a Budweiser out of the South Hampton 7-Eleven under a sweatshirt, sticking a *Penthouse* into a copy of *OMNI* for camouflage and walking out of the Ideal. I abstained, and Sidney Poitier, observing my peers' thievery, kept silent, merely clucking his tongue occasionally. I had only tried to steal something once. And I had learned my lesson.

THE GREAT COCA-COLA ROBBERY occurred in the spring of 1985, when I found myself in that most unlikely place, a party. I'd run into Bobby one afternoon at Tower Records on Sixty-sixth Street. I was looking for a Depeche Mode twelve-inch; he was down from Scarsdale to buy U.T.F.O.'s debut album. We rarely saw each other during the school year, but quickly picked things up again as if we'd ridden through the Hills the day before. As we were about to split, I removed all tagalong/mooch emanations from my voice and asked what he was up to that night. He said, "Going to a party. Wanna come?" And maybe that was a kind of theft, because with the finesse of picking a pocket I'd spared myself a night at home watching cable.

The party was a few blocks away from my house, on Ninety-eighth off West End Avenue. Bobby went to a prep school in Riverdale that had a mix of city kids and Westchester kids. I met up with him in front of the McDonald's outside the subway. "Karen's parents fly away every weekend," Bobby told me, "so she has a lot of parties." I pictured weekend after weekend of parties, Friday to Sunday bacchanals where kids smoked weed and drank beer in full Kid with the Empty House liberation, a notion reinforced when we walked in and saw everyone lounging on couches, or leaning against walls in mellow affect. It seemed they had been there for days in a perfect habitat of cool poise. Bobby introduced me around, and I was greeted with genuine, nonjudgmental interest. New York private schools all drew from the same pool of well-scrubbed scion, but these people seemed nicer than the reliably dismissive brand at my school, like they'd make space for my tray and scooch over if I walked by their lunch table, or make fun of my clothes in a way that said, We're close enough that my joking reveals our human connection, as opposed to, You're a jerk and I'm an asshole. I thought to myself, I could get used to this. I went to look for a beer, and there I stumbled on the Fort Knox of carbonated beverages.

A few weeks earlier, the Coca-Cola Company had discontinued their signature cola. They'd lost market share to Pepsi. Diet Coke, the sister brand, had been too successful, luring away consumers with the promise of thinner thighs, a figure more in line with that Aerobicized You. The higher-ups hit upon a catastrophic solution. They decided to replace the most famous drink in the world with an impostor.

I had been addicted to Coke for years, with a two- or three-can-a-day habit since the fifth grade, starting around the same time my schoolmates started stealing, now that I think about it. When my sister told me not to be so hyper, or my parents told me to knock it off, I vibrated with the strain of keeping still, and wondered why nature had cursed me so—it wasn't until I was in high school that I learned what caffeine was. My love for Coke went beyond mere buzz, however. How could one not be charmed by the effervescent joviality of a tall glass of the stuff—the manic activity of the bubbles, popping, reforming, popping anew, sliding up the inside of the glass to freedom, as if the beverage were actually, miraculously, *caffeinated on itself.* That tart first sip, preferably with ice knocking against the lips for an added sensory flourish, that stunned the brain into total recall of pleasure, of all the Cokes consumed before and all those impending Cokes, the long line of satisfaction underpinning a life. What forgiveness for the supreme disappointment of a fountain Coke that turned out to be fizzless and dead, or a lukewarm Coke that had been sitting for a while, falling away from its ideal temperature of 46.5 degrees Fahrenheit/8 degrees Celsius, all the bubbles fled, so that it had become a useless mud of sugar. Which is what New Coke tasted like, actually.

I remember when I first heard that they were changing the formula. April 23, 1985. It was dinnertime and I'd wandered into the living room to ask my mother a question—I can't remember what it was, as it was erased by the terrible information. Dinnertime custom had Reggie and me eating in his room before an array of sitcoms, the *M*A*S*H*s, the *'KRP*s, while our parents ate in the living room watching the evening news. (I moved into my sister's room when she went to college, but Reggie got to keep the TV after a series of negotiations too Byzantine to go into, higher-level even-Stephen stuff beyond mortal ken.) I walked in just in time to hear the newscaster say, "A surprising announcement about an American classic." Somehow I knew. I stayed through the commercial break and watched as Roberto Goizueta, the CEO of Coca-Cola, cheered the end of the world. It was inconceivable, like tampering with the laws of nature. Hey, let's try Gravity-Free Tuesdays, buckle up, motherfuckers. From this day on, water is incredibly flammable, see how that goes. I slunk back to my room, dizzy and confused. It was as if someone had popped the top of the world, and let all the air out.

Within days, I'd cornered the local market on Old Coke in a grid defined by 106th Street to the north, Ninety-sixth to the south, and from Amsterdam to the river, buying up what I could from the corner bodegas, the increasingly slick delis popping up on Broadway, and the assorted stationery stores of the 'hood. By the time New Coke started to appear, a few days after the announcement, I was well prepared, with a huge stash in my closet, a prayer against Doomsday. (A secret stash, Klepto-style.) I had no dreams of profiteering, of selling my stock at a dear price to aficionados when the day came that the people of Earth discovered the treasure they had destroyed, as if the cola were an exquisite lizard or spiny bivalve driven to extinction in our race's savage drive to ruin. No. I wanted it all to myself, like an art thief who steals *Nude Descending a Staircase* or some key Picasso and hangs it on the wall of his own private gallery, for his wicked and ingrown pleasure, at peace with the fact that the world is unaware of his activities, and perhaps that is actually the point of the entire exercise—although such a sentiment is probably not too surprising coming from a boy whose main recreation was masturbation.

When I'd finished my scurrying up and down the avenues, and hauled my six-packs back to my lair, it seemed as though I had enough Coke for a lifetime. But of course it went fast. I tried rationing myself to one can a day, but that didn't last long. I couldn't keep my hands off the stuff. My parents had a party, and my mother asked if she could "borrow" a few cans for mixers. Borrow! How did she even know about my stash—if she knew that, what else did she know? There were magazines in my possession I should maybe hide better. What could I answer but yes, since she could not see or just plain ignored the desperation in my eyes. What a horror it was to see all those half-finished cans strewn around the house, it was a battlefield, my own Gettysburg, and I learned that day what it is to mourn when I heard the sad, exhausted hissing as I poured the remains down the sink.

I was susceptible, then, when I went into Karen's kitchen and someone opened the cabinet next to the sink and I saw a flash of red. As if in a dream, I knelt down to see and there it was, six-pack upon six-pack of Sweet Brown Gold. I was astounded—yes, there was more Coke in the world, but more important, there were others out there like me, those who had been disappointed by life but who did what they could to beat back chaos. I drifted away from the kitchen to let this revelation settle in. As I hung out with Bobby's friends and talked and joked with them, my dream of being adopted by their clan faded away. The cans, the cans kept returning to my mind, like a red curtain falling down to hide the world. After two beers I knew what I had to do. I'd never had two beers before.

I retrieved my jacket from Karen's parents' bedroom, which had been commandeered as the coat room, and slipped back to the kitchen. A boy and a girl talked close together next to the fridge. I tossed some ice into a glass, loudly and emphatically, and declared, "Just looking for mixers," and they smiled and moved away. Obscured by the cabinet door, I wrapped a six-pack in my jacket and pulled the next six-pack forward so that it appeared as if nothing were amiss. My crime might not be noticed for days. I stood. No one had noticed me.

I walked very "act naturally" out into the living room. My plan was to stash the goods in a safe area in the coat room, and exit calmly with the stuff at the end of the party. The living room was quiet, the talking room as opposed to the dancing room, Karen's bedroom, where the music was cranked up. Which is what made the crash that much more loud. In my nervousness I had clumsily wrapped the six-pack, and when I adjusted it as I walked across the room, the cans slipped out in the slow motion that is the speed of humiliation. They clattered against the hardwood floors. Everyone looked over, but my crime was so inexplicable that outsiders could not comprehend what had just happened. They returned to their conversations as I picked up the six-pack. All of them except for Karen. She looked into my face and shook her head ever so slightly in sad assessment. She took the Coke from my hands and said, "I think you should go now."

In the following days, I don't know what I regretted more—my exile from those who might have been my new friends, my classmates from the school I might have gone to had I chosen differently, or the loss of six Cokes. Frankly, it was a toss-up. Bottom line, the episode put an end to my troublemaking efforts. What was the point? Move. Don't move. Act. Don't act. The results were the same. This was my labyrinth.

NP PLACED HIS MOTHER'S PINT of ice cream in the freezer out front, to keep it out of the way.

"I think I might have a hot dog," I said.

"*In a waffle cone?*" Meg shrieked malevolently, and we cracked up. My hand instinctively shot up to cover my mouth.

My mouth. Is it possible I haven't mentioned my mouth yet? My mouth was everything you have ever found repellent gathered together, piled in a cauldron, melted down by sadists into an abhorrent alloy, and then shaped into clips and wire for placement on my teeth. I wore braces, you see, tiny self-esteem-sucking death's-heads all in a row, turning my smile into a food-flecked grimace. Oh, I kept them pretty clean, but a series of corn-on-the-cob-related incidents had planted the seeds of a neurosis, and every so often, if the psychological weather was right, my hand darted to cover my smile from view. So I guess something was brewing that day, because to observers it appeared as if I were sniffing my palm.

"Why are you sniffing your palm?" Meg asked.

"Nothing!" I said.

The families started trickling in, the early eaters full of pizza slices and fried miscellany from one of the seafood restaurants on Main Street that changed names and owners every summer. Only the distributors of processed frozen-fish parts remained the same, eternal in their way, maintaining supply lines season after season. Bert emerged, attended by his sound effect, a flushing toilet. He mopped his forehead with a wet towel and told me to take the garbage out back.

The sky was getting dark. "Is it going to rain?" I asked Nick. The sole grace of the waffle apparatus was its proximity to the window, allowing a prisoner's view of the outside and inspiring many a waffle-duty space-out.

"Not yet, but it's all cloudy."

If the rain came quickly, we'd have an easy night. I took out the garbage. Now I'm no chemist, so I can't break down the reaction with any real authority, but I'd have to say that Bristol's had been forced into an unholy pact when they devised their ice-cream formula. In exchange for supernaturally delicious flavor, the ice cream could not survive for long outside its containers. It started rotting immediately when exposed to room temperature. Standard Deal-with-the-Devil trade-off stuff. By the evening, that morning's ice cream reeked like curdled hell.

There was always a hole somewhere. I dripped a multicolored trail above the previous day's dried trail like a dipshit Jackson Pollock, along the Promenade, around the back of Bayside, to the official Jonni Waffle Dumpster. With some difficulty, I tossed the heavy bags inside, turned—and saw Gabe across the street, leaning against the door of the Tuck Shop, eyeballing me. I looked down, took a step, looked up again, and he was still staring at me. And that expression on his face—was it disapproval?

Not only was my Jonni Waffle T-shirt stinking but now it blazed an obnoxious neon red, the white logo blinking its message: Traitor, Treason, Traitor, Treason. No, we didn't visit Gabe anymore. Once in a while we'd get seized by nostalgia and walk in to play a video game. The place was always empty. The games seemed so silly. How could we have spent so many hours in there, standing like morons, our fingers tapping, eyes glazed? I walked back to the store, looking at the ground. I remembered an incident from a few weeks ago, when Gabe had stopped me on my way to Jonni Waffle saying, "Hey, you guys never come in these days," jabbing his Pall Mall toward me. And I said, "Yeah," not even stopping to be polite. I was late for work.

I made it past the Tuck Shop, ignoring Gabe's stare. Who wouldn't be mad at being replaced? Just another smear under Martine's steamroller. Pat pat. "Whatever happened to the Tuck Shop?" you'd hear in the coming years. It was "destroyed by fire." Next summer it was a health-food store.

The wind was picking up, the sky over the wharf a dirty gray foam. Although I'd only been gone four minutes, the store was packed. Often they came out of nowhere, at the behest of a signal out of range of human ears. Bert caught my eyes as I wriggled through the crowd. "Incoming!" he yelled from the other side.

Incoming, exactly. War and siege analogies came easily in there, during a rush. I was most partial to a scenario I called the Zombie Hideout, given my early training in horror movies: the human beings in the house, the furniture nailed up against the doors and windows to repel the living dead. *Dawn of the Dead*, with its consumer-society subtext, had its particular lessons. For those who may have missed it, basically the dead have come to life and desire human flesh. In ballerina costumes, policeman uniforms, and terry-cloth robes, the dead roam the streets in search of prey. Once they were normal people. In this entry in the *Living Dead* series, human survivors have barricaded themselves in a mall, a micro society with all the packaged food and consumer items they could want. At one point in the film, as the characters stand at the doors and look at the hundreds of mindless zombies gathered outside, they wonder what drives them. "It's some kind of instinct," one of them says. "This was an important place in their lives." Their brains are gone, but they retain this one thing. I know now that when the living dead come, it will not be at the mall that they gather but at the ice-cream shop.

Once in a while, in the city, I'll come across a white person, and Sag Harbor will come up and they'll say, "Oh, I didn't know black people went out there." Which I always find funny, because until that summer, I thought all the white people I saw in town were townies. Townies with checkered pants. That's how we saw things from our neck of the woods. Working at Jonni Waffle taught me that all those white people who came in couldn't have been townies because if the tiny hamlet had been home to that much miscreancy year-round, it would have been swallowed by the Earth long ago.

They took a number from the pink plastic dispenser and waited, the entire Hamptons. The smell of the waffle cones drew them inside, the same way we had caught minnows with old sheets and bedspreads—they flung themselves toward the open seas of their desire. They wore flip-flops that smacked like wet lips, they shuffled forward in tasseled loafers, in white tennis sneakers, and their polo shirts prowled the entire pastel spectrum, from lime green to Creamsicle orange to baboon-butt pink. They were members of varied fraternities, yacht clubs, golf clubs, secret-handshake groups, they were strivers, inheritors, and the privileged bored.

All kinds of flies out there in the summer, stuck to the gently swirling brown strips.

We served them. Gardeners who spent the afternoons shepherding rows of tomatoes to a vulgar fullness through elegantly gritted overpriced gloves. Retirees shaking their heads over the weekend traffic and hissing invective at the young, young street cops and their new regulations, these peach-fuzz constables who treated them like newcomers even though they'd been coming out for years. The I-Remember-Whensters lumbered in with their musty catalogues of the bygone, dragging IVs of distilled nostalgia behind them on creaky wheels, looking down on the new money and reminiscing about the silent Main Street of yore, when you could walk whole yards without being insulted by sniveling little emissaries of the upstart future. There were people who emerged from big old cars that they don't make anymore, which sat under tarps in immaculate garages waiting for the three days of the year they gulped and started down the lanes, these gawked-at luxury rides of the dead, slowly tooling down the main drags of the towns for all to see and ponder.

They came from all over the East End. The youthful princes who swerved drunkenly down the back roads and were written up by eager deputies who saw their reports crumpled up by wizened sheriffs with a curt "What are you, stupid?," as the police blotters of the weeklies detailed tawdry domestic disturbances next to tear-out coupons advertising "2-for-1 Nite at Jonni Waffle." Indeed police-blotter habitués staggered into the store in between capers. "I think I know that guy." Those deposited by helicopter, those who putt-putted down 27 in jalopies, those who blessed the Earth with every footstep, those who deigned, those who stooped to, those who would get their pictures next to their obituaries in the *Times*, and those who would lie on the floor of their abject rooms for days before being discovered.

You got to know the locals. There were people who had uprooted their lives at great cost, the converts who had just become year-rounders with schemes of belonging. Entrepreneurs who fell in love with the silence and the sunsets and convinced themselves that their establishments would succeed against the odds—restaurants serving lovingly produced food of a specialized bent, curio shops whose shelves buckled under knickknacks that were physical manifestation of their owner's psychology. The shopkeepers who shivered with desperation and pounced whenever a visitor roused the sleepy bells over their front doors, the shopkeepers who would take until grim October to accept what was obvious, when they frantically tried to renegotiate their leases, and came into Jonni Waffle less frequently as the summer wore on, as they started to cut back on extras, and when has ice cream been anything but the definition of extra?

We didn't discriminate, we scooped. For the burnouts, the flotsam, the human tumbleweeds who were all of us but for our choices, who found purchase in Springs, outside Amagansett, between towns on dirt roads, in little rooms above Main Street storefronts, in basements of bleak illumination. Magazine editors who assigned articles on the hot spots in order to avail themselves of comps thereafter, oh how they waddled in. The caretakers of other people's property, the people who lived on boats, the painters out to capture that fabled East End light, stoop-shouldered writers ironically digging the affluence while sniffing around for patrons. Posers. Celebrities in shades. Sailors without ships. Descendants of locally famous whalers, whose names hung on street signs to remind people of what they had never known. Potato farmers deliberating offers from developers, the summer influx of help, the waitresses and bartenders and sous-chefs flapping in on their annual migration. Deckhands of yachts on the lookout for wedding rings on fingers, the easy prey, those well-acquainted with knots of all kinds, au pairs stumbling in high heels on their night off and wearing too much makeup and helplessness on their faces. Two scoops, please.

They pointed through the glass and ordered us around. C-list celebrities visiting the houses of their B-list friends, hovering impatiently at the counter as they tried to juggle condescension and confusion at the same time. Old ladies with oddball things on their heads: turbans, pillbox hats fresh out of mothballs, floppy wicker creations that drooped over their big dark sunglasses. Weekend houseguests full of love and ideas and fretful talk of schedules, the train on Sunday that would take them away too soon. Weekenders, weekenders of every disposition, saying, Look at this, Check this out, Isn't that the cutest, the quaintest, dawdling before window displays while the ice cream melted in sweet rivulets over their fingers, Isn't this the kind of thing we can display in our houses and have a little story about if anyone should ask, and we hope they ask, because if they don't there is this great abyss of us we must navigate. Young enthusiasts of fudge. The smeared, the daubed, the ugly eaters out for their favorite treat.

They wanted ice cream and we served them. We scooped and scooped. For crumbling entities held together only by the energy of their fierce disdain, who were often, paradoxically, nice tippers, go figure. Heiresses tugging dour poodles from place to place—"It's good to have someone to talk to"—and grizzled he-men who worked with their hands, sneering at and ripping off their clients, those pampered city infants whom they overcharged for wood and nails and spackle so that they could afford a special oil to rub into their calluses. The kept, the models and rent boys and sundry amenable, as if we were not all kept by this place in some way, so who were we to sneer. The strange cheerleaders and the weirdly smiling, the victims who just bobbed along on the current one time too many. Wasted clubbers drifting over from Bayside with eyes the color of raspberry sherbet, who pressed their noses up to the glass to view the stark majesty of the vats and shuddered at the plenty.

They handed us money and dropped coins into the tip cup from time to time. Scrabbling creatures with power of attorney, swaggering instigators who would emerge unscathed from impending savings-and-loan disasters, cagey VP's of inscrutably named corporate divisions who skipped into the store half levitating on their own magnificence and sneered with impotent disdain at the numbers on the paper tickets. Renters whose thin complaints echoed in the halls of awesome mansions, renters in shabby clapboard shares that didn't have enough bathrooms, renters of total dud houses with overburdened septic tanks and serious drainage issues. Weekend hoboes without a place to stay, who hitched a ride on the five o'clock from Penn, jumped off and prowled after fun, caroused, fucked or did not fuck, found a bed or sofa or floor or slept on the beach and miraculously did not get molested in any way, dozed late and started again on Saturday, with more or less success in their adventures, and took the early train back Sunday morning reeking of their ills and hopes, nodding off in bliss.

And there must have been creatures of such affluence that I cannot even speculate about their day-to-day, outside the fact of their sweet tooths. They lived over in South Hampton somewhere, on estates guarded by solemn hedges, an army of little green petals repelling all invading eyes. I imagine steaming mud and hairless reptilian creatures swooping down low from between fanlike prehistoric leaves. Beings emerge from the gray muck, raising their great eye-domes above the silt, flicking tongues. The exact shape of their bodies, the number of gills in their neck and suckers on their mottled digits, I cannot say, because in order to mingle with Earth people they needed to wear human-flesh costumes, for only then could they walk among us, and of course eventually they came through the doors of Jonni Waffle like all the rest, like all of us, and I served them ice cream.

But not that night.

The lights went out at 8:30, just when things were getting good and horrible in their familiar way. The pink paper tickets fluttered to the floor, stuck fast to melted goo. The hands received the cones. A stray boob collapsed against my elbow and I felt a tiny flutter in my groin. Sorry, sorry. Another sensory organ piped up: my nose. The smell of burned waffle turned the air acrid. NP was on the grills, displaying his customary pride in his job. I looked up and saw him toss a charred Frisbee into the trash—it dissolved into a black vapor as it flew through the air.

Choppy waters. Bert performed a course correction, putting me on the grills to head off disaster—peril, thy name is waffle shortage. I traded places with NP. He handed me the apron. I put on the apron. He handed me the gloves. I put on the gloves. As I reached for the ladle, I glanced to my right, into the twinkling eyes of a towheaded urchin who looked up at me in wonder, a flying buttress of clear mucous attaching his nostril to the plastic barrier—and the lights went out.

The only illumination was the crimson eye of the power indicator on Nick's radio. They wailed—inside the store, the evening strollers out on the Promenade and the wharf, the mid-amble folks on Main Street. Bert grumbled in the dark and appeared with some flashlights and we finished out our orders, on the house since the registers were out of commission. We banished the rest of the unfortunates from the premises. They milled around in the corridor outside, clutching their numbers as the news sunk in.

"Thank God," Meg said.

"It was starting to get crazy in here," Nick said. "Look at them . . ." Headlights washed over their bodies, producing scary silhouettes.

"We're closed! It's a BLACKOUT, shit," NP shouted.

Keep your voices down, I murmured to myself—the living dead will know we're inside. Bert locked the front doors for added protection and told us he was going to try to get Martine on the phone.

"Maybe we're going to close early," I said.

Nick fiddled with his radio and found WLNG. "The power's out in the Town of South Hampton, and we're getting reports that the lights are out everywhere from Quogue to Amagansett . . ." It hadn't started raining yet, but obviously the storm was doing some damage up-island.

"Martine must be freaking out," NP said. "Blackout on a hot night like this—all this ice cream is going to be puddles, yo."

"Sucks for him," Meg said.

All of it was going to be soup if the lights took too long to come back on. That was a lot of money.

Bert returned, flashlight under his chin to give his face a ghoulish cast, and told us that Martine wanted us to give it an hour to see if the electricity returned. Then we'd call it a night. Even if the lights came back on in a few hours, the night was a wash. Everybody was going to stay home in case the juice went out again.

Who knew what was going on out there? It sounded wild. People whooping, cars honking at things that darted past in the night. The DJ was excited. Nothing ever happened, now this to savor: "We have a report from Eric of Watermill, who's standing outside the Candy Kitchen, and he says all of Main Street Bridgehampton is dark." Bert told us of the last time he was in a blackout, a story that involved two Swedish exchange students, a borrowed Volvo, and two bottles of Jose Cuervo. "We didn't need lemons, if you know what I mean," he said. I didn't. Outside the windows and beyond the glass doors of the store, the figures loped in the darkness, caught by random slashes of illumination. We heard their voices as they ran into comrades and shared info, trading disappointments. All in it together.

The phone rang a bit later. "That's it, we're done," Bert said as he came back out.

"Shift over?" Nick said.

"Our master has spoken."

"Master?" I asked, before NP beat me to it.

"It's a figure of speech."

"We better get paid for a whole shift," NP said.

"I'm sure you'll get your $8.35," Bert said, to our general contentment. Like I said, the money added up.

We cleaned up what we could. Special blackout procedures called for us to lay down garbage bags on top of the open containers in the vats, to add another layer of insulation. Keep the cold inside where it belonged. Bert double-checked the bags when we were done, tucking their edges down tight. "He's going to freak if he comes in tomorrow and all this is melted," he said.

I was wiping down the waffle apparatus when the door started rattling. "We're closed, damn it, shit," I said.

"Let me in, fool!"

It was the other cousin, Marsha. "You guys got off lucky," she said when I opened the door. She'd come to fetch Meg. She and her date, and one of her date's buddies, were waiting outside.

"Hey Bert, can I go?" Meg asked. She rearranged the slash of hair across her face, but given the lighting conditions, her lazy eye wasn't going to be an issue that night. There was a moment in the dark when I had pictured her giving me a ride home (had she driven to work? I didn't know) and then various things occurring. She grabbed her bag and was gone. "See you later!"

Soon the rest of us were out on the wharf. The wind cooled the sweat that had soaked into our Jonni Waffle T-shirts. Folks were drinking beer and looking at the stars. The people on the boats had their radios up loud, the mandatory Motown faves from *The Big Chill* soundtrack overlapping each other in the night. A few yards away, the windows of the Long Wharf Restaurant glowed from the tiny candles on the tables. Bert said he was going to head to the Corner Bar. His friend was bartending. It wasn't the first blackout night he'd spent there. Nick went over to the Long Wharf Restaurant to see when Randy was getting off. Maybe we could get a ride home or maybe there was a plan brewing.

NP cursed. "Yo, Bert, can I get the key? I left my pint in there." He disappeared into the Promenade with the keys. I was surprised that Bert just tossed him the keys. Of course NP wasn't going to steal anything, but I was always surprised by these little trusting gestures from white people in authority. Like when Gabe went outside the Tuck Shop for a smoke, full of faith in our character. I shouldn't have been surprised. We had earned it by being good boys. And look at Gabe now.

NP returned. I said, "Damn, I forgot my mix tape! Can I go and get it?"

Bert shook his head and handed me the keys. "Hurry up, man. I need a goddamn beer."

I can't explain what happened. I can only tell you, the best I am able, about how I used to live.

Mix tapes were the perfect alibi. All of us in the teenage crew had them, they were a snapshot of this month's soul translated into music and arranged in perfect order. We let everything else go but we were fascists about our mix tapes. They were our necessary evidence. We took turns, sticking them into Nick's radio when it was our go, to make somebody listen finally. I had a fall guy in NP, who by his own admission had returned to the freezer to retrieve his pint. I unlocked the front door and stood before the mammoth freezer. You had to really pull hard on the freezer doors. They were designed to stay shut and make a strong seal. I pulled them open and the cool air tumbled over my face. I couldn't see it, but I pictured the white mist in the darkness spilling out in chilly, ghostly tendrils. The heat and humidity reached inside, brushing their fingertips along the side of the cans and transforming the frost there into beads of water. It was an exchange, the outside coming inside and the inside entering outside, like a tiny darkness that grew and then spread to cover whole towns. I left the doors open, first at a ten-degree angle, then a twenty-five-degree angle. Like that.

I gave the keys back to Bert. He slapped us five and padded over to the Corner Bar, the headlights of the creeping cars lighting his way. At the intersection, a cop waved a glowing red cone around and around. Nick had some Budweisers in his hands, a bribe from Randy for us to wait until he finished his shift. I was tired and I smelled and I decided to go home.

It was so different walking home without streetlights, especially once I got past the marina, where people had their boats lit up and were having a high old time, drinking and laughing. Surely the young ladies at the Cormaria Retreat House were dancing with their candelabra under the stars with extra passion tonight. The farther I got from town the darker it got and there were fewer cars slowly nudging their way through the dark to light my path. The rain still hadn't come, but the wind fussed the trees and this was the only sound I heard. The candles and kerosene lanterns burned in the windows of the houses, pulsating in orange and yellow, showing the way, just as they had a hundred years ago. I couldn't see the power lines and telephone and cable wires and I couldn't make out the fancy cars in the driveways. Events had pulled the plug on the modern world. As if it had never been. The lights in the windows of the familiar old houses had guided the men home when they returned from sea, the earthbound constellations they recognized and trusted and steered by. I knew where I was. I had walked these streets my whole life. For a few minutes I was a true son of Eastville, returning with my brothers in the dark down Bay Street and Hempstead Street after a good day's work.

The lights were on when I woke up the next morning. The rain never made it. Reggie and I spent the afternoon cleaning up the house, undoing the mess of our days. Our parents arrived that evening and it all started again.

I didn't work that weekend—Nick had asked for my Saturday night shift to help pay off his gold—and when I came in Monday there was no mention of the open freezer and the ice cream inside, solid or otherwise. I didn't ask about it. Jonni Waffle was a family, and my experience of family was that you didn't ask too many questions. A few days later, on the wall above the desk in the back of the store, Martine taped up a sheet with a list of Blackout Rules, the last of which was: DOUBLE-CHECK THAT THE FREEZER DOORS ARE SHUT! The following summer, the list was still there, and next to it was a picture of Martine and his brother, taken at a family reunion "back home," or so he told us. They had their arms crooked around each other's necks and cups of pale beer in their hands. They looked a lot alike in the face and had the same smile. If you disbelieved what people told you, all you had to do was look at the smile. His brother was black as hell, no joke, with a crazy crown of kink on his head.

The Coca-Cola Company brought back Coke—now called Classic Coke—soon after the blackout, on July 10, 1985.

I worked at Jonni Waffle for another two summers, eating ice cream all shift, every shift. The smell of the batter haunts me still. My metabolism was such that I never got fat, but eventually my gorging turned into a form of aversion therapy and made me hate ice cream, the very sight of it, and this hatred spread to the entire dessert world, and most sweets. It's a terrible thing to hate dessert, to remove yourself from the ways of civilized people. You learn to see things differently from the other side, standing there behind the protective plastic, looking at the normals and their easy pleasure in simple things.

From time to time, I think of the freezer and have a vision of the catastrophe. As the night grows long, the containers at the bottom of the pile start to buckle under their burden. What is inside has gone soft and weak. The bottom cans collapse under the weight of their brothers and the ones up high tumble out of the freezer, knocking the doors wide, the lids of the cans popping off. The cans splash out their guts, one after the other. It's dark, and no one can see it but me, I can see it, the rainbow calamity on the tile, the green mint and bloodred sherbet and other assorted plenty in a cookie-clotted sludge oozing out across the floor, marshmallows floating like broken teeth, all this in a slow and ugly wave, reaching toward me like a hand.

The

Gangsters

ALL THE ILL SHIT WENT DOWN ON THURSDAYS LIKE clockwork. Mondays we slept in, lulled by the silence in the rest of the house. The only racket was the carpenter ants gnawing the soft wood under the deck, not much of a racket at all. It was safe. When we met up with the rest of the crew, we traded baroque schemes about what we'd get up to before the parents came out again. The rest of the week was a vast continent for us to explore and conquer.

Then suddenly we ran out of land. Wednesdays we woke up agitated, realizing our idyll was half over. We got busy to cram it all in. Sometimes we messed up on Wednesdays, but it was never a Thursday-sized mess-up. No, Thursday we reserved for the thoroughly botched, mishaps that called for shame and first aid and apologies. All the ill shit went down on Thursdays, the disasters we made with our own hands, because on Friday the parents returned and our disasters were out of our control.

The first gun was Randy's. Which should have been a sign that we were headed toward a classic Thursday. I never went to Randy's—he didn't have a hanging-out house. But everybody else was working. Nick at Jonni Waffle or in the city buying stuff for his B-boy disguise, Clive barbacking at the Long Wharf Restaurant, Reggie and Bobby at Burger King. I felt like I hadn't seen Reggie in weeks. We had contrary schedules, me working in town, him off flipping Whoppers in South Hampton. When we overlapped in the house we were too exhausted from work or gearing up for the next shift to even bicker properly. I had no other option but to call NP, not my number-one choice, and his mother told me he was at Randy's. Normally I would have said forget it, but there was a chance they might be driving somewhere, an expedition to Karts-a-Go-Go or Hither Hills, and I'd have to hear them exaggerate how much fun they had.

Randy lived in Sag Harbor Hills on Hillside Drive, a dead-end street off our usual circuit. I knew it as the street where the Yellow House was, the one Mark James used to stay in. Mark was a nerdy kid I got along with, who came out for a few summers to visit his grandmother, who was of that first generation. When I turned the corner to Hillside, I saw that the Yellow House's yard was still overgrown and the blinds were drawn, as they had been for years now. I hadn't seen Mark in a long time but a few weeks ago, by coincidence, I'd asked my mother if she knew why he didn't come out anymore and she said, "Oh, it turned out that Mr. James had another family."

There was a lot of Other Family going around that summer. People disappeared. I asked, "What happened to the Peterses?" and my mother responded, "Oh, it turned out Mr. Peters had another family, so they don't come out anymore." And what happened to the Barrowses, hadn't seen those guys in a while, Little Timmy with his crutches. "Oh, it turned out Mr. Barrows had another family so they're selling the house."

For a while it verged on an epidemic. I found it fascinating, wondering at the mechanics. One family in New Jersey and one in Kansas—what kind of cover story hid those miles? These were lies to aspire to. And who was to say which was the Real Family and which was the Other Family? Was the Sag Harbor family of our acquaintance the shadowy, antimatter family or was it the other way around, that family living in that new Delaware subdivision, the one gobbling crumbs with a smile? I picture the kids scrambling to the front door at the sound of Daddy's car in the driveway after so long (the brief phone calls from the road only magnify absence) and Daddy taking a few moments after he turns off the ignition to orient himself, figure out who and where he is this time. Yes, I recognize those people standing in the doorway—that's my family.

How extensive was the transformation? The rules and decor and entire vibe changing from house to house. In that other zip code, Daddy was a pipe-puffing teddy bear in a sweater vest, a throwback to a sitcom idea of genial paternity, peeling off wisdom like "You know, son, sometimes a body's got to stand up for himself" and "We all get bruised sometimes, but then we dust ourselves off and say, Golly, tomorrow is another day." Mommy was always taking the bird out of the oven, she dolled herself up on Our Anniversary and they walked out arm in arm, they never missed a year. Everyone tucked in tight. The family ate together and communicated. And then Daddy lit out for this zip code, changed his face, and everything was reversed. One man, two houses. Two faces. Which house you lived in, kids, was the luck of the draw.

You might call this speculation dumb. Each house made the other a lie. None of it was real. I'm not so sure.

Randy and NP were in the street. They were bent over, looking at something on the ground. I yelled, "Yo!" They didn't respond. I walked up.

"Look at that," NP said.

"What happened to it?" I asked. The robin was lying on the asphalt, but it didn't have the familiar tread-mark tattoo of most roadkill. It was tiny and still.

"Randy shot it," NP said.

Randy grinned and held up the BB rifle to show it off. It looked real, but that was the point. If it looked real, you could pretend it was real, and if you had a real gun you could pretend to be someone else. The metal was sleek, inky black, the fake wood grain of the stock and forearm glossy in the sun. "I got it at Caldor," he said.

We looked down at the robin again.

"It flew over and landed on the power pole and I just took the shot," Randy said. "I've been practicing all day."

"Is it dead?" I asked.

"I don't see any blood," NP answered.

"Maybe it's just a concussion," I said.

"You should stuff it and mount it," NP said.

I thought, "That's uncool," a judgment I'd picked up from the stoner crowd at my school, who had decided I was "okay" toward the end of the spring semester and let me hang out in their vicinity or at least linger unmolested as a prelude to a provisional adoption by their clan next fall. (They had a Weed for Nerds charity and a strong commitment to diversity.) I liked uncool because it meant there was a code that everyone agreed on. The rules didn't change—everything in the universe was either cool or uncool, no confusion. "That's uncool," someone said, and "That is *so* uncool," another affirmed, the voice of justice itself, nasal and uncomplicated.

Randy let NP take the rifle and NP held it in his hands, testing its weight. It looked solid and formidable. He aimed at invisible knuckleheads loitering at the dead end of the street: "Stick 'em up!" He pumped the stock three times, clack clack clack, and pulled the trigger. And again.

"It's empty, dummy," Randy said.

We headed into his house to get some more "ammo." Randy lived at the end of the street in a long green ranch house with fading orange trim. I'd never been inside. He opened the screen door and yelled, "Mom, I'm inside with my friends!," and the sound of a TV disappeared as a door closed with a thud. I didn't know much about Randy's home life, but I knew his father wasn't in the picture.

There were fathers who worked in the city during the week and there were fathers who were a variety of gone. I knew Randy's father came out one weekend every other summer because I'd hear my parents talk about it. "Stanley's out this weekend with his young girlfriend/expensive car/speedboat," whatever prop he was riding that year. I assumed he didn't stay on Hillside.

The blinds were tilted open, sending planes of light to charge slow-dancing motes of hair and dead skin. NP and I sat on the plastic-covered furniture while Randy went into his room. I smelled dog, and remembered a recent conversation with Randy about his dog, Tiger, a cocker spaniel who had choked on a piece of rope and died two years ago. I noticed some white fur trapped underneath the plastic on the upholstery and experienced a doctor's-office wave of nervousness.

"Can we sit down here?" I asked.

"What do you think the plastic's for?" NP said.

Randy returned and led us out through the kitchen into the backyard. Brown leaves drifted in tiny dirty pools in the butts of chairs. Behind the house was woods, allowing him to convert the patio into a firing range. He'd dragged the barbecue grill to the edge of the trees—I saw a line of ashes in a trail—and around its three feet lay cans and cups riddled with tiny holes. Randy set up a Six Million Dollar Man action figure on the grill's lid. It took a few tries to get him to stand up straight. We'd outgrown tying army men to bottle rockets, failure itself despite our delusions of NASA-like competence, so this was a logical extension of action-figure abuse.

"Lemme get a shot," NP begged.

"I go first," Randy told him, with the imperious tone he'd mastered during his stint as the Kid with the Car.

Steve Austin, the Six Million Dollar Man, who had been rebuilt at great expense with taxpayers' money, stood on the red dome, his bionic hands in eternal search of necks to throttle. Randy took aim. Steve Austin stared impassively, his extensive time on the operating table having granted him a stoic's quiet grace. It took five shots, Randy pumping and clacking the stock with increasing fury as we observed his shitty marksmanship. Steve Austin tumbled off the lid and lay on his side, his pose undisturbed in the dirt. Didn't even blink. They really knew how to make an action figure back then.

"I want to get the optional scope for greater accuracy," Randy explained, "but that costs more money."

"Lemme try that shit now," NP said.

I left soon after. I threw out a "You guys want to head to East Hampton to buy records?" but no one bit. I thought we were past playing with guns. I walked around the side of the house and when I got back into the street the bird was gone.

That was the first gun. The next gun was Bobby's. This one was a pistol, a replica of a 9mm. We were in his room. Bobby had invited me to play Lode Runner on his Apple II+, but when we got up there, he dug under his mattress and pulled out the BB pistol.

I jerked my head toward the open door. "What about your grandpa?"

He pointed to his alarm clock. It was 7:35 PM. Which meant his grandfather had been asleep for five minutes. Bobby's parents returned on weekends, like ours, but in his case he was not completely unsupervised. His grandparents came out for the entire summer to make sure he got fed. But after 7:30, Bobby crawled over the wall.

His grandparents were friends of the first generation, but they'd never bought a house during the gold rush. They stayed with pals on weekends, and then Bobby's parents started renting a house in the '70s, up the street from our old house on Hempstead, which is how he became such an integral part of our crew. His family had built the house up in Ninevah two years ago, an imposing gray beach house overlooking the bay from on high. I remember playing Alien Prison Cell in the cement foundation when the construction workers were off slacking. Splintery and vertigo-inducing stairs led down the dune to the water. It was a big place—most of the first-wave houses were single-story—with a guest room downstairs and three bedrooms upstairs.

Bobby's grandparents stayed on the first floor, so we had a state-of-the-art slipper-on-stairs warning system in case his grandfather, against all odds, was still puttering around past 7:30. In the great local tradition, his grandmother stayed in her room at all hours, occasionally summoning Bobby in for conferences from which he'd emerge with a five- or ten-dollar bill for "treats." I don't think I saw her that whole summer. His grandfather was a real gentle guy, always kind to our mangy bunch when we came over. Gentle in that way that said he'd seen a lot of racist shit in his life and was glad that things had turned out better for his children and grandchildren. That cool old breed. His daughter had married another Brooklynite—not a Sag guy, although he grew up with Sag kids in the offseason and knew the myth—and now they had finally arrived. He had a right to be proud. And a right to get some damn sleep at the first hints of twilight.

"Me and NP went with Randy to Caldor and got one," Bobby said. "He got the silver one, but I wanted the black one. It's the joint, right?" Of course Randy was the facilitator. Seeing Randy fondle his rifle, given its potential, had the paradoxical effect of making him look like a monstrously overgrown baby. He might as well have been sucking his thumb. Bobby's real-lookin' gun allowed him to indulge his hard-rock fantasies and bury his deep prep-school weakness. Hide his grandfather's soft features in the scowl of a thug, the thug of his inverted Westchester fantasies. A kind of blackface.

"Greg Davis's cousin has a gun like this," Bobby said, squinting down the pistol's sight. "I saw it once at his house. You know what he's into, right?"

"No, what?"

"You know, some hard-core shit. He was in jail." He held it out. "Do you want to hold it?"

"No, that's all right."

"What are you, a pussy?"

I shrugged.

"Me and Reggie were shooting stuff over at the Creek today," Bobby said. "He has good aim. He should be a sniper in the Army Corps."

I'd seen Reggie before he went off to Burger King, asked him what he'd been up to. "Nothing."

"Let me see that," I said. It was heavier than it looked. Its insides dense with cause and effect. I curled my finger around the trigger. Okay. Got the gist. I pretended to study it for a few more moments and gave it back to Bobby.

"I'm going to bring this shit to school," Bobby said. He put his crazy face on. "Stick up some pink motherfuckers. Bla-blam!"

Which was bullshit. Hunting preppies—the Deadliest Game of All—would cut into his daily vigil outside the college counselor's office. Despite his recent theatrics. This BB-gun shit was making people act like dummies.

To wit: he pointed it at me. "Hands in the air!"

I shielded my eyes with my hand. "Get that shit outta my face!"

He laughed. "Hot oil! Hot oil!" he said, rolling his eyes manically.

"Shoot my eye out," I said. Reggie had started saying "Hot oil! Hot oil!" whenever I bossed him around or said something lame. After the twentieth time, I asked him why he kept saying that, and he said there was a semi-retarded guy who worked at Burger King through a special program, and he always got agitated when he walked by the fryers, squealing "Hot oil! Hot oil!" to remind himself.

"Don't worry. I got the safety on," Bobby said, pulling the trigger. The BB shot out, hit the wall, ricocheted into his computer monitor, bounced against the window, and disappeared under his bed. "Sorry, man! Sorry, sorry!" he yelped. Downstairs, one might conjecture, grandpa stirred in his sleep.

At least it was a plastic BB. Randy had copper BBs and Bobby had plastic BBs at that point. The plastic ones didn't hurt that much. The copper ones could do some real damage, though, as I saw the next week when I found myself out on "target practice." We were on our way to Bridgehampton to walk around. Me, Randy driving, Clive, and NP. Then Randy pulled into the parking lot of Mashashimuet Park.

"I thought we were going to Bridgehampton," I said.

"After we go shooting," Randy said. He slipped the car keys into his pocket.

We walked into the trails behind the park. NP carried a moldy cardboard box. When I asked him what was inside he said, "That would be telling." I followed behind Randy and NP, and ahead of Clive, according to a beloved survivor scenario from the old days. The trails, you see, were maintained by the wheels of pickups, motorbikes, and ATVs, which ground down foolhardy weeds, churned up the dirt, and snapped off the branches of the sad oaks and sticker bushes to the side. Where the trails opened into small clearings, we discovered proof of older kid/redneck presence—old beer cans and cigarette butts, sure, but also shotgun shells. The woods between towns were the domain of good old boys and their good-old-boy inclinations. Out of reach of the law, out of earshot, they could get down to the business of shootin' things. We never in all our summers came across another soul out there, but such a thing was just a matter of time, surely. Walk toward the rear of the pack but ahead of the last guy, and you had insulating bodies to protect you in case of ambush.

Or so my young self theorized. Today we were armed.

Randy had the spot all picked out. The abandoned Karmann Ghia. It made sense. We'd tried to make a plaything of it many a boredom-crazed afternoon, but it was too rusted to approach and properly incorporate into high jinks beyond throwing rocks through the dwindling windows. We were a dutiful and tetanus-phobic group, lockjaw being the most sinister villain we could imagine. "His face twisted into a grimace of horror." But not anymore. The guns gave us the distance to hasten the car's ruin.

Whenever you saw the red Karmann Ghia, that debased victim of the Rust Gods, some other kids had ripped off another piece in the interim. The hubcaps, the mirrors. One day the windshield wipers were stuck out like antennae, and no one touched them because the effect was cool, satisfying adolescent aesthetics of destruction. Another summer we ventured out and the upholstery hung out of the driver's window like a ghastly tongue. Kids all over like to mutilate it. Since this is a What Happened tale, I wonder how the car got there, who owned it. Abandoned by joyriders, left to die by a summering specimen who couldn't keep up the payments. Had I seen them just the day before, these faceless elders, sailing through the crosswalk in their new fab ride even though I had the right of way, had I served them ice cream at Jonni Waffle for no tip, did they throw a *Hush!* our way when we got too loud at Conca D'Oro? We didn't know each other but we had this hidden link. We were related by rust.

Randy's first attempts were unspectacular. But as his aim improved and he figured out the key pressure points, a BB disintegrated a nice section of the car's weakened frame instead of zipping straight through and leaving a tiny fingertip-sized hole you had to get up close to see. "You see how I pump it?" Randy asked rhetorically. "The more you pump it, the faster the FPS." Feet per second, I guessed, and later confirmed when I sat on some ketchup-stained rifle literature in the backseat of Randy's car. "Low FPS is good if you just want to scare a deer or another critter off your property. Higher FPS is when you really want to send a message." Yee-haw!

NP and Clive took turns with NP's pistol—Randy clung tight to his baby today—and while it was diverting for a while, I started to wonder if we had enough time to drive to Bridgehampton and back before my shift.

"We just got here, dag," NP said.

"I'm not ready to go," Randy said as he reloaded his rifle. His car, his keys.

Clive had taken a few shots. He was the only sensible one among us, but he seemed to be enjoying himself. "Why don't you go and try it?" he asked me. Co-opt the complainer.

I thought about Reggie and Bobby taking potshots at squirrels and dead horseshoe crabs. I took NP's gun. Identical to Bobby's, except in silver. Clive offered the carton of BBs to me. In their small blue box, the copperheads turned molten in the sun. NP said, "Let's break out the stuff," and opened the box he'd brought along. It was filled with items scavenged from his basement, a porcelain vase, a bunch of drinking glasses with groovy '60s designs, a Nerf football with tooth marks in it, a bottle of red nail polish, and other junk chosen for its breakable qualities.

"Here, do the radio," NP said. "Don't shoot!" He dug into the box and perched an old transistor radio on top of the Karmann Ghia. I took my time. I wiped the sweat off my forehead. I held my shooting arm with my left hand, gunslinger style. Drew a bead.

The radio made a sad "Ting!," tottered in cheap suspense, and fell in the dirt. I'd hit the radio toward the top, knocking it off-balance. The words "Center of Gravity" occurred to me, secondhand track-and-field lingo from my vain attempt to place out of P.E. that spring through the glory of high jump. I couldn't throw a ball worth shit with my girly arm but somehow I'd hit the radio. NP and Clive whooped it up, slapping me on the back. Clive offered a terse "Good shooting," like a drill instructor trying not to be too affirming. I grinned.

We positioned the other relics from NP's basement. The vase didn't explode, but each time it was hit, another jagged section fell off so we could see more of its insides. It finally collapsed on its own while we were reloading. I aimed at an old lampshade of rainbow-colored glass, and while I didn't re-create the swell marksmanship of my first attempt, I had to admit it was fun. Not the shooting itself, but the satisfaction of discovering a new way to kill a chunk of summer. It was like scraping out a little cave, making a new space in the hours to hide in for a time.

I placed the final victim on top of the car—the neon-green Nerf football. We'd saved it for last because nothing topped Nerf abuse. It was Randy's turn, but NP established dibs, as it was his Nerf ball. Which, looking back, was a rare case of one of us challenging Randy, since he had the car. It turned out NP couldn't hit it. Time after time. We'd been out there in the sun and were dehydrated. The rush, the novelty, was gone, and we all felt it.

Finally, NP gave up and handed his pistol to Clive. Randy said, "NP couldn't hit the broad side of a barn," that hoary marksman's slur.

NP exploded. He had put-downs to spare, but now he grasped after his trademark finesse. "I could hit your fat fuckin' ass fine, you fuckin' Rerun from *What's Happening*–looking motherfucker."

"What the fuck did you say?"

"You fuckin' biscuit-eatin' bitch!"

Randy's hours of picking off his old toys in the backyard finally found their true outlet. He stroked his rifle, clack clack, and started shooting the dirt at NP's feet. "Dance, nigger, dance!" he shouted, in Olde West saloon fashion, which was pretty fucked up, and the copperheads detonated in the ground in brief puffs. NP skipped from foot to foot, his bright white sneakers flashing like surrender flags. "Dance!" I don't think Randy was aiming at NP's feet, but I couldn't be sure. What if he missed? One of those BBs, depending on the FPS, would rip through the sneaker, definitely. "Dance!" How much deeper, I didn't know.

Clive and me shouted for Randy to knock it off. We were on either side of him, out of range, making it easier to confront him. Clive took a step toward Randy, hands out defensively. He was fast enough to rush him, but nevertheless. Randy glared at Clive, I swear he made a calculation, and then lowered the rifle with a "I was just playing."

NP charged Randy, cursing like a motherfucker. Clive restrained him. "That's uncool," I said, but no one chimed in with the other-shoe "That's *so* uncool." The boys boiled off in their neutral corners and we left soon after, scratching the Bridgehampton excursion without discussion.

I HADN'T SEEN THAT in a long time, that old fighting thing we used to do. We used to fight each other all the time out in Sag. We honed special knuckle punches, wherein the knuckle of the middle finger was cocked underneath by the thumb for lethal blows, according to our lore. Reenacted kung fu poses from Bruce Lee's too-brief oeuvre while wrinkling our faces into Muhammad Ali frowns and trying to remember the positions of key nerve clusters. There were places on the body known to aficionados, vulnerable to a single blow. And that meant me, too, for a time, despite previous descriptions of my temperament and personality. No, really. It's how we were raised.

I got my training early. One night in the fourth grade I was playing with my Star Wars action figures when I heard my father yell "Benjamin!" from the living room. I dropped Greedo immediately. I'd moved on from playing the Caucasian heroes of the Star Wars universe, preferring instead the alien and armored and masked. I'd been Luke Skywalker for a long time, the bright rays of the whole "great destiny" thing appealing to my overcast soul, and then Han Solo, his wisecracking ease in the face of hardship a kind of tutelage. A light saber for a blaster pistol. Then I decided that being them was tainted. I'd seen something on TV about it. One Sunday morning my parents were watching the black affairs show *Like It Is*, when Gil Noble welcomed a psychologist who railed against Barbies and the cult of the blonde. Gray waves swept through his Afro and he wore a green-and-yellow dashiki, a silver Black Power fist hanging on a chain around his neck. Swear to God. He described a study where a group of black children was told to "pick the pretty doll," and when they passed over the brown princesses, time after time, what was there to say? "Why are our children being taught to hate themselves?" Barbie, Luke. Brainwashed by the Evil Empire.

Black was beautiful, but black didn't exist in the pre–Lando Calrissian Star Wars universe beyond the malevolent black of Darth Vader. (And what about Lando's treachery in the Cloud City of Bespin once he did appear? Selling Han out, hitting on his lady. Some role model.) So in my games I became Greedo, the green, scalloped-eared, bug-eyed nemesis of Han Solo, or rather in my mythology, another alien from his home planet of Rodio—Greedo's cousin. Hence the family resemblance and predilection for ribbed bodysuits. He was a good kid, on the straight and narrow, unlike his relative. Or I was a Death Star Droid with human programming (not much of a stretch) or a defecting Stormtrooper, skin obscured behind the armor plates of the Empire. In my room, Greedo's cousin redeemed his people through his private war against the forces of evil. He was "a credit to his race."

"Get in here!" I jumped up.

Someone had ratted me out. Reggie only ratted me out if we were fighting because it was a risky proposition—you never knew when our father would introduce an obscure subclause in the family rules of conduct, something along the lines of "You should have known better than to let your brother do that," whereupon the rat was included in his brother's punishment. Take his belt off loop after loop and beat both of us. Don't cry or you'll get some more. Kept you on your toes. But we'd been getting along, Reggie and me, and in fact I had loaned him twenty-five cents that morning at my usual "it doubles every Monday" interest rate, for him to buy snacks. He fiended for Munchos, blowing through his allowance by midweek like a junkie.

I beat it out of our room and reviewed the last few days for any slipups. I couldn't think of anything. I had thrown two stalks of broccoli into the garbage, but I was sure that no one had seen me, and it had been almost a year since I got into trouble for not cleaning my plate. Maybe that rule was still being enforced, maybe it wasn't, you never knew. The rules came, the rules went, new rules were introduced. Then I remembered that I'd worn slightly wrinkled khaki slacks to school that morning. After being intercepted on our way out the door one day, we'd been admonished (that's not the word but that word will do) for wearing wrinkled clothing and from then on we had to lay out the next day's clothes before we went to bed, for inspection. It had to be the khakis. I'd taken a chance that my father wouldn't check them, and I'd lost.

He was on the couch. The TV was off, a bad sign. He said, "Your mother tells me you got into a fight at school today." I had a bunch of thoughts all at once. 1. My mother had ratted me out. 2. I didn't have to revenge myself against Reggie, and I'd have to save the two or three plans I'd devised on the short walk to the living room for another day. 3. It wasn't the khakis, so I could risk another wrinkled-clothes day in the future. 4. I had no idea what he was talking about. But this was a familiar situation. Familiar as in, family.

I looked at my mother. She didn't move. There was that way she used to sit in these situations, right, I remember now. I said, "I didn't get into a fight today."

He looked at my mother and then he looked at me. He said, "Your mother said some boy called you a nigger at school today."

Oh, he was talking about *that*. A week ago, during snack break, Tony Reece had done something weird to me. It was Tony Reece's first year at our school. His father was a bigwig at the French embassy. The headmaster and founder of our school was French and a number of French dignitaries sent their kids there, which meant that we watched a lot of François Truffaut movies and we celebrated Paris Day once a year, where we ate croissants and pain au chocolat while the French teachers shared some motherland tales, like childhood reminiscences about watching collaborators get their heads shaved. They snatched the hair from the ground as souvenirs. "You Americans were so shocked at Watergate," our music teacher Madame Mamelock told us one day. "We have never believed in the powerful. The powerful are liars." I was six.

Tony Reece only lasted a few years. He was a skinny little boy with dark eyes and a sinister up-curl to the left side of his mouth. On his first day, he ate his lunch on a white handkerchief that he unfolded delicately and placed on his desk. We all laughed at him and he never did it again, but he was constantly en garde from that moment on, fearful of these hot-dog-eatin' heathens and their New World cruelties.

The day my father was asking about, a bunch of us were goofing around during Snack. Andrea Rappaport had just come back from Saint Thomas and her face was pink, brown scales withering on her nose. We hadn't been on spring vacation—she'd gotten her schoolwork for the week in advance and done it in between trips to the pool. That's how her family rolled. There was a discussion about tanning while on vacation, the pros and cons, the various theories of how much was "too much tanning," from which I abstained, and then Tony Reece reached over to my face, dragged a finger down my cheek, and said, "Look—it doesn't come off."

He snickered, the right corner of his mouth curling up to complement the left, and I didn't get his meaning and then I realized, given the context of the conversation, that he was talking about my brownness. The other kids looked at one another, and what do fourth graders know about things, I don't know, but they knew wrongness when it happened right in front of them and Andy Stern who was my friend said, "Shut up, Tony *Reece*," and shoved his shoulder. "Where's your hankie, Frenchie?" Everybody laughed at Tony Reece. The bell rang for Social Studies, and we returned to our desks. I'd told my mother about it an hour or two before I was called to the living room, something to kill the time while she tossed pepper on the pork chops.

I said, "Oh, that was last week." To get the facts straight. This was a misunderstanding. "He didn't say that." I related my version of the incident.

My father looked at my mother and then he looked at me. " 'It doesn't come off,' " he said. "He was calling you a nigger. What did you think he was doing?"

"I don't know" slipped out of my mouth and I knew I had messed up because he hated "I don't know." There was no purchase there. Actually, I think maybe he liked "I don't know" because then he got to pry you open.

"Why didn't you punch him like I told you?"

"I don't know." I said it again, I couldn't help it.

"You were afraid he was going to hit you back."

I couldn't say no and disagree with him. So I decided to agree with him. "Yes." Surely if I stopped struggling, trying to wiggle out of this, I'd quickly be Greedo again.

"Like this?" His fast fast hand struck me across the face and iron rolled around in my head and my cheek pulsed with heat and felt like it had swollen up to twice its size. When I looked in the mirror later, it looked normal, if a bit red, but that's what it felt like. I heard Elena and Reggie close the doors to their rooms, but how could I hear that really, because they were too far away, but I just knew that's what they did because that's what we always did. In these situations.

"Can he hit you harder than this?" he asked, and he swatted me again, harder.

My eyeballs bobbed in their water. In the corner of my vision, my mother uncrossed her legs. I said, "I don't know."

He swatted me in the face again, harder. This time I was ready and I told myself, don't fall over. "Can he hit you harder than that?" he asked.

"No," I said.

"Then there's nothing to be afraid of." A pause. I was breathing a lot through my nose. "Don't you cry now," he said, so I didn't. "Who's going to protect you if you don't do it? Me? Your mother? The world's not going to protect you. That's what I'm trying to teach you."

The lesson was, Don't be afraid of being hit, but over the years I took it as, No one can hurt you more than I can. The same end result, really. The next morning I went up to Tony Reece and punched him in his face and sent him flying against his desk. No repercussions.

SUMMERS WE BRAWLED. We were hungry for slight, for provocations big and small, and when one didn't appear, we trumped up charges. Turf. The more whole you were, the more turf you had. You could tolerate the occasional trespass. But if you had so little turf that you felt like you barely had any air? You told someone they had crossed a line they didn't know existed. Then you punched them in the face.

The first equations of manhood. Generally you punched someone younger and smaller. Common sense. A more even match was sometimes unavoidable. The standard fight was brief and awkward. A quick blow to the face sent you into your favorite stance, one that cannot be found in any boxing primer in the land, or sent you searching after a cherished martial-arts movie pose, Praying Mantis, Turtle Position. The traditional epithets were offered, strange personal oaths muttered, and things quickly degenerated into a slap fight, and then the inevitable pinning to the ground by this day's favored son. The other guy flopped in headlocked futility, dirt mashed into Afro and scalp that would take extra fingernail scrapes in the shower to remove, and we stepped in to break it up.

You never fought unless there was an audience. On the sidelines we picked our boy and heckled. "Oh, shit!" "He fuckin' whopped that nigger!" "Rope-a-dope!" Last week's throw down with one of the fighters came back in a flash—sunlight reeling as your head was knocked back, the arena lights through the leaves—forcing you to root for his opponent. Beefs and disagreements from years past perverted the conventional betting wisdom. We laid our bets based not on speed, weight class, or fighting record, but grudge. In August 1978, Nick broke the fin off Clive's Air Rocket and refused to pay for the damages. Hence Clive's insistence that Bobby "Beat that nigger!" during the Bobby-Nick Pugilists in Polo series of bouts in the summer of 1980. Marcus ate my last Twizzler during a matinee of *Herbie Goes to Monte Carlo*, on purpose even though he denied it, and this was the backstory when I served, metaphorically, as Clive's cut man during the Showdown of '81. But short-term memory entered in as well. Spend a satisfying round of hanging out the previous afternoon with someone, and you were in their corner if something popped off, broken toys and stolen Twizzlers be damned.

The winner was generally whoever wanted it more, and generally that was someone who'd had a bad weekend or knew they had a bad weekend coming up, the Dreaded Impending. Damage reports came in: a ripped-open elbow already scabbing, a torn shirt that would lead to questioning from parental authorities. They dusted themselves off, saying, That was nothing. Losers cast aspersions on their opponent's technique ("He has long nails like a girl"), and winners overexplained their mercy ("I coulda wailed on him if I wanted, but it wasn't worth it"). The mob dispersed, dissecting the fight in smaller groups until some new escapade bulldozed it all. Next time, next time was plotted out that night in bed when the fighters were alone at last, without an audience, under the chilly night breezes of regret.

As we got older we stepped in to break 'em up instead of hooting ringside. Break up someone else's fight and they might return the favor later. Then on universal order we stopped fighting altogether. We were relieved. For one thing, we got bigger, and could do some damage. Sam and TT, two older kids who were brothers, fought one day and Sam whipped TT's face with a piece of electrical cable and the skin on his temple was raw the rest of the summer like a warning. We honed our verbal dexterity instead, learned to signify, studied the uppercut of the quick remark. Discovered that we all had glass jaws and went down like a sack of potatoes at the right combo of words. Also—puberty. That infamous culprit. Hormones rechanneled stray energy toward the groin, and how to use that body part as opposed to the fists. (One day, God willing. All-Powerful Being, Most Merciful, Who in His Kindness might throw a brother a bone every once in a while.) In fact, in the telling it becomes clear that puberty rearranged my brain so thoroughly that this period belongs to another kid's history. What happened to him, Ma? Turned out he was this other boy. He doesn't come out anymore.

I must've liked it, up and hitting someone for no good reason, something stupid. For those few years. Ten, eleven years old. It gave it a place to go. It was somewhere to put it. Our father gave Reggie his own instruction, individually tailored, and on those nights it was my turn to close the door to the room, but when Reggie instigated with someone bigger, I stepped in and fought for him, that was my job, and I got knocked down or I didn't. Sometimes he instigated because he knew I was there to step in, but that was okay. We were in it together back then. Friends became enemies for a day or two and then the boredom was such that you forgot. You needed someone to play with. Or else you were alone.

TARGET PRACTICE BEHIND THE PARK was on a Wednesday. I can't remember what happened the next day. Something bad probably happened to someone. On Monday we were back at the threshold of another empty week we needed to fill. We convened at our place that night. I bossed Reggie around to help get the place in shape. He glowered at me, standard operating procedure that summer. I told him to straighten up our parents' room, since it was his turn to sleep in there while they were away. There was a phone next to the bed, allowing our friends to close the door and prevent us from hearing their bitch-ass responses if they called home and got chewed out for something or other. "Okay . . . okay . . . okay." They emerged with excuses about why they had to suddenly break out. We didn't gloat. Gloat, and karma said next time it was your turn.

I was washing the dishes when he came out and said, "Benji— what do you think this is?" I glanced at it and wiped my hands off so as not to leave any evidence that I'd touched it. It was our mother's handwriting, on one of our father's old pads, the ones we used for scratch after he got his new stationery. It was bullet-pointed in her work fashion:

- yells at me in front of my friends
- mean/verbally abusive
- drinks every day
- blows up and then forgets about it the next morning

I told him to put it back where he found it. We didn't mention it again, according to custom, and when it was my turn in there next week, I looked for it but I didn't see it.

It was getting dark when they came over. Randy, Nick, Bobby, and Clive. Randy brought beer, a new but permanent feature that summer. The drinking age was nineteen, which made Randy legal and Clive and Nick tall enough to buy take-out six-packs at the Corner Bar unchallenged. One beer and I was buzzed; two beers, I was drunk. We asked one another "Which one are you on?" to see who was ahead and who was falling behind. Pointing at the empties for proof.

"Why don't you open the screen door to let the air in here?" Randy said.

"It's a screen door. The air comes through," Reggie said. "Plus the mosquitoes will get us."

"Then leave the lights out. They won't come in," Randy said. "I'm hot."

Reggie opened the screen door and we hunkered in the gloom. We got down to business. We had three days. Clive suggested night bluefishing off Montauk. Nick grumbled about the price, for his own reasons, but the rest of us agreed that it was too expensive to go more than once a season, given the realities of minimum wage, and we'd already been once. Reggie, who this summer decided that he was no longer afraid of the water, disavowing a key tenet of the men in our family, said that we should borrow Nick's uncle's motorboat again. But Nick said his uncle was having the hull refinished, plus he thought maybe his father and his uncle were having an argument, from the frequency with which his father was talking shit about him. Like, hourly. Brothers—what are you going to do? Bobby busted out that old chestnut, Ask Mrs. Carter if We Can Go in Her Pool, but Clive and Bobby immediately said no dice. Mrs. Carter's son had died five years ago. He'd grown up in Sag in a crew with Clive's father and Nick's father, and the last time they used her pool, she kept calling them by their fathers' names and it creeped them out. She saw the brown bodies underwater and thought she knew them. Then these faces surfaced to scream "Marco!" and "Polo!," other boys suddenly up from the deep, and her brain misfired. Creepy, right?

Stumped, and it wasn't even August yet.

"Let's show dicks," Randy suggested.

Cricket, cricket.

"Why the hell would we do that?" Clive asked, finally.

"To see who has the biggest dick," Randy said.

"Next time we go to Karts-a-Go-Go, we should race for money and time ourselves to see who's the fastest," I said, steering the proceedings like a good host. I wasn't much of a go-cart driver, but I thought the novelty of the scheme might appeal.

Bobby turned on his MC voice, "One Two Three, in the place to be," and Reggie said, "Alright!" They started their routine and I rolled my eyes in the darkness. Bobby and my brother had memorized the lyrics to Run-D.M.C.'s "Here We Go" and had to perform it at least ten times a day. Bobby was Run; Reggie was D.M.C. Bobby took the lead, Reggie side-kicking after each line like an exclamation point. Back and forth. Clive kept the beat with his hands. They'd been practicing, because they had it down pat, a real fucking duo.

BOBBY: It's like that y'all
  REGGIE: That y'all!
BOBBY: It's like that y'all
  REGGIE: That y'all!
BOBBY: It's like that-a-tha-that, a-like that y'all
  REGGIE: That y'all!
BOBBY: Cool chief rocker, I don't drink vodka,
  But keep a bag of cheeba inside my locker
  REGGIE: HUH!
BOBBY: Go to school every day
  REGGIE: HUH!
BOBBY: Always time to get paid
  REGGIE: HA HUH!
BOBBY: Cause I'm rockin' on the mic until the break of day!

Run-D.M.C. boasting about staying in school—quaint days in the history of hip-hop. "We played Go Fish before the Scrabble marathon—Ha Huh!" To my chagrin, I had never heard the song before they started singing it. Too much Buzzcocks. I thought I knew all of Run-D.M.C.'s records, the self-titled debut and *King of Rock*, but I was a square. The song was a limited-edition live recording made at a club called the Funhouse, taped "Funky fresh for 1983," according to the lyrics. Any mention of a Real Club bedeviled me with scenes of silver leisure suits and telephone book–sized high heels, imagery drawn from the old eleven o'clock news segments tsk-tsking about "Decadence at Studio 54" that I used to endure before *Saturday Night Live* came on. Years later the sound of the crowd on the recording was a reminder that people were out chilling and I was still home in my pajamas waiting for a good video to come on *Night Flight*.

Bobby introduced the song to Reggie, who dubbed a copy of "Here We Go" on Nick's boom box. Distracted by their rhyme skills, no one followed up on my Karts-a-Go-Go plan, with its money-competition-fame glamour. In my jealousy, I saw Bobby and Reggie performing their bit behind the counter at Burger King, their clubhouse where I was not allowed, in their paper Burger King caps and hairnets, while the retarded guy chimed in with "Hot oil! Hot oil!" like an amen.

We continued to brainstorm. No progress. Then someone said, "We should have a BB gunfight," and it stuck. The only thing to silence the new hunger. That was that. Our house was full of mosquitoes for a week, and me and Reggie had to sleep with our heads under the sheets to keep them out of our ears.

And then I had one. The next day Randy drove me and Clive to Caldor's. After consulting our savings, kept in battered envelopes in top-notch hiding places around the house to prevent each other from skimming some off the top, Reggie and me decided it would be best if we shared a BB pistol, with one of us borrowing Randy's spare for the fight itself. Sharing—the half that is always less than half. This arrangement also allowed me to keep track of Reggie's gun activity. He was going to hurt himself. Bobby'd cook up some dumb idea and Reggie would go along with it and he'd get hurt. I had to look out for him—in fact, the night of the Mosquito Summit, I decided to try and get the BB gunfight scheduled for during one of his shifts at Burger King. We all missed key shenanigans because of work. There was no reason this couldn't be one of Reggie's times to listen to glorious tales and rue his absence until the end of time. The BB gunfight was stupid, but this stupidity I reserved for myself.

Clive rattled a fist on the screen door. As soon as the last micrometer of my body passed the doorframe, he shouted "Shotgun!," dibsing the front seat. Clive was a man of priorities, and a peerless shotgun-caller. Those days, shotgun—calling it, planning for it, successfully disputing outcomes—was another popular brand of sublimated warfare, the brawling urge directed toward protecting front-seat passenger turf. Literally protecting your ass. He rushed ahead of me despite his indisputable victory, jumping into the car and slamming the door shut.

We took the back roads, arguing like real live grown-ups over the One True Route, murmuring the incantations. Right at Texaco, left at Scuttlehole, turn at the Farm. There was a secret combination that unlocked the East End and we all thought we had it in our pocket. The power of pure lore. You truly live in a place when you don't bother with chump stuff like street names, because the names of the streets are irrelevant. The Big Red Barn, the Burned-Out House, the second left, these were inarguable coordinates and all the map you needed.

The old Caldor complex is a big mall now. These days every brand name that ever befouled your mailbox with catalogues has a storefront, but back then there were only three entities of note: Caldor, King Kullen, and the Drive-In. Former playgrounds in less particular times. The Drive-In was closed, and had a postapocalyptic vibe. It was easy to picture the survivors of the Big One congregating in the lot, hair falling off, teeth bobbing in their gums, and flesh ablaze with God-awful rashes as they looked up at the dirty screen for messages from their fallen world. The weeds and grasses broke through the asphalt as if they were the last of their kind, they drooped in the air, fleshy kin to the gray speaker boxes flowing on their iron stalks. In our jammies, under the threadbare summer-home blankets, we'd lived for double features, the scratched-up Disney prints from the '60s and early '70s, then the scary second feature we tried to keep our eyes open for. We'd wake up for a glimpse of low-budget horror, stirring on cue from some lot-wide tremor to see the Good Parts we'd relive among ourselves the next day. Look, it's a young Dirk Benedict from *The A-Team* turning into a human snake, scale by scale.

The Drive-In was closed. Had been for a while.

Dapper dancing hot dogs beckoned us to the concession stand between features and we got lost in the vehicles, desperate for silhouettes of our acquaintance. In the daytime we also got lost and separated in search of food, among the gigantic aisles of King

Kullen. A supermarket, although super is too weak a modifier for the formidable bounty of Kullen's realm. The meat aisle alone was a griller's paradise, a chunk of bloody plenty. We'd rumbled through the aisles, our feet tucked into the rails of the shopping cart. We were there to police our mother, who sometimes neglected to see the wisdom in a family-sized pack of Yodels. But that summer we were past our enthusiasm for that exercise. Downright unmanly, calling shotgun for a grocery trip.

And then there was Caldor, the East End's one-stop emporium for action figures and beach towels, insect-repelling candles and beach chairs, lighter fluid and flip-flops. The maintenance supplies that kept the vacation humming and going, as any lapse in movement forced contemplation of that off-season life waiting on the other side of Labor Day, when nothing in the shelves of Caldor could stop the inevitable written on the snappy breezes and quick sunsets. There was one aisle we never had cause to enter, the Man Aisle, full of accoutrements and props, gas tanks, barbecue paraphernalia of obscure purpose, chrome shapes worked over in the coarse lathe of male id, heavy and gleaming on hooks. And BB guns. That day we passed the toy section without thought, en route to our new toy aisle.

There was no attendant at the counter, and despite my imaginings no red-aproned drone rushed to shoo us away. Randy showed off his knowledge with the arrangements behind the glass. Those are the speed loaders, those are the scopes. And there, my boys, there are the guns themselves. You had to be eighteen or older to buy one, so we handed our ragged, balled-up dollar bills over to Randy and summoned a teenage lackey. She pulled out her key chain to unlock the case.

"Do you want the black or the silver?"

Black, baby. (Internal voice "baby," not external people-voice "baby.")

Reggie and I didn't have toy guns growing up, so we had to catch up. Even when the house was empty, I got nervous walking around with it. Green or orange water pistols had been okay, but anything else sent our father speechifying. "That's some white-man shit," he'd say, confiscating the cap gun from a birthday party goody bag. "Whitey loves his guns. Shoot somebody, he loves that shit. So let him. No kid of mine is going to get that mind-set." I practiced solo, deep in the recesses of the Creek, out of sight of beachgoers and homeowners. Why startle the happy vacationers with the sight of a skinny, slouching teenager, the sun glinting off his braces and hand-gun? All they wanted was to get out of the city for a few days and put their feet up. I rounded up some mussel shells from the dark sand at the edge of the Creek and stuck them in a thin black row. My great aim the first day was just dumb luck, a little taste to get me hooked. I nicked the shells, tinking off bits. The day of the fight, I'd have the bigger targets of my friends.

We armed one by one. Reggie told me he was "going off to prac-tice with Bobby," and disappeared for one of their secret confabs, probably a razzle-dazzle rapping/shooting extravaganza of great theater. It's like that y'all. Anticipating the hip-hop stars a few years off. Not that the rest of us were immune. NP tucked his piece into his belt like a swaggering cop on the take or the cracker sheriff of a Jim Crow Podunk, Clive was observed busting a Dirty Harry move when he thought we weren't looking, and Randy was often found cradling his rifle to his chest, a gruesome sneer on his face as if he were about to take an East Hampton bistro hostage. I myself favored a two-handed promising-rookie pose, favored by *Starsky and Hutch* extras who got clipped before the first commercial and were avenged for the rest of the hour. "He woulda made a good cop, just like his old man."

When we all got together in the days leading up to the event, it was only a matter of time before we started posing for album covers. (The photographer always gets a kick out of taking pictures of these rap guys, they preen and strut more than supermodels.) We stood in a line, in character. The movie and TV comparison is the natural analogy, because back then we were informed by cop movies and cop shows, but given the future of rap music, the album cover is the bet-ter fit. Not one from innocent '85, but a few years in the future, when the music changed. We were a posse: the Azurest Boys.

We'd learned to change the character of our fighting and would continue to do so for the rest of our lives, readjusting for different provocations, different stakes. The music grew up, too, testicles dropping, voice changing, going from this:

Rhymes so def, rhymes rhymes galore
Rhymes that you've never even heard before
Now if you say you heard my rhyme, we gonna have to fight
'Cause I just made the motherfuckers up last night

To this, in so short a time:

"Hey yo, Cube, there go that motherfucker right there."
"No shit. Watch this... Hey, what's up, man?"
"Not too much."
"You know you won, G."
"Won what?"
"The Wet T-Shirt Contest, motherfucker!"
[sounds of gunfire]

Lyrics from the aforementioned "Here We Go" and then "Now I Gotta Wet'cha," copyright 1992 by Ice Cube, born the same year as me, who grew up on Run-D.M.C. like we all did. "Wet'cha," as in "wet your shirt with blood." All of us, the singers and the audience, were of the same generation. Something happened. Something happened that changed the terms and we went from fighting (I'll knock that grin off your face) to annihilation (I will wipe you from this Earth). How we got from here to there are the key passages in the history of young black men that no one cares to write. We live it instead.

You were hard or else you were soft, in the slang drawn from the territory of manhood, the state of your erected self. Word on the Street was that we were soft, with our private-school uniforms, in our cozy beach communities, so we learned to walk like hard rocks, like B-boys, the unimpeachably down. Even if we knew better. We heard the voices of the constant damning chorus that told us we lived false, and we decided to be otherwise. We talked one way in school, one way in our homes, and another way to each other. We got guns. We got guns for a few days one summer and then got rid of them. Later some of us got real guns.

ON WEDNESDAY WE WENT OVER THE RULES at Clive's house. Me, Marcus, Randy, and Clive. Clive's parents worked for the Board of Ed and only came out on weekends, and he had a nice deck on which to discuss matters of importance. The deck furniture was brand-new, fuming up a cloud of plastic musk. We weren't allowed to sit on it. The week before, according to Nick, he'd come over for a visit, and joined Clive at the table. Clive's mother summoned Clive into the house, and when he came out, he went around to the back of the house and fetched an old mildewy chair for Nick to sit on. The forbidden aspect made the meeting seem more official.

No face/No shooting at the eyes, that was a no-brainer. No cheating—if you're hit, you're hit, don't be a bitch about it. Sag Harbor Hills was the boundary of the battlefield, no cutting through to other developments and sneaking back to emerge ambush-style. I said we should all wear goggles just in case, and to my surprise they seemed to agree. There was talk of synchronizing watches, but no one wore a watch in the summer except me, because summer is its own time and I was the only one who didn't know this. When the scheduling question came up, I said, "Tomorrow night?," during Reggie's shift, and everyone at the table was free then so there were no objections. The weekend was out—too many people around—and no one wanted to put it off 'til next week. Reggie was benched and I was glad.

Not that it could have gone down any other way. Although we hatched the plan for the BB-gun war on a Monday, there was no doubt that in the end it would go down on a Thursday.

There was one matter left to discuss. Clive brought out some lemonade. Classy. I took notes. Me and Reggie's house was a hangout pad for the guys during the week, but Clive made better use of his Kid with an Empty House situation, bringing home girls from Bayside and even having girls from his high school out for a few days. He bused them in from the city, and didn't even pay for the Jitney. The boy had style, our Hefner in Kangol.

Sipping his lemonade, Clive raised the issue of Randy's rifle and the FPS. A metal BB out of one of the pistols, at the range we were going to be shooting at one another, hurt a little bit but not that much, according to hearsay. Pump the rifle enough times, however, and a copperhead BB was going to break the skin.

"But if I can't pump, I'll be at a disadvantage," Randy moaned.

"We have to figure out how many rifle pumps is equal to the standard pistol shot," I offered.

"How do we figure that out?" Clive asked.

"We can test it out on Marcus," Randy said.

Marcus said, "Okay," and we headed out into the yard. Midweek, midafternoon, we didn't have to worry about passersby. Marcus took off his shirt.

Randy loaded his rifle. "Let's start at one," he said.

I said, "Marcus, why don't you turn around so it doesn't go in your face or something."

Marcus turned around and gritted his teeth. There was a routine he used to do when one of us got mad at him, where he pulled up his shirt and clowned, "Please, Massa, Massa, Massa, please," anticipating the whip, *Roots*-like. He had the same expression on his face. Randy stood four yards away, aimed, and fired. The BB hit Marcus in the spine and bounced off.

"Shit, that didn't hurt," Marcus said. "Do I have a mark?"

We told him no. Randy said, "Then let's try three times," and stepped closer.

"Ow," Marcus cried. But it still didn't break the skin.

Clack clack clack clack clack. I noticed that Randy kept creeping closer between shots, but I didn't say anything. Neither did Clive.

Five times and Marcus screamed and a crescent of blood smiled on his skin. "So don't pump it more than four times," Clive said.

"Yo, that hurt," Marcus said.

"Let's make it no more than two, just to be safe," I said.

I couldn't sleep that night. The mosquitoes didn't help. Then it was Thursday and its tally through the years. When NP broke his ankle sneaking into his bedroom window after hanging out late at the Rec Room with those townie girls. When I didn't properly hose off the lounge chairs on the deck was a Thursday, and the next day I got confined to inside the property line for a week and obediently stuck around like a fool even when they were out of town and would never know. Fight after fight, too many to count. When the chain fell off Marcus's bike and he smeared his bare feet all the way across the gravel of the Hill trying to stop—that was Thursday all over. Our weekly full moon.

I woke up wrong. I heard noises in the living room. It should have been quiet. "Why aren't you at work?" I asked my brother.

"I switched my shift so I can be in the war," he said. I later learned Nick had done the same thing, making it four on four.

I told him he couldn't go. He'd get hurt. "When they're away, I'm in charge," I reminded him.

"You're not in charge of me."

Odd. It always worked when our sister used that line, like every five minutes. "Yes, I am."

"What are you going to do—tell on me?" he said, and he had me there. I couldn't rat him out or else I'd get it, too, just like the good old days except now I was actually guilty. He went off to get in some last-minute practice.

At fight time, I headed up Walker. I passed the STOP sign at Meredith and noticed it was freckled with silver, the red paint chipped away—target practice for one of our friends, probably Marcus, who lived two houses down. Nice cluster on the T and O. He had good aim, depending on how far away he was standing.

I stood in front of the Edwardses'. They'd been some of the earliest victims of the Other Family bug. Yvonne Edwards was my sister's age, and had a rep for throwing heavy objects when she got angry, usually at her little brother. Ralph, who happened to be my final opponent in the days of summer smackdowns. Ralph was an in-betweener like Randy, too young for us to accept into our plans, and too old for the younger crop of kids. He was harmless, and occasionally we'd let him hang around us, but that had been years ago. I don't know what he did with his days, but with a crazy sister like Yvonne, he probably spent a lot of time ducking.

Like all of our fights, it started over something little. A pebble, actually. He was two years younger than me, and I was a head taller. Which probably enabled me to croon, "You're lost little girlllll," from the Doors record our sister played over and over, when I saw him sitting on the curb that day. Forlorn, with his ashy elbows on his ashy knees and messed up 'Fro. The words just popped out. That's what occurred to me to say as I biked past him.

He gave me the evil eye and threw a pebble at me. It skipped on the ground and jangled about my spokes. No biggie but then I saw Marcus coming down the street, slapping a basketball, so there was a witness. I jumped off the bike and—pausing to knock the kickstand down—said, "What the fuck are you doing?" Like I said, he was smaller than me. I'd wrap this up pretty quickly.

The fight was long and drawn out and went on for miles, if you untangled our paces and laid them out lengthwise. I'd never seen such fury before. In a little person, anyway. I punched him in the face and he took it and retreated, walking backward, and I advanced on him for a while up the road. Then he reached some internal border and started advancing on me, hitting me in the face, and I retreated for a while, walking backward until I was up against my own personal wall and advanced on him again. That's why pro fights have a ring—otherwise people would just walk all over the goddamned place, up the aisle through the seats, out the lobby, and into the avenues. We prowled after each other up and down Walker, back and forth, the moronic pendulum, as my friends came out one by one, sniffing this on the wind from all points and following alongside like a news crew, providing blow-by-blow for the folks at home. His evil eyes on me the whole time. I'd get him in a headlock but he wouldn't go down to the ground like he was supposed to. He was tough! I tried to do an Indiana Jones move, from when he's grappling with the Nazi bruiser on the airplane and slams the guy's head into the wing a bunch of times. I thought this was a spectacular gimmick and tried to re-create it with Ralph's head instead of the Nazi head, and the Andersons' red Volvo instead of the airplane wing. But I couldn't get his head to the metal. His neck was superstrong, probably from dodging his sister's bricks.

Eventually we got tired and put down our fists. He didn't beat me and I didn't beat him, but since I was the older one, the judges called it his way. If anybody asked, I would have said, Look, the other guy wanted it more. He was descended from a construction material—throwing peoples and was in serious training between that and the whole Other Family thing, which he probably wasn't aware of consciously but you know he had to bend before such fierce invisible gravity. Especially if his family was the Other Family in question, with the cheaper presents and fainter hugs. But no one asked. Reggie wasn't there, and he didn't mention it but I know he heard, so in the end I did lose, in the eyes of my inner ref. I cut through the Edwardses' driveway. The summer of that last fight was the last summer they came out.

WHEN I GOT TO CLIVE'S HOUSE, we were all there except for Nick. He'd called, whispering about how his mom was home and he couldn't get out of the house with his BB gun. Marcus suggested we start without him.

"But then we'd have uneven teams," Bobby said.

"One of us can sit out," I said. "Youngest first?"

"Four is better than three," Clive announced, and we caved.

It was going to be dark soon, so we got busy making teams. Everybody wanted to be on Clive's team because Clive's team always won, but Randy was a factor with his rifle expertise. Plus, if you appeared to value his Randy-ness in all its wondrous forms—driver, hunter . . . well that's all I can think of right now—he might rule in your favor during an upcoming shotgun dispute. He threw off years of sturdy mathematics.

Reggie said, "Me and Bobby are a mini-team because we've been practicing together," and I was appalled. We'd never not been a mini-team, what with the whole "Benji 'n' Reggie, Benji 'n' Reggie" singsong thing through the years. The only thought that had calmed me that afternoon was that I could protect him better if he was on my team. Send him on a crazy mission out of the way until it was all over. He didn't look at me.

This historic severing of the Benji-'n'-Reggie alliance went unremarked upon. But who was I kidding? Nobody thought of us as the old unit anymore except for me. Some brothers threw bricks, others simply walked away from each other. The final teams were me, Clive, Marcus, and Nick on the Vice (for *Miami Vice*) and Randy, Bobby, Reggie, and NP on the Cool Chief Rockers. When Nick finally got his ass over there, I pulled out the paint goggles I'd rescued from the cobwebs under the deck and NP said, "Goggles?" I'd brought them for Reggie.

"No one said anything about goggles."

"I don't got goggles."

"I'm not wearing any pussy-ass goggles," Marcus said. And neither was Reggie, I didn't even bother to fight with him about it. I didn't wear them, either.

The sky was getting dark. We went over the rules again and counted to two hundred per the guidelines. Then it was on.

We ran away, scattering according to haywire teenage logic toward the highway, toward the beach. I jogged around the corner, checking to see if I was in anyone's sights, and jumped into the undeveloped lot next to the Nichols House. I waded in deep enough that I couldn't be seen from the road, but shallow enough that I could see anyone coming down Clive's street or the street Mrs. Jenkins's house was on. Fifty-two, fifty-three. Getting there. It was almost too dark to play at this point, but the poor visibility would help me. I was going to wait for one of the Cool Chief Rockers to recon my way and then ambush them, a favorite tactic of mine to this day. Wait for the right moment in an argument with a loved one, then ambush them with some hurt I've held on to for years, the list of indictments nurtured in the darkness of my hideout, and say, "Gotcha!" See how you ruined me. If I was lucky, Bobby and Reggie would stop right in front of where I was hiding, to regroup or break into song, and I'd take them both out.

A firefly blinked into existence, drew half a word in the air. Then gone. A black bug secret in the night. Such a strange little guy. It materialized, visible to human eyes for brief moments, and then it disappeared. But it got its name from its fake time, people time, when in fact most of its business went on when people couldn't see it. Its true life was invisible to us but we called it firefly after its fractions. Knowable and fixed for a few seconds, sharing a short segment of its message before it continued on its real mission, unknowable in its true self and course, outside of reach. It was a bad name because it was incomplete—both parts were true, the bright and the dark, the one we could see and the other one we couldn't. It was both.

I moved closer to the street so I could get a better view and someone hit me in the face with a rock.

Hot oil! Hot oil!

A rock. That's what it felt like. My head snapped back and the top half of my face throbbed like I'd been slapped. I cursed and stumbled out into the street. Who throws rocks at a BB gunfight? I yelled for a time-out.

Randy popped out of the woods on the other side of the street. "I hit you," he said, in surprise and pride.

"Why are you throwing rocks?"

"No, it was a BB."

I poked gingerly around my left eye. He'd hit me in the socket, in the hollow between the tear duct and the eyebrow. There may be a proper anatomical name for that part of the eye socket, but I don't know it. It felt like a rock. I couldn't see out of it. There was stuff in it. Randy reached forward and I batted his hand away. I heard NP say, "What's up?" I traced my fingertip along the lumpy hole in my face, the stinging flesh. It broke the skin. He'd pumped it more than two times.

"What happened?" Clive asked.

"Benji's out. I hit him," Randy declared.

"I'm not out," I said. "He pumped it more than twice! I'm bleeding! He's disqualified!"

Randy took my face in his hands and lifted my chin for a better look. He did this queasy thing. He bent his face down and stuck his tongue in the wound.

I pushed him away. "What the hell are you doing?"

"I was checking the taste to see if it was blood or sweat," he said. "It's sweat. You have sweat all running down your forehead."

I told him to keep the fuck off me, freakazoid. I touched the hole in my face and staggered into the cone of the streetlight. Fat june bugs crawled over one another on the ground in their wretched streetlight ritual. I held up my finger. It was blood.

Bobby and Reggie appeared, and then all the Cool Chief Rockers and Vicers, guns dangling. Reggie grabbed my arm and wanted to know if I was all right. I hadn't heard his voice like that in a long time. I shook my head drunkenly. "What the hell did you do, Randy?" Reggie said.

"He pumped it more than twice," I said. Everybody murmured dag, in their disparate dag registers. When they got a look at the wound, they re-dagged at how close it came to my eye.

Randy denied it, but to break the skin from across the street, he had to pump it a lot more than twice. We all knew it.

I realized the Horrible Thing. I said, "It's still in there." I probed around the wound. The skin was tough and swole up, but beneath that was something harder, like a pearl. I shared the Horrible Thing.

Randy didn't believe it. "Let me see," he said, his hands out.

"Get away from him," Reggie shouted. He stepped between us. "Benji," he started, squinting at the bloody hole in the poor light, "you have to go to the hospital."

"We can't do that," Marcus said. "We'll get in trouble."

"We'll all be in some serious trouble when our parents come out tomorrow."

I looked around. They had decided. Even Clive, who in his alpha dogness could have grabbed Randy's keys and taken me if he wanted, fuck everybody. He was looking down the street, as if he heard his parents pulling up, avoiding my gaze. Half gaze.

Randy said, "How are you going to get there?"

"That's uncool," Reggie said. He was my brother. I loved him. The way he said it, I knew. He'd found stoners. Maybe he was going to be all right after all.

"That's so uncool," I said. Justice according to brothers and stoners: if someone needs to go to the hospital and you got the car, you have to take them.

Reggie said, "Bobby, your grandpa can drive us!"

Bobby got weaselly. "He's asleep—look, it's dark."

"I don't have to go to the hospital. I'm okay," I said. Reggie protested, but everyone else was so thoroughly relieved that it was someone else's Thursday that the point was moot. I'd take one for the team. I didn't care that that's what they wanted of me. I'd take the hit because that's what I did. The other guys turned on Randy for putting them in this position, bitching about the pumping and whether aiming for my face was an accident or not. He didn't give an inch—"It just happened"—but did offer me "automatic shotgun for two weeks" as compensation. But the next week Bobby got his car, and the girls finally appeared, and Randy's reign was over.

My plan was to go home and try and squeeze the BB out, pimple-style. Me and my brother walked away, one palm over my eye and my other hand on his shoulder.

"We can still play three-on-three," NP suggested.

We tried to cut through the Edwardses' house on the way back, but the lights were on. Someone was home. We took the long way around.

In the bathroom mirror, my eye looked disgusting. Like I'd gone a few rounds with a real heavyweight. The socket was all swollen up, and blood trickled over my nose and older, dried trickles of blood. I washed my face off and got a better look. I could feel the BB in there. I couldn't move it. It was lodged in the meat or something. Reggie hovered around, trying to be helpful, but he freaked me out so I asked him to give me a minute. I tried to wiggle the BB again, applying time-honored zit-popping principles of strategic leverage like a modern-day Archimedes. Nothing happened, and the inflamed flesh was so tender that I couldn't really have at it. Blood with dark little bits in it dribbled over my fingers. We'd thought it all out and decided metal BBs were okay because in theory they weren't going to break the skin, but now I had a tetanus-covered time bomb in my head. I was going to wake up with lockjaw and waste away in bone-popping misery. Should I have occasion to fly between then and my deathday, to visit an international lockjaw specialist at his mountain-top clinic, for example, metal detectors would go off and I'd have to explain the whole dumb story.

We drank some of our father's seven-ounce Miller bottles. I put ice on it and we watched the last half of *The Paper Chase*. I'd try again in the morning.

The next morning the swelling had gone down a little and the hole was scabbed over. I tried squeezing it again. The BB wasn't stuck in the tough flesh anymore, but now the "entry wound" was closed over. Our parents were coming out that night and they were going to murder us. Playing with BB guns. Allowing Reggie to play with BB guns when I was in charge of the house. Both of us letting the other play with BB guns when we should have known better. Three capital offenses right there.

I was going to have to get it out.

I had a scalpel from my eighth-grade science class, but it was in the city. Our father's razor blades were the disposable kind, encased in plastic to prevent exactly this kind of misuse. I sent Reggie out to Frederico's. "Get some of those old-fashioned razor blades, the ones people use to kill themselves."

I stared at my stupid face. Some kids rebelled to get attention. I did stupid things very carefully, spending all of my time thinking of ways to engineer small stupid things without getting caught. Things so small that no one else could see them and only I knew about them. But there I was last night, being stupid in a group, and of course that broke my rules and look where it got me. Who holds a BB-gun war at twilight? The dumb and the desperate. I had that thought, What if I could go back in time? Just thirteen hours. A simple time machine was all I was asking, a leftover prop from a science-fiction movie. You had to have real powers to pull that off, George Lucas–type special effects. Take the case of my friend Greedo. In 1997 when George Lucas rereleased his *Star Wars* trilogy, he fixed what he didn't like using modern special-effects technology, erasing the mistakes of his youth. He had a secret compound and an entire nerd army dedicated to this purpose. In Greedo's case, that meant rewriting the alien's history. In the original movie, the green-skinned bounty hunter is going to deliver the reluctant hero Han Solo to the space-age Mafia don Jabba the Hut, so Han shoots him to prevent this. But all those years later, that version of Han Solo, the one who shoots first, didn't fit in with Lucas's idea of how a real hero acts. So he changed what happened. He re-digitized the scene, inserted a laser blast of Greedo shooting first so that Han didn't shoot someone in cold blood. Han was a hero, Greedo the villain. There. Fixed.

Fans were angry. People don't like it if you mess with their childhood. But not me. Greedo didn't change. There was the first Greedo, the one we knew, and the other Greedo, the new one that emerged to change the meaning of things. To me they're both real. It's a simple thing to keep the two Greedos together in your head if you know how.

Reggie returned with a pack of real razor blades, each one individually wrapped like cheese slices. I peeled the cardboard off one. God it looked terrible. It was such a slim piece of metal and yet host to so much more potentiality than the BB guns. And I was going to put it in my face. Reggie's lip was trembling. His eyes watered. He said, "I don't want anything to happen to you."

Don't cry or you'll get some more. "I'll be okay." I kicked him out. I cut a thin line into the scab and I squeezed. The BB didn't move. I cut deeper into it. Nothing happened. So I cut another line, and now I had an X. I squeezed as hard as I could. The BB was too deep. The FPS had been such that it was down in there, and the skin had closed around it in an embrace. I wasn't so much of a psycho that I was really going to dig in there, shit.

We didn't know what we were going to do. Like the good old days when we broke a lamp or put a hole in the couch and ran around each other like crazy cockroaches. Two fuckups waiting for the Big Shoe. Eye patch? We prayed they'd decide at the last minute not to come out. The odds were good. ("Never tell me the odds," was a Han Solo–ism, hero talk.) We cleaned the house extra special, even used Windex for the fingerprints on the fridge. Maybe that would distract them. We stuck the bloody mop of Bounty paper towels and a blood-soaked washcloth into a plastic King Kullen bag and shoved it way down in the garbage.

In the middle of the afternoon, Reggie went out to sell our gun to NP, who bought it for fifty cents on the dollar. We rehearsed cover stories and settled on, We were running through the woods to Clive's house and I ran into a branch that was sticking out! I coulda poked my eye out! That way they could scold us for running in the woods, and leave it at that. But they got home and never noticed. This big thing almost in my eye.

The BB guns didn't come out again that summer. We weren't the only ones to get rid of them. The thrill was gone, plus the girls finally appeared, like I said, contorting our Thursdays into a new sort of miserable. For some of us, those were our first guns, a rehearsal. I'd like to say, all these years later, now that one of us is dead and another paralyzed from the waist down from actual bullets—drug-related, as the papers put it—that the game wasn't so innocent after all. But it's not true. We always fought for real. Only the nature of the fight changed. It always will. As time went on, we learned to arm ourselves in our different ways. Some of us with real guns, some of us with more ephemeral weapons, an idea or improbable plan or some sort of formulation about how best to move through the world.

An idea that will let us be. Protect us and keep us safe. But a weapon nonetheless.

It's still there. Under the skin. It's good for a story, something to shock people with after I've known them for years and feel a need to surprise them with the other boy. It's not a scar that people notice even though it's right there. I asked a doctor about it once, about blood poisoning over time. He shook his head. Then he shrugged. "It hasn't killed you yet."

To

Prevent

Flare-ups

WE WERE A COSBY FAMILY, GOOD ON PAPER. THAT was the lingo. Father a doctor, mother a lawyer. Three kids, prep-schooled, with clean fingernails and nice manners. No imperial brownstone, but our Prewar Classic 7 wasn't too shabby, squeezing us tight in old elegant bones. Did we squirm? Oh so quietly.

The Cosby Show was the Number-One Show in America, leadoff man of NBC's Thursday Night Dynasty. White people loved it, even the ones who took it as science fiction, some colored version of *Time Tunnel* or *Lost in Space*. Who are these people? We said: People we know. And we watched it. People we knew started wearing sweaters with mind-melting patterns, in tribute to the Coz Himself, and the barber shops buzzed up versions of Theo's latest haircut, whatever he and his friends sported on set, in their brief careers, those handsome boys who went nowhere. The young men marched out of barber shops to all coordinates with flattops, fades, hi-tops of Pisan ambition: Theo's army. "They're a real Cosby Family," people said, when acquaintances broke the atmosphere to better orbit. A term of affection and admiration.

From the street, I'd been relieved to see that the bedrooms were dark. A long day at work, then suffering through Friday-evening LIE traffic—my parents were often asleep when I got off the late shift at Jonni Waffle. Then I reached the steps and heard the TV and saw the moths staggering in the light from the living-room windows. My father was awake. "Where's Shithead?" he asked as I closed the door.

"He's still at Burger King," I said. We were a few months into When Dad Called Reggie Shithead for a Year. That spring, my brother brought home two C minuses on his report card, a new record. Reggie and freshman year were not buddies. He flunked test after test, the ones handed out by teachers and the more important ones, the ones given by other students. It was this latter brand of pop quiz that he really cared about, which is a pity because you can never prepare for them. Especially if you were kids like us. These other grades went down on your real Permanent Record, the one you carried on your person at all times even when high school was long over. Everyone saw the marks you got, as if they had X-ray eyes.

Our father reacted with the boilerplate threats and harangues, and finally this renaming. Whenever our father was in the room, Reggie disappeared and in his place lingered this embarrassing, ever-accountable stain. "Is this Shithead's?" he'd ask, holding up a copy of *Spin* that had fallen between the cushions of the couch. Lightbulb burn out? "Shithead's using too much electricity." I got off the hook a lot. I was grateful. We were always grateful when someone else got the business. If I left some dirty dishes in the sink, my father said, "These must be Shithead's," as he passed by, and I took the hint and scrubbed them. It wasn't until Labor Day that I realized that over the course of the summer Reggie had moved most of his Burger King time to the weekend, trading and swapping with co-workers shift by shift to minimize exposure. That night he was at BK like I said, and had arranged for a double on Saturday. That was a big chunk of quality time disposed of right there.

I opened a can of cream soda and leaned against the fridge. My father said, "I was wondering when you were going to stop having me cut your hair."

I ran my palm across my bristly scalp. "Clive has a whole clipper set."

"Look like one of those corner niggers," he said. Groups of brown young men—black, Dominican, Puerto Rican—hung out in alternating shifts outside the bodega on the corner of 101st and Broadway, that locus of licentiousness. Whenever something went awry in the neighborhood, the corner niggers eagerly stepped up for scapegoat duty. Gum mashed into your shoe, runny dog shit in front of the building, transit strike: these were all well-known manifestations of corner-nigger high jinks. They kept their hair grazed down to quarter-inch stubble, and Clive had inducted me into their gang.

"I like it," I said.

"Your head." He shrugged. He leaned back on the couch and returned to the TV. It sounded familiar. I'd seen the movie before.

It was the first time someone else had cut my hair. Since I could remember, me and Reggie had a ritual. When our hair got too crazy, we asked our father to give us a haircut, and he put us off, saying he was too busy or had had a long day at his practice, and over the next few weeks or months we'd ask again, judiciously spacing out our requests so as not to "nag like an old woman," and then eventually one evening he'd come home tipsy after "a meeting" and break out his scissors. Black barbers the world over, they use electric clippers. These are modern times. In many sectors, technological advances are welcomed and embraced. My father, however, loved his special pair of old-school barber scissors, and we loved them, too, because the sound of the long, thin blades sniping against each other was the sound of his undivided attention.

As I sat on a chair in the bathroom, holding the towel tight around my bony shoulders and staring into the black-and-white subway tile, he trimmed and trimmed, grumbling about the light, tilting my head to and fro with a firm push of his index and middle fingers. He drew up tufts with a pick and squinted and clipped. I murmured the Prime Directive to myself, "Don't move your head, don't move your head," even though it never worked. I moved. He always told me I moved no matter how much I concentrated, no matter how many oaths and pledges I devised between haircuts, as if a new arrangement of words might make things turn out differently next time. At some point he'd say, "You moved your head. Now I have to even it out," and I cursed myself as he cut and cut, and my 'Fro grew shorter and shorter and shorter . . .

But when he was done, it was perfect. Like when he grilled—you had to admit that despite everything, he was a master griller. It was one of those things he did well, you couldn't say anything against it, it was a cornerstone of our reality. He gave us miniature versions of his own cut, the same one he'd given himself since high school, when he took over haircut duties from his father. The haircuts remained perfect for whole hours—don't be thrown off by the fact that no camera ever recorded them. The spell broke when you took a shower or slept on them, whereupon all his tucks and pats and proddings were undone and our superb crowns became utterly misshaped and disordered, the underlying principles revealed as counterfeit. What occurred on my scalp could not be called a "style" in any true sense, and it got wilder the longer it got. It was a weird black amoeba testing the edges of itself, throwing out nappy pseudopods here and suddenly there, an unpredictable new direction every day. I swear it lived, and have come to believe that its ever-shifting lumps and tendrils were a doomed attempt at communication with the humans. The tragedy of the day-after haircuts! And all the days after! The months passed until we had to admit to ourselves that the world abhorred us, and the process started anew.

Needless to say, I had no idea how fucked up the haircuts were at the time. To us they were normal. Just how things were done in our house. (Raise your hand if you can relate.) My delusions ended that spring when I was cleaning out my desk during one of my periodic purges of nerdery. My twenty-sided die possessed a curious will, returning to pester and trouble me even though I had thrown it out a hundred times, the specter of D&D games past. This time I threw it out the window. (I found it under the radiator a week later.) I stashed dog-eared copies of *Famous Monsters* in a box at the back of the closet and hid all the comic books I'd bought since the last purge, in case a girl materialized in my room due to a transporter malfunction. I was in a good mood or something, feeling optimistic, like someone had chuckled at a joke that I'd made in Biology, or History, and it had gone to my head.

I came across a packet of fifth-grade class pictures under my copy of *Swamp Thing #35*. It is the nettlesome quality of elementary-school pictures to reveal the true nature of our childhoods. Nothing is how we remember it, and all the necessary alterations we've made in order to survive with semi-functioning psyches are exposed. Best to leave them alone.

Looking back, I think I had what is best described as a prelapsarian fondness for fifth grade, its lack of complication. No more. Miss Fredericks, the Social Studies teacher whose cruel smile had haunted me for years and who was actually the default setting in my nightmares when I needed an evil authority figure, had a melancholy face now that I really examined it. She seemed a bit too skinny, almost ill, and I got to thinking about what her house looked like, picturing the shadows in the kitchenette where she prepared her lonely meals. Two scoops of cottage cheese on a big leaf of wilted iceberg lettuce, and a side of misery. She never appeared in my dreams again.

Scanning the rest of the photograph, it was clear that none of us, teacher and pupils alike, had remained untouched by that horrible epidemic making the rounds back then, '70s fashion, the manic stripes and prints of the shirts and skirts and pants a kind of rash on our flesh that only a new decade could cure. Then there were the kids themselves. No one looked like they were supposed to. These changeling creatures surrounded me in polyester, touching my elbows. Strangers. I traced a finger along their faces like a movie amnesiac . . . that must be my best friend . . . his name is Andy . . . that's the smart girl who sat in front of me all year . . . she ate frankfurters out of a *Bionic Woman* thermos filled with hot oily water. Then there was my own face. My face was not the one I remembered showing to the world. Were my eyes so dark, those days? There was something amiss with my mouth, always my mouth, even before I got braces. My lips were chapped, sure, but the chappiness seemed to have extended its territory, so that a huge white halo encircled my mouth, like I'd been eating ashes for breakfast, lunch, and dinner. And then there was that thing on top.

That really fucked-up haircut.

I recovered from the class picture pretty quickly. It wasn't that bad. Seeing the white letters identifying my homeroom, the construction-paper map of France we'd toiled over that winter, the poster of Neil Armstrong floating down to the lunar surface, I felt a nice warm tingle of nostalgia. The killer was the four panes of wallet-sized photos beneath the class picture. It was just me there. They should have stopped me. They should have stopped me at any number of checkpoints. As I tried to leave the apartment—here, a close relative would have been key. The doorman could have taken me aside. We got along, him and me, trading *hey*s with enthusiasm, or so I thought. But he said nothing. Certainly the bus driver, de facto deputy of the body politic, could've forbid me entry, ripping my bus pass in half and tossing it to the dirty black treads. The security guard outside school should have beat me with his flashlight, and surely my homeroom teacher, Miss Barrett—stickler by nature, wielder of a bifocaled annihilating gaze—should have shoved her big wooden desk up against the classroom door, back brace or no back brace. All of them should have said, What the fuck is up with your hair?

Obviously it had been months since my last trim. Instead of a haircut, the photographer had captured some primordial process unfolding. The universe tugged and pressed on my hair with invisible fingers, the way it had pulled up mountains to the sky and gouged the deepest ocean chasms, where the only living beings are pale boneless things rooting around in everlasting gloom. What else is there to say but that in my vicinity larger forces were at work, the ancient underpinnings of it all. There are natural laws. The Third Law of Thermodynamics says that as temperature approaches absolute zero, the entropy of a system approaches a constant. Sir Isaac Newton's Third Law of Motion holds that for every action, there is an equal and opposite reaction. The entity on my head was proof of another fundamental law: a fucked-up Afro tends toward complete fuckedupedness at an exponential rate over time, as expressed by the equation,

$$AN = F * t$$

where AN is Absolute Nappiness, **F** is fuckedupedness, and **t** is time

The pane of photos was uncut, of course. Who'd want a picture of that in their wallet, poisoning their money?

I don't remember being teased about my hair or my acute chappiness. But surely they made fun of me, the children in the photograph and the strangers out of frame. Surely they had to see it. Why didn't they say anything? I was due for another haircut when I found those pictures, but it never occurred to me not to ask my dad to cut my hair as usual. We'd always done things a certain way. Then out in Sag I was at Clive's house when he was cutting NP's hair, and when he was done he turned to me and asked, "You want me to cut off that jungle bush or what?"

I finished my cream soda and went to wash out the can. Chicken parts bobbed in a big pot of water in the sink, defrosting. He was going to barbecue tomorrow. I made a note.

"He just boiled that dizzy bitch in the hot tub," he said.

Halloween II. "Dag," I said. I sat down on the couch and watched the rest of it with him.

Reggie woke me up with his french-fry smell when he came in. The french-fry smell was almost another person in our room, stumbling in the dark. When I got up, he'd already gone back to work.

It was almost noon, from the noise. Saturdays in Sag Harbor, I liked to lie in bed listening to the weekend rev itself up. First, though, I concentrated on the house noises, to see what I'd be getting into. The screen door slammed shut and someone entered the living room—my mother, from the walk. She made a comment, my father responded in his wisecracking intonation, and both of them laughed. I relaxed. Things seemed okay out there.

I had three speakers—the two windows and the crack beneath the door—that functioned as my tri-phonic hi-fi, filling the room with the melody of an Azurest afternoon. If I closed my eyes, I saw everything perfectly. Things never happened otherwise. Last-minute lawn mowers spun and spat, and a car made a slow turn 'round Terry onto Walker, reconnoitering to see which houses had cars in the driveway. That eternal question: Who's out, who's out? Three houses up, Big Dennis cranked up his Earth, Wind & Fire best of, which by that point in the summer I knew track by track, crooning the next song while this one was still on the second verse. "Reasons, the reasons that we hear." Out on the water, two motorboats cruised in circles, preparing for the busy weekend workout: hauling worthies up on water skis; fishing expeditions in the Great Beyond outside the bay; and slow jaunts around the Neck or into Baron's Cove, depending on one's motives. The weekend jigsaw fit together into the shape on the box, the one we were promised. Then I heard it, a sound the normal person would never notice.

Poomp.

It was the magnet. There was one magnet with which I was well acquainted. It resided in the next room, in the lower left quadrant of the kitchen island, securing the liquor cabinet door. It produced a sound—*Poomp*—when the twin metal strips on the cabinet door connected with the magnet in the cabinet itself. *Poomp* meant the liquor cabinet had been depleted. *Poomp* meant it had started.

I felt a twinge. Then relaxed. It was okay—I'd devised an exit strategy when I saw the chicken in the sink.

I haven't gotten to the layout of our little hideaway yet. The beach house was a ranch bungalow my grandparents built in the late '60s. Long planks stained a deep, earthy red covered the exterior, and the roof sloped at a narrow angle, like a book that had been set face-down. The two small bedrooms faced the street; walk out of them and you were in a hallway with a bathroom on your right before things opened up into the living space. The TV area and encircling couches on the left, kitchen and dining on the right. The north wall was glass, facing the deck, and beyond that stretched the beach and the bay. Visitors coming up from the beach used the screen door, and those from the street used the side door next to the stove. The clomp-ing up the side stairs was an invaluable early-alert system, allowing us to scurry into the back if we decided to pretend not to be home. Which was quite often.

We'd spent three summers there. We used to stay on Hempstead Street, in the old house my grandparents put up when the develop-ments started going. My mother and her sister inherited the two houses, and then in some intricate bad-blood transaction our family got the beach house and my aunt got the Hempstead House. Obvi-ously, from an objective real estate point of view, the beach house was the better property. Location, location, etc. But I'd spent my true childhood at the other place, and I never got over leaving it. My laundry list of psychic injuries aside, the Hempstead House was just bigger. In the new place we were on top of each other. My sister got the second bedroom whenever she came out, forcing me and Reggie to sleep in the living room, waiting for her or our parents to get up so that we could stumble off into their rooms for the short but im-portant stretch of late-morning sleep.

The beach house was still big enough for you to sneak around in, slink into the bathroom, and generally get your shit together before you had to say good morning. This day, I heard my mother talking to one of her friends out on the deck, so I dashed into the bathroom, checked that the coast was clear, and then made a break for it to my parents' bedroom to use the phone.

"James going to barbecue today?" I heard NP's mother ask.

"You know James," my mother answered.

Bobby said he'd pick me up at two o'clock to go driving around. I counted to one hundred, and when I emerged Mrs. Grimes was just disappearing down the stairs to the beach. Good timing. My mother tucked her hair into her bathing cap, an old favorite of hers, white with rainbow-colored plastic flowers floating on it. "Have to get my swim in before those maniacs get out there," she said. In a few hours, the boats would be zipping back and forth, the drivers with one hand on the wheel and the other in the beer cooler, eyes on the rove for the next escapade. There had never been an accident, but an afternoon in Sag Harbor had special pockets of tsk-tsking that needed to be filled.

My mother looked great. Always this magic happened: as the summer went on, she got younger and younger. The sun tanned her skin to a strong, vital brown, and her thin crow's feet disappeared, ushering an impish twinkle into her eyes. During the week she was a mild-mannered attorney, an in-house lawyer for Nestlé. Every few years, I asked what she did there, and she said, "Oh, you don't want to know about that," or worse, explained in full detail, causing my synapses to shut down. Something about international trademarks, the protection of the Nestlé family of products and top-secret formulas. We got a big crate of Hot Cocoa with Mini Marshmallows every Christmas that lasted us all year.

City mornings, she armed herself for the midtown hustle, walking out in her monochromatic business-wear and Nikes, her nice shoes in a PBS tote bag. It's a living. But out there, she was a different person. She'd never missed a summer the last forty years. Her friends on the beach were her friends from the old days. Her crew, like me and Reggie had our crew. She wasn't the only one who went back to the start of Azurest, but Sag Harbor worked on her in a way I'd never seen it do other people. There was a part of her that only existed out there. It made her go.

"Sounds like someone is having a party up the beach," she said.

"That's just Big Dennis and his mix tape," I said. "Where's Dad?"

"He went down the beach to talk to Mr. Baxter," she said. She walked down to the water.

I had the place to myself for a while. I ate breakfast and watched *Young Frankenstein* on Channel 11. Each time I watched it, I got

5 percent more of the jokes. Just killing time until Bobby picked me up. He had a car now, his parents' attempt at seducing him with the sweet nothings of bourgie comfort. I didn't care how the car got there, reveling in the aftermath of our coup. Randy's messed-up jalopy was now in exile, the last-resort overflow vehicle, shotgunned no more. We had reestablished the natural order. Except for the whole girl thing.

The girls just appeared one day, stepping out of their clam. The house came first. We noticed it on one of our early circuits at the start of the summer. It had obliterated a chunk of woods of no special value, bereft of cherished shortcuts and dilapidated hideouts, but it still hurt. It was an '80s prefab joint, no saltbox or rancher, but something you might see if you took a wrong turn and got lost in the suburbs. I'd never been to the suburbs, but I'd seen movies set in sterile subdivisions where over time the dead rotting heart of suburbia was laid bare, and the houses in those movies looked like that house.

The scattered intel and unsubstantiated reports trickled in halfway through the summer. Day One: "There are some girls out," Marcus declared. "I saw some girls walking up Cadmus," Reggie reported. "What, little kids?" "No, our age." "Let's go see." "No, they're gone, man." Day Two: NP alleged that "Their names are Devon and Erica." "Sisters?" "No, man, you see how light Devon is, and then the moms and pops? No way Erica is her sister." Fact: they were cousins, and it was Devon's house. Day Four's debriefing contained more confirmed sightings, bonehead speculation, and then something new—firsthand encounters. The girls hailed from New Jersey, high-school sophomores to-be. Devon had "those big Lisa Lisa titties," Erica "a dick-sucking mouth." "That's too young for me," Clive demurred, "but y'all should give it a shot." "I'd hit either one of those honeys," Randy declared, sharing his enthusiasm for statutory rape. NP presented his conclusion: "Devon would grab your jim with a quickness." I said, "Really?" By Day Five, it was all over. Bobby and NP called a meeting to announce that they were going out with them, following an eventful afternoon when the cousins "went for a ride" in Bobby's car. I hadn't even met them yet! You go to work, scoop some ice cream, come back home, and the whole balance was off. Cars, man.

"That Baxter is a panic," my father said, sliding open the screen door. He had an empty glass in his hand, part of a set we bought when we started staying at the beach house, to replace the '60s glasses with mod designs on them, polka dots and odd geometric forms. The old stuff went in the garbage. "What are you doing?"

"Nothing," I said.

"Time to get a fire started."

He was known up and down the beach as a master griller, the wind itself in service to his legend, bearing the exquisite smell of caramelizing meat through the developments. Every Saturday, every Sunday, in good weather and bad. On good days, the chicken skin bubbled ferociously, sunlight dancing in the juices, and on bad days the rain evaporated on the lid with bitter hissing sounds. He didn't believe in God but was a devout worshipper of Gore-Tex the Miracle Fiber, grilling into autumn and winter while armored in his beloved Windbreaker. "This stuff really works," he exclaimed, angry gusts ripping the fabric back and forth. Nor'easters roared up the coast, bringing minor complications vis-à-vis fire-starting, but he always discovered his personal storm-eye beneath the overhang, amid the bluster, the flames ripping with fury in the wind. Autumn days, ours was the only inhabited house on the beach, the bucket of fire a sign of life and ancient caveman lore. He grilled in a blizzard once, as he liked to remind people, for kicks and to prove that he could. You should be so lucky as to witness such a strange and marvelous sight. Shelter Island, the bay, everything that existed outside our property line, was an impenetrable void, a kind of hungry salivating darkness, as the snow swirled like a thousand fireflies into the light thrown out from the living room. We were the only ones left, the last human beings, or maybe the first. The chicken took longer to cook, but when he brought it back inside it was fantastic.

If you told him you weren't hungry, he didn't care. He'd grill anyway. Eventually you'd eat it.

Poomp! Needing a refreshment. How many was that? The one I heard in the bedroom, and probably a refresher at Mr. Baxter's. Plus this one. Starting at who knows what time that morning. I calculated: almost an hour until Bobby was going to pick me up. I could make it.

Before the *poomp* was the *tock* of the liquor-cabinet door sucking away from the magnet. You could hear the *poomp* all over the house; the *tock* was a slighter sound, inauspicious, given that it was the start of things. It was simultaneously the sound of two things separating as well as the snap of eventualities locking into place. A sequence counting down, tick-*tock*.

To be completely accurate, you heard the ice first, but sometimes ice is just ice and not an omen. I myself enjoyed a nice Coke with ice from time to time. Ice foreshadowed only intermittently. My father rummaged in the freezer, moving the half-full bag of Tater Tots off the ice tray. Then the ice tumbled into the glass. It was a short fall but it seemed longer. The ice cubes jammed in like inmates. Then—*tock!*

The bottle of Tanqueray *thunk*ed on the wood of the kitchen counter, followed by the tinny *rasp* of the bottle cap sliding clockwise. *Crack crack!* The gin shattered the ice, slicing planes through the cubes, but they remained whole, only the thin fuzz of frost melting into the alcohol. The first of the day's many chemical reactions. *Poomp*—the magnet pulled the door shut. He opened the refrigerator door and another magnet, silent in its coat of white accordion plastic, drifted away from the metal frame. The tonic water hissed as the pressure in the bottle fizzed away. The bottle made a slight *ting* as it slid into the rack in the fridge door, next to the relish and mustard.

I was well acquainted with all these sounds and heard the other silent things. This made no sound: my father stirring his drink with his finger. This also made no sound: that dreaded calculation, how many is that today? Certainly this made no sound: the understanding, I'm pushing my luck by hanging around here. And silent now but soon to make itself heard, the chemical reaction in his brain that said, Let's get this hate in gear.

"Can I turn the channel?" I asked. He had turned to CNN. "*Road Warrior* is coming on."

"Go ahead."

We were a made-for-TV family. Every new channel added to our lineup, every magnificent home-entertainment advance increased the possibility that we wouldn't have to talk to one another. If we lived a hundred years in the future, we'd never have to deal with one another at all. Peering 24-7 into our virtual-reality headsets, we'd merely bump into one another every so often, a family that knew itself as kicks in the shin and elbows in the stomach. Although if I stop to think about it, that would probably be more physical contact than we had now.

There's no dialogue in the first ten minutes of *The Road Warrior*, once the narrator sets up the when-where-why. (After Apocalypse-Apocalyptic Wasteland-Survival.) The Road Warrior and his dog scour the desert looking for food and gas. Mohawked madmen ride motorcycles and trucks and souped-up muscle cars, preying on the weak. Things kick into gear when the Road Warrior discovers the settlement, an old oil refinery where a band of humans have cobbled together a community in the void of the world. They live under siege, the leather-clad psychos circling their walls, the outside world hollering in menace. I loved *The Road Warrior*.

Through the glass, my father got to work. First up, grill prep. He wheeled the Weber to the side of the deck and dumped last week's ashes over the rail. They thrashed through the air in gray waves. His eyes were slits. The ashes tumbled into their mound. Ten feet separated us from the neighbor's house, and no one ever walked over there, especially since me and Reggie had outgrown "exploring" the property, pretending the scrub pines and gnarled bushes were alien territory. Trying to make unknown that which was completely known. The mound grew higher all summer, hardening into black cakes when it rained. Off-season, the wind took it away so he could start over again.

Next came the ceremonial scrubbing away of last week's grease from the grill. "Don't want that to flare up when I'm trying to cook some chicken." He cleared the dishes in the sink to have room to work. The SOS pads disintegrated into pink suds and nubs of metal in his hand. Top side, underside, the tiny cracks where the rods met. This took a while. He hummed some Nat King Cole.

I went to the bathroom and when I came out, CNN was on. I turned it back to *The Road Warrior*. He didn't respond.

I wanted something to read. The TV was always on in our house, whether people watched it or not. We needed sound, any kind of sound. Watching TV and reading at the same time was standard op. We didn't have a lot of books in the beach house. There were my mother's Danielle Steels and Judith Krantzs, old horror and sci-fi novels of mine and Reggie's that were neither beloved nor gory enough to reread. I had some old *Amazing Spider-Man*s and *Marvel Two-In-One*s in our bedroom dresser, but the last few months I had renounced all things dorky and was doing quite well at it, my spring nerd-purge and subsequent haircut revelation feeding my resolve.

Which left *The Book of Lists*, that eccentric encyclopedia of the world, boiling down trivia into thick, murky lumps of truth. National Bestseller! It was falling apart. I'd read it many times, but there was always some new list that fell out from between the pages into my lap, tweaking my status quo. Not 6 Positions for Sexual Intercourse or 8 Remarkable Escapes from Devil's Island, I had those memorized. I didn't care that the book was already horribly dated in 1985 (#1 Hero of American Boys and Girls—O. J. Simpson; #1 Most Beautiful Woman of Modern Times—Twiggy). I still respected the classics, like 8 Cases of Spontaneous Combustion and 10 Ghastly Ghosts, which might as well have been commandments carved into stone tablets, eternal and awesome. Spontaneous combustion is a rare occurrence, to be sure, but you never know. Forewarned is forearmed.

Mrs. Gardner padded up from the beach and made her way across the deck. I saw her out of the corner of my eye and ducked into Dr. Ashley Montagu's 10 Worst Well-Known Human Beings in History. (You'd be surprised.) She rapped on the glass. I feigned being startled. She was nice enough—her daughter and son were my sister's age, so we'd had a lot of dealings over the years—but still.

"How you doing, girl?" my father asked cheerfully.

"Just making my way down the beach," she said. "Mind if I use the facilities?"

Another thing, besides the routine quicksand, was that you had to talk to grown-ups all day if you stayed in the house. They came up for a bathroom stop, to say hello and check off this encounter from their weekend to-do list, to grab the drink that was always offered. Back then I didn't realize that most grown-ups didn't want to talk to you as much as you didn't want to talk to them. *Hello, how are you?* The smallest interaction made me shrivel as I considered the consequences. My brother and mother and sister, they were known quantities. I knew how to factor in my mother's rare spells of defiance and Reggie's monkey-wrench ways. These people coming up from the beach were rogue variables, and you couldn't predict their effects. The wrong word, the wrong reminiscence might set the afternoon on a new, choppy course. They might say or do something that started a reaction, either when they were there or after they left, hours later when his brooding had got a hold of it and we were the only audience. The sound of the screen door closing behind them was never much of a relief because you didn't know what they'd left behind.

"You making some of that good barbecue?" Mrs. Gardner asked as she left the bathroom.

"You know me," he said. "Can I fix you something?"

She went off empty-handed—pre-barbecue visits were always shorter than when food was around—and my father went out to start the fire.

"She better not of stunk up the bathroom," he said.

I chuckled.

Tock, thunk, rasp, poomp.

Kingsford charcoal, my father's fuel of choice. When it came to grilling, anyway. The coals rustled out of the big blue-and-white bag onto the grate. Gravity had a design, tossing them in a certain arrangement. My father had his own laws, a precise concept of fire formation honed over the years. To people like you and me, a briquette is a briquette. Not to him. He seemed to analyze each coal individually, taking measure of its strengths, deficits, secret potential. The diamond in the darkness. He knew where they needed to go, recognizing the uniqueness of each cube and determining where it fit with the rest of the team. He assembled the pyramid meticulously, perceiving the invisible—the crooked corridors of ventilation between the briquettes, the heat traps and inevitable vectors of released energy, any potential irregularity that might undermine the project. The sublime interconnectedness of it all. He asserted his order. Built his fire.

The canteen of lighter fluid was an indispensable tool in this enterprise, up there with the spatula and tongs. (He cried "Tongs!" like a TV surgeon demanding a scalpel.) He doused, he drenched, he baptized his creation with a truly fucking gruesome amount of lighter fluid. The fumes were intoxicating, strangely appetizing in their noxiousness, an anti-aroma to the aroma to come, as interlinked as the caterpillar to the butterfly. The coals were so thoroughly suffused with lighter fluid that every so often a pile preemptively ignited itself when a matchbook got within thirty yards, choosing to embrace its destiny with honor. On those occasions when a mound of coals declined to self-immolate, a single match sent it up with a spine-tingling *whoosh*. My father nodded to the fire and let it be for forty minutes to allow it to make peace with its god.

Every so often, one of his friends or a galoot out for the weekend came up from the beach and, watching this ritual, felt inspired to share their fire-starting techniques. "I make what I call a little 'nest' of newspapers under the coals." "You should try one of those chimneys that they have now." My father glared at them like the imbeciles they were, spatula a-dangle. *Make a little nest.* "Whitey invented lighter fluid for a reason," he told them. Who could argue with that?

"James! You up there?"

Mr. Turner's bald head broke the horizon of the deck. My hand whimpered in anticipation of the bone-crushing handshake. He was one of my father's oldest cronies. They went way back, to college, the late '50s, when they were part of a handful of young black men infiltrating the big-time Northeast schools. Brothers from Brooklyn, Harlem, huddling together as the Massachusetts winters, the New Hampshire winters, took a bite out of their asses. What were they doing getting Ivy League educations? They weren't supposed to be there. They hung tight with the five or six other black guys in their school, drank beer with the five or six black guys the next school over. Dated the five or six black ladies at the genteel women's college the next town over, and the other schools on the black network, road-tripping to the big dance that weekend at B.U. or Smith, or up to Montreal, where from all accounts some crazy racial utopia existed, integration of the sort that'd get you lynched in half the South. My father met my mother during that time, on the New England black-college circuit. So that's where all this begins, maybe.

Mr. Turner was also a Sag Harbor guy, son of one of the first families to come out here. I mention this because it was one of those rogue variables with the power to transform my afternoon. My father got to talking, talking got to dredging, and who knew what might happen.

"When did you get out?" my father asked.

"Last night."

My father went to get him a drink. Mr. Turner stayed on the deck and I kept my head in *The Book of Lists* to ward off eye contact. Mr. Turner had his own company, selling package tours to Africa and the Caribbean. See the Motherland, get in touch with your heritage, vacation where everyone looks like you for a change. He dispatched fleets of rickety buses to chug-chug up scrabbly mountain roads, kickbacks deciding where they stopped for lunch. He negotiated deals with trinket outposts hawking authenticity in many forms, bead necklaces and fertility symbols, the omnipresent masks reflecting back the faces of sentimental longing. When you went to someone's apartment, you never asked, "Hey, where'd you get that cool African mask from?," because the answer was always, "Mike Turner's tour." There were Kenyans driving BMWs up to their mountain villas, big satellite dishes in their backyards, because black Americans needed a little whiff. He provided a service.

I hadn't seen him since he came over to our apartment to apologize for how things went on our Jamaica trip last Christmas. He'd booked us into a crumbling all-inclusive in Montego Bay where the roaches were as big as lizards, the lizards were as big as bats, and the bats had such an impressive wingspan that you wanted to ask them for a lift back to JFK. Everybody got food poisoning one night at the crappy buffet, except for me because I was working a not-eating-salad angle that winter, inexplicable looking back these years later, but fortuitous. "I don't work with them anymore," he informed us. "The son has really run that place into the ground." My father had cursed his name for weeks, but after he apologized they went out drinking and it was like nothing happened. They went way back, like I said.

My father tossed him a Budweiser. "My son got himself one of those haircuts like the boys on the corner," he said, making sure I heard.

"Corner . . . ?" Mr. Turner sucked his teeth. "Man, all the kids have that now."

Now I had to go out and say hi. He pulverized my hand, but not as much as usual, thanks to my recent fortifying regimen of ice-cream scooping. "Looking like a man now, huh, Benji?" he said. "You got yourself a girlfriend?"

"No."

"Shit, if I were you I'd be all over the girls they got out here. When I was coming up, shit." He winked at my father.

6 Fake Smiles in Benji's House
1. To Patronize Grown-ups
2. On Hearing Cruel Put-down of Family Member
3. False Front of Invulnerability
4. When All Else Fails
5. Bizarro Form of Cognitive Dissonance
6. To Avoid Being Next

"That reminds me," Mr. Turner said, lifting his eyebrows, "you know who else is out?"

"Who?"

"Mabel."

"Mabel Jackson?"

They snickered.

"Haven't seen her in years," my father said.

"I know she don't want to see you, boy," Mr. Turner said.

My father shrugged. "Shit, I can't help what I am. How she look?"

"Like her husband left her ass for that young thing, what else she going to look like?"

"Back when, though."

"Damn."

I went inside to call Bobby. He was late. His mother told me he'd already left. He'd honk his horn any minute and I'd be free. Maybe we'd go by Devon and Erica's or something. Maybe I wouldn't even have to suggest it, he'd bring it up and I could maintain an air of disinterest. I hadn't been inside Devon's house yet, torturing myself that I missed the Hanging Out in Their Basement period, those four fabled days cut short once Devon's father got wind. Word was he was "really strict."

"I better go down there and see what these people are getting up to," Mr. Turner said. He shook his beer can to see how full it was.

"Come back and get some chicken when you're done struttin' through your coop," my father said.

He checked the fire, spreading his hand over coals. "Mabel Jackson is out." He shook his head and smiled. "Back in college, she was fine . . ." He stopped. He looked at his palm. "That's why you should marry a virgin," he said. "People talk about you. You want to be out with your wife and have some fool whistling about what he used to do?"

"Right. I mean, no."

"What you do follows you, that's what I'm trying to tell you."

"Right." He headed for the kitchen. Ash nibbled the corners of the coals. One of my mother's friends walked down to the beach along the side of the house, dragging a beach chair across the cracked paving stones. Early Saturday afternoon, there were distractions. A cocktail party up in Ninevah, or a birthday luncheon at the Salty Dog, but the beach was HQ. Things always ended up on the beach, in front of our house.

When I walked inside, he was getting out the chicken. CNN was on. I turned back to *The Road Warrior.* He didn't say anything, but I could've turned on MTV at full volume and he wouldn't have heard. Everything ceased to exist when he spiced up the chicken. His world shrunk to the size of the aluminum tray before him, a type of screen. He scrutinized the limp rows of chicken parts as his hand jagged over them. There are those among us who put their faith in marinades. For others, barbecue sauce—Texas-style tomato-based or North Carolina vinegar-infused—is the order of the day. My father didn't truck with any of that. "Salt. Pepper. Paprika. That's all you need. All you ever do need." First one side, then he flipped them piece by piece and did the other side. As a concession to the rest of humanity, he'd brush on some barbecue sauce at the end if you asked for it, but it was obviously beneath him and a betrayal of bedrock values. Slap on some store-bought Heinz crap, to show what he thought of you.

He kept changing the channel out of habit. CNN and the Nightly News were the only things he watched. To him, the faces on the screen—the anchors, the newsmakers, this day's victim, and all the everyday heroes—were a parade of shifting masks. Props of an idea, like the souvenirs our friends and neighbors brought back across the Atlantic. He saw the true faces beneath and called them out. He didn't need a teleprompter; he knew his commentary by heart. A Televangelist snuck his hand into the collection box. "Problem with black people is that they waste all this time praying to God when they should be out looking for a job." Welfare Moms exposed! "Nobody ever gave me anything. Didn't ask for anything. Some people need to get off their asses." A Hot Young Thing sued her boss for squeezing her behind. "Women always talking about how they want to be equal, but they get mad at you if you don't hold the door for them." The Undersecretary of Bullshit explaining why he wanted to bomb some country. "Whitey always trying to blow somebody up. They should put all those warmongers on an ice floe in the North Pole with the penguins, let them blow each other up and leave us the hell alone." He was our talking head. The only channel we got.

Tock, thunk, rasp, poomp.

Nobody ever gave him anything, and he never asked. His parents died before I was born. I didn't know much about them because he never talked about them. I knew his stand on every issue, but his parents were a blank. Except for the fact that they never gave him anything. He washed dishes at an uptown restaurant to pay for college, the first one in his family to go. After that, grad school. "I didn't know I could do anything else," he told us. "Back then if you wanted to make something of yourself you went into the Sacred Seven"—he ticked them off on his fingers—"Teacher, Preacher, Doctor, Lawyer, Nurse, Dentist. Undertaker. If white people aren't going to do it, we have to do it ourselves. Separate and as equal as we can make it. I looked around and thought, Everybody gets sick. And all the black people I knew, they had bad feet. So I became a foot doctor." He did two days a week at Harlem Hospital and three days at his office on Morningside Drive. I never saw it. I assume it existed. He made a good living. He was right—black people had some bad feet, although it should be pointed out that he worked with a self-selecting sample.

I will add here the personal observation that being a podiatrist taught you how to really put your foot up someone's ass.

My mother returned from the beach.

"You finish making that macaroni salad?" my father asked.

"It's here in the fridge," she said.

"Your mother makes the best macaroni salad."

She poured herself some white wine. "It turned out to be a nice beach day."

"They're all down there?"

"Where else would they be?" She looked over at me. "You going to stay inside all day?"

"Bobby's coming over. We're going driving around."

"You're going to stay for some barbecue?" my father asked. "I got that good chicken 'comin' right up.' "

"I already talked to him."

A shadow crossed his face but then that gene we shared kicked in, the one that said, Don't show it. To see his expression, he was back at his timetables, when to put on what, turn this, take off that. He was a master griller. It was good I was getting out of there.

The fire was ready. He scraped the pile into an even red layer—none of that hoity-toity direct/indirect heat-zone crap for him. Behind him, this old lady I didn't recognize came up from the beach, her gray-purple hair poking out from beneath a big floppy straw hat. Bet me money and I would have guessed she was in her sixties, but I found out she was twenty years older. She carried her age in her movements, in her tiny hesitant steps and the tremble in her hand as it skipped along the rail. "Gail, is that you?" she said, trying to see into the living room. "Louisa said you might be up here."

My mother rushed out to the deck. "Mrs. Russell!"

"Natalie," my father said. "How you doing, girl?" They gave her big hugs. She had to be an Azurest old-timer to get this kind of treatment, one of my grandparents' friends, which was confirmed when she looked around and told my mother, "I remember when your father started clearing this lot." No matter how old you were, you remembered the trees going down.

"Benji—come out and say hello!" my mother said.

When I shook her hand, Mrs. Russell winced. "That's some handshake."

Was that some kind of a joke? She told me she hadn't seen me since I was a baby. "Your grandfather—he was just the nicest gentleman that ever came out here. A real one of a kind."

"Doesn't she look good?" my father asked me. "I swear you haven't aged a day, girl."

"I do miss coming out here," she said, almost blushing. "I should make more of an attempt."

"You're always welcome around my house," my father said.

"Is that *Finn's Spirit?*" Mrs. Russell pointed out to the water. A big white yacht crawled slowly across the water toward the Long Wharf. I couldn't see anybody on it. Big yachts were a rare sight back then, drifting around like rumors.

"I saw it out here last year," my mother said. She went to fetch the binoculars.

"It's a big one," my father said.

"It's from Holland," Mrs. Russell said.

"If you got a yacht like that, you might as well show it off."

"Is it too big for the yacht club? They're pretty strict there, I know," Mrs. Russell said.

After my mother and Mrs. Russell went back down to the beach, my father told me, "That's what you look for in a woman—good DNA. She really hasn't aged a bit. If you want to know what a woman is going to look like in thirty years, look at her mother. It's all passed down."

"Right."

"That way you don't make mistakes. Her mother, too—she was a knockout. Old as hell when I met her, but still. Classy. A real lady. She was *dark*. That's why she was always nice to me. I wasn't one of them, either. She wasn't one of these light-skinned pussies they got out here. I don't know where the bitch was from, but it wasn't no Sag Harbor, I'll tell you that."

I thought, This is where the day curdles. It was in his posture, this rigidity. He stared down the beach. From up there, it all spread before him, the slow-moving pageant of an Azurest Saturday. "All these bourgie bitches out here . . ." He lifted the binoculars. "Who's that down there by the Rock?"

He passed me the binoculars. "That's Sherry. She's friends with Elena."

"She's going to be fat when she's forty." He took the binoculars back and looked at her again. "Gotta watch for that. Don't want people talking about how you got a whale for a wife. It's in the genes, I'm telling you."

Bobby honked his horn. I ran to the bathroom to check myself out in case we saw Devon and Erica. Not bad. I was liking my haircut more and more. When I got to the street, the girls were indeed there. Devon in the passenger seat next to Bobby, and Erica in the back with NP.

It was the first summer Devon's family came out, which was why we'd never seen them before. According to my mother, Devon's father used to come out sometimes in the '6os, so the family had some bona fides, but that was way before my time. I had finally gotten a gander at the famous twosome when NP brought them by the ice-cream store to show them off. I had the usual disreputable smears on my Jonni Waffle T-shirt and was manhandling a sundae. Good timing.

The answer was obvious: Erica. I'd listened to the Devon versus Erica debate for a long time, managing ever-morphing portraits of them in my mind, each new opinion or report sliding their features around, adding and subtracting baby fat, tinting the flesh. Depending on your hardwired tastes—a little light or a little dark, plump or lean, preppy or an iota less preppy—you sided with one cousin or the other. (Am I talking about chicken? If you delete the preppy stuff, I mean. I have chicken on my mind today.) Erica was skinny, like me. We'd make a nice skinny couple, never taking up too much room and passing the days discussing our spiffy metabolisms.

I crouched so I could see everybody in the car.

" 'Sup, Benji?" NP said.

"Hi, Benji," Erica said.

"Ben," I said.

"What?"

"What's up?" This was Bobby.

"Just hanging."

"Your dad barbecuing?"

"Mr. Cooper makes the best barbecue," NP informed Erica, tapping her forearm.

"He's a real pistol," Bobby told Devon.

"He's a trip," NP said.

Erica said, "Oh."

"So what . . . ?" I didn't know who to talk to. I'd made plans with Bobby, but I wanted to maintain an easygoing manner for Devon and Erica's benefit so that I looked like a regular guy that people wanted to be friends with, and part of that entailed acknowledging NP's presence, even though NP never should have been there in the first place. I was supposed to be in the back with Erica. My eyes jumped from face to face as I bobbed between the windows.

"Look," Bobby said, "we're going to have to catch up with you later, okay?"

"We're going to the ocean," Devon said, bored. Yeah, forget Devon. Devon was totally second-tier, especially since Erica had laughed at my joke the other day, bonding me permanently to her. See, we were at Conca D'Oro and NP pulled out his wad of Jonni Waffle pay, riffling through the bills like a big shot, so I said, "What are you, Phil Rizzuto from the Money Store?" and Erica laughed. Her smile was incredible, so incredible that my hand shot up to cover my braces. In my book, we'd been married for years. NP was sitting in my seat.

"You going to be around later?" Bobby asked.

"Yeah."

"I'll drive by later," he said. "Try to save me a piece of that good chicken."

"Bye, Benji," Erica said, her words barely escaping the window before they pulled away.

Tock, thunk, rasp, poomp.

No, it wasn't possible to hear that all the way out in the street. I rocked my heels on the curb. I didn't have to turn around. I could've walked to town for a slice, picked up a science-fiction novel at Canio's and taken it to Mashashimuet Park. Checked out the developments to see who else was around. But I didn't. This was where I lived.

"You sticking around?" my father asked.

I nodded. The trays sat on the table next to the grill, the chicken parts in formation on the aluminum like fighter planes waiting for takeoff. He whistled "Lady" by Kenny Rogers. Maybe the cloud had passed. He'd had a good time with Mr. Turner and Mrs. Russell, and with Mr. Baxter earlier. I decided to play the odds. I went inside, back to *The Road Warrior*, the first batch sizzling behind me.

I'd watched the movie so many times it was shameful. I saw every smashup and crash-up and spinout before it happened, but still got pumped like I was back in the East Hampton theater seeing it for the first time. An alert went off in my head, warning me that this was as bad as comic books, but I put off making a ruling on the matter. Call the movie sci-fi or fantasy or what have you. Now that I'm older, I put it up there with Beckett as pure realism. But then, most days I'm up to my neck in sand.

My father stood in the doorway. "What do you want? A breast and a wing? A bunch of wings? I'll do those first."

"I don't care."

"That's not an answer. What do you want?"

"Some wings."

I knew white kids in school whose parents didn't let them watch TV, these urchins with scabbed knees who always had their hands out for crumbs when you mentioned Potsie or Chachi. Still meet white people who crow, "We don't let our kids watch television." Can't say I've ever heard a black person say that. Maybe I should travel in different circles. Perhaps one day, as the forces of racial progress transform every corner of our nation—can you hear it, the inspirational "overcome" music?—we will cross the color line in TV prohibitions. What black person didn't like laughing at the shenanigans white people got up to on TV? White people were black camp, our native kitsch; white sitcoms magnified the campiness to grotesque proportions. Hug. Talk it out. I'm here for you. What kind of shit was that?

You could only laugh. Sitcom white folk, movie-of-the-week white folk were our coon show. Judge's Daughter Hooked on Pot, Teenage Runaway Sent to Reform School—these earnest cautionary tales played like pure vaudeville, especially the opening minutes, with the montage sequences establishing the Perfect Home, the Perfect Family. Like, they ate meals together. Come on, now. And then the puzzled reactions once the crisis boiled over. "I found this in your room. Where did you get it?" "I got a call from school today. They say you haven't been in weeks. What's going on?" Things went down differently in our house. These were transmissions from a distant star.

My father stuck his head inside. "Do you want barbecue sauce or no barbecue sauce?"

"I don't care."

"It's a simple question. An idiot could answer it. Do you or do you not want barbecue sauce on your chicken?"

"No."

"I'm going to put a little on some pieces, because I know people like that."

The Cosby Show cornered us, forcing us to reconsider our position. That was some version of ourselves on the screen there. After so long. My mother told us that when she was growing up, whenever a black face appeared on television, you ran through the house to tell everyone, and they dropped what they were doing and gathered around the RCA. If you had time, you hit the phone to spread the word. You could plan your day around it—*Jet* kept a list of upcoming appearances of black people on television, no matter how small. Nat King Cole, Diahann Carroll in *Julia*. Make some room on the couch to verify that you actually existed. My generation had *Good Times* (six seasons) and *Baby, I'm Back* (one-fourth of a season), shows that honestly depicted how the black community lived in this country. Like, what to do when the heat goes off in the projects in the middle of winter. How to sort things out when your deadbeat husband returns after seven years with a jaunty "Baby, I'm back!" Hence the title. The practical matters of the black day-to-day, don'cha know. Me and Reggie and Elena tuned in, making room on the couch to verify that we didn't exist, while my father restrained himself from kicking in the set: That's not how we live.

Cosby presented a problem. What did it mean when millionaires said, "I'm going for a little bit of that Cosby thang"? Standing there in some fucked-up sweater. Hungering for validation after all they'd accomplished. If a sitcom had this much influence, then there was nothing to make fun of. Such things were possible. The box contained things of value. Where did that leave us when we looked around our own houses? The reception was terrible.

In the end what happened was, my father put some macaroni salad on a paper plate and as he walked back out to the fire, the plate flipped over and the macaroni salad fell on the deck. I saw him standing there looking at it when he called out, "Benji!"

I jumped up so fast I got a head rush.

"Go tell your mother I need her," he said. He turned to the grill and stuck the tongs into the smoke.

I walked slowly. I breathed loudly through my nose. My heart was pumping fast, thanks to the adrenaline, but when the blood reached my head it turned to lead so that everything above my shoulders was unbearably heavy. At the bottom of the stairs, my mother and her friends sat in their familiar circle, with magazines in their laps and plastic cups by their ankles. Wide wet circles bloomed on the backs of their beach chairs, their afternoon swim drying in the sun. Mrs. Burnett was telling a story when they looked up and saw me. My mother shooed a horsefly from her foot.

I gave a general hello to the ladies in the beach chairs and said, "Mom, Dad has a question for you."

She looked at her legs to reaffirm that she was good and settled, and sighed. She stood. "Probably wants to know where the other bag of charcoal is," she said.

Her friends nodded and looked at one another.

We walked up, me ahead walking faster. I wanted to get inside before she got there.

"What happened?" she asked, seeing the macaroni salad.

"I thought I didn't want you buying these cheap paper plates anymore," my father said. "Look at this. Why didn't you listen to me? What do you think I am? You treat me like I'm some kind of goddamned pussy."

"I went to King Kullen—they were out of them."

" 'Out of them.' You should have gone earlier. You were sitting around here all morning on the phone, talking horseshit with your friends. You should have had your ass in the car on the way to King Kullen. True or not true?"

"I had a lot to do today."

"True or not true?"

"True."

She backed away, toward the living room. To keep her friends from hearing. As if they had not heard. He advanced. She was in the living room. Then he was, too.

My mother had been playing the odds. Earlier in the summer, he'd thrown a fit over the poor quality of Dixie brand paper plates and banned their use. In his extensive battery of tests, they couldn't support the weight of chicken and a side of macaroni salad or Ore-Ida Tater Tots. They buckled. Moisture quickly crippled them. You required three, possibly four to achieve adequate firmness. My mother had played the odds that a month later he'd forgotten about his ban and it was safe to buy the most available brand of paper plate. It was one order among many, after all. So she gambled. I saw how it went—my mother nervous while buying the Dixie plates a few weeks after the first incident and holding her breath when he started up the grill. Nothing happened and she relaxed. We'd been using the Dixie paper plates again for a while. Maybe she felt a twinge the first few times, but now it was almost August. Surely it was safe. We all played the odds in our little ways. Sometimes just walking into a room was playing the odds. Eventually the odds caught up to you.

They were inside the house with me. After the quick flash of relief that it was someone else's turn today, I had to face practical matters. Other times, I could close the windows and try to contain it, but it was an Azurest Afternoon. Everyone was out. People coming up from the beach or the street, walking along the side of the house—there were too many, too close. I couldn't leave the house because I had to act like nothing was going on. I turned into a rock. I focused on the TV. I turned up the volume. The more I concentrated, the less I could see. The movie spoke of mayhem. There were hunters. There were pursued. They killed each other in the winding-down world.

"We talked about this. These plates are cheap. I need the plastic ones. That's all I ask. I'm trying to cook for my son. Did you go to Schiavoni's?"

"Schiavoni's doesn't carry that kind. All they have is those."

"If Schiavoni's doesn't have them then you should keep looking until you find them. I'm trying to grill here. What am I supposed to put the food on? This flimsy shit? I spend all this time—why can't you do what you're supposed to do? Are you telling me that there's nowhere on this island that has plastic plates? What about South Hampton?"

"I don't have time for that."

"You have time to sit on your fat ass and talk to your friends. 'Yeah, yeah, uh-huh, uh-huh.' You were sitting on your ass just now."

"James," my mother said.

This was how my mother disappeared, word by word. She got older by the second, that magical Sag Harbor effect fading. Something happened to my mother in her life that she never defended or protected herself. That she never defended or protected us, when it was our turn. I don't know what it was. I suppose it was the same thing that prevented me from defending or protecting her, once I was old enough. I kept my mouth shut and watched TV.

8 Most Common Silences in Benji's House
1. Just Poutin'
2. Really Wounded
3. Apprehension of One's Weakness
4. To Avoid Further Provocations
5. Indexing of Grudges
6. Preamble to Explosion/Eruption
7. Stunned in the Aftermath & Reeling from the Ferocity of the Attack, Especially When You Hadn't Really Done Anything
8. To Accompany a Furtive There-There Glance of Sympathy

"You think you'd be sitting down there talking all that horseshit if I wasn't doing what I'm supposed to? All week long slaving for this family. I'm not like all these other pussies out here. I work my ass off. I don't ask for anything except I don't want cheap shit in my house." I saw a head appear above the beach stairs, a torso in a cherry-colored polo, and then whoever it was backed away.

I burrowed, I burrowed deep into *The Road Warrior*. No words. Just cars smashing, metal crunching into metal, bullets and arrows piercing flesh. Grease and blood. We had reached the saddest part of the movie in my book, the death of the Road Warrior's dog. He was named Dog. A mutt, the Road Warrior's only friend. They shared expired dog food out of rusted cans. Nothing else to eat in the wasteland. The Road Warrior gobbled down the gray paste with a smile, as if it was the best thing he'd ever tasted, and Dog nosed after the stuff at the bottom. Together they eliminated their enemies, Dog jumping out to startle the punk holding the crossbow at the right moment so that the Road Warrior gained the advantage. He was a cool dog to have, Dog. He had your back. I wouldn't mind having a dog like that.

Then I remembered that I hated dogs. Because dogs hated me. My whole life they chased me like I was made out of kibble. They bared their teeth and slick pink gums, excavating harrowing sounds from deep in their bellies. Big dogs, small dogs. They smelled it on me. Fear, some kind of weakness. They sensed the part of me that relished being crushed and destroyed. It was always in there, the goblin mind, salivating and rubbing its claws together, waiting for the dinner bell announcing it was time to feast on my humiliations. They barked and snarled at me with the brute understanding that this was all that I wanted and deserved.

"Now clean that up and get me some goddamned plastic plates."

A few years ago, me and Reggie went exploring on our bikes. We'd run out of places to make ours, so we struck out where it had never occurred to us to go. We went down Division Street, in the white part of town. We didn't know where it went. We just knew we were sick of our old places and tired circuits around Sag Harbor.

It's a small town. Once you're off the highway, you can go for a long time without a car driving by or someone coming out of their house to get the mail. We only went a few blocks, but even one avenue off our map felt like miles. Reggie and me smiled at each other. Pedaling off into adventure.

The Doberman galloped out into the street and we were paralyzed. It stopped two feet away, muscles vivid under the skin, bright yellow teeth snapping. Time stopped. Its paws scraped on the asphalt in its furious half steps. I thought it was going to rip us to shreds. Doberman pinschers had replaced the German shepherd as the most fearsome dog around, in those quaint days before the pit bull hit the big time. We'd heard the stories. It was ready to leap up and tear out our throats, first me and then my brother. There was no one around. No one called him off. No one cared.

We didn't say anything. We backed up a slow inch at a time. For the first few feet the Doberman stayed with us, continuing his threats. Eventually he reached the end of his territory and stopped. We left him there in the middle of the street, us going backward on our bikes, paddling our feet on the pavement, until we got around the corner. We went home and gulped down a lot of Hi-C to replace what we'd sweated out, and told the story of Division Street to our freaked-out friends, who were envious that we had something to talk about. They said, "Wow."

When our parents came out that weekend—this was when Elena was in charge during the week—our father told us to get in the car and show him where it happened. We were scared until Reggie pointed out that the dog couldn't get us through the car. We kept the windows rolled up and locked the doors just in case.

"You see that there," he said.

"What?" I waited for the Doberman to come loping out.

"That." We hadn't seen the lawn jockey the first time. The little midget stood in the middle of the lawn holding a gold ring, grinning in his bright red getup. Shining, well-polished.

"That's how they train it to attack black people," he explained.

"That cracker in there tosses raw meat by the lawn jockey, the dog eats there every day and then when it sees black people it thinks, Food. You're lucky it didn't tear you apart."

I looked at Reggie and Reggie looked at me. Dag.

"It's not the dog's fault. It's how it was trained." He stepped on the gas. "I want you to stay away from that house," he said. "I don't want you coming here again."

The *Road Warrior*'s score thundered now that the yelling was over. I turned down the volume.

"Look at this," he said, holding up the first batch. "I love it!" He transferred the chicken into a glass bowl. "I'd grill on the moon if I could," he said wistfully. And Mars and Saturn and beyond. Is there grilling in Heaven? Who knows what angels eat. But I know there's barbecuing in hell, and its your very guts and inner stuff blackening before your eyes.

"You ready for some good chicken?" he asked.

"Yeah," I said.

We were a made-for-TV family and when he called "Action!" we hit our marks and delivered our lines like pros. The scripts were all the same. We had the formula down.

Mrs. Gardner returned to use the facilities. "Where's Gail?" she asked, knocking the sand off her feet before she stepped inside.

He didn't answer so I said, "She had to run to the store. She'll be right back."

She nodded and went into the bathroom. When she came out, he stopped her. "Girl, you best take a wing if you know what's good for you," he said.

"Mmmm," she said. "I was hoping to get a piece of that barbecue." She grabbed a wing and topped off her white wine before rejoining the ladies on the beach.

For all his fear that people were watching all the time, that people will talk about you unless you're vigilant about what they see, no one was watching at all. No one cares about what goes on in other people's houses. The grubby dramas. It was just us. The soundstage was empty, the production lot scheduled for demolition. They'd turned off the electricity long ago. We delivered our lines in the darkness.

"Here you go," he said, handing me a quadruple-reinforced paper plate of chicken wings.

You have a fucked-up haircut and everyone knows you have a fucked-up haircut. But no one says anything. You don't know you have a fucked-up haircut, or know it and can't admit it. Until one day you face the fact that you have a fucked-up haircut and you get a new one and everyone says, Good job, as if they'd been waiting for it. As if they cared.

"How is it?" he asked. He held the next tray of chicken in his hand, one foot inside the house and the other on the deck.

I took a bite. It was like biting into sand. The juices had boiled away or splattered the coals, leaving these dried-up shreds sticking to bone. I looked at the other wings on the plate in my lap. They were charred and shrunken, the lot of them, crumbling into black specks. I chewed up the sand and swallowed.

"It's great," I said.

Breathing Tips of Great American Beatboxers

THE HIGHLIGHT OF THE SUMMER WAS THE U.T.F.O.— Lisa Lisa concert at Bayside. Lisa Lisa and Cult Jam headlined, thanks to their crossover hit "I Wonder if I Take You Home," but U.T.F.O. was the real draw in our neck of the woods. They'd ruled the winter with "Roxanne, Roxanne," a lamentation about a fly girl who wouldn't give them the time of day. In the tradition of the Village People, they employed theme personalities. The Educated Rapper boasted of his capacious intellect ("She needs a guy like me, with a High IQ"), Doctor Ice wooed her with his knowledge of the medical world ("Dermatology is treatment of the skin ... There's anesthesiology, ophthalmology, internal medicine and plastic surgery, orthopedic surgery and path-o-logy"), while the Kangol Kid put his faith in . . . his Kangol, though frankly one should never underestimate the power of accessories to help one stand out in the crowd. Mix Master Ice, their DJ, kept silent, preferring "to speak with his hands," as they said in his milieu.

A young lady calling herself Roxanne Shanté released an answer record called *The Real Roxanne*, a Rashomon-style revision of her dealings with "dictionary breath" and his friends. Answer records to answer records escalated matters, with Roxanne's "parents" chiming in, her big "brothers," far-flung second cousins, and the occasional bystander, culminating in "Roxanne's a Man," which, like a hip-hop Hiroshima, stunned all involved and effectively ended the conflict. In revisiting the Roxanne Wars of the mid-'80s, I know I run the risk of stirring the deep and fierce emotions associated with that unfortunate episode, but I feel the background is necessary to explain our excitement. U.T.F.O. (Un Touchable Force Organization) represented teenage striving, youthful perseverance against the odds, and goofball personas that made our own stabs at reinvention look like genius. Bayside advertised the concert in *Dan's Papers* all summer, so by August we were in a bit of a froth.

You had to be eighteen to get into the club. It was a former roller rink, a kinda sketchy operation where the skates squished unwholesomely moist on your feet and the squirrelly DJ often disappeared, putting *Off the Wall* on repeat and slipping out the back. Since the revamp, we'd been barred. The more adventurous among us tried all summer to breach the walls in a string of legendary failures involving strategic facial hair, studied nonchalance, and some inspired business about the Make-A-Wish Foundation. It was sad to see Clive and Nick get into character and shuffle up to the velvet rope only to twist back to Earth with melted-off feathers. If they got in, it was like all of us getting in. When they failed, we accepted our portion of shame.

By the time the big day rolled around, the only person with a real shot was NP, who'd been bribing Marlon the Bouncer for weeks with the Long Wharf's top currency—ice cream. Marlon came into Jonni Waffle a couple of times a night, NP ducking supervisors as he fixed him a cup with a conspiratorial nod. Marlon resumed his post, slowly eating his Banana Mint as a gaggle of preening Hamptonites queued up for inspection. He sucked on the tiny spoon with a pensive air while appraising those before him, some nice theater that lent his judgments the air of demented caprice.

"I know I'm getting in—I set him *up*!" NP told us.

"Better hope Freddie isn't on that night," Marcus pointed out. "He'd be like, Nigger, please, Nigger Please."

Freddie was this big bruiser from Bridgehampton, known for his martial-arts expertise. In addition to working Bayside, he bounced some nights at the Reef, a club on 27 where Marcus had worked earlier in the summer during one of his short-lived gigs. ("The barback said I stole two bottles of peach schnapps, but I was framed.") "He has this case in his trunk where he keeps his nunchucks and sai and throwing stars," Marcus warned us. "One night Freddie was working the door and this redneck got up in his face so he busted out his sai like *boom-bip!* and sent that bitch into traction." Adding, "High all the time on coke, too." All I knew about him was that when he ordered his Orange Sherbet, he never tipped, avoiding the sight of the tip cup as if it contained pictures of his pre-dumbbell, ninety-nine-pound weakling self.

"Marlon's working that night," NP said, "I already checked. I'm not worried."

I NEVER TRIED TO GET IN. My daily routine already generated plenty of embarrassment—why get greedy? But as August got closer, I fixated on the concert, drawing up plans for one, determined sortie. Not being particularly tall, and possessing a prepubescent mien I found impossible to shake, my idea was to wear some preppie camouflage to help me fit in with the stream of East End swells— no mummy-bandage Chuck Taylors or Flipper T-shirt—and hold my advance-purchase ticket as if it were identity papers at a border crossing. Since I'd come over time to believe that no one was particularly interested in what I had to say, I tended to mumble or talk fast in an attempt to help people more easily ignore me, so I practiced adamant phrasings of facts like "I bought this ticket" and "I paid money for this ticket." I also crossed my fingers that the no-doubt-complicated refund process represented a bureaucratic hassle the bouncer didn't want to get involved in. That's all I had going.

The night before the concert, I walked up to Bobby's to begin the hunt. A normal person would've picked me up at my house, but Bobby, like so many before him, was lost in the moral fog of first-car ownership. Apparently I have issues in this area—why did a change in circumstance mean a change in character? It seemed a brand of weakness. His recent promotion probably had something to do with it. He'd been kicked upstairs, from Little Bobby to just Bobby. Given the strict hierarchy of age classes out in Sag, nomenclature problems arose from time to time. If kids in two different age groups had the same name then, logically, one was Little and one was Big. Big Bobby was in my sister's group, a few years older than us. Since his day of birth, our Bobby had been saddled with the Little sign hanging around his neck.

There was one easy rule: if there was a Big X, and a Little X, they had to have night-and-day personalities. Big Bobby was a jerk, no dispute. He cut in line at the video games in town, whet the sadistic aspects of his personality on Marcus with cool diligence, and was known to rip the heads off Han Solo action figures and eat them. I had actually witnessed this last despicable act, and it haunts me still. But Big Bobby had stopped coming out, you see. Working in the city, whatever, so Bobby was unqualified, just Bobby, and free to unfetter his character. Bygone Little Bobby, he was like me—a nice kid, conveniently invisible, beloved by aunts and uncles, perpetually pre-wince in anticipation of having his plump and inviting cheeks pinched by some elderly relative with boundary issues. Now, he could be a jerk. It wouldn't have surprised me if there was another Bobby playing in the sand of the Sag beach, thus crowning our Bobby Big Bobby, and this hypothetical tyke donning the nice-kid mantle. Nature abhors a vacuum.

As I passed the Sag Harbor Hills beach, the stragglers were folding their beach chairs and whipping the sand from their blankets. The gnats gathered in bobbing clouds and in the long grass the chittering insects saluted twilight. It was getting dark earlier, the endless summer days no longer so patient with our attempts to cram it all in.

I climbed the steps up to Bobby's house. His grandfather let me in. He hadn't shaved, a thin white fur covering his cheeks, and he looked harrowed in his faded blue Morgan Stanley T-shirt, a souvenir from his daughter's job. I didn't know he'd returned—two weeks earlier, he'd had some kind of "health scare" and gone back to the city to get checked out. He slid the screen door wide, smiling, but I noticed a new, gingerly quality in his movements, like he had broken glass in his slippers.

He told me Bobby would be right down. He asked after my parents, and Reggie, and then said, "Been doing any fishing?"

"Not this summer, no." Six years ago, he'd taken me and Reggie and Bobby out to the Long Wharf to fish for snapper and porgies, calling a huddle to share his method for threading the bait securely through the hooks. "If the eye pops out, you know it's good and tight." Except for night bluefishing off Montauk, which was an excuse to stay up until 4 AM and drink seven-ounce Millers, I hadn't fished since that day.

"Your grandfather loved to fish out here. We used to go out all the time on that little boat he had back then."

I nodded.

"It's nice to see the young people following in the tradition. I know he would have liked to see you out there, dropping a line like we used to."

"I like fishing," I said. I heard Bobby thumping around upstairs so I sent a telepathic blast to make him hurry. My grandparents died before I was born and I didn't know how to feel when people talked about them. I had this thing in my head where they sat me down and laid it all out, the way things work, how to move, what to be, but I'd never get that information now. Except the hard way. I picked a burr off my socks, but didn't know where to put it, so I just held it in my hand.

"That's the beauty of coming out here," Bobby's grandfather said. "Having this place. People like your grandfather working hard to make something for his family, and passing it down to your generation." He suddenly realized how the dark had crept in around us and he groped under the lampshades. "You're lucky, you know that?"

"Yes."

"To have all of this."

"Yes."

When Bobby and I got in the car, we tried to come up with a plan. Everybody was working that night except for us and Nick, but Nick had gone to the city to buy records. (Sounds, the East Hampton music store, didn't cater to us unless we wanted something Top 40.) We needed beer. The quest for beer, with its daily intrigues, reversals, and cliff-hangers, had become our favorite subplot. How to get it, who to buy it, where to drink it, starting all over again the next day. Our tall friends weren't around. We'd drunk a few of my father's beers already that week, and I didn't want to push it. It was a long shot, but we finally decided to hit town, and then the other key places, like the 7-Eleven in South Hampton, to see if any amenable parties materialized. Like one of my sister's group, or Orrin. Orrin was this older white hippie guy who oozed around the towns, perpetually en route to or in between odd jobs and escapades, and he'd buy a six-pack for you if you listened to his latest sad story of "I was just minding my own business when." He smelled like a backed-up sewer, but it was worth it.

"They have these place mats at the Corner Bar," Bobby told me as we broke out of Ninevah, "that have the history of the Hamptons written on them and they said that Sagaponac is an Indian word meaning 'the land of the big brown nuts.' I was eating a hamburger and just busted out laughing."

"That's funny."

"I was like, 'I got your big brown nuts right here.' "

"Your sacadiliac," I said.

He looked over at me. I told him, "Like in 'The Message' by Grandmaster Flash and the Furious Five, when Melle Mel raps"—I tried to get it right—" 'Neon King Kong standin' on my back, Can't turn around, broke my sacadiliac.' His nut sack. He's saying everything's so tough, it's like getting kicked in the balls."

"I never knew what he was talking about there."

"Yeah, well."

Bobby turned into Azurest and informed me that he was going to drive by Devon's house to see if she was back from her family outing. "If she's there, I gotta give you the boot, dude." I'd just dragged myself to his house. I thought: Chaotic Evil. I hadn't done that in a while, tripping down the alignments. During my big D&D phase (October 1981–April 1983), I'd taken the game's classification system to heart, doling out alignments to the world. See, according to *The Player's Handbook*, people and monsters can be broken down by their inner natures, with Good, Evil, and Neutral on one axis, and Lawful and Chaotic on the other. Lawful Good, for example, described a knight's dutiful temperament, and Lawful Evil the personality of a dictator or evil king—they had an order they obeyed, sticking by their rules whether it called for them to save people's asses or cut off their heads. Neutrals bent toward Good or Evil depending on whether they dabbled in the occasional altruistic act or had a penchant for stabbing people in the back. Robin Hood was a Chaotic Good type, lawless and unpredictable but lending a helping hand, and Chaotic Evil was the banner of twisted prankster, like the Joker in *Batman* comics. Or guys with their first cars.

I took this taxonomy seriously. It just made sense: people had alignments, an essential nature. If you could see who and what they were, you'd be better equipped to deal with them. Before my sister became a potential girlfriend and they had to treat us better, the Older Boys of Sag were Chaotic Evil through and through. Coming across a group of them hanging out on the corner of Terry or Milton, you had to steel yourself. They'd say, "Nice bike! Can I see it for a second?" and then book up the hill, seesawing on your tiny Huffy, leaving you in the midst of their howling cronies. You'd discover it dumped on your front lawn hours later with grass smeared in the pedals, just when you were about to rat them out. Marcus was their plaything, abused and disrespected. They tripped him and sent him sprawling into the sharp gravel, pissed in his Coke, stomped his kites. Chaotic Evil, like I said.

The first week of eighth grade, I leaned over to Andy Stern in the middle of second-period Science and whispered, "Don't you think Dr. Nadler is Lawful Evil?" Yes, Dr. Nadler, the dragon waiting deep in the cave of junior high. We'd heard the tales for years, and now here he was, with wild red eyes and scaly armor. A late lab report knocked your grade off five points, five points that could only be earned back through extra credit. An unyielding faith in a bogus system. Lawful Evil.

"What?" Andy asked, wincing.

"Lawful Evil, man."

"Shush!" He looked around for eavesdroppers and ignored me the rest of class. This was my first indication that I lagged in lame/not-lame knowledge, what could be said when girls or cool kids were around, and what couldn't. Mentioning D&D, you might as well fart while playing seven minutes in heaven, not that I'd ever played seven minutes in heaven, but I had spent some time thinking about it and it had occurred to me that farting was something you shouldn't do, if the occasion arose. I'd have to get used to it, falling behind, because this was no temporary condition. The guy dropping off the weekly pamphlets outlining the shifting teenage codes and edicts skipped my house, or someone stole them from my doorstep before I got up.

I was undeterred. Taken with the reassuring clarity of the alignments, I didn't stop with people, proceeding on to label inanimate objects, abstract systems, and states of being. A nap—Lawful Good, certainly. The Assassination of Betamax at the hands of dastardly VHS—that was Lawful Evil all over, for what was capitalism but malevolent design exercising its power? Getting up for school was Neutral Evil by my sights, the blank slate of the day with its possibility for fun or misery Neutral in itself, the Evil creeping in with the school thing, being forced to play my part in the social apparatus. I was a dork, not a cog.

D&D had few other real-life applications, except as a means of perpetuating virginity and in its depiction of existence as a never-ending series of grim adventures in dungeons. I rued the former, embraced the latter as an elegant metaphor. (Or, in my language of the time, "Yeah, man, that really sums it up.") Eventually I forgot about the alignment thing. I lost my taste for nuance once I became a teenager. Nuance got you nowhere. Either/or was where it was at.

We hit Meredith Avenue. "NP's going to get me and the girls into U.T.F.O.," Bobby said. "They have to give it up after that."

"Right," I said.

The lights in Devon's house were out, and Bobby drove by without comment. The hunt was on. Halfway up Bay Street, we rolled up on this guy walking back from town under the weeping willows. It was dark, but I thought I knew him. Our eyes locked when we passed each other, and even though he didn't recognize me, I asked Bobby to turn around. "That's my uncle," I said. This went against my strict rules for avoiding all but the most inevitable interactions with grown-ups, but for some reason I wanted to say hi. I think I wanted to show off that my friend had a car, that we'd entered the next level.

"Maybe he can buy us beer," Bobby said.

"Are you crazy? He'll tell on us." Everyone over the age of thirty was in cahoots in my book, Telexing reports to the command center so that the colored pin on the wall map held my current position. "Suspect is walking gawkily in a south-southeasterly direction."

"Uncle Nelson," I said. "It's Ben. Benji."

He peered into the car. "Where's Reggie?"

"He's working at Burger King."

Uncle Nelson nodded. He'd settled into a bearish pudge since I'd last seen him, his polo shirt tight on his chest and exposing a centimeter of belly when he moved. His hair thinned in the same pattern as his father's, the gray retreating from a shiny atoll of scalp. I'd always liked Uncle Nelson, rascally Uncle Nelson with his shitty luck and wide, eager face. He was my mother's cousin off some branch I couldn't keep track of, the important part being that his parents and my mother's parents had been part of the first Sag wave. Mention his name and heads shook, hands wrung. My mother's family was proper, well mannered, raised right. Uncle Nelson was "bad," in their classification system. "That's where Nelson drove up on the lawn," my mother reminded us whenever we went down Sagg Road, in tribute to that summer scandal of yore. He'd dropped out of dental school (the horror), played house with That Spanish Woman (cringe, cringe), and worst of all, Moved to California, which was code for smoking pot and group sex. All this was in the '60s and early '70s, before I was aware; I received these stories as pure history, When Uncle Nelson Sank the Chris-Craft up there with Washington Crossing the Delaware and Jimi Hendrix Choking on His Own Vomit, of equal import. I hadn't seen him in years. It had been a while since he came out to make the rounds. Chaotic Good, I would've said—bucking the bourgie system, but daring and bighearted.

"What are you boys getting up to?"

"Just going for a drive," I said, as if I were some South Hampton fossil taking out his Model T. "You staying over at the Yellow House?"

His eyes dipped and he said, "I'm hanging out at Eddie Baxter's this weekend, seeing what he's up to. But they're putting the grandkids to bed, so I decided to go out for a little bit. I'm too old for—"

"Do you think you can buy us some beer?" Bobby asked.

"I'll buy you some beer," Uncle Nelson said, in a blink. "Just don't tell your mother, Benji. I know I'm her favorite cousin, but she'd still wring my neck."

Bobby'd asked the only old-time Sag Harbor guy who'd do it for us, as if recognizing Uncle Nelson's mischievous bent right off. I wanted to punch him in his face, like the old days. I think he wanted word to get back to his parents, to prove that despite accepting the car (and gas money, despite his constant tithing of us), he could still bring them misery. Bring, in fact, a new kind of misery.

I offered Uncle Nelson the front seat but he wrinkled his face. I remembered the time he squeezed in with us at the kids' table during a family reunion, begging, "Lemme in here, I'm one of you guys." We laughed, and he entertained us for the rest of the meal, clowning around. Off behind him, his father grimaced as he watched Uncle Nelson's big legs bouncing on the tiny chair.

He leaned forward, jamming his elbows into the front seats. "You just have to do me a favor and take me around the Hills when we're done."

"Bet."

"Uncle Nelson used to have an MG," I said. There was a picture in the Hempstead House of him leaning on the hood of this emerald Speed Racer vehicle. Cool as hell. He was wearing hip visor shades and had a beatnik V of hair shrouding his lip. No, not exactly in line with the standard Sag Harbor alignment.

"Fresh," Bobby said.

"That was the best time," Uncle Nelson said, "taking that baby up these roads. Getting up to no good." He sat back, smacking his hands on the upholstery. "Long time ago, boy," he said. "Now it's your turn to do all that stuff we used to do." It was quiet back there as we zipped up the turnpike, and I kept my mouth shut in case I said something kidlike, and he changed his mind.

After we went to 7-Eleven and came back and dropped him off, Bobby and me went over to my house and drank the beer and watched *Hooper* and *Terror Train*. "That's the killer, right?" he asked after every suspicious twitch, and I said, "Keep watching." We didn't stay up late. We had a big day tomorrow.

I WORKED THE NEXT AFTERNOON. Change had come to Jonni Waffle over the weeks, autumnal telegrams to remind us of the fleetingness of the season. The new Soft Serv machine arrived, a single nozzle delivering chocolate, vanilla, or strawberry with the press of a button. It buzzed all day with an unholy power. Jonni Waffle HQ sent over a box of T-shirts with the new logo—a smiling cone with spindly arms and legs. More than one customer remarked that it looked like a dancing dildo. I didn't know what a dildo was, so I had to ask. The customers were always right in Jonni Waffle. And finally, the cousins were gone. Martine fired them after they'd robbed one too many Reddi-wip cans of its N_2O, causing the white liquid to pour over the cones and boats instead of producing a handsome, vertical swirl. Yeah, Meg and Marsha had developed quite a whippets problem to cope with the stress of life in the waffle-cone trenches, and polite society rendered its punishment. My elbow tingled occasionally in phantom arousal and to this day remains charged, a shameful erogenous zone.

Taking their shifts was Jen, a redheaded local girl and student of New York State's labor laws, especially with regard to the duration and frequency of breaks. She declared, "I'm going on my break," as if daring the manager to stop her, and when no one said anything, because no one was paying attention, she added, "We're allowed two ten-minute breaks per shift!" before storming away. For some reason I can't fathom, she was a tip magnet, which was fortunate because we divvied up the tip cup evenly, a nice system for someone like me, who sent customers' change plummeting down their pockets.

D-day, I was on with Jen and NP. The start of the shift was so uneventful, I almost forgot it was a weekday. Then Jen said, "The Boat People are here."

The Boat People, done picking Main Street clean, came our way to continue their destruction. What I knew about Connecticut could fit in a thimble, or more properly, a sugar cone or blue eight-ounce plastic serving dish, but I did know this: every weekday morning, residents of that fine state boarded a ferry for an outing to the Hamptons. That the boat didn't sink is a wonder, given the stupendous human mass that poured down the gangplanks onto the Long Wharf at noon. They raided the curio shops, stopped traffic as the slow herd of them meandered across the street, dawdled in glassy-eyed pleasure at the kitschy whaling paraphernalia and WASP accoutrements in the windows. They stopped to eat. They rose from the tables in unison, greasy napkins falling from their laps like a flock of doves in sudden, communal heart attack. They strolled back to the ferry up Main Street, up the asphalt of the Long Wharf, patting their bellies, which gurgled with fish-and-chips and fried clams and battered cod, the bottom halves of their bodies busy with digestion and their brains full of that peculiar melancholy that marks the end of an adventure or of an exploit winding down. Then they smelled it. The waffle-cone aroma dancing on the sea breeze, and they were renewed, stampeding into Jonni Waffle with their tongues hanging over their lips.

Boat People rushes were brief—no one wanted to be left at the end of the wharf, waving at the disappearing ship—but the departure-time anxiety made the customers all the more boorish and bullying. It was overwhelming. I reminded myself that it would soon be over. The assault had a finite length. I used that rationalization a lot in those days. When things wound down, I drifted into one of my midscoop space-outs. Sometimes when you had your head down in the vats, time stopped. The swirling white mist stalled in the air, hanging like ribbons. All sound dropped out, the whirring of the blender and the radio, and even the static-y buzz of your own thoughts. I don't know where I went during those spells. They only lasted a few moments yet they contained a little scoop of the infinite, a waffle-perfumed eternity.

I heard a knocking on the glass and assumed it was the customer scolding me for scooping the wrong flavor, but it was Erica, frantically waving hi once I looked up.

"You're really working in there!"

I was still partial to Erica's charms, but had put aside my fantasies of her dumping NP and then in the exhilaration of her new freedom realizing my virtues. It didn't seem like the NP-Erica unit was going anywhere, making it hard to look at her sometimes, especially when she had her hair in a ponytail and her face became a still life of teenage promise, dark and benevolent. If I had a coffee shop or dry cleaners, I'd put her head shot on the wall by the register even though she wasn't a celebrity. NP'd stopped giving us updates on whether he had touched her tit or whatever, adopting a reserve and circumspection we'd never seen in him before. His elaborate yarns dried up, at least when it came to stories about girls. Is tamed the word? He came out from the back of the store and we took our breaks, Jen nodding with proud, motherly encouragement.

Outside, Devon waited with Bobby. Devon wore a blue polka-dot bikini top, khaki shorts, and red toenail polish; Erica wore a red polka-dot bikini top, khaki shorts, and blue toenail polish. It had been a busy morning. Devon smiled at me while radiating that familiar school-year vibe that she was very, very unimpressed with me. I was standing out in the sun, the seagulls pecking a few feet away, but I could've been back in the city, stumbling like a clod through the hallways of my high school. Picture the great factory churning out the women who would never smile my way except in condescension, the busy assembly lines, the intricate distribution plan that ensured that my vicinity was well stocked. Erica, at least, would chuckle at some oddball comment of mine. Devon didn't understand a single word out of my mouth, but she was raised right and didn't express her revulsion overtly. I think she was simply puzzled by me.

We stood on the little strip of green across from Jonni Waffle, me and the double-daters. The thing about dating cousins, I observed, was that it generated a lot of nonverbal communication, bushels of quick glances and raised eyebrows, as the boys reassured themselves that their banter and posturing was working, and the girls checked in with each other to make sure they'd made good choices.

It was a famous part of the Sag Harbor experience, dating within the developments, swapping spit with other chosen ones. Your own kind. There were famous local teenage pairings that went on forever, led to marriage, repopulation of the neighborhood, extension of the brand. NP's parents were one such Golden Couple. When they first started coming out, their houses were across the street from each other—see them waving at each other before they turned in at night, the mosquitoes hopping on the screens. Everybody knew everybody's family, so partners came prequalified and notarized. Whether things worked or not, you were going to be in each other's faces for the rest of your lives. The double-daters had to ask themselves, Where is this going?

The bridge to North Haven was a long white frown before us. From time to time, suicidal painters and playwrights (few artists from other disciplines partook for some reason) flung themselves from its concrete heights, but the water wasn't very deep, and they usually ended up being dragged by a gaffer's hook onto a passing motorboat, or wading out dejectedly, pissed that they'd lost their wallet. A few yards from our feet, seagulls staggered and pecked at a fallen waffle cone—run the film backward and the bits fly up into the hand of an anguished child, un-breaking and fitting together as his face transforms from anguish to absentminded, Oreo-licking ecstasy.

Bobby rubbed his leg and told us a story about how on the way out of the house, he tried to jump into his car like Crockett and Tubbs when he slipped. "I almost crushed my sacadiliac," he said.

We all laughed except for NP, who said, "Saca-what?"

"My nut sack," he said, gesturing at me for backup.

I said, "I read a book about Sagaponac by Honoré de Ballsack," but that only confused things more so Bobby explained about the big brown nuts and the rest. "Look it up."

"In what?" NP asked. He was right—no one had a dictionary out there. Maybe an old Scrabble dictionary, missing half its pages and frothing with silverfish, but that was it. "I'll bet you a hundred dollars you're wrong," he said. From time to time, this competition emerged between NP and Bobby over who was the alpha dog in this double date, complicated by the fact that Bobby had the car keys. A hundred-dollar bet was a serious escalation of stakes, three weeks' wages.

Bobby couldn't back down. His girl was watching. His girl's cousin was watching. He looked at me for reassurance, and I shrugged, but it was already too late anyway. He was committed. The money was in the bag—if you can't trust a nerd with a big word, who can you trust?

The hydraulic wail startled us and we turned as the big tour bus pulled up in front of Bayside. Destination: CHARTER. Roadie-looking guys in black T-shirts stepped out and Erica squealed, "It's them!"

Devon said, "I have to get a look at the Educated Rapper," starting a discussion with Erica over who was "all that," him or Doc Ice.

We walked over, halting at an invisible line by the planters that we sensed civilians shouldn't cross. We waited for a glimpse. "I'm going to get y'all in," NP said. "I got the hookup. Except for you, Benji. I don't have that much of a hookup."

I wasn't offended. I had my own scheme, and even though it cycled between doom and sure thing every five minutes, I was going to execute it. I wanted in. But to say it was to kill it, to express a want out loud was to be slapped back down. I kept my mouth shut.

When no one else got out of the bus, I said, "Maybe it's just their equipment." Devon scowled at me as if I were their tour manager, arranging their travel to stymie her. It was exactly the sort of buzz-kill comment a puzzling fellow like me would make.

We gave up. NP and me returned to work, and Bobby took the girls home so they could "get ready for tonight." Perhaps something else of note happened in the next hour and a half, but I don't remember because Lisa Lisa and U.T.F.O. walked in.

Yeah, we got celebrities in Jonni Waffle. Nowadays Bayside is this big theater, so there's always some actor or actress who's doing a show there, hanging around the wharf, plus Sag Harbor itself is not the same place, so the ambient celebrity quotient has gone up, our baseline celebrity presence, but back then it was different. They came for Bayside, to club, and sometimes they came into Jonni Waffle. F'rinstance, do you know the actor Saul Rubinek? He always plays the weaselly lawyer guy, the supporting player who double-crosses the leading man, like in *Against All Odds*. Anyway, he starred in this romantic comedy called *Soup for One*, which I don't think got a big release, but I saw it on TV during one of my many becalmed afternoons and not long after, he walked into Jonni Waffle.

"Hey, you were in *Soup for One*," I said.

He seemed dubious. Or even disappointed for some reason. "Where did you see that?"

"Cable," I said. He looked sad. I didn't give him free ice cream. Karen Allen from *Raiders* walked in once and I gave her free ice cream, because who in the world didn't have a thing for Karen Allen, who literally would have been the coolest girlfriend in the world. Punching out motherfuckers, shooting Nazis. She had these incredible freckles covering her face like sprinkles. Some other celebrities came in, drunk or high after going a few rounds in Bayside, and scooper-customer confidentiality forbids me from naming them, but let me just say that you'd be surprised (Lori Singer). The biggest sighting, of course, was when Lisa Lisa and U.T.F.O. walked in that day.

Lisa Lisa was shorter in person, but her chest was bigger. I signed off on that. She wore a red leather jacket with long fringes and tight tight jeans rhinestoned down the overworked seams. Cult Jam, the two guys who were her backup players, weren't with her. They were probably putting on their mascara, a lengthy process judging from the music video. There weren't any other customers, but Lisa Lisa ripped a number from the dispenser anyway and looked at us meaningfully with tender puppy eyes. Jen jumped up. She didn't recognize her.

U.T.F.O. was dressed in Adidas track suits, out of character—Doctor Ice's stethoscope and white smock waited in the wardrobe trunk—except for the Kangol Kid, who wore his trademark chapeau. NP and me rushed to take their orders, giving cool-cat head-nods by way of introduction.

"So you guys are playing tonight, huh," NP said, grabbing a scooper from one of the tiny sinks attached to the vats.

The Educated Rapper grunted and tapped the glass above Mocha Praline Surprise.

The Kangol Kid asked for two scoops of Strawberry with M&Ms. "In a waffle cone?" I asked.

"What's that?"

"It's a cone made out of waffle."

"Yeah, one of those."

I made it for him and he told me, "Mix Master Ice will have two scoops of Fudge Ripple." I hadn't heard the DJ speak.

"In a waffle cone?" My eyes darted between the two men.

The Kangol Kid checked in with his partner. Mix Master Ice blinked slowly and tilted his head ever so slightly. "Yes, a waffle cone," the Kangol Kid said.

I dug into the vats with NP. "This is cool," I said.

"I'm going to ask the Educated Rapper."

"Ask him what?"

"About the sacadiliac," he said. "I ain't losing no hundred dollars."

"Why don't you try Doc Ice instead?" I suggested. "Since it's a part of the body."

"Good idea."

He handed Doc Ice his cone and said, "Can I ask you a medical question?"

"Shoot."

"What's a sacadiliac?"

"Excuse me?"

"The sacadiliac."

"Perhaps you're referring to the sacroiliac joint, between the sacrum and the ilium. Is that possible?"

NP looked at me. "Is that it?"

I said, "You know, from 'The Message'?"

"Oh yeah, Melle Mel is always going on about his back problems. The *sac-ro-i-li-ac*. Can I help you with anything else?"

We shook our heads and Doc Ice reached into his pocket.

"No, it's on the house, brother," NP said. "No problem." Doc Ice thanked him, and NP quickly snuck in, "But there is one thing . . . since we're helping each other out here, you know . . . can you put me on the list tonight? So that I get in? I've been like dying to see your show all summer."

Doc Ice glanced over at his crew. They licked their ice cream. Mix Master Ice nodded.

"I can do you plus one. What's your name?"

"NP."

"NP what?"

"Just NP. They know me there."

After they left, he said, "Just in case." Now that the day had arrived, I wasn't going in for that if-one-of-us-gets-in crap. I was pissed at the thought of them inside and me standing outside the club like a fucking jerk. We leaned against the counter. The new Soft Serv machine hummed ominously, underscoring the emptiness that was our lives in the aftermath of a celebrity sighting. C-list, but still.

Jen said, "Sacadiliac?"

AT HOME, I laid out my costume. I dug in the closet and retrieved a pair of Sperry Top-Siders from two summers ago. They didn't fit, but I could fake comfort until I got inside. I grabbed one of my father's Ralph Lauren polos, my skinny arms poking out like sticks. I inspected the pleated khaki shorts my mother got me at the beginning of the summer. She bought them on automatic pilot as if I *still wore clothes like that*, hoping that my bummy phase had exhausted itself. I had five hairs on my face, two on the left, and three on the right, which I hadn't shaved since July, in anticipation. I pepped them with my fingernails so they stuck up—grotesquely, in retrospect, but I was satisfied with the effect. With any luck, I wouldn't have to speak, just hand my ticket over and shuffle in. Because of my fucking braces.

It was Thursday night, but weekend traffic clotted the intersection of Bay and Main. One of the town cops chopped at the air to keep things going. They were already gathering, lining up outside and packed in little groups, waiting for the rest of their party to arrive, having a cigarette, sucking at the damp end of a roach. I scanned the crowd, assuming they'd gone in without me, but then I saw Bobby and them over by the windmill. From their body language, things were boiling over, with Bobby and NP angled into each other, and Devon and Erica patting each other's arms in support.

"You know he's not a practicing physician," Bobby said.

"But he had to read all those medical books to come up with those rhymes, so that's where he got it from," NP responded.

"I'm not paying you shit until I get some more proof."

"You better give me my money, with your cheap ass."

"You boys use some foul language," Erica said.

I said, "Hey, guys."

After a few remarks about my costume ("Spaz," "Poindexter," "Warren T. Higginbotham the Third"), we headed over to Bayside. "Where's Marlon?" Bobby asked.

The inside man was nowhere to be seen. Squatting on a red stool at the palace gate was Freddie the Fierce, just now grabbing an ID from a quivering anorexic who'd been in a terrible hair-spray accident. He shook his head dismissively. These were his despised Boat People, disheveled travelers from the dead kingdom of boredom, with their desperate faces and Day-Glo attire.

"I thought you said you were going to get us in." Devon pouted.

"He probably stepped away for a second," NP said, rubbing Erica's back. "Plus, I'm on the list."

"That's you," Bobby said. "What about us?"

We got in line behind a coked-out couple. The guy had a Mercedes-Benz logo on his T-shirt, Ray-Bans covering his eyes, while his girlfriend wore Daisy Dukes and fishnets, one shoulder poking out of her sweatshirt. In those one-bared-shoulder days, it was easy to picture her hidden shoulder white and veined from lack of sun. I stood up straight and my back cracked, my lungs confused at this sudden roominess in my chest cavity. I felt like a giraffe, with my three extra inches of height, but I fit right in with the freakish menagerie around me. There were the standard-issue older guys wearing white jackets over monochrome T-shirts, *Miami Vice*–style, the white fabric giving their overtanned flesh a reptilian cast. Their arm candy tottered on the sidewalk with teased-out ostrich hair, in leather pants, snakeskin pants, motley-colored pantaloons, their blouses open to the navel and shoulder pads sticking out. The ubiquitous pastels reigned that year, and oversized jewelry, bracelets as big as inner tubes flopping on wrists and belt buckles like license plates sparkling in the streetlights. Looking back, there must have been some underlying theory to it all, an agreed-upon notion, but like I said, I wasn't getting those weekly updates, and in this case I wasn't missing out.

Devon and Erica checked the tails of their white shirts, flattening them against their matching pink corduroy skirts. "Get ready," NP said. "Benji, why don't you stand behind us and, uh, let us go in first?"

I said to myself, I paid for this ticket with hard-earned money.

The four of them stepped up and Freddie scrutinized them as if mulling pressure points and nerve clusters to jujitsu.

"Where's Marlon?" NP asked, cozy. Bobby extended a manly head-bob.

"He got arrested," Freddie drawled, looking at Devon and Erica.

"He was going to hook us up," NP said, whispering. "I work next door and he always comes in."

"I don't know anything about that." He flicked his head at the girls. "What are they, thirteen?"

"We're on the list," NP said. "U.T.F.O. put us on their list."

Freddie roused a paw and consulted his sheets. Perhaps he'd had an earlier career in civil service. "They don't have anyone down here."

"We have to be there," NP said, a bit frantic now.

"Even if you were on the list, I can't let these little girls in. You two maybe, but these little girls? They'd shut us down."

Another flameout at the gates of Bayside. We'd seen it before all summer, the broken faces and the inevitable stunned drifting-away. I followed. There was no use. We marched off to the grass.

Erica said, "He called us little girls."

"We're not little girls," her cousin said.

NP straightened. "Well, I'm going in."

"What about us?"

"You heard him," NP said. "They'd get shut down. I'm sorry, baby." A soldier explaining the facts of war.

"You can't just leave us out here."

"What do you expect me to do? Miss the concert?"

"Bobby," Devon said, "I want you to take me home."

"Me, too!"

Bobby looked like he'd swallowed a bucket of fishhooks.

"We're not going to walk, motherfucker," Devon said.

. . .

THE GIRLS AND THEIR DRIVER LEFT. I'd like to say that NP and Erica's bond was strong enough to survive this little contretemps, but it was not to be. Shit was tense. In the following days, Bobby's refusal to honor his debt and NP's constant griping that he "need to get paid," pitted the cousins against each other as they defended their boys. Throw in the girls' resentment over being ditched, which they probably egged on between themselves when they got bored, and it was all too much for the young lovers, untested as they were in this arena. A week later, Erica kicked NP to the curb, and Devon realized that it wasn't as fun dating by herself, so she broke up with Bobby as well.

As for my role in the breakup, I can only shrug over my misreading of "The Message." In reconstructing my sacadiliac theory, I have to go back to when I first heard the song, when I was twelve. Melle Mel was on the mike unfurling his litany of urban disquiet—"Don't push me 'cause I'm close to the edge . . . It's like a jungle sometimes, it makes me wonder how I keep from going under, ah huh huh huh"—and when he got to the part in question, I thought he was saying that getting kicked in the balls was on par with transit strikes and getting his car repoed. He added what sounded to me like "adiliac" to "sac," in order to round out the rhyme, some nonsense syllables for rhythm, like "ah huh huh huh." Then over time I forgot how I'd wrassled down that conclusion, and sacadiliac became an official medical term in my mind. On second thought, I take back my shrug. Mishearing song lyrics, making your specific travesty of the words, is the right of every human being. Getting socked in the nuts, the dungeon—these were metaphors that made a lot of sense to me. Blame society.

Every time the doors opened, the music came out in a great gust. "Super Freak" was the tipping point. What is there to say about "Super Freak"? Figure out a way to harness the essence of "Super Freak" and you'd put Exxon out of business. Flying cars, funky flying cities. That was it. I told NP I was going ahead with my plan. "I paid good money for this ticket," I told him.

"Freddie," NP reasoned, "I think I can talk to Freddie. 'And this is our game plan.'"

It was over like that. We got back in line, and when we reached Freddie's stool, he barely glanced at my ticket and waved me through. He waved NP through, too, with a curt, "You better hook me up with some of that shit you sell over there."

And so it came to pass that NP and me were the first of our crew to get into Bayside. That was my only excursion that summer, but NP milked his dual hookup until Labor Day. (Marlon got out on bail the next day.) That fall, in the city, I'd smuggle myself into the Peppermint Lounge and Area a few times, in my different costume of plaid New Wave jacket and combat boots, but they raised the drinking age to twenty-one that December and it was a long time before I got into a club again.

Stepping inside, I saw they'd done a lot of work to the place since its roller-rink days. Instead of bodies drifting in circles, now people's minds performed endless circuits, gliding through need-a-drink wanna-dance like-to-fuck need-a-drink, the club-land loop of desire. People waded in and out of the human surf around the bars, holding drinks above their shoulders to keep them above water. Waitresses in nipple-popping T-shirts, battle-worn from a summer of rough duty, carried trays up to the VIP section on the second floor, the ring of tables circling the dance floor. How nice to look down on those below! Look at her, that one looks like she's into it. The DJ cut it up in his perch, interpreting the crowd through Lennon sunglasses, the twisting bodies like tea leaves. He took counsel from the lady at his side, who stood in the dark as the floodlights zagged around her, hiding her features but casting the eerie shadow of her Afro-puffs against the wall. His muse, the temper of our night. By the stage, techies hunched over the monitors like disco Igors, unwinding the cables coiled around their arms, jabbering into walkie-talkies. Check one, check two. Mix Master Ice's turntables waited at the back of the stage, cross-faders set to zero, black styluses poised like the grim heads of gargoyles.

Rainbow lights strafed our bodies. My head bobbed, with a little extra on the downbeat. Thinking about U.T.F.O. now, it's hard to remember why I was so excited. The beat is immortal, sure, but the lyrics of "Roxanne, Roxanne" are so fucking corny, man. It's a classic because of when it came out, those early days of hip-hop when anything with a bit of novelty was mesmerizing, but it's goofy as hell. Nowadays I read about them doing nostalgia gigs, reunion shows with people like Whodini and Kool Moe Dee and Dana Dane, break dancing on their aching sacroiliacs, busting out their hits for the aging fans. Bringing it all back. For Bobby and NP and Devon and Erica, hearing the song probably calls up memories of their double-dating days, sneaking around after curfew, parking at Haven's Beach in the dark. For me, I'm reminded of a caper that didn't go wrong for once, looking back fondly on a day without injury.

The DJ dropped "Raspberry Beret," to seismic effect. Most of them weren't there to see the concert. It's a safe bet the older white people, the middle-aged East End denizens, were not die-hard U.T.F.O. fans. They showed up because they'd heard that Bayside was the place to be that night. Refugees from the known and humdrum, the smothering day-to-day. I coulda bought a beer, but I didn't want to push my luck, picturing the music cutting off and Klaxons sounding as the bartender discovered I'd made it past security. Everything coming to a stop as they all looked at me, the utter opposite of what was going on now. No one looked at me. I was one of them on the dance floor and they were one of me. I jostled, was jostled in turn, collision as communication: I am here, we're here together. The bass bounced my shirt on my chest. My elbow mashed the rib cage of this forty-something white lady in a green metallic jumpsuit and when I turned to apologize, she simply smiled and continued swaying to the music. At some point I'd started dancing. I was a pretty crappy dancer, but how could I muster shame with that music rewiring my every system? *We can rebuild him.* A plane of blue light sifted through the crowd, dead in my eyes for an instant. NP was off somewhere, getting up to something. I didn't know anyone. And it was okay. Something good was about to happen. I just had to wait. Weird trendoids surrounded me, fearsome geezers, drugged-out wackos, but now we were comrades. We were all there for the same thing. The DJ hovered above us, throwing down his thunderbolts. He mixed in a segment of Debbie Harry singing "Rapture" and they screamed. Actually, I decided, I'm not dancing that badly at all. I thought, This is Good. No qualifier, chaotic or otherwise. Simply: Good.

I knew what Evil looked like.

THE NIGHT BEFORE, after Uncle Nelson bought beer for us, we had to carry out our part of the bargain and take him around the Hills. "I just want to see if some people are out," he told us from the backseat. "A look-see. I'll be quick."

"How come you don't come out anymore?" I asked. I had the six-pack between my feet. If my conversation rankled him, he'd have to fight me for it.

"You know, I want to," he said, "but I have too much stuff to do, I got a lot of stuff I'm trying to get off the ground. Little this, little that. Can't be drinking beer on the beach all day with all these people."

We turned onto Beach Avenue. "Still here," he said.

"Left or right?"

"Right. Up there . . ." he trailed off. The white house was dark, the lawn bushy and monstrous. One of the shutters tilted down forty-five degrees on its remaining hinge, exposing shattered panes and the darkness within. "Guess they aren't around," Uncle Nelson said. "That's Lionel's house. That's where we always hung out. Day and night."

I'd never seen anyone in there. It was one of our haunted houses, with a drooling man-child chained up in the basement nibbling animal crackers or a batty old lady stirring up a pot of Kid Soup. What would our houses look like thirty years from now? We'd still be here, right? Or would we be out in the world like Uncle Nelson, our homes shadowed, the gutters sprouting flora, the driveways buckled and ripped? Haunted by us. And one of the other houses up the block or around the corner the new hangout spot for the next generation. Those future kids tossing pebbles at our windows and running away screaming, or daring each other to knock on the door. Double-dare you—crazy people used to live there and they'll get you.

He resumed the tour of his developments, superimposing his houses over the houses we knew, leading us beachward. When he saw the lights outside the Nicholses', he asked us to slow down. My mother always said, "Looks like someone's having a party," when she saw a line of cars like that, bunched up on the curb. Figures moved in the bay windows and beyond the screen door.

"Here?" Bobby asked.

"I'll catch up with them later," Uncle Nelson said. "There's one more place I want to see."

Bobby scowled and kept driving. We reached the last street in Sag Harbor Hills, the dead end on the water. "Pull up there on the left," my uncle told us. We parked in front of the Lee's, where Abby, one of my sister's friends, used to stay. Maybe he knew her parents from the old days. I turned around to ask him what he wanted to do. He was staring out the window, across the street at the Yellow House, his parents' place. I'd forgotten that's where it was.

The Yellow House was a cozy bungalow, perpetually musty and overstuffed with sailing memorabilia. Rudders and shiny brass cleats owned prime decorating real estate, the remains of beloved vessels long gone. Uncle Nelson's father was one of that seafaring generation, like my grandfather and Bobby's grandfather, hitching his motorboat to the station wagon at the start of the season, chugging out into the deep water to fish, tooling around the Caribbean in the winter. Uncle Nelson had inherited some of that. His old Sunfish spent its final, neglected summers lodged in the beach grass in front of our house, its mildewing white-and-yellow sail collecting dirty lakes during rainstorms. When I was little, our parents hauled us to the

Yellow House to reunion barbecues or birthday parties for some Southern cousin my age whom I'd never met before and would never see again. The kids running on the grass, the parents on the patio, sipping their drinks. So many years ago.

"You getting out?" Bobby asked.

"No."

He sat there looking at his old house, not saying anything. I didn't see anyone inside, but all the lights were on. The bug zapper sparked. "Is your father out?" I asked.

"Yes."

"How's he doing?"

"I don't know."

We called his father Uncle Gideon, which was what our mother called him. Look at Uncle Nelson now and you saw him in there. Although he was as skinny as me when he was younger, Nelson had grown into his father's shape, his belly spreading out, his cheeks rounding into apples. Uncle Gideon didn't have much time for kids, which was fine with me, and I didn't remember that much about him beyond what trickled out in my mother's stories about her cousin's misadventures. "Uncle Gideon was *mad*." "You should have seen Uncle Gideon's face when he got the bill." In my mind he was a character standing to the side of one of the bad-boy anecdotes, tsk-tsking at high jinks. One of the founding fathers, with their ideas of how proper black people should act.

Bobby cleared his throat.

Uncle Nelson said, "He told me, 'Don't set foot in my house ever again.' So I'm not." I stared straight ahead. "That doesn't mean I can't look, does it?" he asked. The developments were usually hopping this late in the season. It wasn't too late. You could count on a barbecue or two at least, winding down to stragglers, a get-together shrinking to diehards, the people with nowhere else to go. But no one was around. I heard nothing except my uncle's breathing. The previous stops had been window-dressing. This is where he wanted to be. "I can look, right?"

An insect sizzled in the zapper, converted to smoke. He flipped a switch in himself. He clapped his hands together loudly and said, "Let's go, boys! If you drop me at the Nicholses', I'll be much obliged, and I'll see those fine fine people and relieve them of their fine fine liquor. It's early yet!"

"Okay," I said.

When we dropped him off, Bobby said, "Well, that was a buzz kill."

I said, "Yeah." But mostly I thought, Evil. Nothing else to call it. I could've made up my own lyrics to what passed between the father and the son, something about misunderstandings, the ones that don't matter and the ones that are everything, but I would've gotten the words wrong. Make up lyrics to someone else's song and you put yourself in there, botching it all.

AS "RAPTURE" TRANSFORMED INTO "BAD GIRLS," NP tapped my shoulder, materializing in the crowd with two Bartles & Jaymes wine coolers in his hands. He gave me one. He started to speak but it was too loud to hear him. I knew what he was saying anyway. It was going to be a great night.

One more thing, before the concert starts, and they're going to go on any second, you can feel it. It's not that important, but in case it comes up—Sagaponac is a Native American word meaning "the land of big ground nuts," not "big brown nuts." The place mats of the Corner Bar contain a world of knowledge, never to be doubted. Bobby misread. I'd hate for you to repeat that in conversation. It might lead to complications.

Now you'll have to excuse me. Can you feel it? It's about to start.

Tonight
We
Improvise

EVERYBODY HATED WLNG. IT WAS SAG HARBOR'S lone radio station, beaming out sentiment at 92.1 megahertz, reverberating through our skins and inner transistors even when the stereo was off. They called themselves a Classic Oldies station, spinning the requisite Motown and Beatles and barefoot singer-songwriters to justify themselves to advertisers, but their specialty was the oddball tune, the one-hit wonders and fluke achievers, the "Popcorn"s, the "Monster Mash"es, the sublimely dreadful "Itsy Bitsy Teenie Weenie Yellow Polka Dot Bikini"s.

Everybody'd heard those goofy songs a million times before, and it was a cold cold heart that didn't hum along for at least a second. What sent people trampling to the exits was a different kind of one-hit wonder, a species of song so cloying and unashamed that the soul shivered in recognition. They came to WLNG to die, these misfit ditties: feverish declarations of affection, tearjerkers about magical last-chance afternoons, odes to the everlasting that were thinly veiled bids for restraining orders. Rented-by-the-hour string sections sawed away at our resistance, lonesome sax solos paraphrased heartbreak. I can't tell you the names of the songs because I don't know, can't say who got the songwriting credit and who cashed the royalties. All I could do was succumb to the LNG Effect when these songs came on.

It proceeded thusly: out of the speakers emerged a song you'd heard only once before in your life, one that left such a faint record in your brain that it was a memory of a memory. Paralyzed by confusion, you wondered, Where have I heard this before? The answer was, Nowhere important. Far from scoring some significant life passage, it was most likely the soundtrack of an anti-event—searching for the matching sock, wiping tartar sauce from your lip—but the deep sense of familiarity and loss was unshakable. That was the LNG Effect—a feeling of nostalgia for something that never existed. It creeped people out. And maybe you'd never even heard the song before, only thought you had and completely invented the connection, so nimble the song's persuasion. There was a quality to the voices of the singers, these faceless warblers and sweater-vested harmonizers, that made their corny scenarios and schmaltzy pleas hypnotizing, transporting. For a few verses, that was you trotting along by the departing train car, coming around to tell the truth after all this time, that was you in the foxhole begging your girl back home to stay true, that was you standing there without defenses for once, in the pouring rain, saying what had to be said. You can't say *longing* without the *l*, *n*, and *g*.

At some weak moment these songs had hit the pop charts, mingling with the more likely pop creations for one brief, glorious instant. Out of place at the party, digging their elbows into the wall and nervously chugging punch before they were found out. They fell out of the Top 40 and tumbled down the rankings, plummeting away from most people's consciousness . . . out of our universe and into another, welcomed into the WLNG firmament the second they hit 41, twinkling in their bygone constellation. I imagine that the LNG Effect was exactly the opposite for the singers. For them, hearing their songs come on wasn't the reinforcement of an illusion but the affirmation of reality—if someone was playing their record after all this time, then they actually existed and it wasn't just a dream, their moment onstage. They heard their words again, restored after being stripped by Muzak-makers and elevator composers, and were made whole.

Everybody hated WLNG because WLNG fucked you up. They turned the station in a New York minute. My friends had no time for it, fiddling for rogue, clear-day broadcasts from KISS FM in the city. My brother was entering a big reggae phase. My mother liked classical music, zooming past 92.1 on the way to all that public radio wine and cheese at the bottom of the dial. And while my father had a well-known weakness for Easy Listening, he loathed the voice of LNG's afternoon guy, Rusty Potz—Rusty Potz!—whom he referred to as "that man" before shutting off the little Panasonic boom box in the corner of the dining area.

So of course WLNG was (one of) my secret shame(s), indulged when I had the house to myself. The songs were too mawkish to be anything other than solo pleasures, savored in private while tickling invisible ivories or fondling a phantom microphone. The furtive way I scoped out the premises, slowly turning up the volume on the radio, wary of every increment, setting it a little higher and higher as I grew bolder, certainly echoed universal porn protocols. Sometimes I forgot to clean up after myself and hours later I'd hear "Who's been listening to WLNG?" from the living room, whereupon I'd walk out and declare "I hate that station!" like a proper citizen. In fact, my father asked the question the same way he asked "Who's been watching Channel J?" in the city, when the dial on the cable box pointed to the local red-light district. Channel J, home of Ugly George and *Midnight Blue*, the porny public-access shows that had been many a Manhattan boy's and girl's introduction to naked moving parts, a stretch of shabby Times Square in the TV lineup. Sometimes I was the culprit, sometimes not. It says a lot about the world that being walked in on with your hands down your pants while Al Goldstein played some grainy action clip of Seka was preferable to getting caught singing along to "Who Put the Bomp (In the Bomp Bomp Bomp)."

I bring all this up because one late afternoon toward the end of the season, I was double-dosing on masturbatory pastimes—listening to WLNG and touching myself. Not touching myself like that, but running my tongue over the mounds and crevices of my teeth and gums. I'd gotten my braces off a few days earlier and was in complete ecstasy over the feel of my new mouth. Look on my Works, y'all, and Despair! Which is not to say that in all probability I hadn't partaken of the more conventional form of self-gratification in the last twenty-four hours, I just wasn't doing it right then. I held masturbation in high esteem, for without it we'd never have developed the opposable thumb, and from the opposable thumb flows all of civilization, the shaping of rudimentary tools, creation of fire for warmth and food preparation, cave paintings, cuneiform, and eventually the Betamax. Think about that next time.

I probed, I polished, I tickled the smooth and lovely surfaces of my naked choppers. They'd never been like that: level, even, sans gusty gaps. Half the reason the braces went on in the first place was to correct my magnificent overbite, which I'd helped buck out when I was a kid. I sucked my thumb well into grade school, popping that little fucker in my mouth at every available moment of alone time. Sucking on the tit that never gave milk. I see I'm going way back with you today, down memory lane where the asphalt stops and it's just dirt leading off, to the origin of this love of solitary consolations. Holy cow, it winds its way back to the crib, this self-pleasuring bent, in the all-too-frequent onanism, the zoning out to sad-sack narcissistic ballads, sucking my thumb—the various strategies of getting a little comfort in this cold mean world. If you had these things, you didn't need anyone else.

I finally started leaving my thumb alone when chicken pox

ripped through my second-grade class and I got little white blisters all over the inside of my mouth from sticking my tainted digit in there. I had the pox on the outside like everyone else, but inside, too, where no one could see. I looked in the mirror, and thought, *Cursed!* Or whatever word second-graders use to nail that feeling of being singled out for a ghastly and specific doom. *Snaked! Goblin'd!* Some say that it's an old wives' tale that sucking your thumb will mess up your teeth, but give me a sandwich board and I'll shill for this theory up and down Broadway. Surely something that felt so reassuring needed to be punished, by deformity, blindness, by a plague of white blisters visited upon the wicked territory of my mouth.

The braces were supposed to come off freshman year, but I never went to my appointments so the treatment stretched on for an extra year and a half. That spring I finally got my act together and started fulfilling my half of the bargain, snapping the rubber bands around the spikes and hooks, showing up at the right time to Dr. Henderson's office. He was an okay guy. I liked the way he said, "You might feel a slight pressure," as if this were a rarity and not a constant state of being.

"How's Sag?" he asked when I clambered into his chair that last time. The summer before, he'd rented a condo in Baron's Cove behind town, and when I ran into him on the beach or whatever, this specter rose before me, him looming in his smock and mask, spiny and serrated implements glinting in the summer sunlight. On those occasions I hummed hello to him, keeping my lips tight.

"The usual," I said.

He got to work with his mallet and monkey wrench and unshackled my teeth. A gruesome funk drifted away from the accumulated microscopic and not-so-microscopic food bits that had been rotting under the metal for years. He cleaned my teeth and my tongue danced over them.

He handed me a mirror. "You're going to be kissing a lot of girls now."

I didn't mind being patronized by Helpful Hints from the back of the *Orthodontists' Handbook*. It made sense to compliment the recently straightened on their new look, to help them appreciate the end result of all their suffering. What ticked me off was the implication that braces were what held me back from age-appropriate shenanigans, the fabled frenching, bra-fumbling, and blue balls. Obviously, it would have been hard for me to kiss fewer girls, basic mathematical properties of the number zero being what they are. In order to improve my portfolio, I needed to dump the braces. But what of the essential me beneath everything? In the logic of my affection, those who would love or kinda like me could see beyond the Iron Maiden embracing my teeth, my incompetent presentation and chronic galoot-ness. None of that mattered. There was something good under there. I had to believe that. If you couldn't see it, you weren't worth being with, right? Not worth kissing. So what people saw of me was a test.

Back at the apartment, I grinned and sneered at myself, practicing with my mouth. I looked at my new smile and wondered what it meant.

I was in the city for four days. On the way in from the island, a perfect orange dome of smog covered Manhattan. The dome kept in the August heat and hoarded the stenches of the city, the decaying garbage and car exhaust, the evaporating essences of those trapped inside. I stepped off the Jitney at Eighty-sixth Street and waded into the bog. It hadn't rained in a while, and miserable puddles fermented along the sidewalks, dark objects bobbing in them and multicolored oil trails hovering on their surfaces. It was late enough in the summer that people were too beaten down by the heat for rage and violence. They gave in, slumping up the sidewalks, martyrs to the choices they'd made.

Reggie had been back a few times to buy records or clothes, but this was my first trip back to the city. My room was a snapshot of my brain circa two and a half months ago, a picture of the mess left behind by the evacuation. Yellowing *Village Voices* lay open to the concert pages, listing the names of bands I hadn't seen and venues I'd never been to. All spring I memorized their addresses and situated them in the amorphous downtown that existed in my head. One day

I'd make it down there after dark, below Fourteenth Street. That hip murk. The records I marathon-taped the night before I left were strewn about, half out of their sleeves, the Birthday Party's *Mutiny*, the first two Stooges records. Stuff I bought because I'd heard it on the mix tape my older sister played when she came back for spring break. Who's that? What's this? Elena was spending the summer away from us, working at a movie theater in her college town. My father made a fuss about that, but what was he going to do, go up there and drag her down?

No one was around in the city, my few friends from school. I wanted to get back to Sag as quickly as possible. I had two more weeks of summer left. I wasn't done with it yet.

WHEN I GOT BACK OUT, the stagehands had moved everything around. Most people, they leave a place for a few days and are reassured on their return that despite their worry, they hadn't missed anything. The legendary party, the life-changing late-night hangout. Not in my case. Not ever. The world really ramped up its carousing when I wasn't around and I had to listen to all the details when I got back. This was especially true toward the end of summer, when things accelerated as they got drawn into that September gravity. Just four days, and Clive was gone. I didn't care for sports, watching or participating, but Clive's fabled basketball camp impressed me as a special calling—he had a higher purpose, going off to fulfill his dunking destiny. In the tradition of Sag friendships, I wouldn't see him until next year. Bobby was in the city, for a few days or for good, it wasn't clear. His grandfather had gotten sick again, so they were all back in Westchester dealing with that. Which left us without a car, as Randy was working double shifts at the Long Wharf to top off his tuition war chest. It might have been December, the desolation we saw when we walked around.

We had one late arrival to replace those we'd lost, Melanie. She used to come out when she was a little girl, according to NP. NP had inherited the nosy-historian gene from his father, who maintained an extensive mental database on everyone in the developments. How long they'd been coming out, which parcels their family had bought and traded over the decades, where their kids and grandkids were going to school, and how much they were or were not raking in from their big jobs. Melanie's family was first generation, NP told me one day as we were wiping down the vats in Jonni Waffle, but they'd sold their house on Cuffee Drive ten years ago. "My dad said her daddy made some bad business decisions." Getting rid of your Sag house, that was unforgivable. Like selling your kids off to the circus for crack money. Mr. Downey was an outsider, you see, and did not understand our ways. How else to explain losing his family's most precious possession?

Now the Downeys were divorced and Mom was trying to reconnect with her heritage. The story was an easy sell in the developments—the wayward daughter back in the bosom and the impostor back where he came from, selling used cars in a cheap suit somewhere. Melanie and her mother rented a house in the Hills, back out for the first time in years. Everyone called her mother "Peaches," a childhood nickname now reclaimed. Peaches put on a good show, insinuating herself into the little klatch on the beach in front of our house. She climbed up on the Franklins' motorboat and water-skied, the only middle-aged lady brave enough to do so when Teddy Jr. was at the helm. The ladies rose from their beach chairs and watched from the shore as the boat hoisted her from the water. Peaches waved at them like a teenage beauty queen showing off during the talent portion, wobbling only a little on the turn. She even got a letter printed in the *Sag Harbor Express* bitching about the weekend traffic, a gesture of righteous outrage that won over anyone still reluctant to welcome her back into the fold.

Her daughter was similarly adept. She hadn't yet claimed her birthright as a proper Black American Princess, the sartorial markers and debilitating stares, so it wasn't until the following summer that Erica and Devon welcomed her into their gang, but Nick quickly scooped her up. So to speak. She became a familiar sight at

Jonni Waffle, poking her head in to coax Nick out for a break on one of the Long Wharf benches and lingering outside at end of shift so that they could walk back in the dark. Her little wheezing laughter signaled her approach, around development corners and the stoops of houses, and then she came into view. She walked in a style halfway between an amble and a sashay—she was edging toward the sashay, getting it down, learning how to put her big hips into it. Next year, whoo-boy.

I first saw her on NP's back patio, early August. She was straddling their old green-and-white lounger and sipping Country Time lemonade. The unmixed bits of the flavor packet swirled around each time she tipped the glass to her plush lips, her long, curly hair corkscrewing into the air. Melanie was soft and round in a sweet, baby-fat way, with this remarkable ability where she converted everything she wore on her legs into hot pants, the press of her thighs turning prim white tennis shorts into Daisy Dukes, the zipper tab of her acid-washed jeans standing at attention like a needle on a pressure gauge.

I didn't remember Melanie from when we were little, but she pulled off a convincing display of insider knowledge like a well-briefed spy. She talked about the "Dancing Popcorn Box and Hot Dog" ads that used to run between features at the old Drive-In, hypnotizing you into a trip to the concession stand, and name-checked Frederico's and the Candy Kitchen with authority, as if she'd enjoyed an unbroken line of hallowed summers. With Devon and Erica making only strategic appearances in our scene After the Breakup, she was usually the only girl around and wasn't bothered by it. The Nick thing helped. I guess she didn't mind that he was technically a townie, or maybe the fact that her own credentials were out of order brought them closer. She feigned interest in his hobbies like a pro, like she'd been married a couple of times and knew how to tolerate the feeble enthusiasms of men. She watched patiently while he adjusted the graphic equalizer on his monstrous radio, furrowing her brow with concentration during his lectures on how this particular setting really enriched the beatboxing in "The Show," but the B side of the single, "La-Di-Da-Di," benefited from a little more treble, to foreground Slick Rick's vocal dexterity.

Although, right, there was that one afternoon of foreshadowing. The gang was eating slices at Conca D'Oro, the orange drops of grease turning the paper plates opaque. "That's not a sample," Nick said, "they did it live in the studio." You didn't want to get Nick started on Melle Mel's studio acumen. I guess Melanie sensed I was looking at her and she turned to me and surgically flicked her eyes to the ceiling. Then she returned, rapt, to his dissertation on "Funky Beat," that old-school master text. But I saw her.

THAT'S WHERE THINGS STOOD that day I was alone in the house listening to the radio. It was the weekend, so Reggie was pulling a double at BK, and it was the third cloudy day in a row so the beach was empty except for the one-weekenders, who had to make the best of it. My parents were off at some function in Ninevah. I was killing flies with rubber bands. I snuck up as close as their hundred-eyed heads allowed, then drew back the rubber and let 'em rip. I'd gotten pretty good at the hunt over the summer, leaving tiny red smears on the windows and walls. My charnel house o' horrors. The light was fading, but I spotted one unlucky dude lingering by the handle of the glass door and I stalked over, my tongue tickling my upper right bicuspid . . . when I suddenly got really depressed. A sadness pumping through my branching capillaries, suffusing my limbs, splashing into the furthest hideaways in my pinkie toes and lumps of earlobe. It was such a profound incident that I imagine the intensity of it left chemical markers in my hair that a high-tech lab could identify, like I'd been smoking some serious reefer, that back-row uptown-theater shit. The fly flew away. I put my hand on a chair to steady myself.

I became aware of the music and understood. I got dinged by LNG, but good. The lyrics carouseled in my head:

Have I a hope or half a chance
To even ask if I could dance with you, you-oo?
Would you greet me or politely turn away
Would there suddenly be sunshine on a cold and rainy day
Oh, Babe, what would you say?

Had I heard this song before? Surely I must have in another life. Another house. The singer croaked out his proposal. His was no velvet instrument, but he made up for it in intensity. The desperation that is cousin to passion. I was there with him at the English seaside resort at the end of summer. The coastal retreat past its heyday. It's the last night at the Dime-a-Dance before they demolish it, the last big concert of the season before they shutter the boardwalk. There he is in his one good suit, seersucker, with shiny elbows and stains from twenty wakes, the widower who has been standing along the wall all night, watching her, looking away when she turned her head toward him. This angel in white with her dark eyes and glowing skin. He saw her at the first dance at the start of the summer—he'd gone on a lark, usually he stayed away from such things—and returned every Saturday night to get a glimpse. Working up his nerve. To risk love one more time. Tonight is his last chance and he gathers himself, rubbing the rim of his old derby with his thumbs and digging his winnowed soles into the dance floor.

Had I heard this song before? I didn't know. Was that a clarinet, that farting sound? I listened to the words and tried to go back. When was it? The phantom when. No, it was a saxophone. The sax player waltzed through his solo, he was up on a tenement roof at midnight, playing for all the lonely ones, who drifted from their beds and moved to their windowsills to hear this more clearly. They couldn't see him. It was the moon itself playing those luscious notes. In the morning they weren't sure if they'd dreamed it. They tried to remember the melody all day and couldn't for the life of them. By lunch, they were thoroughly ashamed for letting him down.

The song ended and the volume spiked up to showcase a commercial for Allen M. Schneider Real Estate. I heard my parents' car in the driveway and dove for the radio, spinning the dial to my mother's Nothing But the Classics. They came up the stairs, and when they got inside my father resumed. It was an argument from inside the car that they'd paused in between closed spaces. Who knew what started it. By then it was deep into the ancient grudges and unforgivable failures. The usual.

I hadn't made any plans. But I did what I normally did not do. I left the house. It was funny—as soon as the door closed, I couldn't hear it. Maybe the wind carried it in another direction. It got windy at sunset that time of year. I was always tormented by the knowledge that the entire developments must have been listening to us, but the screen door wheezed shut and those sounds were gone.

Walking out of the driveway, I tried to get the song out of my head. It didn't work. What if someone came along and heard me humming it? Picking up a ditty from WLNG was hard to explain, like claiming you got VD off a toilet seat in a bus station. You walked around with it to your shame. There were songs that were guilty pleasures, like "Fernando." That ABBA shit. Everybody had 'em. Then there were songs that betrayed fundamental ideas you had about yourself. *Have I a hope or half a chance.* There could be no accommodation for such exposure. My friends wouldn't understand. Reggie would punch me in my face. Certainly my sister wouldn't approve, but I saw her so rarely that I no longer worried about what sarcastic remark she'd throw my way.

I HAVEN'T TALKED ABOUT ELENA much because she wasn't there. I haven't talked about her because she went off to college and never came back. I've mentioned the great migration, when you stop coming out to Sag except for the occasional visit. You got a real summer job in the city, or something on campus, or an internship in the office of a family friend. Common rite of passage. *Enough of this bourgie shit.* You left the place that made you to take your chances in the wide world. But Elena did more than outgrow Sag Harbor. She went off and we saw her on Thanksgiving and Christmas, and sometimes she came back down to New York if she had a longer vacation, but it was never the same. She hasn't been in here much because she'd already moved on.

Elena was three years older than me. Growing up, she was our babysitter, buddy, and bully, according to her needs. Tugging us out of traffic, turning the oven on to 350 degrees so that me and Reggie could slide our Swanson's in there side by side, keeping Mondays at 8 PM in a stranglehold for her beloved *Little House on the Prairie*. Those hard-won frontier lessons. When we destroyed her nerves, she threatened to tell our father, which shut us down like that.

She slimmed down and hipped up when she hit high school, unveiling a cool downtown persona that made the most blasé private-school deb seem like a Kentucky rube. She came home after everyone was in bed and tossed glossy invites from the Peppermint Lounge and Danceteria onto the table in the foyer, where they accumulated like exotic stickers on a steam trunk. At night, strange sounds emanated from her room, bruised melodies wrung from Mission of Burma 45s and ink-black flexis out of British music magazines. There were Friday evenings where she'd psych herself up by playing *Sandinista!* cut for cut, all six sides, and then tromp out of the house in Day-Glo boots to wrestle down the night. Leaving me and Reggie alone in the house with a stack of splatter flicks from Crazy Eddie's, fascinated by ideas of our future, high-school selves. Suckers!

The last few summers, she'd been in charge when our parents were in the city. Now that it was my job, I knew what her expression had meant when our parents' friends asked when our folks were coming out. She was a camp counselor at Boy's Harbor, bossing those kids around all day, which made things easier for us as she was all out of fascist directives by the time she got home. I listened to her sneak out of the house after me and Reggie went to bed. I heard the car door slam as she went off on her secret missions and I put myself in charge of us in the empty house until morning. Her final summer, she was too hip and strange and "white-acting" for the Sag Harbor boys and girls she'd grown up with, and went out to find others like her, her fellow unlikelies. She never brought them around, but she must have found her tribe.

I only saw her once that summer. The week before I got my braces off. Bobby was still out, and we were driving down Main Street, South Hampton, rushing to catch the 7:20 show of *Beyond Thunderdome*. We'd seen it before, but we had nothing else to do. We were about to turn into the parking lot behind the theater when Bobby said, "Isn't that your sister?"

She was across the street, smoking a cigarette in front of one of the fancy restaurants reserved for grown-ups. If our parents took us out to dinner, it was to the Lobster Inn or the latest one-season home-style fried-chicken joint or takeout place. The grown-ups kept the shiny, written-up restaurants for their nights away from the kids. Or away from the wives. She was talking to a German-looking guy with long blond hair and bright white teeth that gleamed from all the way across the street. He had a Eurotrash demeanor I will forever associate with the high-tech terrorists of *Die Hard*, and yeah, I know the movie didn't come out until three long summers later, but what do you want, the movie made a big impression on me, and it is hard to accept the notion of a pre–*Die Hard* world. The cruel efficiency of those guys. She patted his arm and smiled at some little witticism of his, tracing down to his elbow. They were fucking.

They were still there after we found a parking space. Which was good, because I didn't want to have to go inside the restaurant and tell the garçon or whatever that I wanted to look for someone. Her companion spotted me approaching and watched me over her shoulder. His face had that expression I've seen many times, when I'm walking down the street and there's a white person sitting alone in a car. The look on his face was the one they always get before they lock the car doors. Click, click, click up the street as I pass. We were in South Hampton.

"Elena?"

She gave me her hug—I'd forgotten how good it felt—and introduced me to Derek. He lost his squint and shook my hand with a big big smile.

"What are you doing here? When did you get out?"

"I just popped in for the weekend," she said. "I'm visiting Derek."

Bobby checked out her friend, raising a skeptical eyebrow.

I said, "Oh, I didn't know."

"It was a last-minute thing."

"When are you coming over? 'Cause I work—" I began to say. Because I didn't want to miss her.

"I'm probably not going to have time to make it over there," she said. "Probably. It's just a quick visit."

"Oh."

The traffic rushed in the street. Bobby told me he was going to buy tickets and that I should meet him over there. Elena nodded her head toward Derek and he slunk into the restaurant. She had a lot of training with delivering nonverbal directives, working on me and Reggie all those years.

Elena took a drag and exhaled through her nose. "Do me a favor and don't tell Mom and Dad you saw me, will you?" she said. "They wouldn't understand."

"You weren't even going to see us."

"Don't start pouting. Of course I want to see you and Reggie." She squeezed my shoulder. "I'm going to try and come out for longer before I have to go back to school. This was a spur-of-the-moment thing." She stamped out her cigarette and said, "You know how it can be in that house."

"What do you mean?"

"You know what I'm talking about."

She looked through the window of the restaurant after Derek. "Just do me a favor, Benji, and get out when you can," she said. "Work hard and get into a good school. That way you're out of the house and that's it."

"I don't understand."

"Yes, you do."

The next time I saw her was Thanksgiving. She stayed one night and then went to a party in Connecticut some friend of hers from school was having. She was meeting all sorts of new people, she said.

NO, I DIDN'T HAVE TO WORRY about running into Elena with that song in my brain. Those cornball words on my lips. I was out in the middle of the street, a few houses up. Far enough away that I didn't have to pretend I didn't live where I lived. It could go on for five minutes or five hours. This time I was going to stay away.

"Ben." Melanie stood at the corner of Meredith. She was on the grass by the curb, her fingers splayed out on her hips. She wore a white button-down shirt tight enough that it made her look like she'd jumped a cup size. She'd twisted her hair into two long braids that danced on her shoulders when she moved her head. I didn't see Nick.

She prodded something on the ground with her foot. She said, "That's gross." It was a yellow centipede of plastic, clumped with dirt.

"Yeah, you shouldn't litter," I said.

"It's a jimmy hat."

"Right." I hadn't seen one outside the packaging before. Sometimes guys I knew opened their wallets to show off their expectations, and amateurs like me gawked at the outlines of the ring. Now I realized I had seen them before, out in the woods behind the park or deflated on a sidewalk among the other fucked-up New York confetti.

She scraped it with her sandal up the grass and into the woods.

"Nick's at work?" I said.

"I don't know where Nick is. I'm not his keeper."

"Okay."

"What are you doing?"

"Nothing."

"Right," she said. We took a few steps down Terry.

"I can't believe it's almost September," I said.

"Yeah."

I asked her when she was going back. She told me, next week. It was that time of year. At night we started closing the windows. The breezes woke you in the middle of night or startled you at dusk with their sudden lacerations. You remembered packing at the beginning of the summer and trying to figure out how many long-sleeved shirts and sweaters to bring, and realized you chose the wrong number like you did every year. It was almost over. The city rose higher and higher on the horizon.

"You must be glad to be coming out here again," I said. I had a roll of non sequiturs in my pockets and I was just tossing them out across the water trying to get a good skip going.

"It's nice out here," she said, "but it's not all that. Too quiet, you know?" I knew she lived in Queens, and in my provincial head the Outer Boroughs were a hotbed of licentiousness. Sag Harbor people who lived in Queens and Brooklyn were simply cooler. No ifs, ands, or buts. They didn't cage themselves in private school. Their parties ripped the weekend asunder. The standard projections of the repressed. But hearing confirmation from Melanie, who was like a year younger than me, just a freshman, made me feel like more of a stiff than usual.

She kinda squinted at me as we rounded the corner and I remembered the phone call. See, something out of the ordinary had happened the day before. We were at NP's house, me and Marcus and Nick. NP's mother was at a luncheon in the city, so we availed ourselves of his house for a change. We were out on the patio, talking shit, when NP went to answer the phone. He poked his head out of the back door. He looked puzzled. He said, "It's Melanie."

Nick took his radio off his lap. NP said, "She wants to talk to Benji."

Now we were all confused. Nick sat back down, not looking at me. NP shrugged.

The phone was shaped like a banana, a sad, bright-yellow relic of early-'70s design whimsy. The coils of the handset cord were so gnarled and incestuous that I had to pull for every inch. "Hello?"

"It's Melanie."

"Hi." The handset tried to spring away from me.

"What are you doing?"

"Hanging around with NP and Reggie. What about you?" I don't know why I didn't mention Nick.

"Just watching TV."

I looked out the window into the backyard, but I could only see the old tire swing. I fell off it when I was little and scraped up my face and still hated it for chumping me out. "Not much happening here." I cleared my throat.

"It's a boring day." I heard a voice in the background. Peaches. "I gotta go," she said. "We're going to Caldor for slippers."

"Okay."

I went back outside. NP said, "Oh, Heavenly Dog."

"She just wanted to see what was up," I said.

Nick said, "She's all . . ." swatting his hand at an invisible gnat. He wrinkled his face into a well-known expression of male aggravation at the opposite sex, so instantly recognizable that it could have been an international sign for such a thing, hanging in airports and train stations. He didn't seem pissed with me and, in my way, I forgot about the phone call a minute later. She wanted to say hi. It wasn't that weird.

Except for the reliable haunted houses, Azurest was filled up. Every weekend the new arrivals buzzed their hedges into shape, turned the faucets until the rust ran out, exchanged their old mildewed doormat for the latest offering from the Hardware Store in Town. Cars were bumper to bumper in the driveways and clotted the curbs, the vehicles of spectators assembling for the Main Event. The big fireworks show before they had to head back to the city. I realized I was humming that song again and stopped. How long had I been doing that? Had she heard? I said, "You called me Ben before."

"I thought that's what you wanted people to call you?"

"That's right."

"Benji is cute, but I know what you mean. I used to always go, 'Ben-ji! Ben-ji!' whenever you came down the beach with Reggie."

Huh. "When were you last out?" I asked. "I know you used to come out here all the time, but I must have been really little because I can't remember."

She shook her head and smirked. "Just until I was five. But I remember it all. You used to stay at that red house on Hempstead. We all ran around playing red light, green light in the backyard. And there was that old pump that used to be home base."

"You remember that?" I saw it, me and the rest of the gang zigzagging across the grass, saw all their faces but did not see hers.

"You remember that time I kissed you?" she asked.

"What?"

"I was like five or something and I told you we should get married."

"Really?"

"Yeah."

"What did I do?"

"You ran away screaming."

"Really?"

"My mom had to apologize to your mom because I kept following you around trying to kiss you all the time."

"That's weird." Was she fucking with me? That's all I could think. There was that phone call yesterday, and then her telling me this. This was a plot, a conspiracy of city-style, private-school cruelty. No other explanation.

"I thought you were the cutest boy out here," she said. She stopped. "What happened to you?"

"What happened?" I cocked my head back because I felt that was the appropriate response to such a statement. Insulted, etc. What a normal person would do.

"No, I don't mean it like that," she said, chuckling. Her fingers brushing down my arm. "I mean, you just always seemed so happy all the time. You had that *Planet of the Apes* pajama top you liked to wear as a shirt even though it was the daytime, and you were always laughing with Reggie at everything."

"Now I'm all angry and mad?"

"I didn't say that." She bumped me with her hip.

Huh.

We were outside Marv's house. It was a rancher with a long flat roof, painted a robin's-egg color that was what radiation would look like if you could see radiation. Light came from the basement window, through the dirt splashed on by the rain. I thought about Rusty Potz, the WLNG afternoon guy. He coated his voice with so much reverb it sounded like he worked underground, only getting fresh air during one of their remote feeds from the Sag Harbor Masons' Annual Fish Fry. ("Tickets are still available at the Municipal Building on Main Street.") From his hepcat rock-'n'-roll patois, I pictured him with a white beret and satin baseball jacket, standing in front of a few signed photographs of him shaking hands with Bill Haley and His Comets, the Yardbirds, and sundry crooners dressed in matching cardigans. He worked alone in his dungeon, stirring the cauldron, concocting longing for his listeners.

WLNG didn't play hip-hop, of course, outside the occasional spin of "Rappin' Rodney." That's where Marv and his underground operation came in, down in his basement. Marv was an in-betweener, a few years older. He was "street-smart," wielding the latest styles with the unself-consciousness that came from actually being that elusive thing: unimpeachably down. Once he hit high school he stopped coming out, to commit himself to the B-boy lifestyle. He was the first person I met with two turntables. One turntable, you liked music. Two turntables and you were an artist. In the summer of '81, he cut up "Good Times" like a true acolyte of Grandmaster Flash, slashing the fader back and forth in a three-card monte panic, rubbing out a few tentative scratches, zip zip. The famous bass line strutted like a hustler around the room in a beige jeans suit, with an Apple Jack on his head: What can I get up to now? He didn't have that many records in his milk crate, but they all had the name of the song blacked out with Magic Marker. "That's so no one bites me," he explained. We crowded around, watching his magic. After a while he'd say, "I'll see you later—I gotta practice," and he was alone again in the cement room, working solo in his bunker like the WLNG guy. You deliver the news and you do it alone.

Marv's mother still came out. She'd probably covered his DJ

tables with second-home basement crap, old sewing machines and spiderwebbed boogie boards. The stuff you keep around because you convince yourself that one day you might use it again. We all know how that ends. Melanie remembered Marv from the old days and I told her that he didn't come out anymore because he thought Sag was for kids. She told me about her cousin, who was a big DJ at some clubs in the Bronx, and then said she remembered when Marv's mother threw a birthday for him and invited all the kids. One of the big kids started chasing Marcus around the picnic table trying to noogie him, and Marcus slipped and crashed into it, sending the birthday cake flying. "It went all over the place."

I remembered that day. Everybody wearing some form of multi-colored striped article of clothing, that was the rule. Reggie attempted to salvage a clean chunk of cake from the ground. It was something he might do, gather what he could from the mess. Make sure he got his. But I didn't remember Melanie. I tried to put the scene back together, picture the faces under the cardboard party hats. I couldn't see hers. But she had to be there. Was that the day she kissed me? Hovering at my side all afternoon, brushing her arms against me by accident. Then leaning over. I was her husband. It must have happened. Where did it go?

That fucking song scrabbled in the cage of my head, shaking the bars:

For there are you, Sweet Lollipop
Here am I with such a lot to say, hey hey
Just to walk with you along the Milky Way
To caress you through the nighttime
Bring you flowers every day
Oh, Babe, what would you say?

Like I said, I'd been dinged, but good. Now it stirred up all the silt at the bottom. Bringing me around. It was my first kiss I was re-membering, that lost day I recovered. I saw it clearly. The song must have come through the kitchen window that day, the radio set on

WLNG when Marv's mother checked the weather report. She left it there at 92.1 and the enchantments followed. The big kid tormenting Marcus was Big Bobby, no, it was Neil, Neil the pervert who one time climbed up the roof of our porch to peep on Elena and got caught. My parents and his parents didn't talk for two summers. He was premed at Morehouse now, that was the word. Marcus smashed his skull into the table and things went into slow motion as the Carvel cake and Dixie plates and Hi-C tumbled through the air. Someone pulled on my arm, whispering, "Benji."

It seemed impossible not to remember something like that. The first time a girl put her lips on yours. What kind of chump forgot being a five-year-old mack? I would've coasted on that for years if I'd known. But I did know. I was there. What put it out of my mind? I looked at Melanie's profile, the coast of her nose and mouth and chin. She was one of us. A Sag Harbor Baby.

We were at the corner, the end of Richards Drive. The natural destination was town. Where we'd run into somebody and then it wouldn't be just me and her anymore. There was nowhere else to go.

Melanie said, "There it is." I turned and saw the old place up the street and I knew it wasn't her at all.

I will take the world at its word and allow that there are those who have experienced great love in their lives. This must be so. So much fuss is made over it. It follows that there are others who have loved but came to realize over time that what they had was merely the shadow of a greater possibility. These settled, and made do, or broke things off to continue the search. There are those who have never loved, and they walk through their days grasping after true connection. And then there is me. Ladies and gentlemen and all of you at home just tuning in, the angel of my heart, my long lost love, was a house.

There she was, my Sweet Lollipop. Posing coyly behind the old hedges, just a wedge, a bit of thigh, visible behind the trees. When people were inside at night, the light from the windows splashed through the leaves and branches, diluting the darkness. It was always a comfort rounding the corner and seeing that after you'd been running around all day. Soon you'd be inside with everyone else.

The windows were black. Since the swap, where we got the beach house and my aunt kept the Hempstead House, she rarely came out. Occasionally she gave the keys to friends for the weekend, and it was disturbing to see an *alien vehicle* in our driveway. Ours, even though it wasn't anymore. My mother would call her sister to double-check that everything was okay. I hadn't seen anyone there all summer.

"Let's go see," I said. She walked with me without hesitating. The house my grandparents built was a small Cape Cod, white with dark shingles on the roof and red wood bracing the second story. It was made of cinder block, stacks of it hauled out on the back of my grandfather's truck. Every weekend he brought out a load, rattling down the highway. This was before they put in the Long Island Expressway, you understand. It took a while. Every weekend, he and the local talent put up what they could before he had to get back to his business on Monday. Eventually he and my grandmother had their house. Their piece of Sag Harbor.

The hedges out front were scraggly and disreputable, but the lawn was grazed down to regulation height. The house looked like it did at the start of every season, ready for us to open it up. "Do you want to go inside?" I asked.

"Will we get in trouble?"

"No one's using it."

She said, "Okay," and the way she said it zapped my groin, pushing my dick up against my jeans. It was almost dark.

The driveway led to the back patio. Weeds and low flowers sneaked through the cracks in the decaying concrete between the paving stones, and it was still light enough to see some anthills in there, too, the telltale volcanoes of orange dirt. In former days Reggie and me knelt over them with a magnifying glass from the Wharf Shop, tilting the incinerating beam on any unfortunate critters popping out for a hive errand. It was where we had arranged the doomed radio men and bazooka guys from our plastic platoons into the path of Tonka bulldozers, and, farther back, filled bright plastic buckets with water from the hose. The toddler games we found meaning in. We spent drawn-out afternoons transferring water from container to container, spilling some each time until the cement was drenched and we were all out and we cried for a refill. Crawling around like ants ourselves, doing nonsense things like that. Behind the patio, the backyard sloped up, and the pump still stood there like a rusted scarecrow, its underground pipes leading nowhere. I don't know if they ever led anywhere.

The patio furniture was piled on the screened-in porch, a rickety contraption that kept the sun off us on hot days and the rain off us on cloudy ones, the water rolling off the roof into worn-away hollows as we swung on the old rocking couch, watching this and kicking our feet out. The roof of the porch was directly under the upstairs windows and Reggie and me used to sneak out onto the tarpaper in Alcatraz breakouts. Not that we had anywhere to go. Eventually we got big and bold enough to jump over the side, that long seven-foot drop. We wasted a lot of time doing that. Wishing, Maybe this time we'll break something.

I told Melanie to wait there and scuttled through the furniture. We left the window to the junk room unlocked when we lived there. Maybe my aunt did, too. What was there to steal? We were more likely to be accidentally locked out than robbed. I shoved the window open, clambering onto the lumpy guest bed, which was covered with our old board games and my aunt's spy thrillers. Stained shades from thrown-out lamps and busted Weedwackers, fishing poles and plastic boxes full of screws. I walked around to the back door and let her in.

The house looked small from the outside. That was its trick. Step inside and it went on for miles. We were in the kitchen, where the pale green General Electric appliances hummed, the matching dishwasher and fridge and range nestled among the pink Formica countertops. The electricity was turned on and they sparked to life; the electricity was turned off and they shuddered into comas for nine months. The door creaked as I closed it, as it always did. You never forget your first creak. It was the original creak, the creak standard that I would compare all other creaks to. Everything in that house was my model for things out in the world. This is what a doorknob looks like. This is what a drain looks like. The first chair I called a chair was there in the living room, next to my one and only and ever lamp. My feet dangled for years until the floor finally reached up to meet them. Window. Couch. Coffee table. My everlasting objects.

"Cobwebs," Melanie said, scraping her face.

A seafaring sort, my grandfather had paneled the living room in broad, brown planks of knotty pine that made it look like the belly of a ship. A buoy from his old sailboat hung over the couch, the name arcing across it in weathered black paint: MY GLORY. The old horseshoe crab was still there, the dried shell hanging on the nail my father had hammered into the wall after I brought it back from the beach. The only thing I noticed that was different was the TV, but I couldn't believe that the old black-and-white still worked, so I forgave its replacement. It took five minutes to warm up, making all sorts of frantic sounds, like you'd startled the people inside from their dozing. A white dot finally materialized in the middle of the screen. A white dot in a sea of blackness. The first star in the universe on the first day. It grew and spread and the sound came on and eventually the comedian hit his punch line, the weatherman told the future, the monster stepped out of the fog. You had to wait for it to come around.

"Nick's working tonight you said."

"I'm not his keeper," she said.

"Do you want to go upstairs?" I asked. Our eyes were getting used to the dark and a car came up Hempstead, illuminating the room and us in a lighthouse sweep.

"Okay."

This was my old house where all the good things still lived even though we had moved on. Everything as it was. Even the boy, the one who always seemed happy. He had to be here. This was where he lived. Haunting the place in his polyester pants and fucked-up Afro.

Was the same bottle of hydrogen peroxide sitting in the medicine cabinet? The grisly white foam. He was always running around and not looking where he was going. It all bubbled up. I saw it clearly. I thought it had been the kiss that the song retrieved, but it was this place. My lost love's face was the two windows facing the street, the front door for a nose, and the three brick steps for a mouth. Darling. I hummed the chorus and I didn't care if Melanie heard. Certain songs got you like that. You could make fun of them, ignore them, try to tune them out, but the verses still got inside. People you'd never meet offered the words you were unable to shove past your lips, saying what you felt about someone once, or might become capable of feeling one day. If you were lucky. They spoke for you. Gathering the small, rough things you recognized in yourself.

The kids' rooms were on the second floor. I walked up ahead of her, my fingers lighting on the banister made smooth by all our hands, finding the nail heads raised by the settling wood. I anticipated each one before my fingers discovered it. I'd fallen down the stairs plenty when I was learning how to go down stairs. Slamming my stupid head across the steps and finishing in a bruised heap at the bottom. This was the place where I learned to pick myself up, because when I fell the house was always empty.

Elena's room was on the left, me and Reggie's was on the right. The shades at the back of our room were open, enough ambient light sneaking in for us to make out the two beds, the dresser, and the weird vanity table that had been moved up there before I was born, for lack of a better place. The mirror of the vanity was flanked by two mirrored wings on hinges—if you moved them into a triangle, leaving a slot for you to peek inside, the mirrors retreated into endlessness, tossing images of themselves back to themselves in a narcissistic loop. It looked like a tunnel burrowing through the back of the vanity, through the wall, and into an extradimensional beyond. It was amazing how long I could stare at that. The shouts of my friends playing with Reggie came up through the window, or my sister yukking it up with her girlfriends in the next room and I stood there staring.

"This was my bed," I said. I sat down and spread my palm out. The bloom of rusted springs spotted the mattress. She sat down next to me. She said something and I responded, drawing up sentences from a reservoir. I hadn't been on my bed for years. The last time I slept in it—the night of that summer's Labor Day party—I hadn't known it was going to be the final time. A car crept up Hempstead, the headlights casting a window-shaped trapezoid across the ceiling. I knew the circuit—the light traversing the wall next to the vanity, creeping up the white ceiling tiles, then elongating and disappearing in the middle of the room. If the trapezoid blinked off there, the car contained strangers, revving up to 114. If it continued across the ceiling, it was my parents returning after a night out, turning into the driveway, driving the diamond into its home berth above my bed before my father shut off the engine. When that happened, I was safe from all the night sounds that had unsettled me since we were sent to bed. I couldn't sleep, even then. I followed each transit of light, hoping. When the light hovered and stopped, my parents were home and everything would be okay.

"It's quiet up here," she said. Her knuckles rested against my thigh.

"It is, isn't it," I said. She looked into my face. Her eyes glistened in the dark. Then she shut them, screwing them down like she was concentrating very hard, and she pursed her lips.

Why me? She was going out with Nick, but maybe she wasn't anymore. Certainly all the evidence pointed to the conclusion that she wanted me to kiss her. The tale of the childhood smooch, the phone call yesterday, her current pose—oh, let's stop there, I think we have what they call a preponderance, good people of the jury. But why? I reviewed our recent encounters. Had I been cool or said something funny? Accidentally brought forth the winning parts of me? I couldn't think of anything outside of my usual shtick. Maybe my Bauhaus T-shirt was finally kicking in, advertising my sophisticated musical tastes. Did she like Bauhaus, too? It was unlikely. She seemed pretty New Edition. It occurred to me that Nick looked a lot like Bobby Brown. Was she trying to get back at Nick for something? I wasn't the person you made out with to make someone jealous. I was the person you made out with to make someone pity you, like, look how far I've fallen since you left me, what with the far-off stare and general air of degradation. I was missing something. My braces were off. But that seemed such a trivial thing. I was a dummy for skipping my appointments. I could have been doing stuff like this all the time, apparently. I thought of Emily Dorfman sliding her long fingers around mine and now Melanie Downey perched on my bed like a nymph in a painting by one of the Old Masters or like one of the buxom camp counselors in *Friday the 13th*, about to burst out of her cherry hot pants. The girls had to reach out to me. I was too involuted. They had to pull me out of myself. Pull me where? As if it were better outside, with the rest of the world. I needed people to be able to see past my creaky facade in order to prove their worth, but when they did see past it, I refused to accept it. If people looked inside, surely they'd quickly discover there wasn't much to see.

She said, "Uh?"

All this thinking! You understand the impediments I faced back then. Everything came to a halt before this relentless grinding-over. A normal person would have concentrated on the matter at hand, but I came from a degenerate line. I was at a party chatting up a high-probability but got foolishly distracted by the long-shot lovely across the room whose smile kept me on the hook. In this case, the bewitching lass wasn't even a lass at all, but a two-story part-time home with a leaky roof and periodic squirrel infestation. I was part of a dead-end tribe of human beings twiddling our thumbs for extinction. We picked the wrong line in supermarkets, sitting like bags of cement with our meager foodstuffs in our basket, counting and recounting to make sure we had less than ten items, and when we finally resolved to switch to the faster line, it was too late and now that was the slow line. In fact, the act of us joining that line made it the slow line. We peered into the doors of packed buses and decided to wait for the next one, like we had all the fucking time in the world, and looked up the street for twenty minutes for the next one, finally deciding to walk, and then the next bus zoomed past as we galumphed between stops. We sat like idiots as gorgeous girls with big, patient lips offered themselves to us while we reveried over bygone cobwebbed things. We never know when we have it good, and we forget so easily. We will die out. Not that this particular occasion was a chance to pass on my wretched genetic material and extend my kind's useless reign on this earth, but you understand where such behavior leads—eventually the accumulated missed opportunities, shortsighted decisions, and wrong turns will overtake us. We are too stupid to live. It's amazing we made it this far.

Just kiss her. I kissed her. Leaned over, every adjusting spring in the mattress zinging in loutish commentary. It was the house. I could be the real me because this was where I lived, free from what happened and who I came to be. No matter what people saw when they looked at me, there was this man inside.

Did I mention that my eyes were open? I watched her eyes rove under their shadowy lids. Her tongue was soft. Softer than my tongue, or were all tongues the same degree of softness and mine was soft, too? I lifted a hand and rested it on her tit. I squeezed it. Gingerly, like a sailor who'd been thrown overboard and woke to find sand under him. Is this real, the soft stuff between my fingers? She exhaled through her nose. This was a real feeling. The chorus went like this:

> 'Cause oh, Baby I know
> I know I could be so in love with you
> And I know that I could make you love me too
> And if I could only hear you say you do, oo oo oo oo
> But anyway, what would you say?

I know that I could make you love me too. I was wrong again. It wasn't the house I was in love with, either. It was what I put in it. I saw it clearly now, the day I first heard the song, as if I were peeking into the vanity to find the scene unfolding in infinite truth. It was in this very house, many years ago. The sun was bright and every color dazzled. Me and my brother were on our knees on the cement in the back of the house, ramming our toy eighteen-wheelers into each other. Everyone thought we were twins because we were never apart. CB radio was king, and we talked in misapprehended CB lingo. "Breaker One Night, Breaker One Night." I had a red rig and my little brother had a blue one—when our mother took them out of the shopping bag, it was my turn to pick first, so I got the one I wanted. "We got a Smoking Bear on our tail." My sister was lying on the faded green chaise, painting her toenails a brain-splitting red with small, delicate strokes. She and her friends had just discovered nail polish and eye shadow and stuck to a strict practice regimen. She said, "Come here, Reggie, let me do your nails," and he said, "No, no!" My mother flipped the pages of a magazine at the patio table, wearing the white sweatbands that were always on her wrists that one summer she played tennis. "It's good for the heart." She looked so young. She said, "Elena, leave your brothers alone," and turned the page. My father upended the bag of Kingsford and shook a mound into the grill. He said, "The first batch will come off in approximately fifty-five minutes." And I said, "Yay! Yay!" because there was nothing better than his barbecue. We were a family. This was the scene the song gifted to me. The radio played in the kitchen, the black transistor radio sitting on top of the green GE fridge. The man sang through static, "I know that I could make you love me too." That perfect day so long ago when we were all together. The beautiful afternoon before it went wrong.

Of course it never happened. But that was WLNG for you. Got you every time.

I was sucking on her neck. My stomach growled. My eyes were still open. That's how I saw the headlights. The lights moved across the wall, tracing the distance like a needle sweeping across a record. But the lights didn't disappear where they were supposed to. They kept going, to my parents' place, and we heard the tires snapping the pebbles and stones in the driveway.

"Oh, shit!" I said, jumping up as if the house were made of glass and we were suddenly visible up in the air, floating.

"Who is it?"

We scrambled to the side window, which gave us a steep angle on the driveway. It wasn't someone pulling in to make a U-turn. The headlights extinguished and the door opened.

"We gotta get out of here," I said. I was having an action-flick moment, quoting the hero after he discovers the ticking time bomb.

"This sucks!" she said.

I unlatched the windows. She said, "Are you crazy?"

"No, look—the roof." I saw her frown at me. "It's totally safe." Then whispering: "Me and Reggie used to go out here all time."

We heard the front door creak open. That creak! I threw a leg outside and pulled my body through. Melanie banged her head on the frame and said, "Ow!"

"Shh!"

"Ooh!"

"Shh!"

We stepped over the twigs and acorns lobbed from the trees. I led her to the side of the porch away from the driveway. "Now what?" she whispered, looking over.

"We gotta jump for it," I said. More action-flick dialogue. The edge of the canyon, the mercenaries' jeep bouncing closer. The kissing had jostled something loose, some he-man narrative.

"I'm not doing that." A hand downstairs discovered the lamp in my parents' former bedroom, throwing light onto the grass.

"We have to," and I jumped. It really wasn't that far, and my legs knew what to do after so many rehearsals. I'd seen myself jumping off the porch to escape a raging fire or a mass of zombies moaning up the stairs, but never thought I'd be looking up at a girl, saying, "I'll catch you."

I didn't. She knocked me into the dirt like an Acme anvil. She yelped. Loud enough for the person inside to hear. Then we ran. Along the side of the house, dashing across the front yard and into the street. I heard someone yell after us, and snuck a glance back to see a silhouette on the front stoop. But we were around the corner with a quickness.

THE NEXT DAY I SAW MELANIE through the window of the ice-cream store, the lookout by the waffle grill. I took my break. She sat on one of the benches, rubbing her sandals in the dirt, pretty toes poking out. She watched me walk over. A limousine prowled up the lane between us, a slow black shark, and I waited for it to pass. Her expression did not change. I gave her the ice cream I'd scooped for her. Mint Chocolate Chip in a Waffle Cone with Rainbow Sprinkles, what I'd heard her ask for all those times when she came in to see Nick while my head was down in the vats. She said, "Oh, thanks," and extended her soft tongue to the ice cream. "It's hot out today."

I told her that my aunt had let one of her employees use the house for the weekend. She said, "That's okay," and looked past me and Nick materialized and slid up next to her, circling his arm around her and slipping his fingers into the tight pocket of her jeans. He didn't ask about the cone. That was that.

My aunt sold the house a few years later. When I asked her why she'd do such a thing, she told me, "I never went out there. What was the point of holding on to it?" I was appalled, but you know me. I was nostalgic for everything big and small. Nostalgic for what never happened and nostalgic about what will be, looking forward to looking back on a time when things got easier.

She sold the house to that brand who keep it up, diligently mailing checks to the lawn guy and the guy who turns on the water at the start of the season, but who never seem to come out. They haven't done a thing to it, repainted it or anything, so it looks like it always did. When I walk by there now, I could be staring at a photograph of when my grandparents just finished it, them stepping out into the street to admire what they'd accomplished. Or the first time I saw it when I was a baby, aloft in my mother's arms. Far away, then getting bigger and more real the closer we get to it.

It looks like it's waiting.

The

Black

National

Anthem

THE BOYS LINED UP TO RACE. THEY DOUBLE-KNOTTED their shoelaces, the sad noodles gone gray from a summer of tramping, and pulled up their tube socks, which slowly fluttered down their calves and ankles for lack of elastic. They nosed their sneakers as close to the line as possible, newly gung ho about millimeters and the small advantages that get us through life. The red chalk disappeared over the busy day as feet treated it like the dust it was, sweeping it away into the beyond, but for now it was a respected border, cordoning off the picnic tables and red-and-white coolers and spectators from the playing field in the middle of the street. The anticipation. The boys unwrapped their favorite scowls and glares to psych out their competitors. Any second now. And then the false start, from that kid who was you and me. Eager to begin and nervous with everybody's eyes on him and then fucking up. "Dag," the other boys groaned, shaking their legs and gathering themselves anew. Angry as if the whole summer were at stake.

The girls went first. The 5-to-7-year-olds who believed the secret of speed was in the face, in the fierce, scrunched expressions they pushed ahead of their bodies, and then the 8 to 10s, quicksilver in ponytails, and finally the gawky and glorious 11 to 12s, racing for the last time, sprinting desperately into teenage preoccupations and flee-ing the girls they had been. Mr. Grady raised his starter pistol, his other hand cupping the black stopwatch bobbing on his chest. Mr. Grady, year after year. With his brown-and-red skin—half Chero-kee, so he claimed—and skinny arms and legs and potbelly. He was a notorious drinker among unapologetic drinkers, legendary for his annual pass-out in the driver's seat of his dark Cadillac, as the radio played and the motor hummed, too out of it to walk up to his front door. This was his one sober afternoon of the season. He had a duty. His son had been a natural athlete and everybody said he could have been in the Olympics if he'd wanted to, he was that good. But then he fell in with the wrong crowd. After the races, Mr. Grady hit the rum punch in front of the Delaneys' with a quickness, to close the distance. Mr. Grady with his trembling arm sticking up in the air an authority only kids were stupid enough to obey.

They ran to prove who was the fastest, the most worthy, to settle three months of scores, they ran for their parents, who did or did not watch from the sidelines and did or did not cheer them on. First, Sec-ond, and Third Place got medals. Mr. Gordon, the chairman of the Sag Harbor Hills Improvement Association, knew a guy in Wain-scott who knocked them out at a reasonable price. The winners wore the medals all day, pinned to their cotton-poly shirts, looking down to marvel at them when a cloud passed the sun or they shivered from some internal tremor, lifting them up for grown-ups to examine af-ter admiring remarks. Clive always came in First when the mess of us used to pell-mell down the street, except for the year when he twisted his ankle, and he still had them up on the wall of his room, a blue row roused by the draft whenever you opened the door. I never won, but I never expected to. It was okay.

We were the big kids at the Labor Day party now that Elena and her group were off. Watching from the sidelines, jawing, disdainful. We were down to a skeleton crew. Me and Reggie. NP and Nick, who was staying out in Sag in his weird exile after the rest of us picked up our stakes. Time was, we never missed this day. But other things were more important now. Clive and Bobby and Marcus were already in the city. We were growing into those who went away.

When Reggie and me made it over to Sag Harbor Hills, NP and Nick were talking to a tall boy with hazel eyes and rusty curls. His name was Barry David. He wore gray Lee jeans, crossing his arms over a striped blue-and-crimson Le Tigre polo. Also, a constant smirk. He looked familiar and I figured him for someone's city buddy out for the big day, or a Southern relative up for his annual dose of bourgiefication. Labor Day, all sorts of strangers left their mark.

We were learning that it wasn't as much fun watching the races when you weren't running. If the girls were still out, we would've been diverted by social performance, but Devon and Erica had already gone back to New Jersey, and Melanie and her mom's rental was over. Rent your house out for August, sure, but you'd be a fool to give up Labor Day. Watching the little girls tackle the street, it was clear that our group's gender disparity was only a statistical blip— the next group was well stocked. Elena's group had been well balanced, too, and with them no longer coming out, the poverty of our situation was even more apparent. There would be no fashion show this year, and maybe the next few, until the next crop of girls transferred their interests from hopscotch to runways.

"They better have a good DJ this time," Nick said.

"That last guy was illin' with all that Motown shit," Reggie said.

NP said there wasn't going to be a DJ this year. Nick didn't believe it, but my mother had told us the same thing that morning, offering the hypothesis that there wasn't enough money in the budget "because they spent so much on those new Sag Harbor Hills signs of theirs." They were quite natty, the signs, standing at the highway entrances of all the development streets, the jaunty black whale with its come-hither look. Now Azurest would have to get its act together and get new signs, too. It was a cold war, but harmless.

"That's messed up," Nick said.

"That's some bullshit right there," Barry David said. "I thought you said this was a real party."

"There's the bonfire," I offered.

"Wack-ass bonfire," he said. "I'm gonna get me some iced tea."

He walked away and I asked Nick, "Who's that?"

"That's NP's cousin." He shrugged. "He came out for the day."

Out in Sag Harbor, it was good policy to wave at everyone you passed, whether you happened on them as they were removing groceries from the trunk or as they stood in the middle of their lawns with hedge clippers and a vacant expression on their faces, wherever, because there was a good chance you were related. Cousins like crabgrass out there. You never knew how close you were to those you passed. This day, that rule was in abeyance. You'd spend all day bowing and saluting, it was ridiculous. Labor Day, the population was at its highest, with one-weekenders out for their annual visitation, relatives caravanning like Okies to break in the new convertible bed, and the scattered alumni coming around again to see if it was as they remembered. The Sunday of Labor Day weekend we crowded into this one street to see one another and say good-bye.

Ninevah Place, the dead end to the beach the rest of the year, was today the dead end of summer. We could go no further. The next day we'd close up our houses, pulling in the lawn furniture, winding hoses around forearms in messy loops, leaning on faucets with all our might for that extra bit that meant peace of mind for nine months. School, work, autumn. As if autumn was not already here. Nights we zipped jackets to the neck, and days gooseflesh popped on our legs as we tried to squeeze one more use out of shorts we'd never wear again.

But forget all those city intimations. Today was the Sag Harbor Hills Labor Day Party. Card tables replaced the cars outside of houses, set a-wobble by pitchers and Tupperware. We camped out, sharing our food and drink and stories. Mayo glued globs of potato salad to spoons, you had to shake hard to plop it into the compartment on the blue plastic plate. Potato salad, where would we be without potato salad clumped with yellow ladybugs of yolk, potato salad by the bushel and crinkled aluminum tins of greens steaming over Sterno cans of murmuring fire.

Bucket Webers and flat hibachis unfurled magnificent banners of gray smoke. With a plate in your hand, you mixed and matched from experience. There was Mr. Jackson and his grilled chicken. He'd made a name for himself with his Labor Day chicken, the parts marinated overnight in some handed-down Tennessee concoction. He had a long line waiting for a piece. He could hardly keep up. A few houses down, Mr. Turner prodded franks, looking forlornly down the street at Mr. Jackson and his followers and resolving to step up his game, although next year he'd be out with the hot dogs again, jealous again. We plotted and planned and next year came around and we were in the same place. Old reliable. And how could I forget Mrs. French and her cupcakes, soft as the ticking that angels stuff in their pillows. The cupcakes went before three o'clock and her brownies disappeared like that, reduced to smears at the corners of mouths and fingernails and the dirty shirts of dirty kids with no home training. The big bowls of rum punch were refilled punctiliously, in less-regulated proportions as time went on. You knew who to hit up for what.

At any given moment someone was playing "Ain't No Stoppin' Us Now." Labor Day, we cornered the worldwide market on people playing "Ain't No Stoppin' Us Now." It was the black national anthem. The disco version of "We Shall Overcome," courtesy of Mr. McFadden & Mr. Whitehead. It came out of our cars as we drove to the store for last-minute paper plates and ketchup, issued triumphantly from sand-flecked boom boxes on threadbare beach towels, blared out of backyard patios from ancient amps plugged into bright orange extension cords uncoiled for annual duty. There've been so many things that held us down—check. But now it looks like

things are finally coming around—check. We're on the move!—
check. Whether the association was civil rights triumph, busting
through glass ceilings in corporate towers, or merely the silly joy of
gliding around a roller rink as you chased your friends and occasionally held hands with someone, aloft in a polyurethane heaven, the
song addressed the generations. No stoppin'.

Older folks sunk down in beach chairs and did not stir the whole
afternoon, watching it all, waiting for people to come over and pay
respect. They were the only ones able to savor or rue the small jokes
of time. Like, isn't that Sammy Parkerson and James Norton Jr. playing with each other? Their grandparents were pals, the parents
couldn't stand each other, and then the grandkids found each other
one dead afternoon and became buddies for life. The seasons set
everything right again. My parents' generation made the rounds,
popping in for a drink at one of the houses, making carefully timed
appearances at the functions they'd promised all week to attend, hot
on the trail of lost friends rumored to be out after so long. They
checked on their children only occasionally. Why worry today? It was
Labor Day. Nothing bad could happen. They got a break from us. We
got a break from them. Tomorrow it was back to the apartments and
we'd be all over each other for nine months. We'd had all summer to
sew up the tears and push the stuffing back inside, but it was over.
The little kids zoomed. Me and my friends stood with our arms
crossed, shaking our heads.

When was the first Labor Day party? The Last Chance Dance.
Spur-of-the-moment thing one summer in the early '50s, a nice idea,
some friends getting together, then becoming official as it became a
hit, people looked forward to it, with a planning committee and folks
jockeying for their little visions. Foot races for the kids appearing one
year. The fashion show, which I never understood. Was this the
handiwork of famous designers the girls strutted around in, previews from Parisian runways? The girls were game, mimicking poses
from magazines. Throw a kiss to the crowd like I told you, dear. At
dusk the dance party began, on the wooden stage erected the Monday before and sitting in the street all week, teasing, beckoning.

Jump on it to test its solidity. For a few summers we bused in a group of Alvin Ailey dancers—somebody had connections—and they moved delicately in their beige leotards, a slow exquisite display. They used Clive's basement as a changing room, and we crowded around the little window for a glimpse of nip or muff and were run off by Clive's mother. Always, always run off. That was our whole story. The bonfires started again around when the dancers stopped coming.

It was time for the last race. A woman snatched her toddler from the track. Everybody was ready, but Mr. Grady was having a problem with his stopwatch. At the end of each race, he checked the stack of paper in his hand, different colors and stocks from many years, to see if any new records had been set, if the legendary times of yore still stood. "And Stacy Carter maintains the record for girls' 11 to 12s, set Labor Day 1976," he'd announce for the people in the stands. We looked around for Stacy Carter, now in her early twenties, a child on her shoulder, smiling at the mention of her long-ago feat, those next to her slapping her on the back. She ran this street, too, back in the day.

We waited. There was this new gang of kids, boys and girls I hadn't seen all summer. Where did they come from, these cocky little shits, acting like they owned the street? As if these were not our races they were running. Where had they been hiding? Biding their time all these months, on Azurest Beach while we tried to claim the ocean beach, spinning the comics racks at the Ideal now that we had abandoned them. They prowled around on their bicycles looking for the next caper or disappointment, floating above the seat, assaulting the pedals for a few seconds and then gliding for a while, savoring this process. Ditching their half-eaten slices at Conca D'Oro when their lookout finger-whistled of our approach. They bristled at the line while Mr. Grady dicked around reciting the rules they already knew. Our replacements.

"I should get in there and win that medal," Barry David said. "Take that shit."

"You're too old," Reggie said. He didn't like this kid.

"I know that, shit. I was just saying." He poked the last bit of hamburger bun in his mouth and licked his lips.

Mr. Grady took his time. We grew impatient. Let's get this show on the road. We were all there. It was where we mingled with who we had been and who we would be. Sharing space with our echoes out in the sun. The shy kid we used to be and were growing away from, the confident or hard-luck men we would become in our impending seasons, the elderly survivors we'd grow into if we were lucky, with gray stubble and green sun visors. The generations replacing and replenishing each other. Every summer this shifting-over took place in small degrees as you moved closer to the person who was waiting for you to catch up and some younger version of yourself elbowed you out of the way.

Where was my replacement, then? Which boy was it, standing with the others at the starting line. Waiting for it to begin. Probably that knock-kneed creature in the green mesh T-shirt, with the scabbed knees and telltale messed-up Afro. Just looking at him, you knew he wasn't going to win. It was in the way he carried himself, last place before he'd taken a step. But he'd give it a good try. Like he always did. They hadn't beaten that out of him yet.

"Get on with it, Grady!" someone yelled, and the grown-ups laughed.

And who was I replacing? According to this scheme, he had to be here on this street, chowing down on some of Mr. Baxter's pork ribs. Was he one of Those Who Didn't Come Out Anymore? Had he been happy out here, or was he out in the world never speaking of this place just as it did not speak of him, the one who did not turn out as expected. Did he find someone? Was he here watching over his kids to keep them safe and reminiscing with the old pals, shaking hands that were cold and wet from beer-snagging dips into coolers, catching the eye of his wife from the other side of the street. She smiles back and they share this moment in the crowd. Maybe he didn't exist and I was the first of my line. The mutant strain. Or I was in his vicinity, but I couldn't recognize him because I didn't believe I could grow into that one day, smiling and assured and at peace. That sleeping part of me finally roused to action. Maybe I saw him every day out here, passing him by, I was looking at him now, and I pitied the very sight of him, too scared to acknowledge how I would turn out.

The pistol sounded. They ran down the street, all the boys 11 to 12, minus the asthmatics, slapping down the pavement in their cheap rubber. The obvious winner, the tallest kid, the most put-together kid, the one who knew how to move through the world, quickly pulled out in front. The kid I put my money on, the one in the green mesh shirt, didn't come in last, but just barely. He hunched over by the finish line, panting. Tough race. The first time we ran it, I remembered, this street was still dirt. They finally put some asphalt down and then people started retiring out here, staying past Labor Day and through the winter. It wasn't their summer place anymore. It was their home.

The winner jumped up and down. Mr. Grady said, "Almost beating Gary Osgood's famous record from 1981, but not quite, is Little Clive of Azurest!" There was a Little Clive? How could there be more than one Clive, it was ridiculous. The recent overlap in Mohammads and Malcolms made sense, times change, but how could there be another Clive?

With the races over, the crowd reclaimed the street after being penned in the sidelines, bumping their butts against the folding tables and old ladies' chairs. I caught sight of my runner as the people hustled in. He turned from his friends and a darkness churned through his features for a moment before he found his mask again. Yeah, he had to be me. That was me all over. The look of fret when he slips up and for a second other people can see it. Sometimes you recognize yourself in other people right off and sometimes it's subconscious. When you get older, you gather friends and lovers for reasons other than the accident that your houses are close together. There's an affinity, stuff you share in common and things you seek out in other people. Something drew you together but you didn't understand that secret undertow until one day after years and years of talking, it comes, the key story that lays it all out. Who could know at the start of that innocent evening that this was the night to make it plain. They tell you what happened and you think, we're more alike than I knew, but of course you did know, it's what brought you together. Incomplete children become incomplete adults. You can see it. You find each other.

Maybe my earlier model, the jolly son of Sag Harbor I was replacing, was looking at me in that moment, a can of Budweiser resting on his paunch, bad mustache shrubbing his lip, thinking, Why is he standing around when he could be out having fun? Such a chump. I can relate. Talking about that summer all this time, sometimes I have to stop and say, I don't know who this Benji kid is, either. Certainly he would not recognize the man he came to be. The poor sap. I need him to figure out how I got where I am, and he needs me to reassure him that despite all he knows and has seen and feels, there is more. I can listen to him. But of course he can't hear a damn thing I say.

"You can run, but can you jump? Look at you. You can run, but can you jump?" Barry David was playing keep-away with Little Clive's First-Place medal. The younger boy grabbed for it and Barry David snatched it higher. Was there anything worse than a bigger kid playing keep-away with your stuff? That dreary rehearsal for adulthood. It wasn't something we'd do to the little kids. Well, some of us, maybe. But never on a weekend, when parents were around. Barry David didn't care who saw. Little Clive's cheeks reddened. "Look at you!"

I was about to say something when Barry David went stiff, like he'd been zapped by one of those mythical fallen power lines we kept being warned about after a storm. An old lady had him, I didn't know her name. She was one of the great shrunken matriarchs of the community, the ones who only came out of their first-floor rooms in the back of the house one day a year. They had seen it all, witnessed the earth cool and the newly amphibious heave themselves onto sand. The uneasy birth of the developments. She snapped Barry David's arm securely in her claw and said, "Stop that this instant! Stop it! Listen to me when I'm talking to you."

Barry David looked at his arm, confused. His mind couldn't

process this interference. I looked around for NP's mother, tensing myself for the spectacle of her disciplining her nephew in front of everyone. He lowered the medal down to Little Clive.

"Where are your parents?" the old lady said.

For a second there, I thought he was going to whop her. It was a bizarre idea. Such a thing would never happen. But what he did do was almost as improbable—he wrenched his arm free and disappeared into the people and I didn't see him until the bonfire. The old lady harrumphed and lowered herself into her chair. She picked up her fan and waved it across her face and breast. It wasn't that hot. She smiled.

THAT NIGHT, you could almost call it cold, so we eagerly watched Mr. Nickerson arrange the wood of the bonfire while we rubbed our hands together. Clouds overtook the sun late in the afternoon and we were all zipped up now. The bonfires came back to Azurest with the return of the Nickersons. Mr. Nickerson started coming out as a kid, the same time as my mother, then dropped out for a stretch in the late '60s and '70s. California, divorce, regroup. After his parents passed, he reopened his ancestral beach house. "It's good to be back," Mr. Nickerson kept saying his homecoming summer, to let us know how grateful he was. He reinstituted the bonfires that Labor Day. While we were in Sag Harbor Hills, he was here in front of his house with a shovel digging out the pit, throwing the sand into a mountain beside him. His son Nat used to pitch in, but Nat was in college now.

We'd hid some sixes of Strohs in the woods and made forays back and forth, the cans bulging in the pockets of our Windbreakers. "Can you see it?" we asked one another, tilting into the light to see if the outline was visible. We sipped them with theatrical furtiveness when we thought no one was looking. Me and NP made one more run into the woods before Mr. Nickerson started up the fire. I scraped the leaves off the six-packs, our careful camouflage. "We can each have three," I said.

"I put in more money than anyone, so I'm going to have four. Nick only put in two dollars."

"Okay," I said. I was getting my three. I didn't care what other people were doing. As we walked down the steps to the beach, I said, "You should keep an eye on Barry David."

"What for?"

"He's acting all wild. He's going to get into trouble."

NP shrugged. "Can you see it?" he asked, pointing to the beer in his pocket.

The crowd around the fire was smaller than it had been the last few years. There were fewer teenagers in need of an anchor for their night, and not many grown-ups, as the Gardners were having a cocktail party up the street on Walker. That's where our parents were. Unlike us kids, the parents saw a lot of each other in the city, for business, for meetings of their various clubs and fraternal organizations. The Gardners' party was the first item in the new social season while down on the beach the younger set foraged the scraps of the summer. The smaller kids, the ten-year-olds and whatnot, scrutinized every detail of bonfire-construction with dedication, remaining behind an invisible line of safety as if their parents were waiting for an excuse to grab them away from the fun.

Over time I have learned that what makes a man is not his ideas or his words, what makes a man is the ability to squeeze out a ferocious stream of lighter fluid from a can and throw a match on it. Mr. Nickerson was a man. The heat felt good. We spread our fingers out, pushing against the warmth. Sparks twisted on their turbulent currents of heat and dark knots exploded in the wood. As our eyes adjusted, the darkness ate up the world outside the light of the bonfire, the glow of East Hampton over the Point, the white pinpricks from town. Our faces came up out of shadow and you started to learn other people's outlines, the way they walked in the night. You saw a shape, and then it was someone you knew dipping in for a minute. Then they returned to the shadows.

"When are you heading back?" we asked, over and over, chirping it like crickets. The master question of the summer had been re-placed with this one, nothing left to wring out of the summer except practicalities. Early tomorrow, late tomorrow, Tuesday morning "to beat the traffic." Traffic was the entire perversity of the world shrunk down to a long bead of red lights, and if you could beat that, you could do anything. It was a kind of greatness we aspired to.

"Is that one of our beers?" I asked Barry David. He drank it out in the open, without a smidgen of shame.

"What is this," Barry David said, "Nag-a-Nigger Day? He said I could have one." He nodded to the darkness. There was no one there. As long as I got my three.

After throwing a final raft of wood into the fire, Mr. Nickerson told us he was going to the Gardners'. "Let it die out," he instructed us. It wasn't late, but given the turnout, and his son's absence, I gather he was resigned to the fact that this would not be one of the infamous Nickerson bonfires, with shoving matches ("She nearly fell into the fire!"), undying declarations ("I've always wanted to get with you, ever since we were little"), and new lovers slipping away into the night ("I don't think they can see us"). Something about this day was off. No one had even brought out a boom box. That's how depleted it was. The summer of *Purple Rain*, we kept flipping the cassette over and over, singing at the top of our lungs. Maybe next year.

It was only a matter of minutes before we disobeyed him. The final aunts and uncles and random grown-ups who stopped by briefly to check out the fire were gone. The prepubescent girls disappeared in a huddle, for one last segregated Labor Day evening before things got complicated. Then one of the little boys had a tiny twig in his hand. He ran up to the fire, pretending to throw it in, and scrambled back to his friends, who squealed with joy. He did this a few times, the others daring him, and finally he threw it in for real, saying, "It was an accident! It was accidentally!"

Soon it was dried clumps of beach grass, those weird-looking black crabs I've never known the name of, and crinkly fistfuls of seaweed. The little kids stopped retreating after making their contributions, as if they had thrown their fear in, too, standing close to the fire to verify that every last bit turned to ash. They nodded.

"What we need is some fireworks," NP said, like flint.

"Does anybody got some M-80s?"

We shuddered at this diabolical proposition. *To . . . actually blow up the fire!*

"M-80s would tear that shit apart."

"Place them at strategic points."

"Holy shit!"

"Wicked!"

"What about this," one of the kids said. He held up an Eveready nine-volt battery for our consideration.

"You can't throw that in there," his friend said, full of gleeful hysteria. "It'll explode!"

"It's not going to explode," Reggie said.

"Shit, I'll do it," Barry said, swiping it and tossing it into the fire. We jumped back—"She's gonna blow!"—but nothing happened.

I said, "What's next?" I wasn't trying to up the stakes. I was just saying what we were all thinking and feeling. It wouldn't stop there. It was our last night.

Barry David stepped into the light with a thick gray rope. It had nestled in a dirty lump up in the beach grass by the Nickersons' for years, washed up after a nor'easter or discarded after someone's inscrutable mission. He heaved it in, half of it falling into the red heart of the fire and the rest landing at the edge of the pit, launching a plume of sparks. We whooped. We high-fived. We dagged in our fashion. It made rustle-y noises as it went up, it whistled, a chemical inside it producing brief blue jets. Barry David flopped the rest of the rope into the fire with a branch. Then he threw the branch on top of it, too. Barry David said, "What's next? What'll I do next?" He stepped into the darkness.

"That nigger's crazy," Reggie said.

"Yeah," I said.

Not long after, we heard a shout and then three loud thumps.

Something on the stairs. The shadow that became Barry David stomped down the bulkhead stairs, dragging a long red bench. Part of someone's patio set.

"He's going to burn up Mr. Nickerson's bench!"

He lugged it across the sand. We told him it was a bad idea and he said, "Don't worry, it's not his bench, shit." He held it over his head and we shut up and he threw it into the fire. It made a nice light as it went up, opening new stretches of the beach. I looked around, trying to see if there were any grown-ups coming. There was no one but us kids.

"That's one patio set—burnin' motherfucker," NP said.

"With his monkey ass," I added, because the insult would have been naked just sitting there, on this chilly night.

"Where'd he go?" Nick asked.

Soon after, we heard the thumps again, but this time the light from the renewed fire was such that we had no problem seeing it clod down the steps. It was the twin of the first bench. I pictured the picnic table desolate in the middle of blue-and-pink paving stones, mourning its fallen brothers. I'd told myself that Barry David had raided somebody's garbage out on the curb, stuff they were getting rid of at the end of summer, but obviously that wasn't true. The benches were new, fresh from the Outdoors section of Caldor, discounted for End-of-the-Season Savings. He held the bench over his head, tottering, and he let out a Tarzan yell and tossed the second bench into the fire. It banged against the first one and slid off, knocking apart Mr. Nickerson's careful edifice in a blazing cascade. The little kids loved it and hopped up and down amid the sparks. Little Clive high-fived Barry David, his new hero. He threw his medal in the fire. It curled up on itself and became a black spot.

Barry David picked up a beer from the sand and took a big swig. He started up the steps.

This time we followed him, all of us, the kids satellites around him and our crew keeping a little distance, as if we'd be able to disavow being accomplices if someone caught him. Who was this gang of little kids cheering him on? Were they more bloodthirsty than us, or just less scared and more dumb? If there was a Little Clive, then why not a Little Nick, Little Reggie, and of course Little Me, skinny body shivering in his Azurest sweatshirt and not so glum in the light of the fire, energized by this escapade. Me and my gang should have stopped Barry David, but it was hard to resist the pleasure of watching someone fuck up so colossally. Can you believe this guy? What's he thinking? What's wrong with him? As if we didn't know. As if we weren't jealous of someone who just didn't give a fuck.

Reggie said, "He's going to get into a lot of trouble."

I told NP, "You should really stop him."

"What for?"

"He's your cousin."

"He's not my cousin," he said. "I thought he was your cousin."

"I've never seen him before in my life."

"That's what Nick told me," he said. We dashed ahead to catch up.

He'd taken it from the Gardners'. Everybody's parents' cars stretched up and down the street in front of the house. The music was loud, the '70s soul classics everybody knew by heart because of nights like this, when they played in a holy loop. A big glass wall overlooked the patio on the side of the Gardners' house and we could see them all in there, laughing, bobbing to the music, sipping cocktails. Everybody's parents, all the parents enjoying themselves behind the glass as if it were a TV screen. I saw my father talking to Mrs. Greene, with his sly smile, and my mother deeper in the room, carrying an ice bucket. She placed it on the table and tucked her hair behind her ear. We kept ducked down behind the cars so they couldn't see us. Barry David walked up to the edge of the patio, just inside the square of light cast from the room, and he lifted the edge of the red wooden chaise lounge to test its weight. It had wheels on one end, and he pulled it off the patio and onto the grass. The music didn't skip a beat. No one inside noticed him at all.

He maneuvered it around the parked cars and dragged it into the middle of Walker, singing "Darling Nikki." The wheels squeaked hideously. The little kids clapped their hands and giggled. He could go all night. Sure, there was a finite number of patio sets in the developments, but more than enough to keep the fire going. Unless someone stopped him. There was a serious lack of supervision, you could say. I heard Nick tell NP, "He's no family of mine, shit." The cushion fell off, and the little kids picked it up, holding it between them like pallbearers. Barry David, the ghost kid who was all of us and none, everybody's cousin and no one's, pulled the red chaise down the street.

When we got to the Nickersons' driveway, I tapped Reggie's shoulder. "Let's get a beer," I said.

Reggie stopped. The group left us behind, marching ahead to the beach. He said, "Okay." Usually we had to bicker over stuff like that, me making him miss out on something. As we walked away, we heard it thumping down the stairs to the beach. The kids counted off every crash and screamed when it hit the sand.

There were still a few beers left. I'd already had my three. I took another and gave Reggie one.

"That was crazy," Reggie said.

"Yeah."

He took a big sip. "I like Miller better."

We heard them shout down on the beach, the loudest cheer yet.

"There it goes," Reggie said.

Then it died out. It was quiet. At some point that day, I'd heard my last lawn mower until next year. Lawn mowers all summer, and now they were finally silent. If your shit wasn't in shape by now, it was never going to be.

"Are you ready to go back to the city?" I asked him.

My brother took another sip. "Yeah, I'm pretty sick of Burger King."

We drank. A gray Volvo came around the corner. They were playing "Ain't No Stoppin' Us Now" at loud volume. As if it could have been otherwise. We held the beers behind our backs. I couldn't see who was inside but I waved. You never know who might be at the wheel, and how close you are to them.

Late that night, when the fires were long down to ash and the last limes were shipwrecked at the bottoms of the last drinks, and all the lights were out, I was still awake in my bed. Like I always was. The shadows from the trees trembled on the ceiling. Next year, Reggie was going to get the bed by the window. Even Stephen until the end of time. I thought, It wasn't that bad, sleeping in the other bed. I'd get used to it.

I thought about school.

I had a week to get a new plan together. I had to get some new records. I was tired of all my tapes. I needed new clothes, too. First thing Tuesday, I was going to head down to the Village and check out Bleecker Bob's and Tower to track down that Live Skull record, and then head over to Canal Jeans and get some new clothes. It came to me in a flash: combat boots. Why couldn't I wear combat boots? The dress code said we couldn't wear sneakers to school, but there was nothing about combat boots. Like leather ties—we had to wear ties, but there was no rule specifically forbidding leather ties, so people wore them all the time and the administration couldn't say anything about it. Unless they changed the *Student Handbook* over the summer. I'd cross that bridge when I got to it. First day of school, I'd walk in with a new jacket, some plaid New Wave number, and my new pants, and combat boots. Start things off right. Girls would take this as a sign I was different. That was another thing: make out with three girls a semester. September, October, November, December. Four months. That came out to one every five or six weeks. At least! Spring semester was longer, so that was like one every seven weeks. Six girls. Quite the regimen. Was that too ambitious? I could do it. People called me Benji but that didn't mean I wasn't Ben. A lot had happened over the summer. It didn't work out the way I had envisioned but you had to admit some stuff happened. I got my first job, and now if someone said, Hey, look at Benji's right arm, it's bigger than his left because he jerks off so much, I could say, No, that's from scooping ice cream. You have no idea what a relief it was to have an excuse for a question no one would ever ask. I got my braces off. I kissed Melanie Downey and touched her tit. Not under her shirt, but still. I was definitely more together than I was at the start of the summer. It didn't seem like that much time had passed, but I had to be a bit smarter. Just a little. Look at the way I was last Labor Day. An idiot! Fifteen looks at fourteen and says, That guy was an idiot. And fifteen looks at eight and says, That guy knew so little. Why can't fifteen and three-quarters look back at fifteen and a half and say, That guy didn't know anything. Because it was true. Two a semester. But it had to be two different girls. Or not. No need to go crazy. But definitely Tuesday, hit the Village and get this year started right. I'd be sixteen in November, old enough to get into CBGB's and Irving Plaza. Finally start seeing some concerts. Go to more parties. That was the key. I had to go to more parties. Other schools' parties, where I had no rep. Crash, whatever. Lay off the Cokes. I could do it. It was going to be a great year. I was sure of it.

Isn't it funny? The way the mind works?

PERMISSIONS ACKNOWLEDGMENTS

"Top of the World" by Richard Carpenter and John Bettis
© 1972 Almo Music Corp. and Nails Music. Copyright renewed.
All rights controlled and administered by Almo Music Corp. (ASCAP)
Used by permission. All Rights Reserved.

"Now I Gotta Wet 'cha"
Words and Music by O'Shea Jackson
© 1992 WB Music Corp. and Gangsta Boogie Music
All rights on behalf of Gangsta Music. Administered by WB Music Corp.
All Rights Reserved (contains samples from "Aqua Boogie" and "Get Out of
My Life Woman" by George Clinton, Jr., Bootsy Collins, Bernard Worrell
and Allen Toussaint).
All Rights Reserved. Used by permission of Alfred Publishing Co., Inc.

"Oh Babe What Would You Say"
Words and music by E.S. Smith
© 1972 (Renewed) Chappell Music Ltd.
All Rights Reserved. Used by permission of Alfred Publishing Co., Inc.

"Here We Go"
Words and music by Joseph Simmons and Darryl McDaniels
© 1983 Rabasse Music Ltd.
All rights administered by Warner/Chappell Music Ltd.
All Rights Reserved. Used by permission of Alfred Publishing Co., Inc.

Acknowledgments

I'd like to thank my family and all the good people of Azurest, Sag Harbor Hills, and Ninevah for all the adventures, and especially my brother Clarke, who is the best. George Chavez, owner of Big Olaf Ice Cream, helped by giving me three summers of research for chapter three. He was a great boss and if you're in the neighborhood, you should stop in for a cone. Tell 'em Chipp sent you.

A shout-out to the old crew: Jeff Goins, Billy Pickens, Julius Ford, Lee Bostic, and Evan Cotman. I hope you all are well and BB-free.

A shout-out to the new crew: Kevin Young, Richard Nash, Nathan Englander, and Nicky Dawidoff. Your help on the book is very much appreciated. Also, no BBs for you.

A million debts are owed to superagent and superfriend Nicole Aragi, and those wily desperadoes Lily Oei and Jim Hanks.

Doubleday is awesome, and Doubleday people are the most awesome of all. It's an honor to be published by the likes of William Thomas, Alison Rich, and Melissa Ann Danaczko. It has been a lovely ten years.

I am lucky to have received support from the Mrs. Giles Whiting Foundation and the John D. and Catherine T. MacArthur Foundation over the years. Truly, "This program was made possible by." The Cullman Center for Scholars and Writers was immeasurable help, and I'd like to thank Jean Strouse, Adriana Nova, Betsy Bradley, and Pamela Leo for making it such a swell place.

And much much love to Natasha and Maddie.

Mount Laurel Library
100 Walt Whitman Avenue
Mount Laurel, NJ 08054-9539
856-234-7319
www.mtlaurel.lib.nj.us

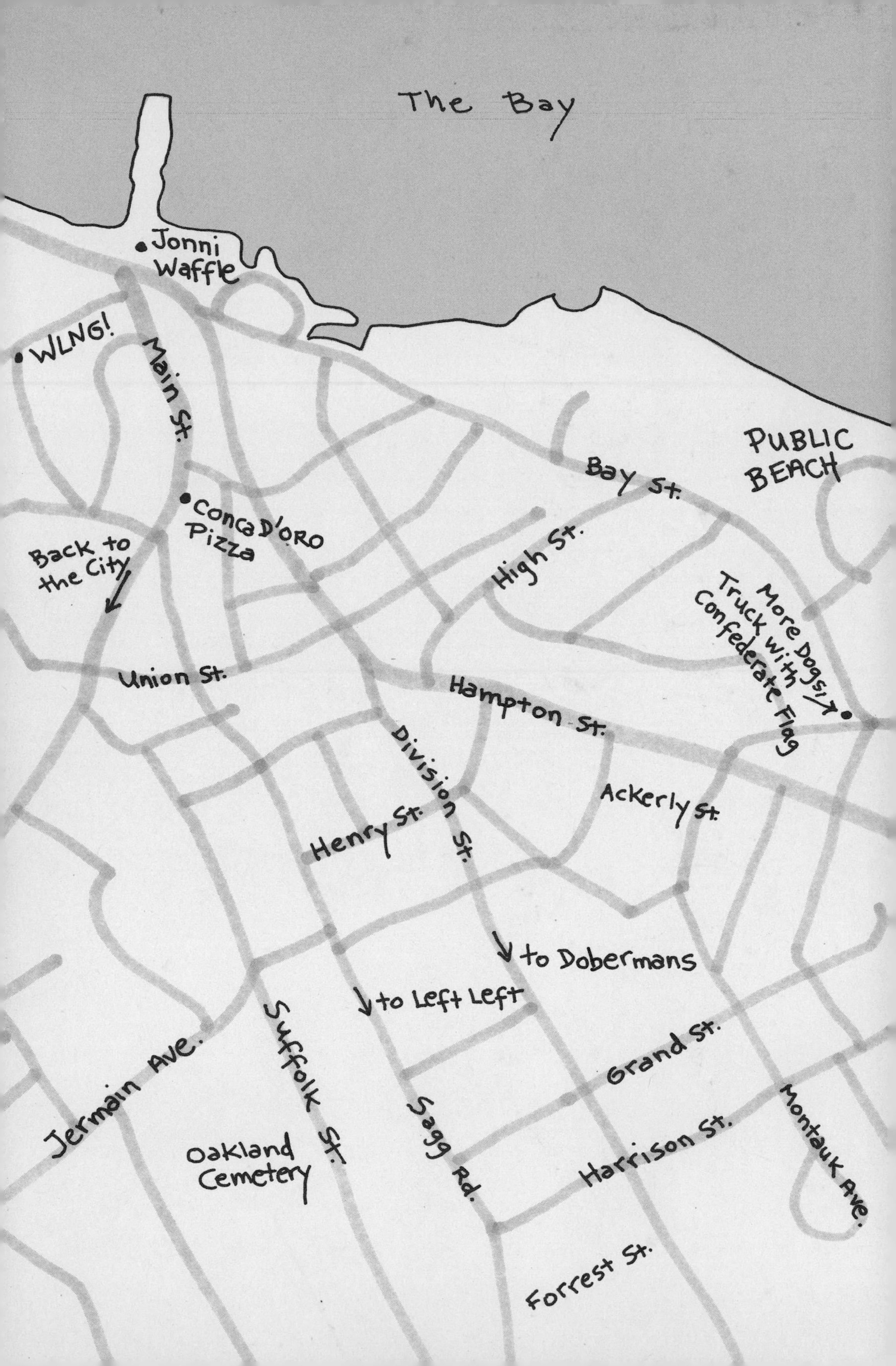
The Bay
Jonni Waffle
WLNG!
Main St.
Conca D'Oro Pizza
Back to the City
Union St.
Bay St.
PUBLIC BEACH
High St.
More Dogs,/ Truck with Confederate Flag
Hampton St.
Division St.
Ackerly St.
Henry St.
to Dobermans
to Left Left
Grand St.
Jermain Ave.
Suffolk St.
Sagg Rd.
Montauk Ave.
Harrison St.
Oakland Cemetery
Forrest St.